"Y...   ...ver want to leave."
                              ...*ork Times* bestselling author

"Erotic and darkly bewitching . . . a mix of magic and passion."
                —Jeaniene Frost, *New York Times* bestselling author

"Yasmine Galenorn is a hot new star in the world of urban fantasy."
                —Jayne Ann Krentz, *New York Times* bestselling author

"Yasmine Galenorn is a powerhouse author; a master of the craft who is taking the industry by storm, and for good reason!"
                —Maggie Shayne, *New York Times* bestselling author

"Spectacularly hot and supernaturally breathtaking."
                —Alyssa Day, *New York Times* bestselling author

"Simmers with fun and magic."
                —Mary Jo Putney, *New York Times* bestselling author

"Yasmine Galenorn's imagination is a beautiful thing."
                                                —*Fresh Fiction*

"Galenorn's gallery of rogues is an imaginative delight."
                                                —*Publishers Weekly*

"Pulls no punches . . . [and] leaves you begging for more."
                                                —*Bitten by Books*

"It's not too many authors who can write a series as long-lived as this one and make every book come out just as interesting and intriguing as the last, but Yasmine Galenorn is certainly one of them . . . Her books are always enchanting, full of life and emotion as well as twists and turns that keep you reading long into the night."   —*Romance Reviews Today*

"Explore this fascinating world."   —*TwoLips Reviews*

"As always, [Galenorn] delivers intriguing characters, intricate plot layers, and kick-butt action."   —*RT Book Reviews* (four stars)

Panther Prowling

An Otherworld Novel

YASMINE GALENORN

JOVE BOOKS, NEW YORK

THE BERKLEY PUBLISHING GROUP
Published by the Penguin Group
Penguin Group (USA) LLC
375 Hudson Street, New York, New York 10014

USA • Canada • UK • Ireland • Australia • New Zealand • India • South Africa • China

penguin.com

A Penguin Random House Company

PANTHER PROWLING

A Jove Book / published by arrangement with the author

Jove Books are published by The Berkley Publishing Group.
JOVE® is a registered trademark of Penguin Group (USA) LLC.
The "J" design is a trademark of Penguin Group (USA) LLC.

For information, address: The Berkley Publishing Group,
a division of Penguin Group (USA) LLC,
375 Hudson Street, New York, New York 10014.

ISBN: 978-0-515-15476-4

PUBLISHING HISTORY
Jove mass-market edition / February 2015

PRINTED IN THE UNITED STATES OF AMERICA

10 9 8 7 6 5 4 3 2 1

Cover art by Tony Mauro.
Cover design by Danielle Abbiate.
Map by Andrew Marshall, copyright © 2012 by Yasmine Galenorn.

Dedicated to:
Meerclar, my own little black panther.
It's been a long run, pumpkin.

ACKNOWLEDGMENTS

Thank you to everyone who has helped me get to this point:

Samwise: my lover and consort. Meredith Bernstein: my agent. Kate Seaver: my editor. Tony Mauro: my cover artist. Marc Mullinex, Andria Holley, and Jenn Price: my assistants. My furry "Galenorn Gurlz": my feline brigade. Ukko, Rauni, Mielikki, and Tapio: my spiritual guardians.

To my readers: Your support by buying my books helps keep me writing. You can find me on the Net on my site: galenorn.com. You can also find an Otherworld Wikipedia on my website.

If you write to me via snail mail (see website for the address or write via the publisher), please enclose a stamped, self-addressed envelope with your letter if you would like a reply.

The Painted Panther
Yasmine Galenorn

War is the trade of kings.

JOHN DRYDEN

Clever tyrants are never punished.

VOLTAIRE

Chapter 1

❧❧❧

"Do you think she knows what we're up to?" Menolly fretted.

She hiked herself up onto the counter of the newly reno-vated Wayfarer Bar & Grill and leaned back on her hands, swinging legs. The bar had been rebuilt, revamped, and revitalized, and tonight we were going to rock the block with a grand reopening party, welcoming back—we hoped—all the regulars who had made the Wayfarer their local watering hole. The doors opened in twenty minutes and we were just killing time as the staff finished last-minute touches, which included sorting out a massive number of balloons for Camille's birthday, which also happened to be today.

I sat on one of the barstools, absently flipping through a book I'd picked up at the pet store: *How to Take Care of Your Mouse*. I had no plans on raising pet mice anytime soon—that idea could too easily turn into a disaster. No, my friend Misha, a mouse who had helped me out in a sticky situation, had just died. I wanted to look after her children . . . and her children's children. The micelings were still frightened of me, but I'd managed to keep my promise to her and never once had chased after her extended family when I shifted into cat form.

"Probably. Camille makes it her business to know everything about everybody. She can't help it. It's the control freak in her. You know that by now. So, did you have any luck finding a new guard?" The portal to Otherworld downstairs needed constant watching, but Menolly had recently gone through a turnover in staff and now was shy not only an evening bouncer, but someone to watch over the portal during the morning shift.

She grumbled. "Not yet, and it worries me. I don't like leaving just one person on duty—not after what happened to the bar. But there's nothing I can do. At least Derrick and I can take care of tossing out the troublemakers during the evening shift until we find someone, though."

Hunger pangs hit my stomach and I ran my tongue over my teeth. I'd just had them polished and the dentist had been a nervous wreck the entire time. Even though he was Supe-friendly, my fangs were sharp, and while not overly large, they didn't retract like a vampire's. Slicing a finger open would be all too easy. I could feel him tense up the entire time he was checking through my mouth.

Occasionally I cut my tongue on them, but I figured that was all part of being a werecat. What was *really* dicey were blow jobs. Shade and I had worked out a system where I managed not to hurt him most of the time, but in the end, it was easier to focus our attentions on other forms of love play, given the risks.

"I'm hungry, you have any snacks in this joint?"

Menolly leaned over and flicked my nose. "Doofus. I'm surprised you aren't packing a candy bar. Go check near the birthday cake in the kitchen—we have plenty of cupcakes and one or two won't be missed. We won't be firing up the grill till it's officially opening time, so if you want, grab yourself one . . . or some nuts from the bar." She smiled and let out a satisfied laugh. "Kitten, I can't tell you what a relief it is to actually *have* a decent grill to go with the name."

Before an arsonist had torched it, the Wayfarer Bar &

Grill's kitchen had been barely passable. The cook had managed a few simple things like fries and burgers, or grilled cheese, or cold sandwiches. Standard dive food: filling, but nothing to write home about.

During renovations, Menolly had consulted with the architect and they'd redesigned the entire joint. She had commandeered the upper floor and ditched her attempts to turn it into a bed-and-breakfast. Instead, they'd relocated the kitchen upstairs, added an elevator, and revamped the staircase to make it user-friendly. A dumbwaiter and intercom system completed the cooking arrangements. They'd gutted two of the bedrooms in order to create a large private meeting room, to be rented out as needed.

"Are you going to miss having a bed-and-breakfast?" I glanced around. While the outside of the building looked the same—red brick, old, and historic—inside, the Wayfarer had a far different feel than when we'd first come Earthside and Menolly had started working as a bartender for her cover job.

"No, I don't think so. I barely had one anyway. The bar had its charms, but now it's *my* vision, through and through." She glanced around, a satisfied look on her face. "As painful as the fire was, at least I was able to rebuild and put my own stamp on it."

She bit her lip, drawing a drop of blood with her fangs. That they were showing told me she was stressed. Vampires had retractable fangs and they only came down during hunger, arousal, or stress. I knew she was thinking about the lives that had been lost during the fire but I said nothing. No use in scraping an open wound.

The walls were covered with postcards and wine labels, and the bar itself was polished to a high sheen, as were the bar stools. Two large tables, each seating up to ten people, took center stage. The booths had been rebuilt, their upholstery now a supple black leather. All the tables on the floor were new, the wood was a deep mahogany, rich and warm.

Menolly had asked the contractor to build a dance floor, and to replace the antiquated jukebox, she'd installed satellite radio. Large-screen televisions were mounted on the side wall of the bar for the sports freaks who occasionally came in—she kept the sound off, but they were continually running different games.

But despite all the Earthside trappings, everywhere I looked, I could see touches from Otherworld, giving the Wayfarer an exotic feel. Star crystals from the mines of the Nebulveori Mountains. Woven lattice tapestries from the shores of Terial, the Eastern Port on the Mirami Ocean. And sand-cast urns holding dried flowers, potted from the dunes of the Sandwhistle Desert. The Wayfarer Bar & Grill had become a beautiful hybrid between the two worlds.

"Well, I approve of the kitchen. I approve of anything to do with food." I reached out and ran my hand along the red brick of the wall. There was a lot of brick in this building, and together with the warm wood and muted lighting, it gave the bar a cave-like feeling, but in a cozy, protected manner.

Menolly sobered. "To tell you the truth, I don't think that I could rebuild as a bed-and-breakfast. No matter how much people say the deaths weren't my fault, I'll never be able to forget." She gave a quick nod toward the new waitress. "I just hope she works out."

I followed her gaze. Jenny was an FBH—full-blooded human. Camille had met her at Broom Stix, a magic shop, and Jenny had taken Chrysandra's place as head waitress. She was a good worker, eager to learn, and just as eager to be out of her stepmother's store.

"She'll do a good job. She's sincere. But I'm surprised you hired another FBH, given Chrysandra . . ." I stopped at the stricken look on my sister's face. "I'm sorry . . . I didn't think." Great, I was just making things worse. I had a knack for opening mouth, inserting foot.

After a moment, Menolly shrugged. "What can I say? Her death will always weigh heavy on my shoulders. Especially at the end." She flinched. "But you're right, Jenny will do a good job. She's smart, personable, and sassy enough to handle the customers. The vamp crowd will love her." She glanced at the clock. "So when does the birthday girl arrive?"

"Camille and Smoky are supposed to be here in about ten minutes. Smoky said he'd have her here right before the opening. They'll come in the back, so the crowd out front doesn't swarm in behind them. You have a fan club waiting, you know." I jerked my finger toward the front of the building.

"I'm surprised anybody's showing up. The final count was twenty-five deaths, you know. Including vampires." Again, the haunted look.

I wanted to wipe away the memory, to wipe away the guilt Menolly felt, but there was nothing I could do. Only time would help her sort out everything that had happened.

So instead, I forced a bright smile. "Well, *I'm* not surprised. People love this place. And they love you." I reached out, patted her hand. The coldness of her skin had ceased to bother me. She was my sister, even if she was a vampire.

I wasn't lying. There *was* a crowd out front. A number of vamps—I assumed they were vampires by their pallor—had shown up to show their support for the Wayfarer. There were also a number of Weres and Fae. All in all, there must have been fifty people outside, waiting in the rain-soaked January evening.

But tonight was more than the reopening. Tonight, we'd planned a special surprise. Since it was also Camille's birthday, Smoky had volunteered to keep her occupied while the rest of us decked out the bar for both the reopening and her party.

"I'm not so sure about this, Delilah. You know Camille isn't much on surprises. You think we can pull this off without a hitch, given our track record?"

I wrinkled my nose. "Our parties always suck. Why should this time be any different? At least this time nobody's hired a stripper."

It was sadly true that we seldom had people begging us to throw another shindig. But it was also true that there was no stripper in a fringed G-string for me to attack as my fluffy-butt tabby self. Although the balloons were mesmerizing, I could keep a handle on myself unless the ribbons were left dangling. Then all bets were off. *Candy in front of the baby time.*

Shade sidled up to me and slid one arm around my waist. He nuzzled my neck and I planted a kiss on his cheek. We were officially beyond the honeymoon stage, and had been together almost a year and a half. But as I leaned my head against his side, the warmth of his musky scent quickened my pulse. I'd never experienced this kind of love before we met. He was sweet and funny, and sexy in that easy, comfortable way. And I could be myself around him.

Shade reached into his pocket for something, but at that moment, Jenny came scurrying out from the back.

"Your sister is here." Her eyes were wide. Camille had cowed her at one point, and Jenny still seemed to be scared of her.

"Thanks, we'll take it from here. You go ahead and finish checking all the booths and tables to make sure everything is ready." Menolly jumped off the bar. She glanced around. "Everybody here?"

I counted. Trillian and Morio were in the corner— Camille's other husbands. She had three of them and they were all very happy together, if at times a little loud.

Vanzir and Roz were playing darts together. We called them the demon twins because Vanzir was a dream-chaser demon and Roz was an incubus, and they liked to hang out together, like a couple of slightly demented frat boys. Hanna, our housekeeper from the Northlands, and Maggie, our baby calico gargoyle, sat at a table with Iris and Bruce.

Nerissa—Menolly's wife—carried the cake down from the kitchen. She placed it on one of the large tables. Everybody was here tonight, including Erin, Menolly's middle-aged "daughter"; Roman, the son of the vampire queen; and Chase, the FBH detective who had become part of our extended family. Even Mistletoe and Feddrah-Dahns had traveled over from Otherworld for the party, though having a unicorn at any function was always problematic.

"Everybody's here and we're good to go." I motioned to Jenny. "Will you ask Smoky to bring her in?"

Whatever excuse the dragon had made for keeping our sister out of the way appeared to have worked. Menolly doused the lights, and a moment later, a rustle told us they'd entered the room. But as she flicked the lights on again and we all yelled "Surprise," we found ourselves shouting and throwing confetti at one very nervous toadsquatter.

"Ah, hell!" Menolly launched herself forward, but just then Camille and Smoky followed the creature through the door.

"Stop!" Camille grabbed the arm of the toadsquatter, yanking him out of the way. The squat goblin-like figure let out a shriek and hissed at her. "Shut up, you little weasel." She swatted his nose as Smoky loomed up behind her, all six-foot-four of him.

"What the fuck?" Menolly pulled back. "What's *that* doing in my bar?"

A whiff of the toadsquatter's stench hit me and I gagged. *Lovely.* Cross a patch of skunk cabbage with a lumberjack who's gone a week without showering and that's pretty much what the creature smelled like. My stomach lurched.

Derrick Means, one of the bartenders and a werebadger, stared at the thing with a horrified look on his face. He leaned over to me and asked, "What the hell is that? It looks like a goblin that's been squashed and deformed."

"Toadsquatter. From Otherworld. A mutant version of a goblin. Goblins use them as slaves, and the toadsquatters hate them as much as we do. The little creeps aren't blameless, though. They can be nasty tempered, fickle, and they're all a pack of thieves." Which begged the question: Why was one of them standing in the bar, and why had Camille protected him?

Derrick, whose ponytail was black streaked with white, shook his head. "Guess it's no worse than some of the things we have over here. I bet you have no clue how many strange beasties we have running around the woods."

"I'll bet you're right." I grinned at him. Derrick was usually pretty grumpy, but he was fair, honest, and respectful. And that was more than we got from a lot of the Earthside crowd, FBHs *or* Supes.

Camille was trying to calm the toadsquatter, who was disturbingly close to tears. And trust me, a crying toadsquatter wasn't any more appealing than a happy one. "Don't upset him any more. He has important information for me, or so he says."

Menolly paused. "Information?"

"We think he may know the name of the sorcerer who is tracking Camille." Smoky glared at the toadsquatter, obviously not thrilled with this turn of events.

Camille knelt down by the creature. Toadsquatters were about four feet high, and squat. And butt-ugly. "Listen, calm down. I warned you people would react this way, so chill out. I promised you that if your info was worth it, I'd give you a reward, didn't I?"

He nodded and, in a halting variant of the common tongue from Otherworld, said, "Yes, yes . . . You promised. You also have to promise they won't kill me, though." He jerked his finger toward us. I'd say *thumb*, but since he had six or seven digits I wasn't sure which stood in for what finger.

"I promise." Camille stared at the rest of us, and we slowly nodded our heads. Nobody seemed too enthusiastic, though. While toadsquatters weren't inherently evil like their brother race of goblins, they *were* sneaky and reminiscent of cockroaches. They might not do anything to you, but they were so nasty you just kind of wanted to squash them on principle.

She straightened up and looked around, her gaze falling on the cake. "Oh, hell—birthday party? For me?"

"Yeah, but you kind of blew that one out of the water." Menolly laughed. "Let's get drinks started, Derrick. Camille, take that . . . thing . . . to my office. I don't want my customers coming in here and finding him."

Camille grabbed the toadsquatter by the hand and started for the back.

Menolly turned back to us. "Delilah, carry the presents to my office, please. We don't want them to get stolen. It's time for me to unlock the doors. Luckily, I ordered a gigantic cake. One big enough to include my patrons. But Jenny, would you move it out of sight till we're done talking to that creature?"

And with that flurry of orders, Menolly headed over to unlock the doors. I gathered up the presents, then paused, watching as she inserted the key to open the Wayfarer to the public for the first time in over two months.

The crowds flooded in, swamping the staff. Once it appeared everything was going off without a hitch, I headed for the back, presents safely in my arms. Menolly motioned that she'd join us in a bit.

The office had been expanded during renos, and we all managed to fit in, albeit a little snugly. I set the gifts on the desk, and Camille walked over, looking at them. She seemed preoccupied.

"Anything wrong?" I glanced over at the toadsquatter but he was ignoring us.

She frowned. "There was someone in the bookstore today who made me uneasy. He was looking for a rare grimoire and was very pushy about it. He acted as though he thought I was hiding a copy from him, when I told him I didn't have it and didn't know where I could get one."

"What's his name? Did he have a demonic feel?" The fact that that question was always one of our first considerations now saddened me, but we always had to take it into account, given what we were facing.

She paused, considering. "No, he didn't—I think he was FBH, but he did have a lot of magical energy, and there was something off about him. I think . . . he introduced himself as Jay. And he said he'd heard about my store from a friend . . . but that could be anybody."

I sighed, leaning against the desk. "Has he been in before?"

"I don't think so. But I don't trust him."

"Keep an eye out." I leaned against the counter. "If I'm upstairs in my office, you can always call me down next time he comes in. And tell Giselle to do the same."

A garbled grunt interrupted us. We looked over to see Smoky holding the toadsquatter in place, his hand firmly on the creature's head. The toadsquatter wasn't moving, but neither did he look like he wanted to be here and I didn't blame him. He was in the middle of a group of hostile people who could easily make mincemeat out of him without so much as a blink. His gaze flickered toward the door.

"Easy, boy. You're not going anywhere. Not yet. So what's your name?" Smoky asked.

Shifty-Eyes thought for a moment, then sighed. "Rataam."

"Well, Rataam, give us the information we're looking for and you get to leave here alive. *However*, if I discover that you've gone back to whoever you've been snooping for and ratted us out, I'll personally track down your family and there will be no more little Rataam babies in the world. Do I make myself clear?" When Smoky played hardball, he didn't hesitate to break heads.

The toadsquatter seemed to realize this was no idle threat. He gulped and nodded.

Smoky let go of his head. "Tell us what you know, then. If it's worth it, we'll pay you for your knowledge."

Rataam ducked his squat head. He really did look very toad-like, and for a moment I felt sorry for him. It was a scary thing to be surrounded by people who could pull you apart. I'd been there. But then he let out a noise—I didn't know what it was and didn't want to—and a vile stench filled the room.

"Oh, dude, that's *nasty*. Do you have to do that?" I blurted out the words before I could stop myself.

Rataam scowled, but ignored me. Instead, he turned to Camille. "The sorcerer following you is named Iyonah."

Iyonah? We'd had a run-in with the woman recently. Or rather, Camille had. But none of us realized she was anything other than a blip on the radar of "potential issues." That she was following Camille and potentially out to kill her was a step up in the game.

Camille blanched. "Oh, fuck. I *knew* there was something about her! But how do *you* know this? How do you even know about me?"

"I only know about her because I was paid to find out. I never heard of you before my employer paid me to look into the matter." Rataam shifted, obviously uncomfortable.

I blinked. Someone had paid the toadsquatter to snoop into Camille's life? That alone was unnerving. Apparently, Camille thought so, too, because she knelt beside him, pale and looking worried.

"And *who* is your employer?" She took his hand in hers, unleashing her glamour, which immediately seemed to have a calming effect on the creature.

He let out a long breath. "Promise you won't tell them I told you?"

She held up her hand. "On the Moon Mother's honor."

Rataam scuffed his foot on the floor, then shrugged. "Raven Mother. She asked me to find out who was following you, and to warn you."

Startled, Camille withdrew her hand and stood up. Raven Mother could be bad news when she wanted to be, but for some reason, she'd decided to help us out. That didn't mean we could trust her, though. Raven Mother was wily and cunning, and she had so many hidden agendas that our enemies looked like simpletons compared to her.

Camille had been getting to know more about the Elemental than she had ever wanted to know—she had no choice given the way events had been turning. As a result, Menolly and I'd been privy to a number of late-night conversations. Intrigue seemed to run rampant in the whole Raven Mother–Triple Threat–Moon Mother triangle that was going on.

"Did Raven Mother tell you *why* she wanted you to spy on me?" Camille's eyes flashed—they were a vivid shade of violet, and now silver flecks appeared. No, she wasn't happy, and her magic was rising.

Rataam shook his head. "No, but she made it clear it was important. She threatened to destroy my family if I didn't do what she asked." He sounded so disheartened that I instantly felt guilty for feeling so uncharitable toward him.

Smoky and Camille looked at each other, and she slowly nodded. There was no real way of telling if he was lying, but odds were, Raven Mother hadn't told him *what* Iyonah wanted. Her motives might be questionable, but she wasn't stupid by any means.

Smoky let out a grumpy sigh. "All right, we will pay you well, but only if you vow on your family's life to keep your mouth shut about everything that's happened. As long as you keep your bargain, we won't tell Raven Mother that you told us it was she who hired you." Smoky nodded to the door. "Come, I'll take you to a portal, pay you, and you can return to Otherworld immediately."

Camille kept her mouth shut until Smoky escorted the creature out. Then she let out a slow whistle. "I should have known Iyonah was up to no good. I think I did, I just didn't realize she was after *me*."

Irritated that we had to focus on enemies, even on our birthdays, I shook my head and gave her a hug. "Well, we should be able to take care of the matter as long as she remains clueless to the fact that you know about her. We'll go over there tomorrow." I pointed to her presents. "Meanwhile, birthday party."

"You didn't hire a stripper, did you?" She stared at me pointedly.

I blushed, but then swatted her playfully. "No, and I'm not going to turn into a cat and go lunging after the customers tonight either. But can you imagine Smoky walking into the room to find a guy jiggling his junk in your face?"

Trillian meandered over, laughing. "Oh, I'd *pay* to see that." He, Smoky, and Morio had a good-natured rivalry going on. While they were all married to Camille and she loved each of them with a passion, they still sparred at times. But when push came to shove, they had one another's backs, and together they surrounded her with a ring of protection that sometimes chafed at her.

Feddrah-Dahns spoke up. For a unicorn, his voice was simultaneously melodic and authoritative. "This Iyonah—I will send Mistletoe home right now to do research on her. Don't take her on until we've dug up everything we can. I don't want you in any more danger than you already are. If she's truly a sorcerer, chances are she's fairly powerful. And powerful sorcerers are danger incarnate."

Before Camille could say a word, I interrupted. "She

promises. She'll be good and wait. Now, can we go join the party? This is Menolly's special night, and it's also special for Camille. We don't get many celebrations. Please, let's enjoy the ones we can." I pushed Camille toward the door, and for the moment, the issue was shelved.

The party was rocking, the music loud, and the bar crowded.

The two large center tables were reserved for our party, but most of the booths were full, as were the counter stools. People had packed the joint, showing their support for Menolly.

In one corner, Marion Vespa—the owner of the Supe-Urban Café—and her husband were ordering drinks. Jonas and his werebear buddies had crowded into a booth and were eating burgers and fries, along with giant steins of beer. At a table near the door, Frank Willows, the leader of the Supe Militia, was holding court with three other werewolves.

And, of course, Roman, the son of the Vampire Queen, sat in the most luxurious booth, along with several of the higher-ups from the Seattle Vampire Nexus. Menolly was his official consort, and boy, did she walk a tight wire between her wife and Roman. All in all, the bar was crowded. The look on Menolly's face made me happy. She'd expected people to ostracize her after what happened, but truth was: none of it was her fault. Maybe tonight would drive that through her thick skull.

As we gathered around the tables, Jenny brought over the cake. Camille winked at her, and the girl, flustered, stuttered out a "Happy Birthday" and immediately left.

"Hey, I wanted to order—" Camille laughed. "I'm going to have to do something to put Jenny at ease, it seems." She stood up, looking over at the bar.

I motioned for her to sit down. "You're the birthday girl. I'll get a waitress. What do you want to drink? Do you want anything to eat?"

"I want a Goblin Blaster and can you order me a grilled cheese and fries? We'll cut the cake while we're waiting for the food." She was eyeing the massive sheet cake like I eyed catnip. Normally Camille didn't go for sweets but Earthside store-bought birthday cake had proven to be a weakness for her.

I motioned to a different waitress and gave her Camille's order, and my own. Grilled cheese sounded good, so I asked for two. As the others ordered their food, I pushed my way up to the bar. Derrick, along with Digger—the assistant bartender, who was a vamp—were mixing drinks as fast as they could.

Derrick winked at me. "What do you need?"

"Camille wants a Goblin Blaster. For me? A Kahlúa and cream, please." I didn't drink a lot, but when I did, I preferred my booze with something to soften the impact.

He raised an eyebrow. "She wants a Goblin Blaster? We don't get much call for those. They're an acquired taste, that's for sure." As he began mixing up the basil liqueur with orange juice and both light and dark rum, the drink took on an earthy, pungent smell. The drink almost glowed green, and I grimaced. I preferred my drinks sweet.

Derrick added a twist of orange to the glass, then whipped up my Kahlúa and cream, and slid both drinks across the counter. I started to thank him but he had already moved on to his next order.

I picked up the drinks and carried them back to the table, handing Camille's to her. She took a long sip and closed her eyes. Something about the basil and orange really appealed to her. Like me, she wasn't much of a drinker, but ever since Menolly had concocted the recipe, Camille had, for the most part, stuck to a standing order.

Over the past few weeks, Menolly had gotten so irritable without the Wayfarer to distract her that she'd turned her lair into a makeshift bar and had managed to get just about everyone in the house drunk at one point or another, experimenting with new recipes. The upside was, the drink menu at the Wayfarer had increased by at least fifty percent.

While we waited for the food, Camille cut the cake. The frosting was an inch thick and my taste buds were doing a happy dance on my tongue. Camille's favorite flavors were strawberry and lemon, so the cake was strawberry with lemon icing. There were chocolate cupcakes for those whose tastes ran to the more traditional, but I wasn't picky. If it was cake, I'd eat it. And I did. Two pieces of cake and three cupcakes.

Menolly climbed on the counter and whistled to the bar. "Listen up! Tonight's not just the reopening of the Way-farer, but it's also my sister Camille's birthday, as you may have surmised. We have a lot of cake here, so feel free to drop by our table for a slice. It's free till it's gone."

A general round of applause and a chorus of "Happy Birthday"'s rang through the bar as I settled in beside Camille and Menolly with a sigh of satisfaction. Despite the toads-quatter, everything had gone off without a hitch.

A little voice in the back of my head kept whispering, *Don't let down your guard*, but I was tired of always being on alert. I decided, what the hell, for once I'd ignore the warning and let down my hair. That was more than a cliché. I actually *could* let down my hair more than usual, because I'd started growing it back in. I was sporting a chin-length shag. Shade liked it, and while I wasn't sure I'd ever grow it long again, it was fun for a change.

I downed the Kahlúa and cream and got a second, then a third round of drinks for Camille and myself. A fourth followed shortly.

The volume of noise had risen to a steady buzz now as more people crowded into the bar, and I blinked, realizing that I wasn't following any particular conversation, but instead, I just sat back, taking it all in.

Menolly was beaming. Another round of drinks later, and the party was growing louder.

Wild Cherry came over the speakers, singing "Play That Funky Music." Nerissa grabbed Menolly's hand and dragged her up to dance. Nerissa towered over Menolly in her tawny, werepuma glory, but the two could boogie it up good. In a skintight hot pink minidress, with golden hair and gold spar-kling heels that sent her over six feet tall, Nerissa was a strik-ing sight.

Camille and Trillian followed, spinning onto the dance

floor in all their fetish goth-glory. Dark and vampy, they made one hell of a pair. I blinked. Trillian cut a damn fine figure, now that I looked at him through my Kahlúa-colored eyes. The song shifted to "Super Freak" by Rick James, then it was fully into retro city with "Electric Avenue," followed by "She Blinded Me with Science," then "Whip It," and of course, "Safety Dance."

I polished off my drink and grabbed Shade's hand. "Dance with me."

He blinked. I danced, but it wasn't a common request, considering I preferred curling up on the sofa with television and junk food.

"Are you sure, babe? You look a little flushed." His voice sounded huskier than usual and I wanted nothing more than to press up against him.

I glanced down at the glasses on the table, counting them. Apparently, I'd had seven rounds, not four like I thought. But though my mind was a little fuzzy, more than anything, I wanted to dance with my lover.

"Dance. *Now!*"

We whirled out on the dance floor, but I whirled a little too enthusiastically and would have gone toppling over except that Shade had a tight grip on my hand.

He pulled me back into his arms and we began shaking it up to "Elevator Man" by Oingo Boingo.

But as Shade spun me around, I began to realize that maybe I really was a tad drunk. Booze hit my system overly fast and I hadn't planned on having seven drinks—that was for sure. Not entirely certain what I was doing, I just attempted to stay on my feet. I probably should have asked Shade to take me back to the table, but I was so light-headed I couldn't seem to form the words.

The next minute, none of that mattered.

The door burst open and Daniel, our Earthside FBH cousin, darted inside, followed by what looked like a very angry Viking. The muscle-bound man wearing the leather breeches and tunic grabbed Daniel by the collar and lifted him over his head.

Shade let go of my hand and I was so startled that I tripped back into the crowd, taking down a couple of vampires who were dancing. We hit the floor as Daniel sailed across the room, the Viking tossing him like a Scotsman tossing a log in the Highland Games.

As Daniel landed in a shuddering heap by my side, Camille darted toward the northern intruder, but the man took one look at her, then at the rest of the bar, and vanished from sight, as if he'd never existed.

Chapter 2

Shade reached down to help me to my feet. The shock of landing on the hardwood floor and of seeing Daniel used as a giant
football managed to jolt some of the alcoholic haze out of my
system. Though I was a little unsteady on my feet, my head
had cleared considerably, probably thanks to the adrenaline.

Camille knelt by Daniel's side, helping him sit up. He
looked dazed and confused. Smoky reached down and slid
his hands under Daniel's arms, hoisting him to his feet,
while Morio brought him a chair.

"Are you all right, sweetheart?" Shade looked me over.

I nodded. "I think so." Tentatively, I tested out my limbs.
Feet, ankles, legs—okay. Arms, torso—okay. Neck—a little
stiff, but okay. "Yeah, I'm fine. No damage done. But who the
hell was that? And where did he go?"

"I don't know, but I imagine Daniel can provide some
sort of answer. Maybe." He took my hand and we threaded
through the crowd that had gathered around Daniel. By her
quick glances around the room, I knew Menolly was keeping a watch out for anybody else looking to stir up trouble.

"Daniel, are you all right?" Camille leaned over him. "Can somebody bring him a glass of water?"

Our cousin had a slender build—one might almost call him effeminate until he spoke. Lithe, blond, and in his mid-forties, Daniel was related to us on our mother's side. He was also an internationally known cat burglar who had belonged to the ISA—the International Security Agency—which meant he'd done some pretty shady stuff in his life. The ISA trained killers, snipers, and assassins, and carried out coupes unknown to even the heads of governments, until they were successfully done and over with. There wasn't a lock in existence that Daniel didn't have a good chance of getting through.

He winced, rubbing his neck. "I'll be all right, I think. I took a good blow to the shoulder, though."

Chase joined us. "I looked for the guy but couldn't find him. I suppose I could put out an APB on him—he wouldn't be hard to spot."

Camille glanced at me, then shook her head and turned to Chase. "No . . . Chase, that wasn't any ordinary person. Leave it be for now. Trust me?"

He shrugged. "Whatever you say, but if some lunatic is running around the streets of Seattle—"

"I don't think we have to worry about that. We'll talk later. Why don't you go home with Bruce and Iris? We're going to probably be late, and I'm sure Iris can use her sleep. Hanna needs to take Maggie home, too." Camille caught Chase's questioning gaze with a shake of the head.

He shrugged. "No problem. We'll talk later." Returning to the table where Bruce and Iris were waiting, he whispered something to them and they gathered their things and headed to the door, Hanna and Maggie in tow.

Camille flashed them a wave, then motioned to me. "We should take Daniel *in back* and get him some ice for his shoulder." Which was code for: *We need to talk in private.*

"Yeah, you're right. Let me get Menolly." As I headed back to the bar, I motioned for Digger and Derrick to join us. Menolly's gaze flickered over to Daniel as she wiped her hands on a bar towel and leapt over the counter.

"We need an ice pack for his shoulder. And Menolly, we need to find out what's going on. In your office, if you get my drift."

"Right. Derrick? Grab an ice pack and bring it to the back. And you and Digger keep a close eye on the crowd just in case anybody else decides to stir up trouble. Send someone to get us if there's a problem."

"Got it. But Menolly, Delilah?" Derrick's voice was gruff but firm. "That was no drunken brawler. That was a ghost." He voiced what I suspected we'd all been thinking.

I clapped him on the arm. "Yeah, we know, but don't say anything to anybody, okay? Just do your best to convince them he was a drunk who vanished into the crowd. Say whatever you have to say. We don't want questions until we have some answers to go along with them."

"She's right." Menolly removed her apron and handed it to Derrick. "Just keep a close watch on things, do your best to squash any rumors, and come get us if all hell breaks loose."

We navigated our way toward the back, passing the stairway leading down to the portal. As I glanced down the steps, I realized I'd rather be talking with the toadsquatter instead of doing this.

Apparently, Menolly felt the same way. "I really do not want to be dealing with ghosts again. I hate those fucking things." She paused as Derrick approached, ice pack in hand. "Thanks. This should be fine."

As the werebadger made his way back to the bar, I let out a long sigh. "Yeah, I've had my fill of them, too. We've dealt with so many spirits over the past year that it feels like we live more in the world of the dead than the living." Then, realizing what I'd said to her, of all people, I started to laugh.

Menolly broke into a grin. "Yeah, ya think so? Maybe just a little? Let's see, Camille and Morio are steeping themselves in death magic. I'm a vampire so, technically, yeah, I'm all the way to the left of the spectrum—dead and then some. And you're . . . what? Right! A Death Maiden. Maybe there's a reason we keep tripping over them?"

"Oh, shuddup." I playfully swatted at her. She knew how to be snarky when she wanted to.

We reached her office—along with Smoky and the rest of the guys—and Menolly handed Camille the ice pack. Daniel let out a groan as Camille placed it over his right shoulder and the back of his neck.

"Well, that feels lovely, in a masochistic sort of way. I'm going to have a lump on the back of my neck tomorrow, that much I can tell you." He winced, trying to hold it into place.

Camille found a strip of cloth—what looked like a long tea towel—and fashioned a tie to keep the ice pack in place. "There. Just don't move too fast and it should stay put."

We gathered around Daniel, Menolly taking her place behind her desk. She leaned back and put her feet up on the mahogany surface, ignoring Camille's frown. "*My* desk, *my* feet. So, Daniel, care to tell us just what the fuck was going on out there?"

Daniel shrugged, then immediately let out another groan as the ice shifted slightly.

"You shouldn't do that." I was feeling all too perky, given the mix of adrenaline and alcohol. Or maybe, *impertinent* was the right word. The evening had been a bust, but not in the way we'd expected.

Daniel stuck out his tongue at me—an uncharacteristic move. "Well, thank *you*, Captain Obvious. I never would have thought of that." He sobered. "All right, here's the deal. I need your help. I was on my way to ask you when . . . when . . . well, you saw what happened."

"You were being chased by one butt-ugly big Viking and we're pretty sure it was a ghost. That's what happened. Care to tell us where you picked him up and why he was after you?"

The fact that Daniel was coming to us for help could only mean that he'd gotten himself in some sort of trouble he couldn't handle. And since he normally ran on the shady side of the law, that also meant he couldn't go to the cops.

He let out a long sigh. "Okay, the thing is . . . I think I'm in trouble. Big trouble. And the only ones I know who might stand a chance in hell of helping me are you guys. Because this trouble? Is the kind I know nothing about."

"Meaning supernatural."

"Right." He shifted again. "I fully admit to ignorance in this venue. I have never been one to pretend to have knowledge that I don't. That sort of arrogance gets you killed very quickly."

Trillian let out a laugh. "I like you, Daniel."

I caught Camille's gaze and grinned at her. Our cousin and her husband had a great deal in common—they were both mercenaries, of a sort, and both were arrogant but it wasn't the blustery know-it-all machismo that drove us nuts. No, they knew what they were capable of, and they were honest about what they couldn't do.

Daniel took a deep breath and let it out slowly. "All right. Long story short: I came across a sword—a very old one. And now I think it's trying to make me do things against my will. And that Viking? I *think* he was one of the sword's protectors. I have no clue as to what I've gotten mixed up in, and for the first time in my life, I'm up against something I can't fight. Will you help me?"

Camille pinched the bridge of her nose and winced. "By 'came across,' you mean you 'stole it,' right?" We all knew what Daniel's shorthand meant. But to our surprise, this time he shook his head, looking serious.

"I did *not*. You know I'd tell you the truth if I had, but no—I didn't steal this sword. And now, I don't know how to get rid of it."

Menolly let out a long, exasperated sigh. I whistled, low and long. We didn't even have to consult over this one. Daniel was blood kin. He and his sister were the only blood relatives of our mother's that we had ever met. Whatever he'd gotten himself into, we were going to help him. With our family so rapidly diminishing, we wanted to keep everybody as intact and safe as we could.

"Of course we'll help. Start from the beginning." I settled down in one of the chairs as everybody else found a place to sit. "And Daniel? Don't leave out anything."

* * *

So I'm Delilah D'Artigo. Over in Otherworld, my name is Delilah te Maria. We take our mother's first name as our surname over there, but when my sisters and I came Earthside, we adopted her surname for our own. Camille, Menolly, and I are half-Fae, half-human.

Our mother, Maria, was human. She fell in love with our father—Sephreh ob Tanu—a full-blooded Fae from OW. He took her home with him and she willingly sacrificed her Earthside life for him. They settled down to live happily ever after, and promptly had four daughters, including my twin, who died at birth. Mother fell from a horse and broke her neck when we were very young, and Camille took over the household, because our father retreated emotionally. We had a rocky time of it, but at least we had each other.

We work for the OIA—the Otherworld Intelligence Agency. Or rather, now we *run* the Earthside division. Our jobs have gone through a major shift since we first crossed through the portals from Otherworld.

Camille is the oldest. She's a witch, and a Priestess to the Moon Mother. She has three husbands—Smoky, Morio, and Trillian—and together, she and Morio work death magic. Curvy and busty, Camille has long raven-colored hair that reaches mid-back. Her eyes are violet, an unnatural but gorgeous color, and when she runs magic heavily, they become tinged with silver. Camille lives in corsets, skirts, and heels that would break my ankles. She's shorter than me—five-seven, and not nearly as athletic.

Menolly is the youngest. At barely five-one, Menolly is thin and petite; she was a jian-tu for the Otherworld Intelligence Agency until she fell into a nest of vampires. Dredge, the biggest, baddest vamp in OW, caught hold of her, and after the longest night of her life, he raped her, tortured her, and then turned her into a vampire. The motherfucker scarred every inch of her body except her hands, feet, and her face, leaving intricate swirling designs that were as beautiful as they were deadly and macabre.

There's no way Menolly can ever fully let go of all the baggage, but we dusted Dredge a few years back, and it helped free her from her past. She's married to a werepuma—Nerissa. They're madly in love, though they have their problems. Menolly is also consort to Roman, the son of Blood Wyne, Queen of the Vampires—and Queen of the Crimson Veil, the sacred realm from where all vampires draw their power.

Then, we come to me. I was born a werecat, and as I said, I had a twin, but Arial died at birth. When Camille, Menolly, and I were sent Earthside, I ended up pledged to serve the Autumn Lord—an Elemental Lord. At first I thought it was inadvertent. Turns out? Now I'm thinking, not so much accident as destiny.

The Autumn Lord sparked off a change in me so that I now have two Were forms—the tabby one I was born with, and a black panther who primarily emerges during combat situations. I'm engaged to Shade—a half-dragon, half-Stradolan (or shadow walker), and he, too, is bound to the Autumn Lord. I'm destined to bear the Autumn Lord's child via Shade, but I'm hoping that's a ways in the future because right now? Children? Not such a good idea, considering what we're facing.

Ever since we came Earthside, we've traveled quite the winding road, but I have the nasty feeling we have a long ways to go before we see the light at the end of the tunnel.

When we were first assigned to come over Earthside, we thought we were on an enforced sabbatical. We tried, but just weren't the most effective at our jobs—no employee of the month awards in our trophy case. But as I said, once we were here, life took a major detour.

Now we're embroiled in a demonic war. Shadow Wing, leader of the Subterranean Realms, is trying to break through the portals, in order to pour his hordes Earthside. Meanwhile, he's managed to send one of his minions through to OW to start a horrific war. They've pretty much devastated the Elfin race at this point. The Demon Lord intends to take over both Earthside and Otherworld to make them his private stomping grounds. And all the nukes the humans have won't be able to stop him.

We've lost our Father, and a number of friends due to collateral damage, but along the way, we've also met some pretty incredible allies. We're holding on as best as we can. Where this will lead? Anybody's guess right now. But we'll fight to the end, because really, that's the only thing we can do.

Daniel cleared his throat. "So, yes. Yesterday, I was on a consultation with a potential client—"

"You mean, you were making a deal to steal something for somebody. Let's be blunt here, Daniel; we're not prettying up what you do." Camille let out a snort.

He flashed her a bad-boy look, but just smiled. "As you wish. Anyway, during our meeting, I noticed a sword hanging on the living room wall next to a painting. I prefer guns and other more portable weapons, so for the most part, I ignored it. But something about it stood out. Almost like it was calling to me. I ignored it, but it kept . . . I swear the damned thing was whispering to me." His voice trailed off and he shook his head. "One thing you need to know about me: I never steal anything from my clients. That's a firm rule. You consult with me, you're free from me ever taking anything you own."

"Okay, so what happened?"

"I don't remember the rest of the meeting, nor do I remember leaving. I must have, but the next thing I knew, I was on the side of a road up in Shoreline. I have no idea how I got there, but my car was out of gas. I had meant to fill it up before the meeting but forgot. Anyway, I managed to flag someone down and get gas, but then I remembered I'd promised to do something for Hester. By the time I finally got home, I found out my apartment had been ransacked. The alarm system had been mangled, and the security tapes showed nothing." Daniel shrugged, looking both irritated and confused.

That someone had the guts to break into his place was odd enough, but to ransack it? They either didn't know Daniel very well or they considered themselves stronger and more dangerous than he was. "Someone ransacked your apartment? For what?"

"I don't know. But it only gets stranger. When I went back out to my car, I found the sword in the backseat, covered up by a blanket. I don't know how I got hold of it—I honestly don't remember."

I cocked my head. "And the sword is the same one that was in your client's living room?"

"Yes. But there's more. I didn't call the cops about my apartment, obviously. But I was going to phone Le—my client—and tell him I had the sword. That somehow it had gotten into the backseat of my car. But when I tried his number, nobody answered." He paled. "That's when I found out that he's in the hospital. Somebody hit him over the head a good one. He claims he can't remember who did it. What if . . . what if that someone was me?" He drifted off, staring into space and it felt like he'd vanished down the rabbit hole.

"Daniel?" Camille leaned forward. "Daniel?"

He barely registered her words.

I frowned. Daniel was one of the most focused men I'd ever known. It wasn't like him to lose track of conversations, let alone anything else. He'd been part of a squad so elite that there was no record of it on the books. Trained to absolute discipline, nothing save for an enchantment or spell should captivate him like this. And he usually never lied about what he did, so why would he lie about what had happened starting now?

Leaning forward, I shook his arm. "Daniel? Can you hear me?"

He jerked, startling out of his reverie. "What . . . ?"

"You tranced out when you were talking about the sword."

"The sword?" He paused. "Oh, yes. That's right. It's really beautiful, isn't it? Makes you want to just hold it . . . " Again, he started to drift.

"So you found out your client was in the hospital. What did you do then?"

"That was late last night. Given the state of my apartment and what happened with the sword, I decided to stay in one of my hideouts for the evening. Today, I checked on my client—

he's all right but apparently he either really does have amnesia or he just doesn't want the cops to know about our talk either. I thought about it, and decided that I'd ditch the sword down off the docks, into the Sound. I normally don't go in for antics like that, but this whole mess has just weirded me out."

I glanced at Camille. She looked as clueless as I felt. Turning back to Daniel, I asked, "So what happened, and why was a ghost chasing you?"

"Okay, I headed down to the docks—I still haven't gone back to my apartment but I guess I'll have to pretty soon, if only to clean up. On my way down to the pier, I had a flash-·back to my time in the ISA. And . . ." He paused, and a worried look stole over his face. "I don't even like talking about this."

"You'd better, if you want our help." Menolly noticed his water glass was empty and pulled a bottle of water out of the mini-fridge in her office. "Drink."

He sipped it, a few drops dribbling down his chin. Absently wiping them away, he continued. "All right. But it's not pleasant."

I eased out a faint smile. "We're used to unpleasant. Go ahead, Daniel."

"Well, you know that I did everything I could to extricate myself from the ISA. I was and am a dangerous and deadly man, and I don't try to cover that up. When I was given a job, I did it, regardless of how distasteful my orders were. I've done things that I regret. That still haunt me in my night-mares. There's nothing I can do to ever make up for some of the atrocities I committed. That's why I went to such lengths to get out without the ISA killing me. I couldn't face the job—or myself—anymore."

Daniel had set in place a system where, if the ISA had him executed, news would be leaked as to some of their more covert activities, which would go down with the pub-lic about as well as public lynchings and the poor house.

"But this afternoon, I had a . . . it was like a flashback. A surge of that ruthless spark. I started thinking maybe I should keep the sword and . . . here's where it gets really weird. I had the urge to rampage through downtown with it, mowing down people. Almost a craving. Now, even when I was in the ISA, I viewed it as a job. I didn't enjoy what I did. Today I was craving the rush . . . the kill . . . After a long struggle, at least an hour of going back and forth with myself, I managed to get a hold on it. But this scared the fuck out of me."

As he once again drifted into silence, it struck me that Daniel was a pressure cooker. As long as he kept the valves running free, he was fine, but clog up the works and he was destined to blow.

Members who had belonged to the military, whether they were secret service or not, always faced the danger of returning to combat mentality. When you added in assassination and sniper skills, along with whatever else Daniel had done, it made for a volatile cocktail. I frowned. Daniel, when I thought about it, had the foundation to become a highly dangerous and skilled serial killer. Or mass murderer.

As if reading my thoughts, Menolly pushed through to Daniel's side. She took his hand. "If anybody knows what the fear of becoming a monster is, it's me. I live with that possibility *every day.* I live with that choice *every day.* Because, Daniel, *I am a monster.* I keep control by conscious decision. You have a choice, and you made that choice when you left the ISA. It sounds like something has triggered you back into that mind-set again. You're going to have to wrestle with your inner monster again, I fear."

Morio nodded. "I think she's right. And I think the sword has something to do with this. Daniel, what about the Viking ghost? Have you ever seen him before? What happened to cause him to chase you tonight?"

Daniel cleared his throat and smiled, squeezing Menolly's hand before he let go and readjusted the ice pack.

"No, I've never seen him before. I've never seen any ghosts before, that I know of. I think the Viking is like . . . a guardian for the sword. As I said, I was going to drop it into Puget Sound. I stopped down by one of the piers and started to take it out of the car when I heard a noise."

"The Viking?" Smoky asked.

"Right. I turned around to see the Viking. When I realized I could see through him, I figured he must be some sort of spirit. I was holding the sword, by my car, when he came charging toward me. Discretion is the better part of valor, they say, so I decided to get the hell out of there. I tossed the sword back in the car and slammed the door, managing to lock my keys inside. By that point, he was almost to me, and I didn't have time to use the code to get my keys and get the fuck out of there, so I ran. I remembered your invitation to Camille's birthday—which I apologize for not responding to—and decided to head to the bar. Ghosts and spirits are right up your alley, so I figured you'd be able to help me. Or at least, protect me. That damned Viking followed me the entire way. Luckily, I'm fast." Daniel's eyes were wide, his pupils dilated.

"Well . . . it's a good thing you got here before he managed to catch you." I leaned forward, resting my elbows on my knees. "So the ghost may be attached to the sword."

"One thing is for sure—we won't be able to tell until we examine it." Camille tapped her finger on the desk. "So, to be clear, the only time this Viking has ever shown up was tonight, when you were about ready to get rid of the sword?"

"Right. I'll be honest about something else. I don't even know if I *could* have let go of the sword. I don't know if I could have actually dropped it into the Sound. There's something about it . . . But that's what I was determined to do. I haven't picked up a carbon copy of the *One Ring*, have I?" Even though he tried to make a joke, it was obvious that Daniel was shaken up.

"Luckily, Tolkien made up the ring. Kind of. But there are other things as dangerous . . . even more so." As Shade spoke, I knew we were all thinking of the spirit seals and what would happen if Shadow Wing managed to collect all nine.

Nine parts to an ancient artifact, the spirit seals had divided the world into Otherworld, the Subterranean Realms, and Earthside. The ancient Fae Lords had driven the Great Divide with a fury and passion, ripping apart the three realms in order to lock away the demonic threat. But now the spirit seals were coming to light. We'd found several, but only managed to keep hold of three. Shadow Wing had come to possess three. There were three more up for grabs. If they were reunited, the resulting apocalypse could destroy the portals and rip the veils separating the realms. And Shadow Wing could break through without a problem.

Daniel didn't know anything about them, though, or about Shadow Wing, so none of us said what we were thinking.

Shade cleared his throat. "Do you remember what was running through your mind right before you saw the ghost coming toward you?"

Daniel rubbed his temples. "I believe what I was thinking right then . . . yes, I was thinking how I couldn't wait to get rid of the sword."

"I think we're right, then." Shade let out a long sigh. "The ghost is some form of protector, and when you started thinking about disposing of the sword, your intention summoned him to attack you. Which means that somehow the sword may have taken a liking to you. And that might not be a healthy thing. Let's hope it's not permanent."

I stood up. "Before we go any further, I think we'd better make sure the sword's still around and that nobody has broken into your car. Whatever the case, it's obvious the blade is a powerful piece and we need to know more about it. We don't want it falling into the wrong hands. We also need to figure out if you're the one who attacked your client. If you did, and he remembers, he might just send somebody after you, thinking you did it on purpose." I stood up. "Let's take a trip down to your car, Daniel."

Menolly patted Daniel on the shoulder—a rare gesture for her, but one that I'd seen more of since she'd gotten married to Nerissa. "I have to stay here and watch the bar—I really can't run off on opening night. But Camille and the others will take you. Camille, do you want to take your gifts with you?"

Laughing, Camille shook her head. "Why don't you bring them home when you come? If I bring them now, we'll probably end up in a fight and they'll get destroyed somehow."

"Are you coming back after you look at the sword?" Menolly opened the door to her office.

Camille shrugged. "Hard to tell, but I doubt it. We don't know if Viking boy has friends, or if he'll still be hanging around. We don't even know if he's really a ghost or some other kind of spirit. So if we don't make it back, please rescue the rest of the cake because I plan on having more than one slice of it."

With that, we trooped out to our cars. The lot on the other side of the street had been razed. The building had been old and crumbling and nobody had wanted the lease on it, so a developer bought it and put in a parking lot. At the rates Seattle parking went for, it would likely bring the new owner a pretty penny—a lot more than a storefront would have.

Nerissa stayed with Menolly, as the rest of us piled into our cars. Camille and I were sober by now—Daniel and the ghost had seen to that. Camille's husbands rode with her. Shade rode up front with me, and Vanzir and Roz rode in the back. Daniel squeezed in between them. And at precisely nine thirty, we pulled out of the garage and headed down to the waterfront.

Along the way, Daniel seemed agitated, and the closer we got to his car, the more agitated he seemed, muttering under his breath and shifting in his seat. I could see him through the rearview mirror. Finally, Shade glanced over his shoulder.

"What is going on, man? What's all the muttering about?"

Daniel grumbled. "I just feel terribly uneasy about the sword. This is not how I usually am. You know me enough by now to know that I'm almost always in control of myself."

"True." Shade glanced at me and, in a low voice, whispered, "Should we do anything?"

"What *can* we do?" I whispered back. It wasn't like we could sedate him. All we could do was hurry to his car and clean up the mess he'd stumbled into, if we could. But truth was, I found myself eager to see the sword and figure out what was going on. At least we weren't facing Shadow Wing's demons, a nice change of pace, ghostly or not.

"Daniel, what was the name of the person you stole the sword from? We should do some research." I glanced over at Shade. "Take notes, love, please?"

"No problem." Shade pulled out a pen and notebook. I'd gotten him in the habit of carrying them wherever he went. I still liked the solid feel of paper, though when I had my new tablet with me, I often used that. But you didn't need to worry about the battery going out on a notebook, and you didn't need to worry about work getting erased.

Daniel let out an exasperated sigh. "I've never given away the name of a client before, you know. I treat everything confidentially."

"It's not like we're setting him up to be arrested." I snorted. "Dude, you either want our help or you don't, and the way things sound, you *need* our help. So cooperate and hand over his name."

Daniel let out a little huff. "His name is Leif Engberg. He lives at the Vista View Towers over in Kirkland." He pulled out a small tablet and began zipping over the surface. "I do extensive research on every single person that I take on commissions from."

"Daniel . . ." I couldn't take it anymore. I had to call him out and make it stick this time. "We're done with the charade. We *know* you don't like facing the truth; that much is obvious. But it's over. You can't fake it with us. You're a professional thief. If you walk the walk, at least talk the talk." I cringed, I hated that phrase—it was so slick and easy, but sometimes? It was also true.

"We don't approve of what you do; you know that. *But* we also know you don't steal from poor people and you aren't leaving anybody hungry. So we're not going to get on your case as long as you're honest. Get it?"

Finally, Daniel let out a long breath. "Got it. All right, no white gloves. When I'm casing a house, I also case the person. The same with my clients—it never hurts to be as knowledge-able as you can. Usually the people I interact with—on either side—have extensive security systems. And for what it's worth, you're correct in that I would never steal from anyone who was poor. Televisions? Stereos? Even jewelry, I don't bother with. For one thing, I wouldn't ever want to put a family at risk for food or cause them to lose a valuable memory."

That made me feel a little better. At least he wasn't being a prick. "So you only go after art objects?"

"Usually. Art. Antiquities. An occasional jewel, but usually it's a rare specimen and not set into jewelry. The people who hire me aren't looking for objects to sell. They're almost always looking to add to a private gallery. They don't want a two-thousand-dollar ring from the local jewelry shop." He shrugged. "They have the money to pay me what I need to support my lifestyle."

I sighed. He had really built up a business, all right. "All right, so the places you go into are highly secure. Meaning your skills are put to the test. And you need to know about the client so you have every resource at hand. That makes sense. Tell us about Leif."

"Leif is the son of a Norwegian immigrant. He's first-generation American. His father, Karl, ran a highly successful technology company over in Oslo. He moved it to the United States shortly before he was killed in a plane crash—pilot error. Small craft. It went down twenty minutes after it left the ground. Leif was an only son, and his mother was dead, so he inherited a great deal of money, as well as everything his father owned. He's on the board of his father's company, but he doesn't take an active part and enjoys a rather freewheeling lifestyle. He just wants to party, play with pretty girls, and spend money."

That gave us a pretty clear view of Leif. "Do you know how he came by the sword?"

Daniel consulted his tablet. "Yes, actually. In my research on him, I found out that he inherited his father's property and it was part of that. His father was an art collector, but apparently the sword is a family heirloom. Another reason why I'd never consciously steal it."

As we pulled into the parking lot near the pier, we saw one

car—a black sedan. It could be any sedan, which surprised me. I'd expected to see Daniel in a Porsche or something fancy, but then I realized, he wouldn't want to be noticed. Not in his profession. The less attention he drew to himself, the better.

As we stepped out of our cars, the chill hit me. I shivered, looking at the mist as it rolled in off the Sound. Filtering up from the water, the wisps of fog boiled along the asphalt of the parking lot, reaching out with ghostly tendrils. Daniel hesitated for a moment, then walked over to his car and punched in a code on a small panel against the driver's door. The lock beeped, and he opened the back left door. After a moment, he emerged, his keys dangling from one hand.

"Found them."

"I thought you couldn't lock your keys in the car anymore," I said.

He shrugged. "Generally most models are set up to where you can't, but I've modified my car. You can lock it without the key. I realized that I didn't have time to hunt for my keys with the Viking coming after me, so I punched the 'lock' button that I had installed on every door. That way, I can lock it and run if I have to, then use the code access panel to unlock it when I return."

He turned back to the car and withdrew a long scabbard, leather inset with sparkling gems. A shiver ran down my back as Lysanthra, my sentient dagger, woke up. She stirred, and an alarm ran threw me as she whispered in the recesses of my mind, *Blood . . . the blade craves it. And it will not rest until the spirit within is freed and his thirst quenched.*

Startled—she'd never really talked to me before like that—I withdrew her from the sheath, about to say something when a noise behind us startled me.

"There!" Daniel gasped, pointing.

As we turned, I crouched into attack position. Three Viking warriors stared at us. And I knew, in the pit of my stomach, that they weren't human, if they'd ever been.

Chapter 3

~~~~~

"Looks like we have some action," Vanzir said, cracking his knuckles.

But the figures paused as if awaiting our next move.

Keeping his gaze warily on the ghosts, Shade let out a grunt. "True enough. But since they're already dead, we can't just take them out. They really are spirits of some sort, but I don't think they're your garden-variety ghosts." Stepping back, he motioned for me to follow. Over his shoulder, he added, "Morio, any clue?"

Morio narrowed his gaze. "You're right. They aren't typical ghosts. I don't think the sword is haunted, not in the way we were thinking. At least, not by whatever these spirits are."

"What can we do about them?" Camille moved up to Morio's side. When it came to hauntings and spirits, they worked together as a unit. I secretly pictured them almost like Bonnie and Clyde, only with magic instead of guns.

"I suggest we try to communicate first." Smoky moved

forward. "Aggressive spirits usually attack first, and so far, they've been hanging back."

Shade nodded. "Let me try." Shade understood spirits far better than most of us. I might be a Death Maiden, but I ferried the living through the veil, and that's where my job left off. Shade had grown up in the Netherworld.

He walked toward the ghosts. They weren't all that tall—my height or less, and I was six-one. But they were big and burly, and looked primed for fighting. Wearing heavy leather armor, all of them looked like they'd seen the wrong end of a battle-axe or hammer. Their faces were ridged with scars. In fact, none of them looked healthy. In fact, they all looked very dead, as if they were still in the shape they'd been in when they'd been killed.

I shook my head. "Something is off. Spirits usually look renewed—like they did during the prime of their life. Either that, or they become some freakshow monster, morphing out of a twisted soul or horrendous trauma. Look at them. They look . . . like corpses but they haven't putrefied."

"Interesting observation." Shade approached them slowly, hands up. He stopped when they started to raise their weapons, and they froze. He took a step back, and they waited. A step forward and again, they raised their weapons again.

"Bring me the sword." He held out his hand.

Daniel edged forward, the look on his face one of both wonder and fear, but I could tell he didn't want to get any closer. I started to take the sword from him, but the moment my hand neared the pommel, a tingle warned me back.

"The blade is iron. I don't have gloves with me, so if I touch it, I'll get burned. You'll have to give it to Shade."

Daniel swallowed hard, then straightened his shoulders. He moved toward Shade, one deliberate step at a time. Shade took pity and reached for the sword, then motioned for him to back away.

"They really are *dead*, aren't they?" Daniel eyed the warriors as he backed away. He was no fool. He knew to watch his back with predators on the loose.

"That would be a big 'yes.' In fact, I'd say these men met

their end a long, long time ago. And I have the distinct feeling they went down, not in battle, but in sacrifice." Shade motioned for me to stand near him. "Let's see how they react to the sword."

I wasn't sure what he was up to, but I trusted him. I glanced over at Morio and Camille, who were watching every move the ghosts made. With a flourish, Shade unsheathed the sword and raised it into the air.

Gasping, the Vikings dropped to their knees, staring up at it like they were cats caught in a sunbeam. Their hands placed on the tops of their axe handles, tips of the blades resting on the ground, and bowed their heads in a reverent silence. Their ghostly cloaks floated in an astral breeze. The scene felt like it had shifted into a surreal, sacred space.

I stole a sideways glance at Shade. The look on his face was one of mild alarm.

"Are you all right?" I kept my voice low, not certain just how much the ghosts could understand of what we were saying.

In a low voice, he said, "An odd feeling is racing down my arm—like something is trying to squirm out of the blade and into my hand. It sure as hell isn't pleasant, and if I wasn't who I am, whatever it is might be successful." He gave an almost imperceptible nod at the sword. "Look."

"What the hell?" I stared at the sword's blade. It was glowing. My dagger was usually surrounded by a pale blue nimbus. She was sentient and an artifact. I also knew Lysanthra had other qualities though she hadn't fully revealed them to me. But this . . . this was different. The sword's blade glowed with an unhealthy green light, almost sickly, and it reeked of death.

The sword was iron, of course, and the blade itself was about three feet long. It was double-edged, with a firm hilt and a small pommel that was intricately etched with runes. The guard was short, and slightly bowed, and the sword— while old—looked well taken care of. It hadn't spent time in a burial mound or under the dirt until some archaeologist turned it up. In fact, if it hadn't been one piece and all iron, I could easily have believed it to be modern make.

Shade was frowning now—full on, scowling. "I better sheath this *now*, because I don't fancy a struggle to keep whatever's in it from escaping. And whatever it is, is putting up a damned good fight. Luckily, I'm half-dragon and not much can stand up against a dragon."

"What will they do if you sheath it again?" I gave a surreptitious nod to the ghosts. They were still staring at the sword, rapt.

"We're going to have to find out, aren't we?" Shade's gaze flickered toward the Vikings. "Be prepared, just in case they decide to rampage once their love interest vanishes." He cautiously sheathed the sword again while I kept an eye on our burly visitors.

They immediately rose to their feet again, hoisting their axes, waiting. They looked a little dazed, but they made no move to attack us.

"They're waiting for our next move." I wasn't sure how I knew it, but I did. The ball was back in our court again.

"What the hell do you make of this?" Camille's voice was soft but clear.

"Daniel, is there *anything* else you know about Leif?" I took a step back toward our cousin. "Can you think of anything at all that came up in your research?"

"No . . . except that he inherited the sword. It was a family heirloom." He paused, his voice uncertain. "This bothers me for so many reasons. One—as I said, I *never* steal sentimental objects, even if they're worth a lot of money. It's just a policy of mine. When I went into our meeting, I already *knew* the sword had been passed down through his family. Two—did I really attack him, and if so, what the fuck is going on? If I'm having flashbacks to my time in the ISA, I could end up being very dangerous. And that . . . " He paused, then hung his head. "That would be very bad and I'd have to consider my next move, quickly, before I killed someone."

Shade let out a sniff. "Daniel, don't be so quick to blame yourself. I don't think you're entirely responsible for this one. Something made you grab that sword—and the fact that you have no memory of it might indicate that there is magic of some sort involved. Have you ever had a flashback or memory loss like this before?"

Daniel shook his head. "Never. Not once."

"Then I think we need to look at this very carefully. You could have been targeted. Whatever is in this sword wants out. Maybe it found a way to charm you into taking it or something. And I'm fairly certain that our unwashed friends here are watching out for the blade—guarding it against destruction. They must have sensed your intention to toss it in the water. You'd better let us hang on to it because whatever is locked inside is looking for a way out, and if you keep it, it might try to use you as a conduit."

"With pleasure. I never want to see the thing again." He paused, then slipped over to my side. "I'm sorry I got you involved, girls. I would never put you in danger knowingly. I had no clue where to go and I was close to the bar so . . ."

"Don't worry about it." I wanted to give him a hug. I was still the tiniest bit buzzed and it seemed like a good idea, but then I remembered Daniel wasn't exactly a huggy type of person. "You're our blood. We take care of our own."

He looked a little skeptical but smiled. "Yes, well, I appreciate it."

Shade held up the sheathed sword and took one more step toward the warriors. They waited, eyeing him carefully.

"I'm going to take the sword home with me and protect it. Do you understand?" He spoke to them, but the words carried more weight than just their verbalization. They echoed through the parking lot, and behind them, their intent followed on the breeze.

One by one, the warriors stood down, lowering their axes to their sides. And then, when Shade stepped away, backing toward the car, they silently vanished from sight.

I stared at the empty lot. "Where'd they go?"

"I don't know, but they aren't far away. That much I can tell you. I can feel them coiling around the sword, actually." He paused, then held out the sheath. "Whatever is going on with this, it's beyond me. We'd better do some research. Even as I hold the blade, I feel unsettled. There's a force in this sword, and I have a feeling it's getting bored with being locked away."

"Possessed?" I stared at the scabbard, wondering just how old it was.

"Maybe. Possibly."

As the men headed back to our cars, Camille and I turned to Daniel. "Everything will be all right," she said. "But keep in touch. We need all the info you can get us, so call tomorrow. Chaos has been our best buddy lately, and I'm not sure that you just giving the blade to us will remove you from the situation that's playing out."

He nodded. "I don't know what to think. I'm not going home tonight—whoever ransacked my place was looking for something. Maybe . . . the sword?"

There was a whole 'nother can of worms. "If so, that means that they had to know you would have it, which means they had to be involved in the theft. I wonder . . . maybe it wasn't the sword trying to free itself via you, but somebody who wanted the sword knew that you were going to be visiting Leif. Can you think of anybody? How do your clients find you?"

Daniel frowned. "That's another good question. Leif . . . How did he find me? Let me look." He pulled out a tablet and quickly tapped away on the keyboard. "Well, hell. I can't remember right off the top of my head, but I always keep that sort of information. But . . . it's gone. There's a folder for it, but the folder's empty—whatever was in there has been erased."

"That cinches it. Somebody set you up to steal the sword somehow, and they don't want you to know. The fact that you can't remember who the connection is points to either drugs or magic."

"There are drugs that can wipe memory, but they're hard to come by unless you want to rely on roofies. This is getting odder and odder. Contact me tomorrow? I need to go back to my hideout and call a couple friends to go over to my apartment with me. Muscle, just in case." Shaking his head, he headed toward his car, turning to shrug and smile. "Well, this still beats my time in the ISA." And then, he hopped in the sedan and pulled out of the parking lot.

Shade stored the sword in the backseat of the Jeep with Vanzir and Rozurial, so it wouldn't have the chance of bumping against me. "Don't want you getting burned while you're driving, especially. The last thing we need is an accident."

As we all fastened ourselves in, I let out a long sigh. "I don't know what we're up against, but I'm convinced that Daniel was charmed into stealing that sword. Speaking of . . . " I glanced in the rearview mirror. "Do you think that keeping that sword in our house is dangerous? What if whatever's inside gets out?"

"I know it seems dangerous, but I think it's far more dangerous to leave it with Daniel. We'll figure out what to do with it when we get home." Shade glanced over at me. "Delilah, if we leave that sword out in the wild, and something cruel picks it up—if the energy trapped inside the blade gets out and finds a host with a thirst for blood, it could be very bad. The blade is hungry."

When I thought about it that way, I could see we had no other choice. Shade was right. Neither Camille nor I could touch it without hurting ourselves. But humans could, and that meant that any FBHs who stumbled on the sword and were the least bit psychic could be in danger. Or any vampire. Or Were.

"I guess we have no choice." I focused on the road, and the rest of the way though no one said much of anything, the presence of the sword weighed heavy, like the white elephant in the room.

By the time we got home, any buzz from the alcohol had long worn off. In fact, the appearance of the ghosts had pretty much taken care of that. Nothing like a dose of spirits of the dead to chase away spirits of the vine.

Hanna was busy in the kitchen. Maggie was asleep in her crib, and Bruce, Iris, and Chase had gone home to their babies. Hanna immediately set the kettle to boiling and then pulled out a couple of pans.

"I'll just whip up a late-night supper for you." And that was that.

I gave her a quick hug before we went into the living room. I dropped my backpack on the chair and sat down next to it.

Shade laid the sword on the coffee table and we sat there, staring at it, not quite sure what to do next. I put in a quick call to Menolly asking her to come home as soon as she could after the bar closed and gave her a rundown of what had happened.

"So we have a possessed iron sword and a bunch of dead Vikings. That sounds about par for the course." She laughed. "I swear, the weirdest shit happens to us."

"That's the truth." As I turned around, I saw that Roz and Morio were leaning over the sword, staring at it intently. Camille was staring at it like it was a snake about to bite her, and the others were just sitting there with blank looks on their faces.

At that moment, I got a text and pulled out my phone again. It was from Daniel. He'd sent me all the information he had on Leif. It might not tell us much, but it was at least a place to start. Feeling tired, I pulled up a chair at the new desktop computer we'd bought for the living room and flipped it on.

I glanced back at Camille. "I'm sorry this happened on your birthday."

"Not a problem. If this was the worst of the night, then we're doing well, given the past few months."

"At least open your presents. You do have them with you, right?"

"No, I left them at the bar, remember? Menolly's going to bring them home." She shrugged, grinning. "I'll have to wait."

"Well, not for one." I crossed to the fireplace and picked up one solitary wrapped package. "Menolly and I didn't want to chance taking this to the bar. Here—open it." I stood back, waiting. Menolly and I had taken a risk on this gift, but we thought we were on the right track.

Camille tore the wrapping paper, then opened the box. As she unfolded the tissue paper inside, her lip began to tremble and she glanced up at me, her eyes misty.

"Oh, Delilah . . ." In her hands, she held a small framed picture. It was a photograph of our parents. Mother had taken a camera to Otherworld, in hopes that it would work. With older technology, sometimes the gadgets would function, and the camera had. Mother had persuaded Sephreh to sit for it with her.

She'd also taught herself how to develop pictures, and taken a lot of them during our childhood.

The photograph had hung over our fireplace in our home in Y'Elestrial. I'd contacted Aunt Rythwar to send it over. Menolly and I had it restored—it was very old by now—and framed in a hand-carved frame Trillian had bought for us when he was over in Otherworld looking for Darynal.

It was our parents' wedding picture. Mother's wedding dress—the same one Menolly had worn when she got married to Nerissa—flowed around her in a billowing cloud. She was laughing, and our father looked like he had found the rarest gem in the world. He had. He'd loved our mother with every ounce of his being and never gotten over her death.

"You like it?" As I stared at the photograph in her hand, I felt tears of my own welling up.

"*Like it?* I would never have dreamed . . ." She glanced up at me. "I am *not* keeping this in my room. We'll hang it on the living room wall. They'll always be with us." And with that, she crossed the room and hugged me.

We stood there, arms wrapped around each other, a bittersweet embrace. The loss of our mother had been a long time ago, but Father had died barely two months back and all three of us felt the impact keenly. Even though Menolly wouldn't admit it, we knew she did, too.

"Happy Birthday," I whispered to her. "Blessings this and every day, my sister." The standard Otherworld greeting sounded oddly out of place, and I suddenly longed for the days when we ran free through the fields, before Menolly had been turned, and before we knew about the demons.

With a dizzying flash, I found my thoughts roaming back. After finishing our daily chores, we'd race out to the wide expanse of grassland bordering our house. I'd scramble for the tallest tree while Menolly would turn cartwheels across the grass. And Camille, she'd whirl, dancing like a spinning top, making herself so dizzy that she'd fall over, laughing. We'd spend the day picking berries or fishing, or telling each other stories. In winter, we'd build forts out of the snow and wage war. There was never a clear winner, but we battled it out with all our might, pummeling each other's kingdoms with snowballs.

In the evening, at the dinner table during the nights Father was home, he'd ask us what we'd done, and we'd be at a loss to tell him. He didn't belong in our secret little world, and we didn't belong in his. So we'd talk about school, and Camille would talk about the Coterie of the Moon Mother . . . and then Father would take over and instruct us on the politics of the Court and Queen Lethesanar and the Guard Des'Estar.

Camille must have been reading my mind, because she laughed and stroked my face. "At least we have each other still—maybe not like in the old days, but we're still together. You, Menolly, and I still form the core of the family. We always have, you know. *Lavena ka seva, ter naksa ter las . . .*"

A smile broke across my face. It had been years since any of us had uttered those words—but they'd been our watchwords. Our comfort, our pledge. *"Lavena ka seva, ter manoz ter vey . . ."*

Sisters we are, through pain and through joy . . .
Sisters we are, through life and through death . . .

"Always." She shook her head, smiling through what appeared to be a glaze of tears, but she dashed them away and looked back at the sword. "Back to reality. So what the fuck are we going to do about this?"

"Let's see what I can find." I returned to my search as Hanna brought in mugs of hot tomato soup and grilled cheese sandwiches. Leif Engberg was well known among several factions. One, for being his father's son. Karl had been quite the businessman and a leader in the IT world. But

Leif had made *several* names for himself and not all of them were good.

"It seems Leif was a playboy and a heartbreaker. There's even a website out of Seattle focused on women who've been used and jilted by him. They call themselves *Leif's Leftovers*. How delightful." I smirked. "Our boy has a penchant for handing out engagement rings, then running off a few days before the whirlwind wedding was to take place. He's left a trail of broken hearts across the country."

"Look into his family history," Camille said. "If the sword came to him from his father, chances are it might be a true artifact. Daniel said it was an heirloom."

"Good point. I'll start checking up on his father, too." I pushed the keyboard back and stood up. "Meanwhile, what *do* we do with the sword here? There's somebody in there, and whoever it is, I'm guessing we're not going to want him for a houseguest too long."

"Especially since he's trying to get out." Shade frowned. "We could stash it in the safe room down at the Wayfarer. The guards watching the portal will make certain nobody goes back there. They're down there twenty-four/seven as it is, and besides Menolly and you girls, they're the only ones who know the codes to enter the safe room."

"That's a good idea." I walked over to stare down at the weapon. The sword practically hummed. At that moment, Lysanthra—which was still strapped to my leg—began to vibrate. Curious, I unsheathed her.

"What's going on?" Camille asked.

"Lysanthra's trying to tell me something."

She snorted. "What? Is Timmy down the well again?"

I was about to snark back at her when my dagger gave me a nasty jolt and I almost dropped it. "Hell, what the—"

Lysanthra let out a high-pitched keening and Camille covered her ears, as did Trillian and Morio. Vanzir and Roz were wincing, and Smoky and Shade immediately took up battle stance.

Another moment and the shrill note died away. Lysanthra's glow dissipated. I glanced at the sword and—once again—it just looked like a sword. I had no clue what had just happened, but whatever it was, I didn't like it.

"Before your dagger started screaming her lungs out, I thought I saw the sword move." Morio frowned, crossing his arms as he examined the weapon.

Camille dashed into the kitchen, then returned, pale. "The wards went off. We better check the boundaries of the land, but I think it was in response to whatever the hell just happened."

Shade nodded. "Better safe than sorry. But Morio, the sword didn't move. It was the energy *within* the sword. Whatever is in there was making a play to escape, though I'm not at all certain what's preventing it. But the sooner we get it down to the safe room at the bar, the easier I'll feel. Whatever is going on, it's dangerous." Shade turned to me. "Call Menolly. If she's still there, ask her to wait there until we bring the blade."

Smoky stepped up. "I'll take it through the Ionyc Seas. Whatever is in the blade, I can handle it. If it happens to free itself during transport, better it be out there in the Ionyc Seas than here at home." He picked up the sword, and before any of us could say a word, he vanished.

"I guess that takes care of that." Camille pulled out her phone to call Menolly.

I stared at the computer. "This is going to take longer than an hour of surfing the Net, I'll tell you that." My shoulders ached from getting knocked down, and I suddenly felt tired and let down. "I'm going to bed. There isn't much more we can do till tomorrow anyway."

Camille glanced over at Morio. "You're staying up for a while, right?"

He nodded. "I need to do some research, so yes. Want me to fill Menolly and Nerissa in on everything that happened, just in case Smoky left out something?"

"Would you? I think we're all pretty beat. And tell Smoky that Trillian and I went up to bed? You coming, too, Kitten?" She glanced over at me and I nodded, suddenly tired. I wanted to sleep, too.

"Will do." Morio kissed her and waved to Trillian.

Camille put her arm around my waist. "Let's go. The research will wait. The sword is in a safe place and dreams are calling."

I hugged her. Then, motioning to Shade, we followed her and Trillian up the stairs, Shade and I continuing on to the third floor after they turned off on the second.

As we undressed by the glow of candlelight, I glanced over at my lover. I loved the coffee color of his skin—like a rich caramel latte. And his hair was the color of amber honey. In Otherworld, nobody really cared what color a person was. What mattered was *what* they were like. And often, which race they were. But the races in our world weren't defined by their color base.

Oh, we had our own types of prejudice. There was no denying that and it was as bad as Earthside. My sisters and I were routinely discriminated against because of our half-blood, but skin color? Made no sense to us. Over here, however, even though Shade was as far from human as Smoky was, he could pass in society. It wasn't easy—not for any of us—but we could manage if we worked at it hard enough. There were some days, when Shade and I walked down the street together, where we received looks that made me want to bash a few heads.

He flipped on the stereo and crooked his finger at me, daring me to come closer. As he stripped off his shirt, his chiseled abs smooth and glimmering in the dim light, all I could think about was how magnificent he was. Oh, he had scars here and there, but they just made him look more rugged.

I yanked off my shirt and moved over to him, turning around. "Unhook me?"

He unfastened my bra and I slid the straps off, one by one, then dropped it to the floor. Shade wrapped his arms around my waist, pulling me close. I leaned against him, my back warm against his chest, and he buried his nose in my neck, tickling me as he brushed against my hair and swayed gently to the music.

"I love that you're growing your hair out," he whispered.

I closed my eyes, drifting in the feel of his embrace. There was something so right, so strong, about us, and it felt like it was growing every day. Ever since Lash, his sister, had arrived, things had been different. Shade had finally begun to open up around me.

A throbbing drumbeat echoed out from the stereo and I leaned my head back and began to shift my hips to the rhythm. For so long, I'd run from my sexuality in human form, too timid and awkward to open up. And then, with Chase and Zachary, it had been good but not right. But Shade? Shade was my match, and now that the fire of the Autumn Lord flowed in my veins, so did his passion, and I responded to my lover's touch and presence.

"Big Stomp" by Motherdrum came on, and our swaying became a dance. I shifted my shoulders to the rhythm of the drums as Shade let go and began to circle me, like a tiger circling his prey. I turned, following him as he moved, arching my neck and letting the beat take control of my body.

Shade darted toward me, and I jumped to the side, teasing him, beckoning him to follow. I backed up, still moving in time with the music, and he followed, crouching, a look of pure joy in his eyes.

The music shifted to a faster, upbeat drumming song and I began to laugh as I shifted from retreat to outright dancing. I reached out and grabbed Shade's hand and dragged him to me. He pressed against me, and I could feel his arousal as I draped my arms around his shoulders and we began to grind to the beat together.

With one hand, he reached down and flipped open the button on my jeans, then unzipped them, sliding his hand down beneath my panties to finger me. I shifted, my hips picking up both his rhythm as well as that of the song's. As my breath began to come faster, he moaned in my ear. I rode his hand for a moment, then I let go of him and reached down to unzip his pants. We stumbled our way over to the bed, and then in a flurry, jeans came off, and my panties and his boxers and we were entangled on the sheets, with me on top of him.

I wasn't in the mood for romance. I straddled him, leaning back as he raised his arms and I took hold of his hands, balancing myself on his strength.

"Come on, baby. Ride me down." His voice was smooth with a little spice, like cinnamon on cream, and I shivered. Leaning down, I ran my tongue along his chest, stopping at his nipple, which was pierced. I gently tugged on the ring with my teeth and he let out a groan as I dropped it and moved on, my breasts brushing along his stomach until I was eye level with his cock.

I cautiously licked him long and hard, stroking him with my tongue, taking care that my fangs didn't scrape along the delicate skin. We'd played that game before, and I'd learned how to be more careful, but Shade could also take more of my mistakes than my other lovers had been able to. He moaned softly as I worked him, the pulse of his hunger running beneath the strain of his erection. Drops of pre-cum hung on the tip of his penis, and I sucked them off, his taste salty and warm in my mouth.

"Come up here, Pussycat." His voice sliding over the words like honey oozing out of a pot, Shade leaned up on his elbows and arched his eyebrows at me. "Climb aboard."

Giggling, I straddled him again, easing down as he guided his cock into me. He was thick and hard and stretched me deliciously wide. I settled down, rocking my hips to pick up the pace. He grabbed me by the waist, his hands holding me firm, fingers digging into my sides. I leaned forward, my breasts brushing his chest, and lowered my lips to his. As we kissed, I ground against him, and he thrust upward, ever deeper inside me.

All laughter vanished then as the energy thickened, coiling like vines growing up from the earth. Thick, like mist rolling along the ground to blanket the world and muffle all sound and sensation except what was directly before us. The world receded and there was only Shade and me, only us— only our passion.

Then, once again *he* descended to join us. Hi'ran, the Autumn Lord, was there, embracing us, surrounding us with the warmth of the bonfire, with the glow of autumn leaves. He was everywhere and nowhere. He did not manifest this time, but he was in every breath we took, in every sound we uttered. We belonged to him, and he had come to bless our connection, to remind us who our master was.

Love swelled in my heart. Love for Shade, love for Hi'ran, love for the fact that I was one of the Autumn Lord's chosen—a Death Maiden. I leaned back, letting out a long growl as the orgasm ripped through my body. Shade let out a guttural cry, bucking beneath me as we rode the waves of autumn where our desire and hearts were anchored. Afterward, I rested on his chest and he wrapped his arms around me, and as we fell asleep, I wondered just how I'd come to this place in my life.

Chapter 4

I was on the edge of the jungle—a jungle I recognized from many times before. The trees seemed particularly tall, but that was because I was Panther, and I was on the path leading to Haseofon.

By now, I knew the way. *Through the jungle and over the bridge to the Autumn Lord's temple we go . . .* There were other paths leading there through the astral, but I'd settled on this route as the most expedient and it was also the one that calmed me most. The thick jungle foliage was lush and vibrant, dripping with water from the frequent rains. I wasn't sure where exactly *here* was, but it had a feed directly into the realm of the Autumn Lord, where the temple of Haseofon—the temple of the Death Maidens—existed.

I had been summoned. Either Greta needed to talk to me, or there was something I needed to learn. As I inhaled, a sharp tang hit my lungs. Mostly, people think of jungles as warm, but here, it was always on the verge of cool, like after a stiff rainstorm, when the air was charged and you weren't sure if the clouds were going to sock in for another good blow.

The urge to roll in the dirt hit me, but I didn't have time, and I didn't want to get my collar dirty. When in panther form, I wore the collar of the Autumn Lord—it was encrusted with rhinestones that mirrored the emerald of my eyes. I was lean but muscular, and as I padded along the path, my mouth opened automatically as I inhaled the scents around me. Leaves and trees and plants were so thick they encroached over the walkway, hiding the roots of the trees that burrowed beneath the compacted dirt. There were animals here— screeching birds and small prey that rustled through the brush.

Again, the urge to chase hit me but I kept myself in check. I had much better control over myself as Panther than I did as Tabby, and thanks to the *Panteris phir*, a plant I'd procured in Otherworld and cultivated at home, my ability to manage my shifting into Panther had steadily increased. The tea was nasty tasting, but it worked, and I drank it three times a week.

The path itself, however, was devoid of other travelers. Once in a while when I came this way, I'd see another person journeying past, but they seldom spoke to me, and often they were ghostly—covered in mist, which told me they were coming in from other dimensions than Earthside.

I loped along, skirting a tree that had fallen since the last time I was here. It was rotten, the stump swarming with termites. Covered with moss and fungi of varying shapes and colors, the bright red of fly agaric caught my eye. I knew better than to eat it, but thought that Camille could use some for her magic. In panther form, however, I had no way of gathering it. I wasn't even sure I could transport it back with me.

The path wound through the forest, then a small clearing where the sound of rushing water hit my ears. I was near a stream that flowed in a narrow channel down a steep ravine. It was always high water season here, and the whitecaps rushed by, churning along over a streambed of sharp rocks and large boulders. The "bridge" was actually an old fir that spanned the stream. It must have been two hundred years old, anchored on either side. The tree was about as steady as it could get. Which was good, because I wasn't entirely certain what would happen to my physical body if I were to fall off, and I didn't want to find out.

I cautiously placed one paw on the tree trunk. My fear of water remained even in panther form, but it wasn't nearly as strong as when I was back in my two-legged shape, or when I was Tabby.

Inhaling a sharp breath that almost made my senses reel—the cacophony of scents was intoxicating—I stepped onto the log and crossed the stream. I didn't run, but kept an even, steady pace. The trunk was at least five feet in diameter, so it wasn't like I was performing a balancing act, but still—the ravine was deep and the fall loomed like a shadow in the background. But luck was with me, and I bounded off the other side of the log with no problem.

Winding my way through another section of forest, I passed into a patch of thick mist. It surrounded me from all sides, and I could only see the path a few feet in front of me. Keeping my head low so that I didn't wander off the path, I focused on keeping on track. Eventually, though, I came to a pale orange shimmer in the mist, stepped through, and passed through an invisible barrier leading onto the grounds of Haseofon.

The land here was different. I now stood in a temperate forest perpetually cloaked in autumn. The trees were covered in shades of burnished red and orange, and they never changed. Leaves fell, but the trees never emptied. The seasons ceased to move here. Winter never came, and spring and summer had never been. This was the land of the Autumn Lord.

The temperature had dropped abruptly and now, instead of the after-rain chill, it was that misty autumn evening chill. Sometimes, in the afternoons, the sun would shine here. But its warmth was fleeting and the sharp tang of autumn cleaved through the golden light. Now, though, it was late into night, and the mist was rolling along the ground.

However, the temple of Haseofon was still wide awake. Lights shone from within. The great hall was marble, white veined with gray, and the pillars and steps leading up to the main entrance were wide and spacious. It had a Grecian feel to it, though it wasn't nearly as majestic as some of the great palaces and temples in Greece. But Haseofon was beautiful. Lights flickered through the window slits and torches illuminated the steps leading up to the temple.

As I approached, I shifted back into my two-legged form. I assumed the dress of my sister Death Maidens—not the gown we used when we were out gathering souls, but a simple tank dress that flowed to my ankles. Soft and comfortable, it was also pretty, in a hunter green that set off my eyes.

Greta—my trainer and the leader of the Death Maidens—had taught me how to shift my clothing when I was out in Hi'ran's service. It had taken a while but I finally got the hang of it.

As I entered the temple, once again the similarity to an opulent palace struck me. A pale light illuminated the room. Evenly spaced pillars lined the chamber, and a cathedral-like dome arched overhead. Curtains shaded the walls, brilliant shades of yellow and red and pink and ivory. Embroidered in fine detail, the patterns were of trees and vines, and swirls depicting the moon and the stars.

The raised dais against the back wall was littered with pillows of varying sizes, and tables around the room were covered with bowls laden with fruit, and platters of bread and meat and cheese. Benches offered the chance to sit, to take a break and rest or eat in comfort.

One side of the great hall was set up as a weapons training area, and there, the Death Maidens sparred together, practicing their techniques. I had never been invited to take part—not on a regular basis—and I had the feeling the training mats were reserved for all of my sisters in the temple who were actually dead. I was the only *living* Death Maiden.

Tonight only a few of the maidens were here. The others were probably off in their rooms or doing . . . well . . . whatever they did while I wasn't around. Eloise was practicing her rolls on the mats—she was a tall, dark-skinned woman who had been a warrior during her life. And Mizuki, a Japanese girl, was playing a violin in the corner, her eyes closed as she guided the bow across the strings in a trill of fluttering notes. Fiona, as redheaded as Menolly, was playing a game of solitaire at a small table. All three of them jumped up when I came in.

"Delilah! Greta said you would be visiting tonight." Mizuki set down her instrument and lightly ran over to embrace me, the others right on her heels.

I laughed and gave them each a hug. We'd come a long way from the first awkward meeting. I let them draw me over to the dais, where we dropped onto the pillows. Here they lived, and here they served the Autumn Lord, who came to them as lover and liege. Each, in her death, had been marked like I was—with the crescent sickle tattoo on her forehead, and the black and orange leaves tattooed up her forearms. When I died, I'd come to Haseofon, too, to serve with my sisters in the temple.

"So how is the outer world? We heard about your trials in Otherworld." Mizuki always seemed the most interested in what went on over Earthside and beyond. She was, I believed, the newest to be brought into the temple.

"The war rages on. It's horrible. Our father was killed. I had to guide the Elfin Queen through the veils." As I quickly caught them up on what was happening—I had learned how to dish efficiently—Greta appeared from a door to the side. She motioned for me to stand.

"We are always happy to see you, Delilah." She slipped her arm through mine. "You must be wondering why I've summoned you here."

I let out a long sigh. "Honestly? I hope it's not an assignment. I'm tired, Greta, and I really am not up to taking on anything I don't have to." I seldom was so blunt with my trainer, but Greta would know something was wrong. And truth was, I just wanted a break.

"Rest your mind. No, tonight you will speak with your sister Arial. There are things you must discuss. Things that have come into their time." She began to walk me down the hall and, at the sighs of dismay from the other Death Maidens, held up her hand. "Delilah will return soon enough for a coffee klatch. But now she needs to visit Arial. Come, girls, go back to your pursuits."

Greta led me down the hall leading to the bedrooms, then stopped in front of Arial's room. "I will return when it's time for you to leave."

Wondering what could be so important but *not* involve my trainer, I pushed open the door to Arial's bedroom. My twin, she had died at birth and been brought to Haseofon. None of us had even heard of her till a few years back. And our father refused to discuss her or why our parents had kept her secret. Now he was dead and we'd never know why they kept her existence secreted.

I wished that Camille and Menolly could meet her. One day, I was told I might bring Camille with me for a brief visit, but we hadn't had that chance yet. But Menolly wasn't allowed to set foot in the temple because she was a vampire. And outside the temple, Arial could only appear in her spirit form as her Were self—a beautiful ghostly leopard.

I peeked around the corner of the door.

Arial was sitting on the bed. We were almost identical, and from a distance it might be hard to tell the difference. But Arial's hair coiled in long, brunette waves to her lower back. We were the same height, though she was thin and willowy where I was lean and muscled. But Arial didn't bear the tattoos of the Autumn Lord, and she wasn't a Death Maiden. Yet here she lived, serving the others by helping out where they needed her.

She jumped off the bed when she saw me, the smile on her face exploding into joy. "Delilah! You came!"

"Of course." I laughed as she whirled me around in a bear hug. She smelled like cinnamon and cranberries, and I kissed her cheek, as happy to see her as she was to see me.

"But why am I here?" I walked her back over to the bed and sat down. "Don't get me wrong—I'm thrilled to see you, but what's going on? Greta said you had something to tell me?"

Arial closed the door and joined me. Her room was pink. Bubblegum pink. Arial liked ruffles and bows, and anything girlish that she could get her hands on.

She nodded, her eyes wide and solemn. She reached out

and took my hand. "Yes, *Himself* has given me permission to tell you." She called the Autumn Lord *Himself* a lot. I wasn't sure where she'd picked it up.

"What then?" I settled myself down, waiting. Something was up or she wouldn't be this tense. "Are you all right?" On the surface, my question made no sense, but considering things could—and did—happen to spirits, it really wasn't so unusual.

She took a deep breath. "I've been wanting to tell you this since we met, but *Himself* told me no, that it must wait until after . . ."

"After what?" Now I was getting really worried. What the hell was going on, and since when had Hi'ran been whispering secrets to my sister? What did she know that I didn't?

"Until after I passed." The familiar voice boomed through the air, low and deep. I whirled to find myself facing Sephreh— my father. His form wasn't substantial, like Arial, but surrounded in a veil of mist. That meant he didn't belong here at Haseofon. It wasn't his home.

"Father!" I jumped up and started to run to him, but then he held up his hand, a wan smile on his face, and I stopped in my tracks. "Father?"

"Delilah, yes, I am here, but only for a brief time. I will join your mother in the Land of the Silver Falls soon, but I could not rest until I settled unfinished business." He ducked his head, and his eyes sparkled in a way they hadn't since Mother died.

I inched back to Arial's bed, fumbling to sit down. My mind was churning with questions and things I wanted to say, but I wasn't sure if I should. So many things had been left unfinished with his death. Camille and he had barely begun to mend their relationship. He had only skimmed the surface of repairing his relationship with Menolly. And me? Well, Father hadn't betrayed my love like he had theirs, but his belligerence to Menolly and Camille had definitely affected how I felt about him. When he'd been killed in the fall of Elqaneve, it left us all in a tailspin, not knowing how to feel.

Sephreh turned to Arial, then me. "I ask you to relay a message to Camille and Menolly. Please, tell them I'm sorry. I failed them, and I can't ever make it right, but I truly regret the way I acted. I ask for their forgiveness."

His voice, though faint, cracked with emotion and the shimmer of tears shone in his eyes. Father had been a soldier first and foremost. Before his marriage, before his children, he belonged to the Court and Crown. But now he was baring himself, stripping away the pride that had intervened between his calling and his family.

"I wish they could be here, to hear you out."

"I wish so, too, but there are reasons I can't journey to them Earthside. So many things, I wish I could say, but the Hags of Fate stay my tongue, and destiny will play itself out as it needs to."

I wanted to cry. I wanted to shake him by the shoulders and ask what he was talking about. Instead, I turned to Arial. "Is this what you wanted me to know?"

She shook her head. "There is far more. Father and *Himself* gave me leave to tell you. It's easier for me to speak than for Father."

Glancing over at Sephreh's spirit—he didn't seem in a hurry to go anywhere—I bit my lip, then turned back to Arial. "Tell me."

"You asked him several times why he and Mother never told you and our sisters about me, about the fact that you had a twin."

Arial seemed so substantial compared to Father's spirit, that I had to remind myself that she was also dead. But when we dug down to the core, given all the different realms and dimensions, did words like *death* and *life* really *matter*? Death was only in relation to the physical world. Father still existed; he was still here, just in another form. Unless one was obliterated—unless the soul was snuffed out for good, which only the gods and the Death Maidens could do—the essence lived on, transformed but still existing.

I stared at Arial, and she gazed steadily back at me. "Yes, we all wondered. We had a sister and they never told us. I had a twin, and I never knew. Why keep it a secret? What good did it do?"

She bit her lip, then shrugged. "When Mother was pregnant with us, she became very ill. She could have died. The healers were at a loss to figure out what was wrong. So Father did the only thing he could think to do. He called on the Autumn Lord—the only Harvestman he had ever encountered."

Father had summoned the Autumn Lord? I whirled around, and Sephreh gave me a soft nod, his face solemn. "*You* met the Autumn Lord?"

He let out a long sigh. "Long ago when I was young and in danger for my life during a battle, the Autumn Lord came to me. He could have taken my soul then, but he gave me a choice. I could either repay him one day, when he chose, and he would let me live. Or I could go with him then. The payment wasn't stipulated, and so I chose life, never imagining what the cost would be."

Arial continued. "When Father summoned the Autumn Lord, *Himself* told him that he would spare Mother's life. He would make certain we were taken care of. One of us would die at birth, but forever live in comfort in his land. The other, she would be bound to him as a Death Maiden. If Father hadn't agreed, all three of us would die in childbirth. The Hags of Fate had sealed Mother's early death in her tapestry. The threads were woven. While this would only give her more time, not break her Fate, it would also give one of us— you or me—a fighting chance at life."

I stood very still. So both Arial and I had been handed over to Hi'ran at birth. Only Arial had actually died then. I had lived. And Mother—well, she had gained a few more years. Long enough to have Menolly, at least.

After a moment, I turned to Father. "So you faced the Lady and the Tiger. Either give Arial and me to Hi'ran, one of our lives forfeit at the moment, or lose all three of us."

The thought crossed my mind that, if Hi'ran had promised Mother's life for both Arial's and my death, Father still would have paid up. I didn't want to go there but I couldn't shake the fear.

Father reached out, stopping short before he touched

my arm. "I know what you're thinking. I know you think I would have sacrificed you and your sister for your mother's life alone. That if I'd had the choice of only her in exchange for your lives, that I would have given you over like that. Admit it: You believe I would have struck a bargain."

I sucked in a deep breath. "Yes, I do. And in an awful way, I understand."

Sephreh straightened and looked more like the father I remembered when we did something wrong, when he was about to punish us.

"*Delilah te Maria*, know this. Your mother was my light, but I would never have given you and your sister over to spare her life. On my honor as a guardsman. There would never have been a question. The *only* way I could save *any* of you, was to bind the two of you to Hi'ran. Otherwise, you would all have died right there, that day." As he spoke, the truth of his words rang through the room. He meant it. He would have let Mother die to save us.

I swallowed my doubt. "So we were marked from birth. And Arial . . ."

"*Himself* made the choice who would die at birth, and who would bear the duty of Death Maiden. And in many ways, I do not envy you." Arial smiled then. "My life here is pleasant. I come and go as I please, and I can leave in my leopard form to walk the earth. On the other hand, you have to fight demons and face death daily. I already passed through the veil—I will never have to face that fear."

I stared at her, thinking carefully. There was so much to mull over that it would take me weeks to sort out my feelings. "But why didn't you tell us?" I turned back to Father.

"I was bound to silence. The Autumn Lord refused to allow me to tell you until I crossed through the veils. He said it would upset the threads of fate, and the Hags of Fate would have been mightily pissed with him. He sealed my tongue so I couldn't speak about it, and your mother's, too."

"She knew, then?" I wondered what she had thought. It couldn't have been easy knowing that her life had been spared thanks to Arial's death.

"He told her after the fact." Father pressed his lips together and I had a feeling that was the only response we would ever get regarding Mother's part in the matter.

Leaning back on the bed, propping myself on my hands, I closed my eyes. What did this all mean? I wasn't even sure how I felt, let alone figuring out how this was going to affect matters in my life.

"And Shade? Was he part of this, even back then?"

Sephreh moved a little closer, gliding over the floor like a true ghost. "Shade . . . I have no clue how he was brought into your life. Whatever dealings the Autumn Lord might have made with him, it was not part of my covenant. No, I only begged him for help to save your mother, and this is the result."

"But it was more than your plea." Arial's light voice trailed over his. "Don't you see, this was part of destiny? The Hags of Fate decreed that Mother die early. Father saved her, for a time, but she still died young. When she crossed the veils, *Himself* allowed her to visit, to say hello to me, before she moved on to the Land of Silver Falls so she could get to know me. We had a lovely talk."

A shy smile flashed across her face. "I would have enjoyed growing up with her. I would have loved to grow up beside you and Camille and Menolly, but it would have changed our lives, and in doing so, it would have changed destiny. Things would not be as they are now—and right now, you are needed Earthside, to fight the demonic war. You would not have been sent there if I'd lived. All things in their own time. I was never meant to live a physical life, so don't feel sorry for me. I love being here, and I have friends, and a purpose, and so it continues on."

Sephreh smiled then, the first time in ages I'd seen him appear so warm and happy. "I am so proud of all of you. I made mistakes—there's no denying that, but you girls, you persevered in spite of my foolishness. You are the true warriors here. For all my talk of duty, I was a coward when it came to facing my personal life. I paid for it . . . and I will always regret it."

He began to walk toward the door.

"Wait!" I jumped up, panicking. I couldn't let him go—couldn't watch him walk out of my life forever. Even though I had seen his body, he was *here, now.* And I wanted him to stay.

He paused, turning. "Yes, my sweet Kitten?"

"You can't go just yet." I had no clue what to say; there were so many things, but most of them seemed insignificant. I just wanted to keep him there a little bit longer, to talk to him just a little bit more.

"Your mother is waiting for me, and I've said my piece. I've told you what you need to know." But his smile was kind, and his voice comforting. "I love you, my Kitten. And I love your sisters, too. Please, tell them for me—and Trillian, too—I deeply regret how I treated him. Please, make them understand. I hope they can forgive me as time goes on. I never meant to hurt any of you, but I did, and I am so incredibly sorry."

I walked over to him. I wanted to hug him, to kiss him, but it would be like embracing vapor. Instead, I reached out, my fingers inches away from him. He rested his hand over mine, the weight of his misty touch almost unnoticeable.

"I understand. Whatever anger I felt, I forgive you. So will they. We all love you, Father. And we miss you."

"That means everything in the world to me, girl. Then we have said all there is to say. I will give your mother your love. She and I will be waiting for you and your sisters, though I pray that day be long, long in the future." He turned to Arial. "Arial . . . my love to you, too. And when you are ready to join us, when the Autumn Lord frees you, we await you with joy."

Before Arial or I could speak, he turned and vanished.

I stared at the spot where he'd been, uncertain what to do. "How long have you known all this?" I asked, before turning around.

Arial cleared her throat. "I knew from the time I was little. I wanted to tell you when we first met, but . . ."

"But you couldn't." And I did understand. Both she and

Father had been proscribed from speaking about it. Just like I couldn't utter the name *Hi'ran* aloud—my mouth simply wouldn't say the word—neither could they speak until they had been given leave.

Feeling like my world had just been shaken to the four corners, I returned to Arial and sat beside her. And yet . . . what did it really change?

"I don't know how to feel about this."

"Just let the information settle. It will sort itself out in your heart. The only thing different now is you know the reason behind what's happened with us. And you also know that Father regrets his actions. That has to be of some comfort." She wrapped an arm around my shoulder and pulled me close. It was uncanny. Separated from me by worlds, by death itself, yet she was still able to comfort me.

I leaned my forehead against hers. It felt like looking into a mirror as we gazed into each other's eyes. "I wish you could have grown up with us. I want you to meet Camille and Menolly."

"I have, just not in this form. They've seen me in my leopard form."

"Yes, but it's just not the same. I guess that doesn't matter right now. So . . . my life as a Death Maiden was decided from the moment I was born. I wonder if Father knew which one of us would die . . . and which would live."

"No, he didn't. He told me that. And since we weren't born yet, what difference would it have made if he had? He was given no choice in that matter. And before you go and pull any survivor's guilt on me, frankly, I think I'd rather be here than walking in your shoes. Honestly, does it matter whether my life is in Haseofon or over in Otherworld? I exist and I'm happy. That's enough for me." She smiled then, and kissed me on the cheek.

Still trying to sort out my feelings, I shrugged. "I guess . . . you're right. You're happy, and you've never known any other life."

"Neither have you. So . . ."

Darting a glance at the door, I suddenly wanted to be in

bed with Shade, at home with my sisters. Haseofon loomed large and imposing, and utterly cold. "I think . . . I think I need to think about this for a while. To sort it all out. This will most likely change the way I view my childhood."

"Didn't that happen already, when you found out about me?" Arial wasn't letting up on me, but she grinned. "You adjusted to that."

I laughed then. "Yeah, I did. Happily. I just have to get used to the knowledge. My path was destined from birth. It wasn't all just a random happenstance. I have a feeling it was that way for Camille and Menolly, too. We all seem to be playing right into the hands of the Hags of Fate."

"They have a way of beating down the door when they want you for something." Arial languorously stood, stretching. "You should go back. You shouldn't linger here too long while you are still alive. But I'm so glad I could finally be honest with you. I've wanted to tell you ever since we first met."

"I'm glad, too. At least I know what happened. At least Father was able to make his peace, and we know he's headed to be with Mother. He's waited so long, and he loves her so much. I sometimes wonder if I'll ever love Shade as much as he loved her. I mean . . . I love him. Very much, but I think . . ."

Arial shook her head. "From what I've seen, the kind of grand love like Father had for Mother comes around rarely. And I think it's more unstable than grounded love. Grand love is blind and all consuming, and overwhelming. Honestly? I would rather have a love that is truthful and solid. I think it brings more happiness in the long run. Grand love usually leads to tragedy."

"How did you get to be so wise?"

She laughed. "I read a lot. Greta brings me books from both Otherworld and Earthside. I know five languages, you know—English, Calouk, Elfin, Japanese—thanks to Mizuki—and Irish, thanks to Fiona. So I read a lot. Romances are my favorite. I especially love an author over Earthside—Mary Stewart."

Just another little fact I hadn't known. "You play the

harpsichord, you speak five languages, just what else can you do?"

She walked me out to the hall. "I can cook, and I'm pretty good with wrestling—yes, wrestling! I make perfume blends, and I can grow vegetables like nobody else. How do you think we get so much produce here during the perpetual autumn? I have a hothouse where I grow food for the Death Maidens."

I didn't even want to ask how they ate when they were dead.

The chaos clamoring inside of my head began to soften and calm down as she chatted along. She was in the middle of a story about a watermelon fight between two of the Death Maidens by the time we reached the front door. Greta was nowhere in sight, but I felt the tug—it was time to return home.

"I love you." I hugged her. "Thank you—you've filled in blank spots I never thought would be answered."

"Thank *Himself*. He freed my tongue and gave the okay." And then, she kissed me on the cheek. "It's time for you to go."

I nodded. "Yeah. I want to, and yet . . . I don't."

But I couldn't stay there. I gave her one last squeeze and a kiss, then headed out the door. Immediately I was transformed back to Panther and raced through the woods. The trees became a blur, and the next thing I knew, I was waking up next to Shade. I was home again.

As I sat up, rubbing my neck, I glanced over at the window. It was still dark. The clock read 4:00 A.M. Menolly would still be up. Needing to talk to somebody about everything I'd found out, I slipped out from beneath the covers and headed downstairs, leaving Shade breathing easy in the bed.

As I entered the living room, I saw Menolly there, rocking Maggie on her lap. Familiar sounds from the kitchen told me Hanna was up. But that was odd—she usually didn't get up until five thirty, so something had to have happened.

I jerked my thumb toward the kitchen. "What's up?

Why is Hanna awake so early? And boy, have I got some-thing to tell you."

Menolly glanced up at me. "Hanna is up so early because . . . well . . . Roz was in bed with her when Fraale showed up. Things are kind of a mess."

"Uh-oh. So not a good thing." I sat down on the ottoman.

Fraale was a succubus. She was also Roz's ex-wife. She still loved him, and he loved her, but there was no way they could make it work, not after what had happened to them. But with Hanna in the middle . . .

I glanced at the kitchen again. "Are they in there, all three of them?"

She nodded. "Yeah, and though they've kept it down, I know for a fact it's not going easy. I have no idea what to expect."

Just then, Hanna appeared. She was dressed for travel-ing, and a pained look filled her eyes. "I want to go back to the Northlands."

Roz followed her in. "Please, talk some sense into her. You can't go, Hanna. Fraale . . . she's . . ."

Hanna whirled. "She's still in love with you, and I can see it in your eyes. You still love her. I won't be stuck in the mid-dle. No, I want to go home, and I want to go now."

I glanced over at Menolly. "What the hell are we going to do?"

She held Maggie tighter and shook her head. "Don't ask me. I have no idea how to handle this."

Chapter 5

〜✥〜

Roz reached out and took Hanna by the shoulders. "Hanna, love, please—don't go. You can't. We need you too much." He paused. "*I* need you."

"But you don't need *me*." Fraale appeared from the kitchen, her voice bitter and tearstained. We'd been witness to this interlude before. She was a plump, curvaceous succubus with mousy brown hair, but on second look, she was a stunner—absolutely gorgeous. Even to me, and I wasn't bi like Menolly or Camille. Fraale exuded sexuality, and she seemed delightfully touchable.

"I can't *let* myself need you! You know what that leads to." Roz's voice broke as he turned away. "I can't even allow myself to remember what it was like to love you because I still get so angry."

Their story was a true tragedy. Fraale and Roz had been Fae when they'd been married, centuries ago in Otherworld, until Zeus took it upon himself to try to seduce Fraale. Trouble was, Hera was close on his heels. Despite the fact that

Fraale resisted Zeus's overtures, Hera pitched a fit and turned her into a succubus.

Rozurial begged Zeus for help, but Zeus's idea of making things right was to turn him into an incubus. Their marriage had pretty much disintegrated from there. Fraale and Roz parted ways, but the core of their love, and the betrayal of the gods, had never left either one.

Fraale hung her head. "I don't mean to make matters difficult. I just . . . I just wanted to talk to you. I miss you . . . I . . ."

She'd never give up loving him. She'd never been able to move on, while Roz was burying his feelings and calling it closure. Perhaps Arial was right—perhaps all great loves were bound for tragedy.

Roz finally looked at her, with a bitter, lost look. "It's better if we don't talk. Better if we don't see each other. What good can come from it? All we ever do is reminisce about times we will never be able to relive. We lose ourselves in memories, and then we have to face our loss all over again. We can never be who we were. There's no going home. We'll never be able to recapture what we had. The gods stripped all of that from us with their petty bickering. They tore apart our lives. I curse the names of Zeus and Hera every day."

Fraale covered her face and turned away, sobbing. Hanna pushed Roz aside and wrapped her arms around the crying succubus.

"There, there, girl. Come, sit down."

Fraale let herself be guided over to the sofa, where Hanna settled her near Menolly. She glanced over her shoulder at Roz. "How dare you be so cold? This woman loves you."

Roz looked absolutely stricken. "I don't want to hurt her, but . . . I can't live in the past. If I do, the wounds will never heal."

Hanna caught his gaze and stared at him for a moment, a soft smile on her lips. "I lost my love to Hyto. I lost my husband. I lost my children. But the day I ever pretend they didn't exist, may the gods strike me down for dishonoring the memory of what once was. I remember the past, even as I try to make a new life here, now."

"And now you say you want to go back to the North-lands to search for your daughters?" Roz shook his head. "Isn't that just going to lead to more heartache?"

Hanna sighed, still holding Fraale's hand. Fraale stared at her, tears streaking her face. "You are right, of course. It is folly to hope."

Sniffing, dashing away her tears, Fraale's lip quivered. "You lost your children? I never had any."

"Smoky's father murdered my husband. To save my daughters, I was forced to send them into the world alone. I have no idea whether they lived or died—they were young. My son died while we were in captivity. I . . . I . . ." It was Hanna's turn to break down. The woman seldom shed a tear, seldom spoke of her pain, but the heightened emotions in the room seemed to be taking their toll.

"I poisoned my son. The dragon drove him mad. There was no other option. I had to help Camille escape or Hyto would have killed her. I couldn't take Kjell with me—he would have given us away, and even if I'd decided to chance it, I couldn't free him from his cage. He'd lived in that cage for years, like an animal, and was quite insane. I couldn't leave him for Hyto to torture. So . . ."

"You killed him." Fraale let out an enormous sigh. She gazed up at Roz. "And you came here and found love again."

Hanna jerked her head sharply. "Love?" Then she noticed Fraale staring at Roz. "No, not *love*, my dear. Your . . . Rozurial is kind and caring and passionate, but his kind? *Incubi?* He cannot love me the way I would need to be loved, and I make no pretense otherwise. We merely found comfort in each other's arms. But I can see now that it was a mistake."

I was watching Hanna. Her movements gave her away—the flick of her hair, the darting glance toward Rozurial. She *had* been falling for the incubus, even though she tried to deny it. Now she was forced to face the reality of what he was. Fraale's presence had brought that glaringly home. So Hanna was backtracking the easiest way she knew how.

Denial. I wasn't sure if I should say anything, or if this was a tangle better left untouched.

Menolly, though, apparently had no such doubts. She plopped Maggie in my lap and stood up. "Enough. Fraale, you came looking to talk to Roz because the loneliness got to be too much. Hanna, you obviously realize that what you have with Roz is probably doomed. And Roz . . ." She paused, then ducked her head. "Roz, you feel guilty over dallying with Hanna, even though your marriage has been over for centuries. But I think you're displacing your feelings. And I think that you shouldn't lead Hanna on. I know who you have a *real* crush on."

We all stared at her. She looked exasperated, and I suddenly had the feeling that something was going on with Menolly besides the drama of this little triangle—something that had nothing to do with Hanna or Roz or Fraale.

"Menolly, watch yourself," I said in a falsetto, trying to warn her from overstepping the line and making things worse. Her skills in diplomacy? Not exactly the best.

But she ignored me. "No, the truth is you've still got it bad for Iris and you know that's never going to happen, so you turned to Hanna—" As if suddenly aware of what she'd said, Menolly pressed her lips together.

Hanna turned to Roz, confused. "Do you have feelings for Iris?"

Fraale looked just as puzzled. "Who's Iris?"

"Now you've done it." I turned to Menolly, both tired and irritated.

Roz's shoulders slumped. "Don't bring her into it. Iris has no part in this discussion, and whatever my feelings might be for her, I will never bother her with them. Especially now."

Feeling like I was suddenly part of a real-life *Jerry Springer Show*, I took a deep breath and waded into the fray. Maybe I could undo some of the damage Menolly had just done. "Okay—calm down, everyone. Hanna, yeah, we have known Roz has a little crush on Iris for a while, but she never encouraged him. And Roz was gentleman enough never to push it. Fraale, Iris is our house sprite, remember her? She's happily married to a leprechaun and has twins now."

Hanna bit her lip, and I could see the confusion growing. "Then I was just a *substitute* . . ."

"No, no! Hanna . . ." Roz paused, then he let out a huge sigh and dropped to the sofa, looking angry. "None of you except for Fraale really understands what my life is like. I crave sex, constantly. *Every* woman that walks by attracts my attention, regardless of age or looks. All she needs is a pulse and I am aware that she's there and sexual. Not little girls—don't make that mistake. But from puberty on? *Oh, I notice.* And I hate that I notice. I wasn't born to this, but I'm in a continual state of arousal and it's only by very strict discipline that I'm not out every single night seducing women."

Menolly arched her eyebrows. She slowly lowered herself back to her seat. I followed suit and so did Hanna and Fraale. I had no clue what to say next, so decided it was best to keep my mouth shut and just let him finish his thoughts.

Rozurial turned to Fraale. "You understand this. You know the hunger." He stared at her hard, and at first she flinched, but then nodded.

"Yes, I do. It's . . ." She glanced at Menolly. "It's like your thirst, only instead of blood, we crave sex. We live off sexual energy—it *feeds* us."

I held up my hand. "Whoa, wait a minute. What are you talking about? I've seen you put away a meal as big as a house, Roz."

He ducked his head. "Food feeds the body but not the soul. It's true. I feed off sex. I don't have to fuck someone every day to survive, but I *want* . . . I *hunger* . . . every day, all day. Where do you think I go when I disappear? I'm not out shopping, girl." His eyes glistened, cold and glittering, and my panther rose up, recognizing she was in the presence of another predator. I'd never seen this side of Rozurial, but then again, I'd never bothered to look for it.

Menolly's fangs descended and she let out what sounded like a hiss as the tension in the room rose. "I've seen it in you. But you repress it well. Isn't that dangerous?"

"I don't repress it. I just hide it." Roz turned to me and cocked his head, a seductive smile washing over his face. Before I knew what I was doing, I found myself shifting in my seat, biting my lip.

"You see? I could have any woman in this house. But I have never—and will never—force a woman." Roz let out a harsh laugh and turned to Hanna. "I do promise you, Hanna, on my oath. I haven't just been *using* you." The cocky look vanished and Roz dashed his sleeve across his face. "I really like you. I have fun hanging out with you. I thought you just wanted a friends-with-benefits situation, too. Please, don't fall for me. I don't want to break your heart."

Hanna blushed. "Since you are being honest here, then so will I. The truth? Yes, I did walk into this wanting only . . . a bed friend. But you are comfortable to be around, Roz. And I suppose . . . it began to feel like I might have a full life once more."

"You still can." He leaned forward, taking her hands. "There are so many possibilities here. But I'm not your future. I can only ever be someone's present. Never bank on me as a future."

She let out a wistful sigh, then patted his hand. "You have not broken my heart, incubus. But you have cautioned me to guard it with more care."

And the room shifted again.

Fraale reacted to the sudden charge of energy. "Now you've gone and done it. I'm thirsty now." She leaned back and crossed her legs, adjusting the hem of her dress. Her thigh was plump and golden beneath the slit of the dress and she lightly stroked her skin, catching her breath as she did so. "Do you know, Rozurial, *why* I seek you out when the memories of the past begin to overwhelm me? Because you remind me to live in the present. You're my reality check, as painful as it is."

"Life moves on." Menolly pushed back her braids. The gleam in her eye told me she was feeling her predator strongly tonight. "I used to hate what I'd become. I hated myself every day, every time I felt the thirst for blood rise.

But I've learned that you can't do that for too long or you'll kill yourself."

Fraale let out a sharp laugh. "Girl, you haven't even *begun* to feel the weight of the centuries. Talk to me in another five hundred years, when you've had time for your state to truly sink in." She may not have meant it to sound harsh, but it came out like a jab. Menolly's brow creased, but she said nothing.

"So . . . I have a question." I decided to intervene before the conversation took another spiral down. "You feed off sexual energy. How does that work?"

I realized just how little we'd bothered to find out about Roz, which made me wonder about Vanzir, as well. And about our other friends? What secrets did they have that we hadn't bothered to examine?

Rozurial shrugged. "A kiss, a touch, sex . . . anything can siphon off the energy. We can *kill* with this power. We can drain our partner dry, but most of us don't. I'd rather feed off sex with willing women—and there are always women who respond to me—rather than coerce or force it. Not all of my kind feel that way, though."

Fraale shrugged. "Not all our kind feel much of anything beyond the immediate need. I think our past has helped us hold on to our emotions." She rubbed her temples. "In a way, what makes us the most miserable probably makes us the most compassionate for our potential victims." With a melancholy sigh, she leaned forward and rested her elbows on her knees.

Roz winced, then reached out and lightly caressed her shoulder. "There, I agree with you."

I turned away so they wouldn't see the mist in my eyes. I didn't like sad endings, but there was no way Fraale and Roz could have a happily-ever-after.

A moment later, Roz cleared his throat. "So where do we go from here?"

"A question first." Hanna chewed on one lip, as if she were mulling over a thought. "I take it you need more than what you have been getting from me to tide you over?"

Once again, Roz winced. "I've tried to hold out . . . Oh hell, why lie? Yeah, I need more than one woman, Hanna. You're great! Never think anything but that, and you're passionate and sexy." He glanced at Fraale but she said nothing. "It's just that I'm an incubus. It's like being amped up a hundred times more than normal. I need more . . ." Here, he paused—he was actually blushing.

"Juice?" I offered, trying to lighten the mood. "Too bad you can't just plug into an outlet."

For once, my joke didn't fall flat. Roz laughed, and Fraale and even Hanna joined in. The break in tension was a welcome relief.

Roz let out a snort. "That would hurt in ways I don't even want to think about."

A wistful smile on her face, Hanna stood. "Best this come out now rather than later after I let my foolish heart lead me into places from where it would be hard to backtrack."

"Hanna—" Roz started to speak but Hanna held up her hand.

"It's all right, Rozurial. I have survived far worse than the likes of you, and we had fun. I will be all right. I promise, I'm not going to return to the Northlands. But I will not share your bed again, for all I enjoy it. Only a fool returns to a path that leads to certain ruin."

She turned to Fraale. "I'm truly glad we met. And . . . I am sorry for the heartache you've endured. I understand loss too well."

Fraale laughed softly. "I would have you stay with him, Hanna—you'd be good for my beloved Rozurial. But you're right. It would only lead to your heart breaking, too, because it's impossible not to fall in love with the man." She held out her hand and Hanna took it. Fraale pressed it to her lips, then gently let go.

Hanna walked over to Menolly and scooped Maggie out of her arms. "I'll put her back to bed."

Fraale watched her go. "If anyone can weather all the slings of the world, that woman can. She's stronger than I am." With a sigh, she also stood. "I should not have come here, but I'm glad I did. You're my touchstone, Rozurial, my love. Like it or not, you ground me back into reality. Whenever I need a kick in the ass, when I start mourning the past, I just have to show up and everything falls back into place. Even if the kick hurts like hell."

She leaned over and kissed him on the lips, slow and long. Roz closed his eyes and I thought I could see a tear trickle down through his lashes. As she stepped away, Fraale worried her lip, but then let out a gentle laugh.

"I wish . . . But if wishes were raindrops, we'd be in the middle of the fucking ocean. Until next time, all of you, take care of yourselves and your extended family." With that, she waved at Menolly and me, and vanished.

Roz watched her disappear. A moment later, he glanced over at us. "Save your lectures, if you have any, because I'm not up for it. I haven't done anything wrong. I never led Hanna on, and I've never touched Iris or any of you." His eyes narrowed, and he rubbed his forehead. "And I have a headache the size of the watermelon."

I glanced at Menolly, then back to him. "Roz, we're not judging you. I never really thought much about the fact that you're an incubus, to be honest. You never really bring it up, and I guess I never thought about what you need."

Menolly stood, pacing behind the sofa. "I have. And I've been watching Hanna. I could see she was getting too attached but I couldn't just tell her to stop. In a way, Fraale's visit was fortuitous. And before you ask, I had nothing to do with her arrival. I have no clue how to contact her, even if I wanted to."

"You're right about Hanna. As I said, I never led her on, but I should have seen it coming. I guess . . . it just felt like a little bit of normality in my life and I liked it. I like her." Roz stretched and yawned.

"The desire for a little bit of normality . . . that I think we *all* understand." Menolly headed toward the kitchen. "I'm going out for a walk. I've got a lot to think about." And with that cryptic statement, she left the room.

A little worried, I decided to follow her. "Roz, go to

bed. Sleep off the headache. I'm going to catch up to
Menolly. We'll talk later, okay?"

He glanced in the direction of the kitchen. "I'm a little
concerned about her, too, Kitten. She's acting a little pecu-
liar, even for Menolly." And with that, he patted me on the
shoulder and headed out the front door, back to the studio
where he and Vanzir slept.

As the door closed behind him, I entered the kitchen.
Menolly was just finishing off a bottle of blood. She flashed
me a quick smile. "Go back to bed, Kitten." She headed
toward the kitchen door.

I skirted the table, catching up to her. "Wait up. I want to
talk to you." I realized I was still in my PJs, so I grabbed a
pair of gardening galoshes from the back porch and shoved
my feet into them, then pulled on a rain poncho that was
hanging there. It was chilly and damp outside.

"I need to think, Kitten. *Alone.*" Menolly frowned.
"Can we talk later?"

"No. I'm going with you, so deal with it." I crowded in
behind her as she exited the porch, out into the backyard. A
little ways away, beyond the rogue portal—which was still
pointed toward the realm of the Elder Fae—stood Iris's
house, behind a stand of maple and fir. We could see the lights
twinkling in an upstairs window. Chances were, Iris was up
for an early feeding of the twins and Chase's baby, Astrid.

Menolly seemed to get the message that she couldn't
shake me, so she fell into a comfortable silence beside me
as we wandered toward the path leading to Birchwater
Pond. She shoved her hands in her pockets and stared at
the sky, which was misty and cloudy, but no longer lashing
rain down around us.

I shivered beneath the poncho but the fresh air was invig-
orating, and made my nose quiver with all of its scents, even
in two-legged form.

As we approached the trailhead, a pale sliver of moon-
light reflected behind the clouds, casting a surreal glow
over lawn and woodland. The conifers loomed like black
silhouettes against the sky, while the maple and alder rose

bare-branched, spectral sentinels over the land. Spring seemed so very far away at this moment.

After a while, I broke the silence. "Why did you drag Iris's name into that little drama back there? She'd be mortified."

"No, she wouldn't," Menolly snapped.

I stared at her. Something had to be wrong. She was usually brusque but we hadn't had an argument in a long time. Something was brewing.

"Then let me rephrase my question." Feeling on edge now, I stopped in the middle of the path and turned to her. "What's going on? You aren't yourself tonight." The wind picked up and I shivered beneath the poncho.

Menolly continued on for another step or two, but then when she realized I wasn't keeping pace, she stopped and turned around. Her eyes were glowing luminous red, and I recognized the predator rising within her. For a moment, a bolt of fear stabbed through me but then I reminded myself that—vampire she may be—she was still my sister.

"You really want to know?" She scuffed the ground. "You have to promise not to tell anybody. Especially Camille. She'd want to dive in and solve the problem and I don't want anybody meddling until I've figured out what I'm going to do."

Okay, this was sounding serious. "You know I hate promising to keep secrets from Camille."

"Promise."

I frowned, then decided if it was something dangerous, I'd just have to deal with breaking my word. Because if it *was* something serious, I wasn't about to keep it on the down low. "Yeah, fine. What's going on?"

Menolly nodded to the trail in front of us. "Let's walk and talk, to keep you warm."

We started up again, and I felt a hollow ringing in my stomach. I was either hungry, or nervous. Or maybe a little bit of both.

As we headed into the shadow of the trees, she ducked her head. "I'm having problems, Kitten. With my marriage."

I blinked. I had expected her to say something about her

inner predator rising out of control, or maybe Roman and
the Vampire Nexus being too pushy. "What's going on?"

"Please understand, I love Nerissa more than I've ever
loved anybody. But I don't know if I'm cut out for marriage."

Okay, that wasn't altogether a surprise. I knew that Nerissa and Menolly argued a lot, but they always seemed to
resolve things. "How so?"

"I love being with Nerissa, I love having her in my life,
I love *her* . . . but I feel so constrained. I can never do anything right. She's always complaining that I check out—
that I'm not emotionally available. I just don't know what
she means." Her voice cracked. "I don't know how to be
who she wants me to be."

"You've barely been married a year." I wasn't sure what
to say, but even as the words came out of my mouth, I knew
that wasn't the right thing.

"I know!" Menolly whirled to face me. Even in the dim
light of the early morning, I could see the pain on her face.
"That's the horrible part. Our anniversary is coming up and
all I can think about is, fuck, how can I make this special for
her? I have *no clue*. Things like anniversaries don't mean
that much to *me*. But they do to her, and I never know how to
respond. You've heard us argue—over Yule, over our wedding. To me, what matters is that we're together. I just don't
understand why we have to . . . to . . ."

"To make a show of it?" I felt like I'd walked into my
second act on the *Jerry Springer Show,* and right now, I
wasn't loving it so much. On television, it was funny—
easy to laugh at. But this was real life.

"Right. Do you know what I mean?"

I debated on how to answer that. I wanted to show soli-
darity with my sister, but I really felt for Nerissa. After a
moment, I decided to just be honest.

"No, I don't. I care about birthdays and anniversaries and
holidays. So I understand where Nerissa is coming from. But
I also know you, and I know how hard this is for you."

Displays of affection had always been like pulling teeth for
Menolly. Even a hug was difficult for her. And talking about

feelings? A nightmare. And the same with planning special events. Tell her what to do, and she'd happily join in, but she wasn't good at taking the reins. When I really thought about it, Menolly's idea of romance was more skewed than mine. I was happy with a movie and popcorn on "date night," but Menolly didn't seem to understand why date night even had to exist.

She shrugged. "So what do I do? How do I get her to understand how hard this is for me?"

Out of patience, I put my hands on her shoulders and leaned down to stare her in the face. "For someone so smart, you can be a total ass, even if you are my sister. What do you do? You do what Nerissa wants."

Menolly stared up at me, her eyes luminous in the night. She looked ready to argue. "Even though it makes no sense to me?"

Exasperated, I let go and shoved my hands back under the poncho to warm them up. "Get it straight once and for all: Marriage, in fact *all* serious relationships with or without the paper, require compromise. And this is where you bite the bullet and *do what she wants*. If you want Nerissa to be happy, then quit whining. Plan a nice evening—it's not going to freaking kill you to take her on a moonlit picnic or something now and then. You're married, not dead."

I'd half expected her to go all fangy on me, but instead she looked like I'd struck her. "That's a little harsh. Your claws are out, Kitten."

"Menolly . . ." I struggled with a way to phrase it that wasn't accusatory. "You guys have been going round and round for months on this issue. We've all heard it. You shut her out. She cries. You feel bad. Round and round it goes. I'm going to ask you a hard question now. If you just wanted a lover, why did you ask her to marry you? Why bother with the commitment if you don't want to put the work into the relationship?"

A cloud formed across my sister's face and I realized I may have gone too far. We walked in silence a little farther before she said, "If I were a guy, this wouldn't be happening. People expect men to be silent and stoic."

"Wrong again. If Smoky or Trillian or Morio acted like this, you think Camille wouldn't have them by the balls? It's not about whether you have a penis or a pussy . . . it's about respect for something your partner needs. I'm sorry, I'm on Nerissa's side on this one."

But she was being bullheaded tonight, and when she dug in her heels, there was no reasoning with her. "I told you I didn't want to talk, but you insisted."

"Stop." I'd had enough. "I'm going back to bed. I came downstairs with something important to tell you, but after dealing with not one, but two soap operas, forget it. You're being unreasonable and I wouldn't blame Nerissa if she walked out on you. Maybe it would do you some good if she did. In fact, if you're so unhappy, then I suggest you take a break. Then, *if* she's still around when you come to your senses, maybe you can ask her to forgive you. And if not, then your loss, not hers."

Abruptly, I turned and marched back along the path.

"I didn't say *I* was unhappy!" Her voice echoed behind me, but I trudged along without answering.

By the time I reached the house, I was feeling mildly guilty, but I knew that Menolly was stubborn enough that she'd have to figure this one out on her own. I just hoped that Nerissa would still be around when my sister saw how stupid she was being.

But as I headed toward the back porch, I found myself thinking about Shade. Yes, we were engaged, but we'd set no date yet. I knew what my future held—marriage to Shade and a child by the Autumn Lord. And to be honest, that scared the hell out of me. Being a mother, especially the mother to a child of an Elemental Lord, and a Harvestman, would be hellishly hard. Being Shade's wife? Well, it was a lot more responsibility than just dating.

Do I even want to get married? I'd accepted my destiny. But had I really searched my feelings? I loved Shade. He was good for me. He made me laugh, and we had a lot of fun together.

I knew that I wanted children someday, but I'd always

imagined a passel of werekittens running around. And I didn't want to be a mother until I was ready. The fact was that until we were out of the demonic war, having babies was out of the question. I couldn't focus on the enemy if I had to be worried about children. Being a private detective while having children? Doable. Fighting demons while being a mother? Not on my agenda.

As I entered the kitchen, I saw that Hanna was up again. She looked exhausted.

"Go back to bed, Hanna. Nobody in the house is going to starve if you take a morning off. We can fend for ourselves." Impulsively, I wrapped my arms around her from behind and hugged her. "We appreciate your work so much."

She smiled then, softly. "I wonder, at times, if I can ever live up to Iris's reputation. I know how much the woman means to you girls."

"There will never be another Iris, but there won't ever be another Hanna either. I can't imagine life without either one of you. Hanna, you brought Camille safely down off that mountain. You saved her from Hyto. If you don't realize just how much that means everything to us, you're blind."

Hanna yawned but a smile broke through her gloom. "I did what was right. I watched too many girls go to their deaths. Hyto . . . sometimes it still scares me when I see Lord Iampaatar, but then I remind myself that he is not his father."

Smoky looked a lot like Hyto—in fact, so much so that Hyto had used the resemblance to trick Camille. Even though the psychotic dragon was dead, his memory would take a long time to fade.

"Smoky could never be like his father. I think he'd kill himself first." I looked around the kitchen. I was as tired as Hanna, but given that she'd just broken off with Roz, I figured she came out on the worse-for-wear side of things. "Go back to sleep. I'll start breakfast. I can make eggs and toast—I'm not that bad of a cook."

"But toast and eggs won't feed this army . . ." She protested even as I took hold of her shoulders and pointed her toward her room.

"*Go.* We'll be fine. We have cheese, don't we? And muffins?" I opened the refrigerator and peeked in. The shelves were loaded. Hanna was right—we were a small army and we went through a lot of food. "See? English muffins, eggs, cheese, and I see a stack of sausage patties in there ready to cook. I'll make sausage muffin sandwiches, and we can have leftover fruit salad. That will work."

Finally convinced, Hanna allowed me to shove her toward the hallway. "I'll sleep another hour, then be up."

"Don't you dare set the alarm. You sleep as long as you need to." As she vanished into her room, I turned back to the fridge. I had barely started to sort out my ingredients when Menolly came through the back door. I paused, my hand still holding the knife, as she silently approached me.

"Kitten, I'm sorry I yelled at you." She cocked her head to one side, the beads in her corn rows clinking together. "I'll talk to Nerissa. I'll figure out something. I don't want to lose her."

And with that, she turned and went toward her bedroom door, the steel of it clanking as it closed behind her. Even though I knew she meant it, I had a bad feeling about the path in front of the pair. There was something melancholy—almost eerie—about their relationship.

Nerissa really has picked a hard road, loving my sister. Even though she's a vampire and not a zombie or a ghost, having a relationship with a dead person can't be easy, a little voice whispered in my mind. Appalled by my own thoughts, I tried to block them out as I continued to work.

Chapter 6

By the time breakfast was on the table and the others were making their way into the kitchen, I was thoroughly exhausted. It was seven thirty, and I'd been up far too long. Shade gave me an odd look, but I just shook my head and mouthed, "Tell you later." I didn't want to air Menolly's dirty laundry in front of the others, especially with Nerissa sitting right there. But I did go out of my way to give her a hug before tapping Camille on the shoulder.

"I need to tell you something. Can I talk to you and Shade alone?" Arial's revelations were lying heavily on me. While I was glad that I finally knew the truth, it felt like my world had taken a huge shift and yet—nothing was any different except for me knowing more about the truth of my birth.

"We really should get cracking on researching the sword." Morio carried his dishes to the sink. "Should we take care of these before Hanna wakes up?"

"Yes, please. And we won't be long. After I talk to Camille and Shade, we'll plan out what we need to do about the sword." I pushed Camille in front of me, into the living room, leaving the others to tidy up the kitchen. Shade followed behind us. We went into the parlor and I shut the door.

"What's going on? Are you okay?" Worry lines creased Camille's forehead and I realized just how on edge we all were lately.

"I'm fine. Really. But something happened last night." Hesitantly, I told them what Arial had revealed, and that I'd spoken to our father's spirit.

Camille paled, the color drained out of her face. She stared at me mutely, as if searching for something to say. Shade stood, crossing to the fireplace. He looked over at me, catching my gaze.

"Did you know?" It was a question I had to ask. I had to know if he'd been in possession of this knowledge all along.

He inclined his head slightly. "Yes, I did."

Camille flashed him an angry look. "You knew all along?"

I thought about intervening but I wasn't sure how I felt myself. The fact that he knew something so important about my childhood, about my very birth, and hadn't told me pissed me off. But then again, Arial had known, Father had known, and Hi'ran had prevented both of them from saying a word.

"Did the Autumn Lord stay your tongue? Tell us the truth." If he said yes, then I could live with it. If he said no . . . I'd have a lot to rethink.

Shade glanced at Camille, then at me. After a long pause, he slowly said, "I knew. Until your father's death, I couldn't say a word. The day your father's body was returned to you, I thought about telling you. But Arial came to me. She told me that the Autumn Lord wanted her to be the one to tell you. I couldn't very well interfere. I love you, Delilah. But I—like you—am pledged to his service. If he wanted the news to come from your sister, how could I argue?"

I wavered. What he said made sense. In fact, it made more than sense. But I still wanted to smack him across the chest for keeping it a secret.

Camille made my mind up for me. "He's right, Kitten. He's pledged to the Autumn Lord, the same as you. If the

Moon Mother were to force my silence on something—well, I'm her Priestess. I have to obey. Just as you and Shade have to kneel to the Autumn Lord. Like it or not, Shade isn't to blame."

I considered what she said. I wanted to be angry about it. Or maybe I wanted to be angry at someone and I didn't know why. Maybe it was something else that had pissed me off. Whatever the case, I had to acknowledge that they were both right.

"Okay, then. But now we know. We know why Father and Mother never told us about Arial all those years. And we know why she ended up at Haseofon and why I'm pledged to the Autumn Lord. It feels like it should make a giant shift in my life—like it should be this dramatic 'aha' moment."

"But it's not." Shade crossed his arms, gently smiling at me. "Ever since you found out about Arial, this has been a puzzle piece that's eluded you. Now you've solved it, but it changes nothing really."

"Gee, thanks." As he grimaced, I relented. "I'm sorry. I know that you had nothing to do with it. I understand that you couldn't tell me about it, nor could Arial or Mother or Father . . . but . . ."

"What now?" Camille interjected. "Now we know, and nothing has changed. We know, but everything goes on as it has."

"Right." I was getting tired of talking myself into a tail-spin, so I decided to let it be. "You're both right. Nothing has changed. Now we know, and there's nothing . . . earth-shattering that's come of it. I guess we just get on with the day, right?"

"You're disappointed." It was a statement, not a question, as Shade crossed the room and took me in his arms. "You thought it would make everything make sense, but it hasn't. You feel cheated."

I leaned my head against his shoulder. "Yes, and what's worse, I know I have no right to feel that way."

Camille patted my shoulder as she headed to the door. "We'd better get to work on figuring out what's going on with the sword. I'll meet you two in the kitchen. By now the dishes should be done and we can break out the laptop and try to dig up some dirt. Come on, Kitten. You know you love stuff like that."

That was also the truth. I let out a long sigh. "You know, sometimes I wish I could just turn into Tabby and stay there. Life would be so much simpler."

"I think you'd eventually get bored," Shade murmured, guiding me with a hand on my back as we headed out of the parlor. The damned thing was, I knew he was right. *Again.*

"What do we know about the sword?" I booted up the laptop and opened a browser, surfing over to my favorite search engine. I glanced up at the clock. It was around ten o'clock but felt like it was late afternoon.

"Nothing. But we know that Leif Engberg owned it, and that he lives in the Vista View Towers. We also know his father owned the sword. *His* name was Karl." Camille pulled out a steno pad—the kind with pale green paper and a line down the center of the page. She liked them the way some people liked blank books or were partial to one type of pen.

I typed in Leif's name to the search engine and immediately got a string of URLs a mile long. "Well, there's no lack of information about him. Let me add *sword* and . . . what else, to the terms?"

"Try *antique sword*," Camille said.

When I hit REFRESH, the results were a lot more limited. Out of curiosity, I clicked over to the Image function, and scanned through the pictures. If I could find an image of the sword, it might be quicker that way. A moment later, I hit pay dirt. There was a picture, and when I clicked on it, the picture linked to a story in a magazine about antiquities by the name of *Amazing Artifacts*.

Luckily, the back issues were archived online. The story had come out last October—just three months ago—and while it wasn't just about the sword, mention of the blade was also included in the article about Leif's entire art collection. Someone named Davis Jones had written the piece. As I began skimming the article, the phone rang. Camille went to answer it. About three paragraphs in, I found what we were looking for.

> Among his other antiquities, Engberg also possesses a rare find passed down to him by his father: a sword that still bears the blood of its enemies. The sword belonged to Einar den Blodige, or Einar the Bloody as he was known— a vicious, cruel warrior from a rough, mountainous region.
>
> An ancestor of the Engbergs, Einar ruled in an isolated part of Norway during the late 800s CE. Invading village after village, Einar was considered a scourge on the countryside, until he ran into Harald Hårfagre, who went on to unify the country.
>
> Harald's warriors drove Einar's army back into the mountainous lands from where they'd come. There, his enemies closer at hand took the opportunity to strike. Einar's second in command beheaded the Viking chieftain during dinner one night, and took over rule, meeting with Hårfagre to iron out a treaty. A curse was supposedly placed on Einar as he died, but what that curse was, no one seems to know.
>
> Einar's sword was passed down through his surviving kin, and has always been carefully kept and cared for. Engberg laughed off the rumor stating that if the sword falls into the hands of someone not of Einar's blood, then Einar will return to avenge both his death and the loss of the sword. The sword passed to Engberg from his father, Karl, and it does, indeed, still bear the blood of Einar's last victim.

I sat back in my chair, staring at the screen, rubbing my chin. So Leif's sword had belonged to a power-hungry Viking chieftain, who had been betrayed by his closest allies. Add to that a curse as he died. Definitely some bad mojo tied up with the sword. The rest of the article went into some of Leif's other objets d'art, none of which held the remotest interest for me.

Pushing the computer back, I looked up as Camille hung up the phone. She pulled out a chair and sat down, looking rather bewildered.

"Something wrong?"

With a shake of the head, she said, "No, not really. But I have news. That was Siobhan on the phone."

Siobhan Morgan was a friend of ours. She was a selkie—a seal shifter—and she was married to a carpenter named Mitch. Or at least he'd been a carpenter before an old enemy of Siobhan's had left him disabled. Siobhan and Mitch had a daughter, who had been born back in the Isle of Man Selkie Pod, where Siobhan originally came from.

I picked up an apple—it was the only thing close enough without having to get out of my chair—and bit into it. "Is she okay? Are the Meré after her again?" The Finfolk—commonly known as mermen and mermaids by the FBH community—were a vicious, brutish race of water breathers who were pillagers of the ocean. They were particularly vicious toward the selkie.

"No, actually." Camille looked over at me with wide eyes. "Siobhan's been called home to the Isle of Man. Her grandmother died and Siobhan has to take over leadership of the Pod."

Choking on the apple, I spit it out into my hand. "First Sharah, now Siobhan? Is everybody we know closet royalty?" I pushed myself out of my chair and tossed the apple in the compost bucket, then dug a package of cookies out of the cupboards. I loved sweets. I lived on sweets, and I wasn't planning on stopping anytime soon.

"Seems like it lately, doesn't it?" Camille held out her hand. "Give me one of those." As I crossed her palm with an Oreo, she bit into it, wiping her chin as a shower of crumbs fell.

"So Siobhan is going home? Is she going for good?" I liked Siobhan, and would be sorry to see her go.

Camille nodded. "She and Mitch have put the house up for sale. They're leaving in a week. Baby Marion will grow up among her great-grandmother's people, and watch her mother become a queen."

It struck me that we probably wouldn't see her again. Mitch would transfer his allegiance to her Pod, and they'd be halfway across the world. We didn't get to see her very often, but we'd become pretty good friends over the past couple of years, and we'd helped save her and Mitch from her stalker.

"I'll miss them. Are they having a going-away party?"

My voice must have been wistful, because Camille gave me a gentle smile. "I'm sorry, Kitten, but no. At least not for anybody outside the Puget Sound Harbor Seal Pod. She just wanted to tell us good-bye before they left."

I contemplated the news. "At least she'll be okay. At least she's leaving because she's needed—not because . . ." Stopping, I didn't even finish the sentence. No use inviting bad luck.

"I know what you mean." Camille let out a deep sigh, then leaned forward, took another cookie, and motioned to the laptop. "So you find anything?"

"Yeah, here . . . take a look at this." I turned the screen around so that she could read what I'd found. She scanned the words quickly.

"Great. I'll give you one guess as to who's holed up in that sword there. And want to make a bet the curse stuck him in there?" She rolled her eyes. "So we have a crazed Viking chieftain locked in a sword, who was so horrible even his allies decided they could do better without him. Kind of makes me think he's better off staying in the sword. I wonder if his Viking buddies are there to help him out of the sword . . . or keep him in it?"

"Good question. What happens if we give the sword back to Leif? Maybe Einar will calm down?" I usually didn't like passing the buck, but if we could pawn off the problem onto Einar's descendant, I wasn't above at least considering the thought.

Camille burst my bubble, though. "Until Leif dies. What if he doesn't have kids? What if he gets drunk and loses the sword? What if he decides to party it up some night and decides to let his great-great-great . . . whatever Einar is to him, out of the sword?"

"We don't know he can do that. And we didn't even know about the sword until last night—it's not like this was destined to be our problem." I didn't usually argue against logic but truth was, I just didn't want to deal with this.

"Maybe not, but now it appears to have latched itself on to us. At least, on to our cousin. And whoever charmed Daniel into stealing that sword—and by now I think he *was* charmed—may make another attempt if the sword goes back to Leif."

My cell phone rang at that moment, putting an end to our debate. I glanced at the number. "The Wayfarer? It isn't even open yet. Has to be one of the staff." But as I answered, I was surprised to hear Chase's voice on the other end of the line.

"Delilah, I know Menolly's asleep in her lair, but you and Camille need to get down here. There's a situation at the bar. We're headed there now."

"Please, oh please, tell me that the bar didn't burn down again?" The fear that Menolly's bar had been torched again raced through me, and I swear, I stopped breathing.

"No, nothing like that. But someone broke in and they knocked out the portal guard. Derrick says it looks like they were searching for something." Chase shouted something to somebody, then came back on the line. "Derrick says no money was taken from the till, but he says something about the door to the safe room was opened."

"Oh, hell! The sword!"

"What sword?" Now Chase just sounded confused.

"Stay there. Camille and I are on the way. Tell Derrick . . . never mind—we'll tell him when we get there." I ended the call. "Code E—for emergency. Somebody broke into the Wayfarer. Derrick says the basement door is open and the guard was knocked out. The safe room is open."

"Oh hell!" Camille jumped up. "You get Shade. I'll grab Smoky and Morio. Trillian, Vanzir, and Roz can stay here to watch over the house."

I still hadn't told her what had gone down with Roz and Hanna. "Um, let's take Roz with us. Smoky can stay. Always good to leave a dragon around." At her look, I just shook my head. "I'll tell you later. It's a mess, though."

"Okay, I'll go grab Morio and Roz, you get Shade." She crossed to the kitchen door. "The guys are supposed to be over at Iris's today, beefing up the greenhouse . . . so to speak." With a laugh, she slipped out to the back porch.

Shade was in the living room, reading a book—*Quantum Physics in Action*. I did a double take, but then remembered how fascinated he'd been by some of the documentaries we had watched. I'd watched them primarily as a give-back since he sat through *Jerry Springer* with me. I loved nature documentaries, and shows about other countries, but the workings of the universe were a mystery to me. Camille and Menolly liked them, though.

"Get your butt out of the chair, honey. Somebody broke into the Wayfarer, and Camille and I have a nasty suspicion they might have the sword. Chase and his men are down there now."

I grabbed my jacket from the coat rack, as Shade marked his place in the book with a Post-it Note and followed me to the door. Camille was already outside, Morio and Rozurial in tow. Shade and I took my Jeep, while Camille, Morio, and Roz went in her Lexus. We needed her car along since the trunk was secure, should we have to move the sword. And with the men around, we actually could move it, without Camille or me getting burned.

As Camille pulled out of the driveway, I plugged my phone into the car charger, then followed her, easing the Jeep down the drive and onto the road. As we headed toward the Wayfarer, I filled Shade in on what I'd discovered about the sword.

He groaned. "Wonderful. With what I felt from that thing? We're definitely dealing with Einar's spirit, and my guess is the curse served to trap him in the sword. The energy would certainly fit. Especially if he's been in there for . . . oh . . . twelve hundred years or so." He stared out the window for a moment, then turned back to me. "Is everything okay? You seem a little depressed today."

Shade was good at reading my moods. I turned on the windshield wipers as the clouds opened and the rain began to pour. "Honestly, I am a little pensive. After I woke up from being in Haseofon last night, I went downstairs to talk to Menolly, and . . . well . . ." I told him all about the incident with Roz, Fraale, and Hanna, and before I realized what I was doing, I was into the problems between Menolly and Nerissa. I felt a little guilty, but I knew that Shade would never mention it outside the car.

"Wow. That's a lot for one night, especially if you include what went down with the sword." He frowned. "I guess you'll just have to let Menolly and Nerissa work things out on their own. There's nothing you can do to help, sweetheart. And if you try, you'll only end up getting them both mad at you."

"I know—this is their stuff, and I can't do a damned thing. But it got me to thinking about us. You don't feel like I'm pulling away, do you? Because I haven't asked to set a date for our wedding yet?" I hoped with all my heart this wouldn't lead into a big blowup. But I knew Shade, and even when we argued, his responses were measured and level. He never yelled—not at me—and he had never once said anything that left me wondering whether he loved me.

This time was no exception. "We have time, Pussycat. We have plenty of time. I agree, now is not the time to even think of raising a child. I think the Autumn Lord knows that. I figure, we're engaged. You don't seem unhappy. I'm not unhappy. If I was, I'd say so. As long as we keep talking, and we love each other, I'm good. Whether we get married tomorrow, or in five years, I'm fine. I'm half-dragon, remember? We don't always rush into things."

As he laughed, I let out a long sigh of relief. "Then you aren't mad that I'm not beating down the doors of Juanita's Bridal Shop, looking for a dress?" It was the only shop that I could remember the name of that specialized in wedding gowns.

Shade snorted. "I figure, when you start talking tuxes and bows, then we can make all our plans. Until then, I'm just glad you're with me."

I eased over into the right lane, then turned onto Whip-willow Street, on which the Wayfarer was located. On the border of the Belles-Faire District and the Shoreline neighborhood, Menolly's bar was in the middle of the block. Luckily, during the fire, the other buildings hadn't been damaged other than being engulfed by some of the smoke. A few blocks over stood the Indigo Crescent and the Indigo Crescent Coffee Nook, Camille's bookstore and coffee shop. I had taken over the second floor of the same building for my PI shop—Cat's Eye Investigations.

For quite a while, I'd let my business languish, but as the war in Otherworld escalated, I'd felt the need to regroup and give myself something else to occupy my mind. So I'd renamed my business and set up semi-regular hours. I missed having Camille right downstairs as often as she had been, but Giselle—the demon who was running the joint for her—was friendly enough.

Added bonus: Nobody was likely to get past her like the freaks who'd blown up part of the bookstore, killing Henry Jeffries—one of Camille's most loyal customers. Henry had bequeathed my sister the money to open the coffee shop, and she had installed a memorial plaque, commemorating him.

Camille had, as usual, managed to find a prime spot right in front of the bar. She had a direct line to the parking goddess. I eased into the next open space, about four car lengths ahead of her. Shade and I hoofed it down to the bar—Camille, Morio, and Roz had already gone inside.

They were standing by the bar, talking to Chase, waiting for us. Camille motioned me over. Derrick was there, and Peder as well. I stared up at the burly giant. He wasn't huge as giants go, but giants were . . . well . . . giant, so he was still close to eight feet of solid muscle. Peder wasn't all that bright, but he'd worked for the OIA for years, and Menolly liked him. She only talked to him sporadically, though, since he was the dayshift bouncer, and she didn't get to the bar till evening.

Shade and I joined them. Camille glanced over at Derrick. "Tell them what you just told me."

Derrick let out a grunt. "The door to the basement is normally locked from the inside. I ring the bell when I get here, and the guard comes to unlock it after I give him the code word. This morning, I found it ajar when I came in. I usually don't get here till later but I needed to do inventory today, after last night's party. At first I thought it had been pried open but when we looked at the security camera footage, it was obvious that it wasn't."

"What about Lucias? Is he okay?" Menolly hired guards to watch over the portal on a continual basis. Lucias had the evening weekend gig.

"Lucias is all right, but he was knocked out. The medic is down there now with him. He's Earthside Fae, or he might have taken the attack worse for the wear. I went downstairs to check when I noticed the door, and called Chase. The safe room is open."

Great. Just great. "Is the sword missing?"

"Yeah, it's gone." Derrick frowned. "Who knew it was stored there? I knew, and all of you. Since last night was Friday, Tavah and Frith were on duty. So they both knew. But they're both vampires so they had to get back to their lairs. Now, here's the thing. Lucias signed in this morning as usual, on the employee log. Frith and Tavah signed out. I don't think we can suspect them in this."

"You said camera footage. So Menolly installed a security camera when she had the bar retrofitted?"

Derrick nodded. "Yes. Somebody came into the bar—a man; Fae by the look of him. He couldn't be a vampire in any case. So, he rang the bell just like I would. Now here's the kicker—he should not have had the code word, and Lucias shouldn't have opened the door, but he did. The man followed him downstairs. A short time later, he came back upstairs carrying something and headed out back."

"Is there sound on the footage?"

"No, so we don't know what he said to get Lucias to open up."

I turned to Camille. "Did Daniel know where we put the sword?"

She shook her head. "No, he went home before we decided what to do."

"Then we should figure that we were all being watched. Probably by whoever wanted the sword in the first place. The same whoever who ransacked Daniel's apartment."

Chase gestured toward the door. "Let's go down. I decided to wait to question the guard until you got here, so he only has to tell his story once. The lump on his head is pretty nasty, but Mallen says he'll be fine."

We headed down to the basement. Even though the lower level had remained relatively undamaged in the fire, Menolly had asked the contractors to fully gut the old staircase and put in a new one, complete with solid railing, and better wiring. The lighting had been changed, and now the basement had three areas—stockroom, portal area, and the safe room.

The area surrounding the portal to Otherworld had been redone, though, of course, the portal itself hadn't been touched. A desk and chairs for the guards were to the left. To the right, she had put a sofa, where visitors coming and going could wait. A Plexiglas cubicle had been built around the portal, so that the guards could see who was coming through. Menolly had also hired one of the local sorceresses to cast anti-magic spells inside the cubicle, meaning that nobody could gate in, toss off a destructive spell, and then immediately gate out.

The entry to the safe room was around the corner, opposite the entry to the stockroom. Neither door could be seen from the portal. The safe room had also been fitted with a magical punch code, a lot like a security lock. Which meant whoever had opened it had to have known the code. The door was impervious to force up to—and beyond—a demon's capabilities. It was also a magically dampened area, meaning no magic would work within the confines of the room.

The guards were set up with one facing the door of the cubicle, and the other to one side. Anyone coming through the portal couldn't take them both out by surprise. Theoretically, if both guards were at their proper stations, one would be out of range from immediate attack. Of course, we couldn't account for the vagaries of having to go to the bathroom, or getting bored and wandering away from the post. There were always bound to be uncertainties. And right now, Lucias was working solo, so that made the whole situation a lot more problematic.

The guard was sitting on the love seat, ice pack pressed against the back of his neck.

"Before we talk to him, let's have a look at the safe room." I led the way around the corner. The door was, indeed, open, and when we looked inside, nothing had been disturbed except for the sword, which was nowhere to be seen. I knelt down to examine the lock. No breaks, no sign of forced entry. And this lock couldn't be picked—at least not without a working knowledge of magic.

Standing, I crossed my arms, frowning at it. "Whoever it was had to use the code to get in. That's the only thing I can think of."

"Then we're in trouble." Camille glanced over her shoulder. "Because that means either Lucias voluntarily opened it, or he was charmed. And once again, the word 'charmed' enters into the picture. But we need to figure it out soon because the sword, running loose in the wild? So not a good thing."

I nodded. She was right. Either our guard had been blindsided, or he was a traitor. And if it was the latter, then we had a lot bigger problems than just a renegade sword.

Chapter 7

After a thorough look around the safe room to make certain there wasn't anybody hiding behind something, and to ascertain that nothing else had been stolen, we returned to the guard. Derrick had brought Lucias some water and had replenished his ice pack.

We pulled the desk chairs over to their side, and Camille and I sat down. Lucias was sporting a black eye as well as a lump on his head, and boy, did he looked pissed.

"Okay, tell us what happened." I pulled out my notebook and pen.

Lucius muttered a curse as he tucked the fresh ice bag over the lump on the back of his neck. "The bell rang. It seemed early, but I thought Derrick just decided to get a head start on inventory. I asked for the code . . . " He drifted off. "I remember asking for the code . . . and that's the last thing I remember until Derrick found me and helped me up."

Lucias groaned again, then suddenly leaned forward and vomited on the floor. Derrick took one look, and hurried to grab a towel. Mallen pushed in between us to examine him again.

"I think you have a mild concussion, after all. I want to take you back to the FH-CSI for examination. We'll hold you for twenty-four hours to make certain there aren't any other injuries." The elfin medic motioned to one of his helpers and the man exited the basement, calling for a stretcher.

Lucias protested. "I don't need—"

"I'll decide what you need," Mallen interrupted, pushing him back onto the sofa.

Just then, Chase turned as Yugi came down the stairs, calling him over. A moment later, they motioned us to join them, both of them pale. "Can Lucias manage to take a peek at the security files? To see if he recognizes the guy in the footage?"

"He's pretty beat up but . . . " I turned to the guard. "Do you think you're able enough?"

"Hell yes. I want to find that fucker that sucker-punched me. Just get me up the stairs."

Pulling me aside, Chase said, "We found something outside. We have a bigger problem on our hands than your missing sword."

Uh-oh, this did not sound good. "What is it?"

"We found a body—he's out back in the alley, with a broken neck. It's the same man on tape. We need to ask Lucias if he recognizes him at all."

"And the sword?"

"No sign of it."

Camille and I followed them up the stairs, and Mallen had Lucias brought up on a gurney. He didn't like it when Chase told him they'd need to take Lucias out back rather than bother with the security tape, but he went along to make certain Lucias didn't faint.

By the time we stepped out the back door, into the alley, the area had been roped off with crime tape. The rain had let up, and it was chill and damp. Against a pile of broken-down boxes, behind one of the Dumpsters, was a body—a handsome young Fae man, who looked all too dead. Lucias stared down at him.

"Is this the man who attacked you?" Chase reached out to steady the guard but Mallen was quicker.

Lucias squinted again, against the light. Then he frowned and shook his head. "I don't know. I don't . . . I honestly don't remember anything after asking for the code. It could be. Maybe not. So . . . he's the one on the tape who I opened the door for?"

I leaned against the brick, staring at the body. "Looks like that might be the case. When did you come on duty?"

Lucias shrugged. "I always get here around five, to make certain the vamps can have time to get home. In summer, maybe a little earlier. I do know that the man who attacked me showed up about twenty minutes after I did—which is why it seemed so odd to me. Derrick never comes in that early."

"When did you show up, Derrick?"

Derrick glanced at his watch. "I came in around nine. That's when I noticed the door to the basement was open."

"So Lucias was out about three hours? Give or take a few? That's a long time to be unconscious." Camille frowned.

"Not all physical—though, as I said, I think he has a concussion. I sense the presence of Compelling Powder, which can lead to a nasty hangover and memory loss." Mallen rubbed his chin. "If Derrick hadn't brought him around, he probably would have been out another hour or two by my estimation."

I grimaced as Mallen's techs led Lucias back to the stretcher and trundled him out to the waiting ambulance. A thought occurred to me.

I motioned to Camille. "Whoever it was used Compelling Powder. Is there a way to track an energy signature from the use of magic? And can you tell if any Demonkin were involved? You can sense them. Maybe this was . . . you-know-who's doing."

I didn't want to come out and talk about Shadow Wing in front of the others, but we couldn't discount the chance.

He'd been quiet, at least Earthside, for the past couple of months, but we had been warned he was sending new personnel our way, even as his general Telazhar tore a path through Otherworld.

Camille shrugged. "Can't hurt to give it a try. Let's head back to the basement."

Once we were there, she gestured for us to move back, then settled herself in one of the chairs and held her arms out to her sides, palms up. A familiar prickling crept up my neck. I was so used to the feel of her magic by this point that I could tell when she was running it, and right now she'd called it in big time.

The more she worked with Morio and the more she worked with Aeval and the ES Fae Queen Courts, the more powerful she seemed to be growing. Though her Moon Magic still blew up on her at times, she'd found ways to circumvent some of the worst of the backlashes. Although the hail of slugs and frogs a few weeks ago proved she hadn't fully outgrown the half-human problem.

The energy around her spiraled; it was visible in a shower of purple and silver sparkles. At one point, she dropped her head back, and her eyes rolled up in the sockets. The next she let out a slow breath and lowered her hands.

"Whoever it was, I don't think he, himself, is magical. He just used the powder to subdue Lucias and force him to hand over the code to the safe room. No Demonkin, though." She shrugged. "That's the best I can do. Sorry." Then, she paused. "I have felt this before—recently. Hell, Daniel—his aura had the same feel to it. I bet somebody used Compelling Powder on him, too."

Chase leaned on the desk, drumming his fingers on the wooden surface. "So someone stole this sword you had locked up, after injuring Lucias. Just how powerful is this blade? Why do they want it?"

Camille gave him a long look. "We need to fill you in on what we know, but not right here. At this point, we don't know who might want it. But . . . I think we know why. Or at least, one of the major reasons. At first, I thought one of the guardian ghosts may have been up to the theft, but after what we saw—I don't think so now. Ghosts don't usually use spell powders either."

"That sword has gone from a conundrum to a problem child." I shuddered. The thought of Einar den Blodige gaining his freedom to rampage around Seattle in a host body was freaking scary.

"Are you okay, Kitten?" Chase usually didn't call me that anymore, but the look on his face told me he could read my mood and was trying to be helpful.

"I'm just thinking . . ." Shaking my head, I gave him a helpless shrug. "It goes on and on, doesn't it? It's never going to stop."

He reached out and companionably took my hand, squeezing it tight. "It will be all right. It has to be all right." After a moment, he let out a long sigh and straightened up. "There's not much more I can do here. My men will clean up out back and I'll let you know what we find out. I can try to get a match on the face of the man we found out back. Meanwhile, I have to get back to the station. Call me later."

Camille, Derrick, and I were left alone in the basement. Shade, Morio, and Roz were upstairs. The portal glowed, humming away. Just being near it made me nervous for some reason. Usually, I didn't mind. After all, we were used to them. But now? Alone in an enclosed basement near one? What would happen if a troll happened to pop through? It wasn't beyond the realm of possibility—it actually occurred now and then. Or what if Telazhar managed to elude the guards in Y'Elestrial and show up here?

"My imagination is getting away with me," I said, shaking my head to clear my thoughts. "Let's talk about something else."

Camille motioned to Derrick. "Who knows the routine at the bar? Who knows what times the portal guards change shifts? Who even knows about them?"

I glanced at her. "Do you think somebody has been casing the place?"

Camille sat down on the love seat. "Maybe, but I definitely

think whoever has been using Daniel figured out he's connected to us. I think they followed him last night and before they could do anything, they saw us take the sword. But Smoky brought it here through the Ionyc Seas. That means, in order to know about it, they'd have to have been . . ."

I saw where she was going with this. "They had to spy on us. Be looking through our windows. Crap."

"The wards don't guard against all intruders, only those we've set them against. Is a spy an intruder? There are so many variables at play. And what if . . ." She stopped. "I have the beginnings of an idea, but it's not clear yet.

"Well, one thing is for sure. If somebody followed us home after we took the sword and overheard our plans, then they had time to figure out how to get into the bar."

Camille nodded, still frowning. I could tell she was trying to puzzle something out. "The schematics of the safe room had to be built into the architectural plans submitted to the county . . . city . . . whoever. Granted, the thief only had one night to figure out what to do, but if he's good enough to track Daniel and not get caught, then he's smart enough to figure out how to steal the sword. And because he has access to Compelling Powder, we have to assume he's in league with someone who can work magic. Or who has access to it. Next question though . . . Why kill off the man in the alley? He obviously can't be our ultimate target."

"Because . . . he knows who you are. So you kill him after making use of him."

Suddenly, Camille snapped her fingers. "I wonder . . . We went with Daniel down to the docks. Delilah, did you lock your car when you got out, when we went over to look at the sword? I don't think I did."

I shrugged. "I don't remember. Why?"

"Because . . . Get your backpack." She grabbed her purse and upended it on the desk, sorting through the massive pile of things that landed there. "Whoever had access to the Compelling Powder has access to magic, right?"

I opened my backpack and followed suit. I still wasn't quite catching what she was hinting at, but then, I stopped.

Bingo. I held up a small talisman—stone by the look of it, but fully magical. I didn't say a word, though, because I knew what this was.

Camille reached out and I silently placed it in her hand. She turned it over, then nodded. Setting it down on the desktop, she picked up a nearby book and brought it down on the talisman, smashing it into pieces.

Then, and only then, did she speak. "Magic Ears. Simple talisman to make, if you know your spells. Works for a limited amount of time or until broken."

"Then whoever followed us didn't need to be listening at the door?"

"No, they had to be on the property, but whoever it was could hear anything that went on within earshot around your backpack. Was it in the living room when we were talking about the sword?"

I thought back. I'd been so tired . . . but . . . "Yes, I took it with me into the living room. Which meant our spy not only heard Smoky say he'd bring the sword down to the safe room, but he heard Smoky say the guard knew the code to get inside."

We headed up the stairs as Chase called.

I answered my cell. "Yes?"

"The man in the alley? Local thief, named Kendell."

"Well, at least we know his name. Thanks, Chase."

"You know, I have a thought that I'm not sure where to go with." As I followed her, I puzzled through the thread weaving in my mind. "We need to find out if Leif remembers Daniel. And if not, he must be panicking over the theft. And why didn't we hear anything about the loss in the news?"

She glanced over her shoulder, looking tired. "Because we didn't think to look? Because we've been too busy with everything else?"

"And if Leif thinks Daniel took the sword, how come he didn't go to the police?" I frowned. The more we seemed to be on track, the more questions were coming into play.

"That's a good question. I think we need to check up more on Mr. Engberg. We need to do so in person. There are things that computers cannot tell us. Like how someone feels, or whether we can sense them lying or not." Camille frowned. "But just how do we approach him without endangering Daniel?"

"Daniel!" I jumped up. "We need to check how he's doing. The thief—Kendell—was killed over this sword. Just because it's out of Daniel's hands doesn't mean he's out of danger. Let's drive over to his apartment and see if he's there. Can you put in a call to him on the way?"

By the time we got upstairs, Shade, Morio, and Roz were milling around the bar, food in hand. Derrick had found them leftover cupcakes and nuts from the night before.

"We have to book, guys. We have a theory." As we headed to the door, I turned back to Derrick. "You'll have to call someone to take over the guard duty today. But make sure they aren't new hires for now. And double check on them throughout the day. Get on that, would you?" Leaving the bartender overloaded with extra work, we swung out onto the rain-soaked streets.

Seattle during the day can be as gloomy as Seattle at night, and when it's raining, there isn't all that much difference in the amount of light shining down either. Partially overcast or full, the sky stayed a steady gray-silver throughout a good share of the year.

The rain was scattering bullets against the street, pounding down so hard that it bounced off the concrete to spring up again, trying to return to the clouds. It puddled in depressions in the sidewalk, and channeled a river down the sides of the curbs, making stepping out from the passenger sides of the cars an ankle-drowning experience.

It was the lunchtime rush, and pedestrians were hurrying past, some clutching feebly at umbrellas. Umbrellas were a lost cause most of the time in Seattle, with the wind whipping through to rip them apart and blow them backward. Most people just turned up their collars, wore hats and rain ponchos, and hurried along, heads down against the biting sting of the rain. Light rain was no big deal—we were all used to it—but rain like this pelted down hard and stung when it hit hands and cheeks and whatever else might be exposed.

Camille was soaked. She'd been trying to get Daniel on her cell, but now she slipped her phone back in her purse and shook her head, squinting through the rain that poured down her cheeks. I often wondered how she got her makeup to stay and not run, but I was pretty sure she had found some sort of alchemical magic—most likely in a bottle with the MAC or Urban Decay label on it.

"He's not picking up," she said, jumping as a loud rumble rolled through the air. "Thunder!"

We both instinctively began counting the seconds. When I reached three, a brilliant neon flash of blue illuminated the sky and the rain turned from heavy to drenching as the clouds burst open another notch.

"Thor's certainly pissed today," I shouted over another rumble that came through.

Camille laughed as she ran for her car. Morio was already there, and Rozurial was on her heels. She waved at me and mouthed, "Phone," before scrambling into the driver's seat.

While I fared a bit better—my clothes weren't quite so vulnerable to the rain—I still didn't like it. I was a cat. Water and I weren't friends, and baths were an irritating necessity to be gotten over with as soon as possible.

Shade and I slammed our respective doors and sat there, staring at the water cascading down the windshield. A moment later, my phone rang—the ringtone was actually a refrain from "Bad Moon on the Rise" from CCR, and I glanced at the screen. Camille.

"Hey, you wet enough?" I turned on the ignition so I could fire up the heater. It was chilly and getting colder by the minute.

"Too wet for once. Listen, I tried Daniel but could only get hold of his answering machine. I'm worried enough that I think we should drive over to check on him." She paused. "You do have his address, don't you?"

I frowned. Did I? Daniel had never invited us over to his house, and I had the sneaking suspicion that he wouldn't unless we showed up on his doorstep uninvited, like we were planning on doing now. It stood to reason that he liked his privacy, given his background and his profession.

"Let me see." I motioned to Shade. "Can you look on my iPad and find out if I have Daniel's address listed in my contacts?" I still loved my laptop but, like Camille, had switched to an iPad for mobile use.

Shade pulled it out from my pack, which *was* waterproof, thank heavens, and turned it on. A moment later, he was fielding through my contact list. "Here it is. Yeah, looks like you made a note of it. He lives in a condo on Lake Washington Boulevard in Medina."

I whistled. Medina, which was a neighborhood of Bellevue. A pricey neighborhood, where billionaires and millionaires lived—many of them techies who had won at the dotcom game before it had a big bubble burst in the year 2000. Medina was gorgeous, and bordered Lake Washington on Meydenbauer Bay, another famous name over on the Eastside.

As we approached the 520 Floating Bridge—one of the longest floating bridges in the world—which crossed Lake Washington and divided Seattle proper from the Eastside (all making up the Greater Seattle Metropolitan Area), I steeled my nerves. I hated driving the bridge during weather like this. Should the winds reach sustained 50 mph speeds, the bridge would close and they would raise the draw spans, to avoid the bridge twisting and going down. But even during weather like this, the waves would come crashing up over the sides to spray across all the lanes, showering the cars with water.

The wind would shimmy the bridge, and by the time you made it to the other side, you were just so grateful you hadn't somehow managed to drive over the concrete guards lining the sides of the bridge to plunge into the lake that you promptly put the trip out of your mind until the next stormy day you had to cross.

I watched Camille take the bridge before me. It was nearing noon by now, and there was a surge of lunch-hour traffic, but luckily no stall-outs on our side of the bridge. The other side—leading to Seattle—was a solid mass of cars. Some idiot had been speeding, it looked like, and had plowed into the car in front of them, which spun sideways, and now all lanes were blocked as they worked from the Seattle end to clear the accident. An ambulance whirred off into the rain. Apparently there had been injuries involved.

After the bridge, I followed Camille to the exit that led us to NE 28th Street, then we swung right on 92nd Avenue. The heavily wooded suburb eventually led us to Lake Washington Boulevard, where we turned left.

Mansions and extensive condo units lined the streets, but the trees still gave the area a rural feel. To the right, we could see a block or so over, the lake shimmering between the houses and trees. Waterfront access was expensive, and property here cost a fortune. A moment later, Camille turned to the right on a private lane. Heavy lion statues guarded each side of the street, and the speed limit dropped to 15 mph. Another couple of minutes and we pulled into the parking lot of a gated condo community.

Apparently, Daniel lived in the Lakefront Village Condo Community. An extensive lawn led down to the water, where I could see a designated swimming area. Had to be private beachfront for the condo owners. The rain had lessened slightly. Shade and I hurried out of the Jeep and followed Camille, Morio, and Roz, who were hoofing a quick charge toward the building.

The building was only six stories high, but from the outside, it had the polished, high-tech, high-lux look to it. As we raced under the awning out front and approached the doorman, I whispered to Camille.

"How much do you think these run?"

"Want to make a bet you get under a thousand square feet for well over a million dollars?" She snorted. "I can't imagine living in one of these. I get the price, given the area, but it would feel so sterile to me."

I agreed, but kept my mouth shut because the doorman was sizing us up and he didn't look inclined to be helpful.

I motioned to him. "We're here to see Daniel Fredericks. He's our cousin."

"Does Mr. Fredericks know you're coming?" The sneer

lay just beneath the surface, but not enough to call the man out on it—he could easily plead a "I didn't mean anything by it" excuse. I grumbled under my breath. All too often people with jobs that gave them a very minor authority were all too eager to make the most use of it they could.

"No, but we need to see him. We're concerned about his health." A thought occurred to me and I ran with it. "Last night, he was feeling quite ill after a party we held. We came to make certain Cousin Daniel is okay."

The doorman wavered, indecision playing across his face. On one hand, if he let us in, he might be letting undesirables slide through the golden gates. On the other hand, if his tenant was sick, he might be risking trouble if Daniel really did need help. A moment later, he asked us to sign the register and let us in.

"Take the elevator to the fifth floor over there." He pointed to a bank of three elevators. "Your cousin lives—"

"We know, in Unit 507." I swept past him, tired of the game already.

But the fact that we knew the number seemed to calm the doorman down a little and he gave us a smile as we entered the elevator.

The doors closed with a muted *swish*. The carriage was lined with mahogany-colored paneling and what looked like travertine tile above the wooden panels. A brass rail ran around three sides of the elevator, and there was a box marked EMERGENCY on the back wall. I wanted to open it, but thought maybe just doing so would set off an alarm somewhere and that wouldn't lead to good relations with Mr. Doorman out there.

"Fancy . . ." I personally didn't see the need to spend a lot of money on elevator décor but that was just me.

"Yeah, nothing but the best, I guess." Camille punched in our destination. The buttons weren't the typical elevator buttons, but instead, a keypad where you typed in the number of the floor you wanted. There was a Braille system right beside the digital display. As we passed each floor, a soft voice issued from a speaker near the buttons, giving the number.

"Fifth floor." The gentle computerized voice—I think it was supposed to be female—spoke again. "Thank you. Watch your step."

As the doors opened, we hurried off. The elevator gave me the creeps for some reason, but it wasn't like when we ran into a ghost, or some demon or anything like that. It just felt too slick, too elite. Too trendy.

We found the door to Daniel's apartment without a problem. From where we were, I guessed he had a lakefront view, which would mean extra pricey. As we gathered by the door, I rang the bell. I could hear the echo of bells inside. Once . . . twice . . .

"Do you think he really is out? He might be buying groceries or something." I really didn't want to try to enter Daniel's apartment without him being there. Something about the fact that he'd worked for the ISA and knew how not only to disarm traps and explosives, but most likely to build them, set me on edge. "So what now?"

"Pick the locks?" Morio said.

I stared at him. "Do you want to give it a go? Because frankly, I'm about as keen on that idea as I am strong-arming the door and breaking through."

Morio wrinkled his nose, snickering. "Well, we can stand here till he gets home. What about going through the Ionyc Seas?"

Both Shade and Roz shook their heads. Shade spoke up. "You have to know what your destination looks like before you can take a chance on materializing. Don't want to get caught inside a wall and implode the whole damned building."

"Then what do we do?"

Shade motioned us back. "Delilah, kill the lights."

He backed up and closed his eyes. I found the hall light switch and flipped the lights off. I knew what he was doing. A mist began to rise around him—a wispy veil as his body began to vanish, dissolving into the smoke. Within seconds, he was nowhere to be seen as the swirl of brown mist vanished beneath the door to Daniel's condominium.

Chapter 8

Camille glanced at me. "How does he do that?"

"It has something to do with him being half-Stradolan. I know that it takes a great deal out of him, and he can't use it very often. I'm surprised he chose to now, but then again, Daniel is our cousin. And Shade knows how important family is to us."

Morio leaned back against the opposite wall. "I'd like to know more about that part of his heritage."

I let out a long sigh. "Me, too, but he's slow to talk. The dragon in him, I think. You know how closemouthed they can be about things."

At that, Camille laughed. "Oh yeah, trust me, I do."

A moment or two later and we heard the door lock turn. Shade was standing there, looking tired. He nodded for us to enter.

"As far as I can tell, Daniel isn't home. I had a quick look around but didn't want to disturb too much in case he has the place booby-trapped."

Camille looked around. "He's obviously cleaned up

from the ransacking, so he must have been home. As far as booby-traps, I wouldn't put it past him." She glanced back at the door. "I thought he'd have a security system."

"He does, but it wasn't armed." Shade pointed toward the control panel on the wall next to the door. "Which seems odd in itself."

"He wouldn't just walk off and leave the place unarmed. Especially not after being broken into once already. Not Daniel." I shook my head. Something was wrong.

"He might if he were in the bathroom taking a bath." Daniel's voice echoed from behind us. We turned to find him leaning against the wall, wearing only a towel around his waist, with a big-assed gun in his hand. He let out a long sigh and jerked his head toward the living room. "Sit. I'll dress and be out in a moment."

Sheepishly, we filed into the living room and sat down. He had cleaned up to the point of making it impossible to tell he'd been burgled. The place was a tribute to chrome and glass, with all the side tables and coffee tables polished to a high sheen. The glass was spotless. The bookcases were jet black, and it was hard to tell if they were metal or wood, but they, too, had glass doors. Daniel's sofa and love seat were micro suede, in muted gray, and the art decorating the room was one of a kind—obviously high end. I didn't recognize any of the paintings or sculptures but had no doubt they were all originals. Which begged the question: How many of these were stolen?

As if anticipating my thought, Daniel entered the room, dressed in a crisply starched shirt and a pair of jeans that fit so well I wondered if they'd been tailored. His hair was still wet, but brushed back. The gun was tucked in a shoulder holster. I couldn't quite place the make, but it didn't look like a lightweight weapon; that was for sure.

Before he joined us, he crossed to the door and armed the security system. On the way back, he stopped by a minibar and poured himself a drink.

"That's a mistake I won't make again. Can I get anybody anything? Scotch? Vodka?"

We declined. It was a little too early in the day for drinking for us. He brought his drink over and sat on the ottoman opposite Shade.

After taking a slow sip, he frowned. "So what brings you over here on this gloomy day, to break into my condo?" His eyes twinkled, but he didn't sound exactly thrilled about our visit.

I blushed, but Camille just ignored the jab.

"We were worried about you. First, because of the sword. Second, because your apartment was broken into. And third . . . " She glanced over at me. "I suppose we should tell him."

"Tell me what?" Daniel leaned forward, his glass cradled between his hands. "What's gone down now?"

"The sword vanished. We put it in what we thought was a safe place. Someone charmed and injured one of our guards and stole the sword. Whoever it was bugged my backpack last night and followed us home—a magical bug, by the way. We think you're being followed."

Daniel slowly set his glass down on the coffee table, on a coaster with a picture of a wolf on it. He rubbed his chin. "I work cautiously. I'm the best in the business. But as I said, I've had an uneasy feeling . . ." He stood up and paced to the archway leading into the kitchen. "I did some checking into Engberg today. Leif was released from the hospital, but there's been no word from him and when I checked through my private sources, no sign that he's put out a price on my head or any such thing."

"No? Are you certain about that? Enough to bet your life on it?" I appreciated confidence but Daniel was a shade too cocky for his own good. "One hundred percent certain? Would you stake your sister's life on it? Because if somebody is pissed at you, they might take it out on Hester Lou."

That stopped him. He returned to the ottoman and picked up his drink again, taking a sip before speaking. "I'd never bet Hester's life on anything. Let me rephrase that. If someone wants to put out a hit on me, he'd have to take it to the top of the line. And most of the—all right, I'll just say it—assassins who I have met, and who are at that level, are too busy to bother with me. I'm not worth enough for their time, and yet I'm far too dangerous to go after for the lowlife thugs. They know what I'm capable of. But . . . you said the bug was magical? What if it's not somebody I know about? What if it's somebody from your side of the tracks, so to speak?"

"That's what we're thinking. Magic was involved in the attack on our guards. You really haven't had much to do with the magical community—human or otherwise, have you? Do you know if Leif is mixed up in anything like that?" Camille tossed the broken pieces of the talisman on the table. "This is what the bug looked like. Have you seen anything like it?"

Daniel stared at the shards. "No . . . no, I haven't. And I doubt if Leif has any magical capabilities whatsoever, but he might have engaged someone in the Supe Community to help him."

"Maybe. Or a human. . . or something of the like. There are so many magical ways to track lost objects and energy signatures. Heaven help you if Leif decided to employ a sorcerer. They have few scruples and are quite happy to do whatever it takes in order to solve the problem. And you and that missing sword? A problem."

"I'm sorry about your guard." Daniel dropped back to his seat. "I truly am." The reality of the situation seemed to be dawning on him.

"Thing is, Daniel," I said, crossing my legs and smoothing out the wrinkles in my sweater. "The sword also has a mind of its own. We don't know what is going down, but whatever it is? Not good."

He slowly nodded. "I didn't know the sword was magical. Hell, I didn't even know I had it until I got home. I do know the background of it—to a degree. The rumors. Do you think they're real?"

"Yes, bluntly put. They're real and Einar is in that sword." Shade motioned toward the glass. "I wouldn't mind a drink, actually, if the offer is still open."

One thing I'd learned about my fiancé was that he liked fine brandy, a stiff cognac, and he preferred bittersweet dark chocolate, when he ate it. He only ate Cheetos with me to humor me, which I considered an act of true love.

Daniel rose and crossed to the minibar. "What would you like?"

"Brandy, if you have it."

The brandy snifter was so big it would have taken both my hands to cradle it, but Shade was able to do so with one. His hands were large, and firm, and as I watched him gently accept the glass, it struck me just how incredible it was that such a beast—a dragon shifter, even if only half-blood—could handle fine crystal without breaking it. Just like he handled my heart.

Shade stared into his drink. After a minute, he said, "I think Leif has to know the truth—at least about the spirit in the sword. These stories have been passed down throughout his life. They're ingrained into his heritage. Even with humans who are skeptical, family history often forces them into contemplating things they otherwise might not believe."

Morio, who had been silent up till then, spoke up. "Shade's right. Making assumptions can get us killed. I do think it's safe to assume that Leif knows something is strange about the sword. He may even know it's magical. And I think he probably *would* hire someone to track it down, considering what a family heirloom it is. The sword stolen and the Magic Ears talisman in Delilah's pack? These cannot be coincidence. But that means whoever's been following Daniel works fast—and is quick to adapt to the situation. And whoever it was, they put this whole thing in motion. Daniel, have you been able to recall your contact who originally put you in touch with Leif?"

Daniel closed his eyes, his brow narrowing. After a moment, he let out a grunt. "Damn it, I think I have it on the tip of my tongue and it just vanishes."

Camille's phone dinged and she checked her text messages. "Chase has a last known address on the thief who overpowered Lucias. Can we rule out that he had anything to do with this?" She checked the address on her GPS. "What do you know? Kendell didn't live all that far from here. We could check out his house, just to make certain."

"That's breaking and entering, you know." Daniel gave her a sly grin.

"No, really? I had no clue," she shot back. "Just in case there's somebody there, we'll knock first."

"We might as well. Kendell didn't put down any next of kin, but who knows what we'll find when we get there." I gathered my things and Shade finished the last of his brandy. He handed his glass to Daniel, who carried it into the kitchen and rinsed it out.

"Do you want to come with us?" I didn't really want to have him tagging along, but in case he was spooked, I made the offer. We couldn't very well walk off and leave him alone if he was frightened.

But Daniel shook his head. "No, not really. They have the sword, so maybe they won't be following me now. I'm going to do some digging on my end. I also need to revamp my security. One warning: don't try to break in again. Some of my alarms can be deadly. Text me, rather than call, because even if I'm in the shower, when a text comes through, I've got my system wired so that my computer alerts me. The whole condo is wired through with cameras, alarms, and so forth. When the door opened? Even though the alarm wasn't armed, the computer alerted me. Which makes me wonder just how the fucker got in here to ransack my place—there's nothing on the security footage. Absolutely nothing." Daniel paused, then glanced at Shade. "So, how did *you* get in here tonight? The door was locked."

Shade merely smiled—a neutral, not-going-to-tell-you smile. "Texting it is, then. But make certain you take all precautions. Whoever is on the other end of this doesn't have a problem with killing."

On that note, Daniel saw us to the door.

Camille turned before he closed it behind us. "Would you put us on your 'safe' list with the damned doorman? He was unaccountably snide."

"I'll do that as soon as you leave." And with another wave of the hand, Daniel shut the door. We heard the lock.

"Okay, then. Over to Kendell's?"

"Let me tell Chase what we're doing. We still have to fill him in on the sword, but how we're going to do that without exposing Daniel, I'm not sure." I punched in Chase's number there and told him we were headed over to Kendell's last known address.

"Thanks. I was about to send a man over. Just watch your step and call me if you need anything." He sounded tired. "Oh, and Delilah? I want to know what the hell is up with that sword that makes murder an option."

"Promise. But later." As I punched the END TALK button, we headed back to the parking lot. Camille texted me the directions to Kendell's house and we dodged the pouring rain as we ran across the lot to our cars.

She was right. Kendell hadn't lived very far from where Daniel lived, and it took us ten minutes to make the drive, but for the difference in neighborhoods, it could have been ten hours. We ended up in Lakeshore Heights, a seedier area of the city. It wasn't that crime was so apparent, or that the area looked like a dive, but the houses were weathered, the lawns less manicured, the cars cheaper models and makes. And there was a general feeling of unease. I knew that this area was supposed to be rife with gang activity, but if it was, then it was behind closed doors, or kept for the evening.

As we pulled into a driveway, the squat yellow house seemed to be empty. No other cars were in the area, and the house looked silent. But then I saw a child run around from the back. She was about four and she was carrying a ball. Oh wonderful, did Kendell have a family and children? And did they know what he did for a living?

I got out of the car, motioning for Shade to wait. Camille joined me, with Roz and Morio staying in the Lexus. We walked up the sidewalk, eyeing the little girl, who was playing over beneath a tree, ignoring us.

At the door, Camille knocked and I stood back a step or two. A moment later, a woman answered the door, looking frazzled, in a torn pair of jeans and a dirty tank top. Her hair was yanked back into a mop of a blond ponytail, and she was barefoot, and carrying a dust rag.

She gave us the once-over, looking puzzled. "Yes?"

"Hi." Camille flashed her an easy smile. "I'm sorry to interrupt you but is Kendell at home?"

"I'm sorry. He went to work, I think." The woman looked more impatient than ever. "You can leave a message on his door."

"His door?" I glanced at Camille. This wasn't going like we'd planned. "Kendell gave us this address as his."

"Yeah. He rents a room in the basement. Look, I'm busy. I'm sorry, but I'm in the middle of housework, and if I don't get the house clean for company tonight, my mother-in-law is going to make me feel like shit." She brushed a harried hand across her forehead, looking exasperated.

His landlady, then.

"I'm sorry we interrupted you, but Kendell . . . There was an accident this morning and Kendell was . . . he's dead. We were wondering if you know if he has any family in the area?" Camille smiled gently, trying to soften the shock, but she needn't have bothered.

The woman shrugged. "Thanks for telling me. He just moved in a few days ago. Looks like I'll have to put up the FOR RENT sign again. I have no clue about who he was or whether he has kin around here. Send the cops over if they want his stuff. Meanwhile, I have to go." And she slammed the door in our faces.

I blinked. "Rude, much?"

Turning, I headed back to the sidewalk and the others followed me. The little girl giggled and waved, apparently deciding to notice us. When we were by the curb, Camille glanced back at the house.

"Well, then. I guess we should have Chase send some-body over here to pick up Kendell's effects. Maybe they'll hold some clue. Obviously we're not going to get in to look at them."

"I'm at a loss." I frowned, then remembered Lucias.

"You know, let's go to the FH-CSI and see how Lucias is doing. Maybe there's something about the man that he noticed . . . something that he can remember now that he's had some medical care."

"I think that's a good idea." Camille tucked her phone in her bra—her tops were always low cut enough for her to do so—and she hopped in the driver's seat as I returned to the Jeep. I swung into the car and fastened my seat belt.

Shade looked at me. "What did you find out?"

"Kendell rented a room in the basement, and his landlady is a bitch. We're headed to the FH-CSI. Maybe Lucias can remember something else about him now that he's had some time to recover."

The ride there took half an hour. Traffic was beginning to pick up. It was two thirty now, and we were growing closer to rush hour. The rain was still beating steadily, and along the curbsides, little rivers of water were beginning to form. The clouds were socked in so thick that it was already growing dark. Seattle might not be the rain capital of the United States, but we had only sixty-some days that were cloud-free. The rest of the time it was overcast or partially overcast.

Back over the 520 Bridge, and I realized I'd forgotten my Good To Go! Pass, which meant I'd be receiving a bill in the mail. The bridge had been turned into a toll bridge a year or so ago, while they built the new one alongside it. I had no clue when the new one would be done, but it was going to take several years; there was no doubt of that. Back across the bridge, in Seattle proper, we headed toward the FH-CSI, which was on Thatcher Avenue, right over the border in the Belles-Faire District.

The building was four stories, three of them underground. On the main floor was the law enforcement headquarters, and the medical unit. The first floor below ground level was the arsenal. Second was where the prisoners were held. Third was the laboratory and morgue, as well as the archives. There were rumors of another, hidden floor, and Nerissa had all but confirmed that was true, but Chase wouldn't discuss it, saying only that the info was on a NTK basis.

We swung through the front doors, and even though there was no indication, a soft glow of green light from ceiling cameras recorded our movements. But more than that, the cameras had been enchanted so that they could—at the push of a button—let loose a spray of a knockout drug that would incapacitate a giant or an ogre.

We stopped in HQ to talk to Chase. He was flipping through a file, talking to Yugi, when we walked in. Chase had been promoted to director and head detective when his boss had died during a troll attack. Actually, his boss died from a case of stupiditis, but either way—troll or idiocy—Devins had bitten the dust and Chase had taken over, much to his fellow officers' relief.

Yugi, a Swedish empath, gave us a wave as he turned back to his office, taking the file with him. Chase motioned us into one of the break rooms.

"Hey, what's up?" He looked harried, but no more than usual. As he poured himself a cup of coffee and added sugar and cream, we dropped into chairs around one of the long tables. "Coffee?"

As one, we shook our heads. We all knew what the station coffee was like, and none of us braved the mud, unless we were desperate for a caffeine jolt. The stuff was so highly caffeinated and so thick that it made me think of radioactive sludge.

"We wanted to talk to Lucias again, to see if there's anything else he can remember about the man who attacked him. We're kind of at a dead end here for now." Camille pulled out Kendell's file and shoved it across the table to Chase. "Kendell had just rented a room at that address. You might want to send someone over to pick up his belongings. His landlady's a piece of work."

Chase picked up the file and flipped through it, then sighed. "We couldn't find any clue of a relative. Unless there's something in his effects, we're at a dead end there, too. Have you asked the Triple Threat? Is he on the rolls of Talamh Lonrach Oll?"

"No, but that's on the list. We'll tell you about the sword later, but here is not the place. Meanwhile, we'll go talk to Lucias, but I suppose you already have?" I paused, an idea coming to me. "Do you have a mug file for the Fae? Is that how you found Kendell?"

"Yeah. Now we're checking out all known associations he has in the area—especially ones with magical leanings. I've got Yugi on it. If anybody can track down info, he can. Lucias was really banged up. He lucked out he didn't end up dead, girls." With that, Chase headed out the door.

As we crossed out of the CSI division and into the medical unit, Mallen was studying a chart by the nurses' station. The medical unit was primarily for Supe emergencies when it came to crime victims, but lately there had been talk in the Supe Community about the need for a hospital dedicated to Supes only. He looked up from the page as we approached.

"Good to see you again. What can I do for you?" Even though his smile was cool, we knew he meant it. Elves were far more reserved than humans or Fae, and a faint smile from them was as good as a grin.

"We need to talk to Lucias, if he's awake."

Mallen arched his eyebrows. "Just don't tire him out. He's in stable condition but it could easily have been worse. He's in Room 12. Down the hall and to the right. Do you want me to come with you?"

"Do you think he's up to answering a few questions?" I didn't want to charge in there if he was severely hurt and make matters worse accidentally.

"He's stable. I was going to release him at around four, if he continues that way." Mallen glanced up as a chime sounded. "Excuse me, I'm needed with a patient. If you need to talk to me afterward, I'll be around."

We headed down the hall.

Shade motioned to our left. "There it is—room twelve."

I pushed through the door cautiously. The room was the typical two-bed hospital room with TV, nightstands, and medical equipment. The door to a bathroom was off to the left of the entry, and a window with the blinds rolled up was against the opposite wall from the door. Lucias was resting against a bank of pillows on one of the beds. His face looked horrible, now that the bruises had set in. He tried to smile as we surrounded the bed.

"You look like hell." I glanced around and found a chair. "Lucias, we really don't want to bother you, but we have to ask you a few questions. We're trying to find out more about the man who attacked you, but we don't have much to go on. We were hoping that you might remember more about him now? Or is it all still a blur?"

Lucias closed his eyes. "I've been trying ever since they gave me something for the pain. Chase already asked about that . . . but I can't . . . so much of this morning is a blur. The Compelling Powder and the blow to my head worked a good one on me. I have a splitting headache even through the painkiller."

At that moment Chase and Mallen both entered the room. Mallen checked on Lucias's pulse and breathing.

"We have trouble. Big trouble." Chase was carrying a large book and he set it on the bed tray, wheeling it over near the bed.

"That doesn't sound good." I pulled out my notebook and pen. "What gives?"

Chase sighed, shaking his head. He had paled—and with his olive skin that was a feat in itself—and now he looked slightly sick to his stomach. "Fuck. Kendell is the brother of one of the men on the Most Wanted List, and they often work together. I knew he looked familiar but I just didn't put two and two together until Yugi pointed out the resemblance to me. With the way Fae names are, I didn't realize they were related till I looked into it more. We think Kendell's brother is in on this. His name is Aslo Veir. We've put out a Most Wanted alert on him."

That didn't sound good. "You really think he killed his own brother?" I wasn't sure I wanted to know but we had to know what we were dealing with.

Chase cleared his throat. He showed us the picture. Sure enough, the guy looked a lot like the dead Kendell.

"You are looking at Aslo Veir. He's Fae, yes. He's also on watch lists with the FBI's Supe Crimes Unit. Assaults, destruction of private property, looting. You name it, he's done it. Aslo managed to insinuate himself into the radical group known as ANT."

"Who are they? If they're a new hate group, I haven't heard of them."

"Worse. ANT is a full-scale domestic terrorist group. Anarchists Neo Terra. Far more violent than ELF, they stockpile weapons and explosives."

"A Fae hate group? Are they anti-human?"

"Not necessarily. They're anti-everything they decide stands in their way. Word through the grapevine is that Aslo got kicked out. He was too radical for them, if you can believe it, and he went into business as a hired hit man. With his brother, the thief, they made quite a handy pair. Kendell must have botched something royal for Aslo to kill him."

This was getting better and better. An ex-terrorist who even scared his comrades, and now he was running a free-lance gun-for-hire business? Lovely.

"He's known to be in this area?" Shade was scribbling down notes at the same rate I was.

"According to our source, he showed up about ten weeks ago." Chase sat on the bottom of the bed, taking care so he didn't jar Lucias. "Well, then. We need to have a talk. If Aslo is involved in whatever you're dealing with? I need to know everything. And I do mean everything."

Camille walked over to the window. "I could try a Finding spell on him if we had something he touched. Is there anything he left behind?"

Mallen cleared his throat. "It's not exactly something he left behind, but some of the blood on Lucias? Not his. I think that Kendell managed to cut himself when he was attacking Lucias. I have a piece of shirt with blood on it that doesn't match either of our guards."

"Well, it's not Aslo's blood, but since he and Kendell

are brothers, it might work. It's closer to him than any possession could be."

As Mallen left the room, I took a seat in one of the guest chairs against the wall. "What about a misfire? How could this go wrong?"

Camille shrugged. "There's always the chance of backfire, but this once, I wouldn't object to the spell bringing our target to us rather than pointing the way to where he's at. It's not like he's a harpy." Her sly grin didn't go unnoticed.

Chase snorted. "Oh please, not again. If I never see another harpy again, it will be too soon." He closed the file and stood up. "I remember that fucking demon showing up right in front of us."

"You have to admit, we wouldn't have Maggie if my magic hadn't backfired. That was the best thing ever to come out of one of my magical glitches, ever." Camille smiled softly. "Sometimes a mistake really isn't a mistake."

"Maggie could never be a mistake. Or technically, she was a happy mistake. A good one. So Leif may have hired Aslo. I wonder if Leif knows who he's dealing with?" I racked my brain, trying to think of what else we could do right now.

Mallen returned, bloody rag in one gloved hand. "Since we all wear gloves when we treat patients, this shouldn't have anybody else's blood or fingerprints or DNA or whatever you want to call it, on the material. Do you want a pair of gloves?" He offered her the gauze. It looked all gunky—dried blood and a few pieces of hair stuck on it.

Camille shook her head. "No, the more contact I have with it, the better." But she grimaced as she accepted it. "Everybody stand back. We can never tell when I have a misfire what's going to happen."

Everybody took a big step back, leaving her in the middle of the room, alone. Even Morio winced and edged back. With a deep breath, Camille held up one hand as she closed her eyes. The prickle of magic began to spin in the air—she was summoning the Moon Mother's power, calling it into her. I could almost see the shimmering in the air as she let out a long breath and rolled her neck, then brought her head up. As her eyes opened, her violet irises were shimmering with flecks of silver.

Creature of Fae, by name Aslo I call you,
Where are you? Show me the way,
Blood to flesh, an arrow points,
Lady of the Moon, reveal my prey.

As the last word rang out, there was a sudden crash of thunder in the room and a brilliant light flashed out, like a lightning ball, surrounding Camille and temporarily blinding me. She screamed, but in the neon blue glow of the light, I couldn't see what was happening. The next moment, the room was plunged into darkness, and the jar from someone hitting the floor hard shook the room.

Chapter 9

"Camille! Are you okay?" I scrambled to my feet. The room was still bathed in darkness, but the flash of light had left a glowing aftershock on my eyelids. I blinked, trying to clear the haloes that were reverberating through my field of sight.

I heard her cough loudly and then, in a wavering voice, say, "I think so."

Think so wasn't good enough. I stumbled around, feeling against the wall. "Who knows where the light switch is?"

Another moment, and in the jumbled confusion of everybody talking at once, the lights came on. Mallen was over by the door, his hand on the switch. Once again, the sudden brightness made me wince, and I shielded my eyes as I tried to take stock of what had happened.

Morio was on the floor, on his butt, looking confused and a little charred around the edges. A wisp of smoke trailed off his goatee. Rozurial crouched near the bathroom door, dagger out, looking around for whoever had set loose the big boom. Shade was standing beside the window, which was now a makeshift door. His face was bleeding where shards of the shattered glass from the blast had hit him. Mallen was by the light switch, looking relatively unscathed, and Chase was on the bed. Or rather, he was draped over Lucias, butt to the ceiling.

Camille, herself, was standing right where she had been, and she looked like someone who'd put her finger in the light socket. Her hair was frizzed out, she was covered with soot, and she looked like she didn't know whether to laugh or to cry. The cloth she'd been holding had been incinerated.

"Nobody move," she said. We froze. She paused for a moment, closing her eyes, and then let out a deep sigh. "Okay, the energy feels like it's dissipated. I think we're safe enough." After another moment, she glanced around. "Well, that didn't work."

"Damn it, I'm so stupid!" Chase pushed himself off the bed, wincing as he held up his wrist. "Hell, I think I strained my wrist. I've hurt it several times. Mallen? Have a look, will you?"

"Anybody else hurt?" Camille turned to Chase. "And why are you so stupid?"

"Because I totally forgot that we had someone from the Otherworld Wizards Guild in here."

The Wizards Guild was an organization from our home city-state of Y'Elestrial, and was often used by the Other-world Intelligence Agency to magically bug rooms, spy on people, set up the Whispering Mirrors—which were like visual telephones from Otherworld to Earthside. The OIA could make Homeland Security look like kindergarteners when they wanted to.

"What was the Wizards Guild doing here?"

"OIA headquarters sent them over to reinforce our security, now that Shadow Wing has made his move in Otherworld." Chase shrugged. "I forgot about it because it was just one more thing on the list. They installed some sort of anti-magical field or something like that. I'm not clear on what."

Camille snorted. "You'd better get *clear*, then. Usually

we don't work with the Wizards Guild, but I guess the elves can't really send their techno-mages . . . not right now."

"We don't even know how many of them are still alive." Mallen's expression was grim. "Tens of thousands of our people died during the attack. It will take years to sort out the full amount of damage that Kelvashan sustained, and the full number of our losses." A hitch broke his voice, and he pressed his lips together.

It was then that it hit me: Elqaneve had been his home. "You lost family, didn't you?" I did my best to keep my question gentle, not blunt. I was trying to mitigate the bluntness that I could, at times, be guilty of. "*A little tact goes a long way*," Shade was constantly telling me. And I felt I was finally learning.

Mallen gave us a brief nod. "I lost my sister, and I lost my wife and two daughters."

We stared at him. None of us had expected that—hell, none of us had even known he'd been married. I wondered if Chase knew, but he wasn't the one directly in charge of the medical unit. He looked as shocked as the rest of us.

"I . . . I'm sorry . . ." I didn't know what to say.

Mallen gave me a considered look, then shrugged briefly. "What is there to say? They were caught in the fires. At least they died quickly, and not by a goblin's blade. That is my only solace." He quickly changed the subject. "Chase, let me see your wrist."

As the detective showed him his wrist, I walked over to Shade and began to help him pull out the shards of glass. There were at least twenty that had embedded themselves on his face—all small slivers, but they had to sting. After they were clear—none had done much damage, when I really examined him—he washed his face with antibacterial soap.

Camille helped Morio up and we ascertained that nobody had been hurt—not even Lucias. We were all just shell-shocked and a little singed. Chase's wrist was bruised but it would be all right if he was cautious with it for a day or so.

At that moment, Aswala entered. A medic replacing

Sharah, the minute she entered the room, she began to cough. As she caught sight of the window, her eyes widened.

"What the hell have you all been doing in here?" She walked through the debris, over to what had been the window. "Whatever you did, you did it right."

"Never mind that," Mallen said. "Call security, and maintenance, please. Have them clean this up and move our patient here to another room. Make certain it's secure and safe."

Aswala shook her head, then turned. "As you wish."

Mallen dismissed her with a wave. "Thank you."

There wasn't much left to do. "We have a lot to sort out. I suggest we go home. Chase, we'll fill you in tonight on everything. I promise." I glanced at the clock. It was going on three thirty, and I was not only tired, but starved. "I've been up since what . . . four A.M.? And we haven't eaten since breakfast. I want a nap. Let's go home."

"What about the damage?" Camille stared at the window. "I'm sure Smoky would be glad to cover the costs." Smoky was generous to a fault, for a dragon.

But Chase shook his head. "No, don't worry yourself over it. My fault for not remembering about that. And I need to contact them to fix their magical security system. You shouldn't have been able to cast any spell other than healing spells and have anything happen. It should have just fizzled, if I remember right."

As we headed out, Yugi and a few of the other officers came running in.

"A little late on the ball, aren't you?" Chase grumbled, motioning to the damage. "Get somebody over here to fix that today. And make sure that APB went out on Aslo Veir. We want him for murder and theft." Chase was deep in discussion with Yugi as we filed out the door.

By the time we got home, it was 4:00 P.M. and Hanna was busy in the kitchen. She smiled as we came trooping in, even at Roz. Apparently, she wasn't going to let the events of the night before dampen her day.

"Hanna, we haven't had lunch, we've been through the wringer, and we're starving." I gave her my best wide-eyed kitty-cat look and she laughed.

"Go on with you, Miss Delilah. You all get cleaned up and I'll have an early supper on the table in no time."

Camille went to change, along with Morio, while the rest of us washed our hands and faces and gathered around the kitchen table. The living room was nice, but we tended to congregate there in the evenings. The table was for pow-wows and group huddles, and brainstorming sessions. And it was also family time.

"How long till Menolly wakes up?"

"Sunset's around four forty now, so a little more than half an hour?" Rozurial shrugged off his duster, hung it up in the hall closet, and joined us. He turned around to glance at Hanna, who gave him a friendly nod. There was still a hint of hurt in her eyes, but the Northlands woman was resilient, if she was anything, and I had no doubt this was just a blip in the road for her.

Roz settled down. "So what next?"

"Wait till Camille and Morio get back. Meanwhile, somebody grab Smoky, Trillian, and Vanzir. We'll fill everybody in over dinner."

"It's Nerissa's night for training with Jason." Morio grinned. "She won't be home till after eight."

Jason Binds taught martial arts. He was also our me-chanic, and the husband of our friend Tim Winthrop. I'd wanted to take a formal class from him but there was never enough time, so I settled for pointers now and then. But Ner-issa had decided to enroll in one of his classes and she was now going through his grueling 30-Day-Fit-or-Fight Pro-gram, Level A.

Jason taught seven levels of it—the first two each took thirty days, Levels C and D took sixty days each, and the rest were ninety-day-long stints. Workouts were four times a week, two hours each time. If you missed more than three sessions, you had to take the level over again. Nerissa had been going for two weeks now, and while it exhausted even her—a werepuma—she was making remarkable progress under his tutelage.

"Well, Menolly can tell her later, then." I glanced over at Hanna, who was dishing up bowls of stew and pulling a sheet of freshly warmed rolls out of the oven. Camille and Morio returned, both clean and singe-free, and Shade came back with Smoky, Trillian, and Vanzir. Iris peeked in behind them.

"I decided to give Bruce charge over the babies while I came up to visit." She proceeded to help Hanna put the dishes on the table as we gathered around it. Trillian started to help them out, but Hanna shooed him off to go wash his hands.

When we were finally all sitting around the table with food at hand, it was 5:00 P.M. and Menolly was up. We told her what had happened, and the relief on her face when we told her the Wayfarer was still in one piece was almost frightening.

Before we could start eating, Iris spoke up.

"I came up for more than just to get a breath of fresh air. I have something to tell you." She looked so hesitant that a streak of fear hit me in the heart.

"You're pregnant again?" Trillian snorted, but his teasing was with a gentle hand. Iris reached over and thunked him on the head.

"No, you dork. And bite your tongue. While I want more children, yes, I want them several years down the line." She rolled her eyes, pretending exasperation but it was obvious that she was trying not to laugh.

"So what's up?" Camille bit into her roll, closing her eyes as the fragrance of warm, yeasty bread hit the air.

"This summer, Bruce will be going to Ireland for two months. He's leading a group of students on a tour of Irish monuments and countryside. I'd love to go with him, but there's no logical way to do so given the children. The Duchess will be coming back to stay with me, and help out."

Her mother-in-law, who was of leprechaun nobility, had taken on the job of nosy MIL, but she had also been a huge help after the babies were born. She had left for home a couple weeks ago, back to Ireland, and Iris was finding out just how tiring life was taking care of three babies—her own twins, and Chase's daughter. Bruce pitched in willingly, but it didn't take a lot of stress away.

"So he'll be gone for two entire months?" Camille frowned. "That's a long time."

"I know, but the university wants him to lead this program and he really has no choice. I told him it was okay, even though—to be honest—I'm not very happy about it." Iris's expression shifted and she cast her gaze on the floor.

Two months without Bruce meant all the weight would shift to Iris's shoulders. She didn't have to worry about money, but all the decisions would be hers. It was a good thing Chase was living there now, I thought. He was more than willing to dive in and help whenever he could.

As if reading my mind, Iris said, "Thank heavens for our detective. He's been a goddess-send, and I think it's mutual. Anyway, Bruce's tour starts in late June and runs through late August. He'll be back before September eighth, in time to get ready for the new semester."

There didn't seem much to say, other than to comfort her and promise to help her out, so I pointed to the chair next to me. "Sit down. We'll tell you about our day."

As we finished catching everybody up, we ate, while Menolly sipped a goblet of blood.

I buttered another roll. "So what do we do to find Aslo?"

"Hell if I know." Camille gave me a grumpy look. "I'm so tired of having to deal with every penny-ante psycho in the area." At that moment, the doorbell rang. Iris told us to stay seated 'and answered it. A moment later, she was back, with Aeval behind her. Camille immediately stood, curtseying.

"I bring you news about your cousin. Her son Mordred? His body has been found in the realm of Elder Fae. He and his father will rest there together, in the crypt the Merlin was imprisoned in." The Queen of Shadow and Night was a pale beauty, tall and thin, with dark hair and piercing eyes.

Aeval had been old when our father was born, and originally had ruled over the winter months when Titania ruled over summer. With the advent of the new sovereign nation for the Earthside Fae, and the reemergence of Aeval and Titania to their former glory, Morgaine had been brought in as a third Fae Queen, and the winter and summer courts had shifted over to the courts of the hours.

I closed my eyes. The death of Arthur—Arturo as we had known him—had been a total FUBAR situation, and now this was the result.

"How did he die?" Camille had detested Mordred, but near the end, she told me she'd begun to understand him a little.

"We're not sure what got to him. There wasn't much left, but enough to identify." If she felt anything, Aeval didn't reveal it.

"How's Morgaine?" As much as I hadn't liked Morgaine, I still felt sorry for our distant cousin. Morgaine had witnessed Mordred—her own son—killing the man she'd loved for centuries. She'd slipped into a fugue. It had been over three weeks since we had returned from our trip with the Merlin. In all that time, Morgaine had remained in her solitude.

"Lost somewhere in her mind." Aeval's voice was soft, but I had the feeling she was as pragmatic about Morgaine as she was about most everything else. "If you don't mind, I'd like to take a look at the portal on your land?"

"I'll escort you." Vanzir pushed himself away from the table. "The rest of you keep working on our current problem."

Before we could say a word, Aeval had accepted his offer and was following him out the back door.

"I wonder if Morgaine will ever snap out of it." Camille looked like she wanted to cry. "Everything went so wrong."

"Not everything." Smoky reached out to stroke her shoulder. "The Merlin returned. We defeated Yvarr. And perhaps your cousin will return to her conscious mind at some point. It's hard to say, but don't give up hope."

"All right . . . what do we do about Aslo?" With a sigh, Camille carried her dish to the counter and handed it to Hanna. Trillian and Roz began to help clear the table.

"Well, would he have any reason to return to ANT now

that his brother is dead?" I pushed away my dish and opened my laptop, booting up the computer. "Do we have any clue as to why he and his brother would be involved in the theft of the sword?"

"I'd say no to the former." Morio leaned over my shoulder. He had a musky smell but it was lighter than Shade, almost tinged with sunlight and fresh grass. "If he got kicked out, given their history, I doubt they're feeling too friendly with him."

"I wonder why . . . Hold on . . ." I opened six different tabs on a browser and went to the newest search engine that had just come out—Werewyx. It had become popular among Supes because it was the first search engine created and owned by an IT mogul who was, himself, a Supe. It was also extremely accurate and it didn't violate the hell out of our privacy. At least not so far. Who knew what would happen in the future?

I began typing in different search terms in every tab, casting nets out, so to speak, to see if I could reel in any fish.

Camille headed toward the kitchen door. "I need to ask Aeval something—"

"Camille, can you come here?" Iris peeked her head out from the hallway leading to Hanna's room. "I'd like your help with Maggie. She's calling for you."

With a sigh, my sister turned to me. "Would you run out to the portal for me and ask Aeval to come back here before she returns to Talamh Lonrach Oll? I need to talk to her about something."

I stood, stretching and yawning. "Sure. The walk outside will do me good. I was already tired and the meal is starting to take its toll on me."

"Thanks!" As she disappeared down the hall, I slid my jacket on and crossed to the kitchen door. "I'll be right back. Nobody turn off my computer."

It was a quick jaunt through the porch and into the backyard. I was quiet—Weres tended to make less noise than a lot of other Supes, with the exception of vampires. The rain was still beating down and I realized that, even though I'd dried off, I had never fully warmed up. Once I got back inside, I was ready to crawl in a pair of warm sweats and snuggle up with a blanket.

The rogue portal that had appeared on our land sometime back was hidden behind a bunch of out-of-control Scotch broom. We'd cleared a lot of the foliage away from around it, but the damned gorse grew like it owned the place, and no matter how much we cut it back, it returned with a vengeance.

But as I rounded a particularly thick patch, I stopped short. There was the portal. And there was Aeval. And there was Vanzir. And the two of them were in a liplock that would have burned up the screen. Vanzir's hands were on the Fae Queen's ass. One of her arms was around his waist, the other was cupping his junk . . . well, the fly of his jeans behind which his junk resided. The pair looked so hot and bothered, they hadn't noticed me. *Yet.*

Which begged the question: What was the proper decorum when you unexpectedly interrupt the lusty tryst of a Fae Queen? It wasn't like I could tease her like I did Camille. This woman had power and she wasn't afraid to use it. And she didn't have the best sense of humor.

Taking the coward's way out—or as I liked to think of it, the *survivor's* way out—I beat a hasty retreat. But as I neared the porch again, I remembered that Camille really wanted to talk to Aeval. I couldn't just go back to the house without saying a word. Neither did it seem wise to interrupt the darkest of the Triple Threat when she was sucking face with our dream-chaser demon.

After a moment, I decided that my best bet was to make enough noise so they'd hear me and give them time to break up the make-out session. I turned around and, singing off-key at the top of my lungs, headed back toward the portal, making as much noise as I could.

Before I rounded the patch of broom again, I called out, "Aeval? Aeval? Are you still here?" A few seconds later, when they came into my sight again, they were standing at a decorous distance, both looking cool as cucumbers. I wanted to snicker and tell them the jig was up, but I settled for waving.

"Hey, Camille asked me to come let you know that she needs to talk to you before you return to Talamh Lonrach Oll." The Fae sovereign nation roughly translated to the Land of Shining Apples, or some such name.

Aeval searched my face, and I knew she was trying to figure out if I'd seen her and Vanzir. I kept my cat-stoic expression in place.

"I'll be in soon. Vanzir, you will stay here to walk me back to the house?"

He nodded, and he, too, flickered a glance at me, but I pretended not to notice it.

Instead, I gave them a wave.

"Thanks, I'm getting out of this rain." And with that, I hustled my ass back up to the house. As soon as I came through the door, I looked around for Camille. "Where is she?"

Morio glanced up at me, and he cocked his head. "You look kind of funny. Everything all right?"

"Yeah, but I need to talk to Camille. *Now.*" I was working on getting *subtle* down, but still didn't manage it very well, and I knew I had to tell her what I'd seen or I might just bust out with it when Aeval returned to the house.

"She's still in Hanna's room." Smoky jabbed his thumb toward the hall.

I hurried down the hallway into Hanna's room. It was small, but cozy. A double bed stood to one side, with a hand-stitched quilt on it, and Maggie's playpen was beneath the window, near the chest of drawers. The walls were a deep blue, and the trim, white. Everything in the room looked crisp and clean.

Camille stood up from where she'd been playing with Maggie. "Were you able to catch her before she left?"

"*Catch* is the word for it, all right. As in *catch in the act.*" I closed the door behind me. "Listen, I have to tell you something but you have to promise me you won't say a word. Or if you do, you can't say that I'm the one who told you."

She pursed her lips in the Kermit grin—the one Kermit always made when he was trying to figure out what the hell was going on—as she lifted Maggie back into the playpen.

"Okay, but what could be so important?"

I motioned her closer and lowered my voice to a whisper. "I know why Vanzir has been going out to Talamh Lonrach Oll so much."

With a frown, she tilted her head. "I don't think it's our business—if Aeval is training him in some form of magic, then—"

"Oh, she's training him, all right, but I think the only magic they're making is between the sheets."

Camille stared at me like I'd lost my mind. Then, she sat down in the rocking chair. "Say what?"

I knelt beside her. "When I went out to talk to her? I caught her and Vanzir in a liplock so tight you couldn't have gotten a paper between them. He was grabbing her ass and she was cupping his crotch." I had the sudden realization that gossip could actually be *fun*. Maybe that's why I liked Jerry and his show so much? But no . . . I thought. Jerry Springer was just hot to me, very hot. Young or old, didn't matter, something about the man tripped me off.

Camille rubbed her forehead. "Okay then, that just triggered off a major headache. What the hell? Are you sure— never mind. Of course you're sure. You can't exactly mistake something like that."

"Does it bother you?" I suddenly realized that the news might not sit so well with her. After all, she and Vanzir had gotten it on once, and I had the feeling that if Camille wasn't already married to three men, she might have happily added Vanzir to her entourage. With Aeval basically being her mentor and pledged teacher, this could make for a sticky wicket.

She frowned. "I don't know. It's just . . . *weird*. I thought she was helping him with his reemerging powers but now . . . is she just fucking him? Using him? Are they in love? How could they even *be* in love, considering their natures?"

"I thought you should know." Now wondering if I'd done the right thing, there was no way I could really backtrack.

"No, I needed to know. But damn, this is odd. Okay, I'm not saying a word, not till I've thought this thing through. Meanwhile, you don't tell anybody else. *Nobody*. I mean it, Kitten." The *stern older sister* look came out and I knew that I'd better be good and obey. When Camille pulled out that paddle, it was enough to make everybody sit up straight and behave.

"Okay. I promise. You'd better get out there. They're probably back in the kitchen now." I leaned over and tickled Maggie under the chin.

She stopped at the door and glanced back at me. "Great gods, how the fuck am I going to pretend like everything's normal?"

"I say, don't even bother. We don't live normal and you know it. Life's *never* normal for us. Meanwhile, I'm going to plug away on those searches and then take a nap. There's not much else we can do."

"Wrong on that one. I made a decision. After I ask Aeval the question I have for her, I'm going to call Leif and make an appointment for us to go talk to him. We're going to confront him, ask him if he knows who might have hired Aslo, and find out what he knows about the sword and Daniel." She opened the door and, giving Maggie one last kiss, headed back to the kitchen.

All thoughts of Aeval and Vanzir sailed out the window. "What? You mean we're actually going to tell him Daniel stole the sword?"

She glanced over her shoulder with a smirk. "No, we are not going to rat out our cousin. I'll think of something. But we have to find out what he knows and that means actually talking to the man. While I'm talking to Aeval, you search for Leif's phone number. I'll call him when I'm done and try to make the appointment for tomorrow, unless he's willing to see us this evening."

"Tomorrow, please." Fatigue was catching up with me. "I'm tired and I plan on going to bed early." Suddenly too tired to think about Aeval or Leif or anything, I returned to my laptop as Aeval and Vanzir burst into the kitchen. They were both soaked, but neither looked like they cared.

Camille managed to keep her cool, asking Aeval if she could talk to her privately. As they left the room, Vanzir swung a chair around and straddled it. He was eyeing me closely and I glanced up to see the edge of his lip curling into a smirk. He waited but I knew better. I knew that it was too easy to go into a tailspin when you were trying to avoid a subject.

Instead I returned my focus to the laptop, but too tired to think, I limited myself to finding Leif's phone number. Camille returned at that moment.

"That was short." I glanced up at her. "Here, Leif's number." I wrote it down on a Post-it and handed it to her.

"Thanks. I guess I'd better give him a call now." She settled in the chair next to me as I shut the lid of my laptop. It might only be 8:00 P.M., but I was ready for bed.

By the time I headed upstairs, Camille had made an appointment with Leif for 11:00 A.M. the next day. She and her men followed close behind us. We were all beat.

As Shade and I wearily crept under the covers, my mind flickered back to the scene I'd witnessed between Vanzir and Aeval and I shuddered. I wanted to tell Shade, but I figured it was best to leave it for now, if only for Camille's sake. I just wanted to sleep.

Chapter 10

My head hit the pillow and I was out like a light. That is, I was out like a light until 3:00 A.M., when a shriek echoed up the stairs all the way into our room. I shot up in bed, confused, turning on the light.

Next to me, Shade jerked awake, then hit the floor, already sliding into his jeans. I was in my Hello Kitty PJs and I didn't bother changing. I threw back the covers as a black, viscous smoke began to seep through the ceiling, forming a cloud over the corner of the room.

Shade pointed to it. "Fucking hell. Get out of here, Delilah. Whatever that is, it's not friendly."

I had thought at first a fire had broken out, but at Shade's command, I realized that whatever the smoke was, it wasn't some ordinary chimney fire. I hit the deck and raced to the door as laughter ricocheted through the room. The voice was deep and resonate, and the hair on my arms stood up on end.

As I yanked open the door, something stronger than me slammed it shut again, almost breaking my fingers as the knob slipped from my grip. Startled, I let out a scream and turned to see Shade focusing on the cloud. He was changing. Not into his dragon form—he'd wreck the house if he did that—but instead, he was taking on a shadowy nature himself, stretching out, both insubstantial and yet thick, like fog soup. As he rose up, the black cloud rolled back in a wave, then slammed forward, rushing over Shade like waves over the shore.

I half expected to see the cloud and Shade's smoky form blend—but instead, the intruder knocked him back, and Shade very quickly transitioned back to his regular form, landing hard on the ground.

"What the hell—" He looked dazed, shaking his head. Above us, the cloud intensified, and now it sounded like the swarming of a thousand insects. The energy roiling off it was enough to scare the crap out of me—it was bad, big bad, nasty bad. I tried to focus, hurrying over to Shade. Kneeling, I tried to help him sit up.

"Shade! Can you get up?" I realized I was shouting—the sound of the cloud was intensifying and I could barely hear myself think.

"I don't know . . . Where . . . What happened?"

One look at Shade's face and I knew we needed help. He wasn't standing up. He was just lying there, shaking his head like he was trying to clear his thoughts. I scrambled up again, running back to the door, where I tried to yank it open. I managed to get a grip on the knob and, once more, pulled—this time, putting all my strength into it. One inch . . . two inches . . . three . . . I was going to make it this time!

Then, with a giant clap like thunder, the door once again shot out of my hands and slammed shut. I leaned against it, beating on it as I screamed for help. Somebody had to hear me. We might be on the third floor but I had lungs like a banshee when necessary.

"Help! Help! Camille—Smoky! Help us!"

I turned back to Shade, who was sprawled on the ground, holding the sides of his head with both hands. He was groaning, writhing back and forth, and it was then that I saw the cloud had descended and was thick around him.

I gave up on the door and ran back toward it. "Leave him alone! Leave him alone, damn you!" Flailing, I tried to chase it away, but everywhere it touched, I felt a jolt of energy—a thousand pinpricks racing through my body.

My dagger . . . maybe Lysanthra could help. I stumbled back to the bed and grabbed the sheath from where it was hanging on a hook behind my nightstand.

"Lysanthra, help me!" Holding the silver aloft, I charged back toward the cloud, having no clue what I was going to do in order to stop it. A dagger against a shadow creature seemed insane, but it was the only thing I could think. I stabbed Lysanthra into the thickest part that I could reach— a jet-black pillow of smoke.

A second later, a roar echoed through the room and— was it my imagination? I blinked. No, the cloud really was pulling back. It still hovered over Shade, but as I straddled his chest, holding my dagger toward the smoking entity, it kept its ground. We were at a standoff, it seemed. Once again, I started to scream, hoping someone would hear me.

The next moment, another crash broke through the air and the door burst open, splintering as Smoky appeared. Menolly was there behind him, and she pushed through the haze that now filled the room. She dragged me off Shade, motioning for me to run toward Smoky, then she gathered Shade up and draped him over her shoulders. Seconds later, Smoky pushed us all through the broken door, and as we stumbled into the hallway, I stopped short, almost tripping Menolly behind me.

"Get a move on and don't let the vines catch you!" she shouted in my ear. I shook my head, trying to process what was going on as I started up again.

The hallway was filled with vines; they writhed from out of the walls, snaking to cover the old paper and to coil around the railing. The stairs looked tenuous—they were rolling, as if the wood had become liquefied clay. How the hell were we supposed to navigate them without sinking into the mire? But Smoky answered that, hurrying to stop me before I set foot on the staircase.

He swooped down on me, catching me in his arms, and the next thing I knew, we were into the Ionyc Seas, with mist and vapor rolling around us like crashing waves. But within the circle of his embrace, I was protected from the seething energies of the channels that kept the planes of existence from crashing into one another. The next moment, the world appeared once more as he stepped off into the front yard and let go of me. I stumbled, tripping over a tree branch and sprawling to the ground, as Smoky vanished again.

The ground was soggy from the rain, and I was in my PJs, which were rapidly plastering themselves to my body. I managed to scramble up as Camille splashed her way over to me through the mud and the pouring rain.

"Delilah! Oh thank gods, he found you." She was wearing a sheer nightgown, as covered with mud as I was, only she didn't have on any underwear, and the look on her face chilled me to the core. "We thought . . . Morio and Trillian dragged me out but I could hear you screaming."

I grabbed her by the shoulders and shook her. "It's okay! I'm okay. But Shade—something happened to him—"

"I've got him." Smoky stepped out of the Ionyc Seas, holding Menolly and Shade. He let go of Menolly and carried Shade to a nearby patch of grass, resting him gently beneath a tree to try and protect him from the elements. "Is everybody out?"

Camille, her hair plastered to her face from the rain, nodded. "Nerissa, Hanna, and Maggie are over there, under the shadow of the holly tree. Morio's gone to check on the studio, to see if Roz and Vanzir were attacked, too. Trillian headed over to Iris's."

I half heard them as I knelt beside Shade, checking his pulse. He was still breathing, but he was unconscious. "Shade, can you hear me? Shade, please wake up—Shade? Shade . . ." I started to shake his shoulders, but Menolly stopped me.

"We don't know what's wrong with him, so stop that until we make certain he's okay." She pulled me to my feet. "Do you have the keys to your Jeep? We need a blanket for him and I don't fancy going back into the house."

I shook my head. "No, I just have my dagger."

"Camille, did you get the keys to your car on the way out?" Menolly took another look at her, then shook her head. "Don't even bother. There's only one place you could hide them beneath that gown, and I don't want to look there. I think I have a spare key under my car. I'll be right back."

We all kept emergency kits in our trunks—medical supplies, blankets, spare weapons, whatever we might need in order to either take on a battle or deal with trauma. Menolly was gone in a flash. Vampires have the uncanny ability to blur the world around them. In other words, she ran like hell.

Camille huddled with me beneath the tree. "What the hell is going on? What happened upstairs?"

"I don't know . . ." My teeth were chattering as I spilled out the story of what Shade and I had woken up to. In fact, I was stuttering so hard I pierced my bottom lip with one of my fangs. Bleeding, I winced, and pressed my hand to my mouth. "Damn it . . ."

Camille moved closer, and I wrapped my arm around her. She was shivering worse than me. "We had something similar happen. The vines came out of the walls and started attacking us. Luckily, Morio was awake and saw them before they could grab us. He was able to get us out of there. As we headed for the stairs, we heard you screaming."

"What about Menolly?"

"She was running up the stairs. I'm not clear on what went down in her lair, but she dragged Nerissa upstairs and sent her outside while she roused Hanna and Maggie, then she headed upstairs after us. By that point, the vines had started emerging from the walls. Smoky grabbed Menolly and took off up the stairs to help you while Trillian and Morio dragged me downstairs."

I frowned. "Sounds like whatever it was started in the basement and worked its way up. I wonder what the hell is going on."

"I don't know, but once we know we're all safe, then we can figure it out." She huddled next to me, and I wrapped my

arm around her. Menolly returned with blankets and handed
one to us, and draped one over Shade.

Another five minutes saw Morio returning from the studio with Roz and Vanzir, both of whom looked sleepy and
were in their bathrobes. Trillian returned from Iris's.

"Everything is fine at Iris's. Let's get Shade down there,
then we can all dry off and figure out what the hell invaded
the house." He stared up at our home, which had taken on
an eerie green glow—much like what I imagined ecto-
plasm to look like.

Without a word, Smoky gathered up Shade, and we
made the silent trip over to Iris's. As I glanced over at
Camille, I saw that Misty—her spirit cat—was in her
arms. Even our *ghosts* were afraid of whatever the hell had
moved in.

Iris had the kettle boiling by the time we got there. Bruce
was setting out plates of cookies and making sandwiches.
Hanna handed Maggie to Menolly and began helping him
out. The rest of us gathered in the living room, where
Smoky had laid Shade on the sofa. Iris pulled up a foot-
stool to sit by him. She took his hand, and closed her eyes.

"I'm no healer, but I will tell you this: Whatever attacked
him still has hold of him. It's not possessing him, just . . . I
think it's feeding on his energy. Remember the Karsetii
demon? It's not one of those, but it's like that."

I had been attacked by one, I knew what the hell that
energy could do. "What can we do?"

Camille glanced at Morio, who cleared his throat. "We
have to pry that thing loose from the house. If we shake it
up, I doubt if it can also keep its hold on Shade. Tell me
again, what happened?"

I went over it again, one step at a time. "Shade told me to
get out of the room. Something slammed the door shut, out
of my hands. I turned around and saw Shade shifting into his
Stradolan shape . . . he moved toward the cloud, something
happened—I don't know what—and he suddenly material-

ized again and was thrown back on the floor. The cloud came
down on him again, and I grabbed Lysanthra. She seemed to
keep the cloud away from him."

Bruce appeared with Hanna. They were carrying sandwiches and cookies, and Hanna returned to the kitchen for
tea. Vanzir was rubbing his chin, deep in thought. Fleeting
images of him kissing Aeval ran through my mind, but
now it seemed so far away and of no matter.

"I've heard of things like this . . . it isn't Demonkin;
that I can tell you." He frowned.

"What do we do about the house? Menolly's going to have
to find someplace to sleep come sunrise." I was frustrated.
This attack was out of the blue—and what was worse, we
had no clue of who was behind it.

"I can sleep in the safe room down at the Wayfarer. But
I'll need guards on the door during the day tomorrow."
Menolly looked down at Shade. "Or I can call Roman and
head over there tonight."

Nerissa let out a grumble. "I don't like that idea—"

Menolly whirled, her voice rising an octave. "This isn't
about Roman. It's not about you either. It's about me having a
safe place to rest away from the sunlight and potential vampire slayers that want to play Buffy and go all stake-the-vamp
on me. Okay? It's not about anybody or anything except me
feeling safe when I'm at my most vulnerable."

Wincing, Nerissa bit back just as sharp. "*Let me speak*.
I don't like that idea because we won't be able to watch
over you and make certain you're safe."

Menolly stared at her, and a thousand words passed,
unspoken, between them. "I'm pretty sure Roman's guards
will keep me safe."

"Then that's what you should do." Nerissa stared right
back, and I could see a quiver around her muscles. She was
a stone's throw from shifting into her Were form. I quickly
stood, moving to Nerissa's side.

"Let's step out for a breath of fresh air." I steered her
toward the door.

Nerissa allowed me to guide her outside. Once there,

she stalked over to the porch swing and sat down, holding herself, rocking. "I won't shift, I won't shift . . . I won't . . ."

"Take a deep breath and count to five. Then let it out slowly."

She did as I'd instructed. "I'm sorry, Delilah. Sometimes your sister makes me so damned mad. She assumes so much. She finishes my sentences for me. She always leaps to conclusions. Half the time I keep my mouth shut because I know she's going to misunderstand what I say. The other half . . . we argue. I love her, but I'm starting to wonder . . ."

"If you made a mistake?" I hated those words. I hated even bringing them out into the open.

But Nerissa surprised me. "No, never. Menolly, *a mistake*? I can't imagine thinking that. But . . . maybe we rushed into marriage too quickly. We didn't set our ground rules carefully. We've taken everything on the wing and that can be a big mistake. We tumbled into this relationship without thinking of how our differences were going to affect us. And now she thinks that I'm just trying to get back at her because of Roman, but I'm not! I didn't expect to . . ." She stopped, pressing her fingers to her lips.

I straightened my shoulders, icy cold and getting colder. What the hell was going on between them? "What do you mean? What didn't you expect, Nerissa?"

Nerissa hung her head. "You know that Menolly and I agreed on exclusivity regarding women. That's our rule. And we've both played by it—men are fine as a dalliance, but other women? No. As far as I know, neither one of us has ever wanted to break that rule. Then Roman came into the picture, and he's more than a dalliance. I adapted to that—though it did bother me at first, but I'm secure enough in Menolly's love that I got over it. But now . . ."

"Now what?" I wanted to go back inside, to see how Shade was doing, but Nerissa was having a breakdown, and I figured somebody would come get me if Shade took a turn for the worse.

"Now, I've met a man and we get along great. And he's a Were so he understands that side of me. I don't love him,

Delilah, but I think I finally understand what Menolly gets from Roman. He's a best buddy with fringe benefits. Only . . . she's not happy about it."

"Delilah." Iris stuck her head out the door. "Come here. Shade's waking up."

I jumped up, then turned to Nerissa. "Listen . . ."

"Go, be with him. Menolly and I will work things out. But now you know—it's not just me causing problems."

"I never thought it was," I said gently. "I love my sister very much, but I know full well she can be a handful."

"Menolly's guilty of the same feelings she accuses me of. I love her, and we'll get through this, but I think we need counseling." Nerissa nodded to the door. "Now, go. I need to sit out here for a bit."

I hustled through the door, thinking that Menolly led the most complicated life of the three of us. Camille's men were all on board with their poly relationship and really, their arrangement wasn't that confusing. I only had one man—well, technically, but Shade had been sent by the Autumn Lord and Hi'ran would always be part of our relationship. But Menolly and Nerissa? They were walking a tricky path.

When I entered the living room, Shade was sitting up, looking so shaky that I wondered if he could stay conscious till I reached his side.

Chase tapped me on the shoulder. "I've called for Mallen to come out. I think he needs to be looked at."

Slowly, I knelt by Shade's side. "Love, how are you feeling?"

He gazed at me, his eyes unfocused. "Delilah . . . where . . . I feel so strange." Wincing, he rubbed his head. "My head hurts."

Smoky was pacing the length of the room. "Something doesn't feel right—it's not his dragon side, that I know, but there's something . . . off-kilter."

"Dude, he can hear you." Trillian frowned at him.

"Will you all just shut up and let him breathe for a moment?" I seldom made a fuss, but right now, I wanted to smack them all down. "Just be quiet."

Everybody stared at me for a moment, then settled down. Camille moved to stand by my back, and she rubbed my shoulders gently as I held Shade's hands. Right now, all I could think about was wanting him to be all right. He *had* to be okay. He was half-dragon, for Bast's sake. How could anything hurt him?

A moment later, he inhaled a long, shuddering breath. "Something feels like it's missing."

"Missing?" I didn't understand. What the hell was going on?

He nodded. "Missing. Part of me feels like it's missing."

Just then, Morio entered the living room again. "Guys, whatever is going on at our house, it's lit up like fucking Yuletide morning. I'm going to see if Wilbur's home. Right now, we need all hands on deck, whether we like those hands or not. And Wilbur knows magic."

"It's . . ." I glanced at the clock. "Three thirty. You really going to wake him up at this time?"

"Damned straight, I am."

Wilbur was a neighbor of ours whom we sometimes worked with. He was a necromancer who looked a lot like ZZ Top, had one amputated leg thanks to a really nasty pair of sorcerers, and made a play for every woman who came within arm's reach. But he was top of the line at what he did, and he had helped us out more often than not. He lived with his brother Martin, whom Wilbur had raised from the dead after cancer claimed his life. Martin was a ghoul. Wilbur and Martin liked to watch *Jeopardy* together in the evenings, and Martin was a little like a puppy dog in a really sick movie, but what the hell. It worked for them.

"Good idea. Take Menolly with you. She can usually get through to him." Camille waved him off. Then, she moved to one side and pulled out her phone. "I'm calling in Ivana, the Maiden of Karask."

"Oh, how wonderful. She's *just* what we need. But I guess, considering what we're facing, another freakshow in the mix can't hurt anything." I went back to focusing on Shade. I tried to ask him how he was doing, but he just kept repeating that he felt like something was "missing" and that he felt lightheaded. My questions seemed to be making him anxious, so I tucked a blanket around him and held his hand, worried sick.

What if he had been seriously hurt? There were injuries that could harm Supes and dragons far worse than any wound visible on the surface. And I had no idea what might affect his Stradolan side—I was only just learning about that part of him. We'd witnessed some pretty freaking scary things over the years. We'd lost people we'd loved. And right now, all I knew was that the one thing I couldn't do was to lose Shade. I could cope with almost anything, but lose Shade or my sisters? That would be the breaking point.

Fifteen minutes later, Mallen entered the room. He motioned for everyone to get out of the way so he and his tech could examine Shade. We moved into the kitchen to give him privacy.

At that moment, a knock on the back door announced the arrival of Ivana, the Maiden of Karask. Camille quietly excused herself and went outside. She'd borrowed a robe from Chase, so she wasn't so exposed, and while part of me felt I should be going with her and the Elder Fae, I knew I couldn't leave till I found out what was wrong.

After a bit Mallen peeked in, motioning for me to join him. The men had gone up to the house but Iris and Nerissa, who was back inside, came with me.

"I've examined him thoroughly. Whatever it was . . . Delilah, has detached, but it did damage. It drained Shade's powers from his Stradolan side." Mallen's face was void of emotion.

I frowned. "*Drained him?* Could that be why he feels like something is missing? How long till he gets them back?" I turned to Shade, who was resting quietly. "Did he pass out again?"

"No, I gave him a sedative his system can tolerate. He needs to rest." Mallen glanced over at him, then turned back to me. "I don't think you understand what I'm saying. Whatever did this, it drained his powers permanently.

Shade still has his dragon heritage, but whatever powers were fueled by his Stradolan side? His shadow walker self? They're gone. Just . . . gone as if they never existed."

I stared at the elfin medic. "What do you mean, *gone*? Powers can't just disappear like that." But then, I stopped. They could. Vanzir's powers had been stripped by the Moon Mother, but they had come back, in a vastly different way. "Couldn't it just be the shock? Something temporary?"

Mallen shook his head. "I'm afraid not. I can do more extensive testing at the FH-CSI, but I think the results are going to come out the same. Shade is still half-dragon, but he might as well be half-human on the other side now."

I caught my breath. What the hell was this going to do to him? "Can he survive? He's shadow dragon . . . they have a special connection with the Stradolan."

"I know, and I'm not the best one to answer these questions. He really should go home to the Netherworld to be checked out by his people. Both the Dragonkin and the Stradolan. I can heal up his body. He's in no danger of dying. But if there's any way to restore his shadow-walker abilities, I'm at a loss." With that, he stood. "By tomorrow, he'll be up and ready to go. Just don't let him overdo for a day or so."

"Does he know?" I was starting to panic. I wasn't good with comforting people, even the people I loved. How could I tell my fiancé he'd just lost part of himself for good? "Mallen, I can't tell him this. It would come so much easier from someone used to giving bad news. I'm not good with this sort of thing. Can you please stay and make sure that I don't mangle this?"

Mallen shook his head. "No, I don't think he understood me when I tried to tell him—he was too out of it." He patted my arm. "Listen, you'll do fine. Tomorrow, when he wakes up, tell him the minute he's coherent. This is something he needs to know before he does *anything*. We don't know what parts of his routine are from his Stradolan side and what parts aren't. He has to learn how to adjust. It's like a human losing one of their senses. Or if you were to suddenly be unable to shift into Were form."

As the magnitude of the change hit home, I realized that Mallen was telling me that Shade had suddenly—at least for his kind—become disabled. He'd lost the ability to function normally. And that would take a whole lot of getting used to. He would have to learn how to adapt—learn to accept what he could no longer do and work around it. Nodding, unable to say a word, I watched as the elfin medic left.

Nerissa and Iris, who had heard everything, moved to my side. They each took one of my hands.

"He'll manage, Kitten." Iris stroked my hair. "He's a resilient and steadfast man. If anybody can handle this, it will be Shade."

"But . . . how will he figure out what parts of him work and what don't? Is there a guide for which abilities were Stradolan and which came from his dragon mother? I wish he'd told me more about this side of himself but you know how secretive dragons are. They're stubborn and silent and mulish." Another thought hit me. "Oh gods, what about his family? They pride themselves on who they are. Will they even recognize him anymore?"

"I assume you mean, will they accept him?" Nerissa frowned. "I hope they're better about it than my people. In the puma prides . . . well . . . lose your puma side and you might as well leave the clan. They aren't very accepting."

"I know. Remember?" Images of Zachary flashed through my mind. Zachary who had become wheelchair bound, unable to walk. He and I had dated briefly, but Zach lacked the courage to face his future. He was a good-hearted man, but a weak-spirited one. And, when push came to shove, he lacked the courage to face his own disabilities. He'd retreated to Otherworld to remain forever in puma form. While I understood his choice, I also knew he'd done so out of fear of what he'd become in human form, rather than out of embracing the Were side of himself.

Nerissa and Iris both seemed to know what I was thinking, because Nerissa shook her head and gave me a wide smile.

"You know Shade is far stronger than Zachary ever

was. Zachary was weak in spirit even before the accident. You know Shade will pull through this. I think he's going to surprise you. I think you're going to find that he's more than capable of learning a new way of life."

Iris nodded. "Nerissa is right. Shade's not one to feel sorry for himself. And if his family can't accept the changes that have happened to him? Well, will that really be such a big loss? Shade himself has commented before on how little connection the families in the Netherworld have. That being said, I do think he needs to do what Mallen said—go there to assess the extent of the damage."

I pressed my lips together, unsure of how to respond to any of this. But then, a stronger fear took hold. If that creature could permanently drain the abilities of a Stradolan, what could it do to others? Could it drain Ivana's powers? Or Wilbur's?

"Watch him—I have to stop the others—we can't attack this thing till we know what it is and how to kill it. If it can do this to Shade, what can it do to Camille, or Ivana? I can't let them go in without knowing what they're facing." As I slammed out the door, I realized I was still in my muddy PJs but this was no time to worry about that.

I raced into the driving rain, down the steps, and through the mud puddles that had collected along the path up to our house. I wanted to shout, but over the wind and the rain, chances were nobody would hear me.

As I rounded the bend in the trail from behind a thin stand of trees that separated our lawn from Iris's, I saw that the house was lit up like it was on fire. It was glowing, yes, but more than that—the energy oozed off it, rolling like a wave of anger.

I caught sight of Camille and Ivana. They were standing near Wilbur and Morio and the others. I hurried over to them, slipping twice in the mud as I did so.

"Don't go in there!" When I was close enough, I shouted over the roar of the wind that was driving around us. Everybody turned—thank gods they heard me. "That thing eats energy . . . for good."

"What? Kitten, what's wrong?" Camille hurried to my side.

"Shade—that cloud? It drained his Stradolan abilities permanently. Mallen said it drained them dry. He's . . ." I stopped, tired and weary and too jarred to think coherently anymore. Bursting into tears, I wiped my eyes with a muddy sleeve of my pajamas. "Whatever is in there, it can do worse than kill."

Wilbur crossed over to us, a slight limp the only sign of his artificial leg. "I know what that damned thing is, but the weird shit is, it's something that can only be gated in by another spirit. It takes a powerful ghost, controlled by a necromancer, to bring these beasties into this plane."

I stared at him. "Another ghost? You mean a *ghost* summoned this? What the hell is it?"

"A devil-wraith. And you're right, it eats magic, it eats power . . . and the only way to get rid of it is to find a more powerful spirit than the one who brought it here in the first place. In other words, you need a bigger, badder ghost, girls, and a necromancer to wield it. And you're lucky, because between Ivana and me, we might just be able to set you up."

Chapter 11

A devil-wraith? We'd never heard of that before. Or at least, I hadn't. And by the looks on their faces, neither had the others, except for Ivana, who was nodding her head.

"The Mad Man is correct. Devil-wraith, it is. And he's a nasty one. So, Dead Girl . . ." Ivana turned to Menolly. "What needs done, it will be a difficult spell and I must work with this . . . human."

"What kind of bargain do you want?" Menolly glanced over at me. Even she looked exhausted.

"To summon a ghost and bind it to the Mad Man, in order to dispel the devil-wraith? I have one in my garden who can do it, but the Mad Man here must seal it to his will. For payment, I will keep the devil-wraith in my garden once we have collected it. That is my price. Such a lovely toy it will be. Such a trophy—so seldom found."

Well, that was better than her cajoling us for bright flesh.

"That's what you ask? To keep the devil-wraith?" Menolly pressed her. We had to be very clear with the likes of Ivana, because one misstep when it came to the Elder Fae, and we could have a big mess on our hands.

Ivana cocked her head. The bag lady look made her appear both pathetic and grotesquely childlike, but there was nothing either pathetic or childlike about her, when you stripped away the veneer. To us, right now, she looked like a gnarled old bird, her face riddled with bumps and lumps—warty in appearance, though we had no clue what they really were.

Dressed in tattered clothing, from a distance Ivana looked like she was ready to keel over dead at any moment. But all of that was pure illusion. We'd seen her unmasked once, and her beauty was brutal and jarring. She'd put the Fae queens to shame with her brilliance, as alien as a crystal figurine under the night sky.

Ivana cackled. "The devil-wraith is my price. No amount of bright flesh or oinker or moo-cow would ever be as tasty as a devil-wraith in my garden of ghosts. Their screams are delightful . . . a prod with my staff here, a poke of my finger there, and they shriek for hours, begging Ivana to stop. Oh yes, that will do for a bargain."

I swallowed hard. Ivana's garden of ghosts was a terrifying plot of land around her house where she entrapped stray spirits—she said they were all nasty but we could never be sure of that. She liked to torment and tease them. She was a spiritual sadist in the truest sense of the words.

Menolly nodded. "You have a bargain. What do we need to do?"

Ivana turned to Wilbur. "We journey to my garden of ghosts, Mad Man. What do you need for your spellwork?"

Wilbur frowned, and even he looked a little askance. "I should get my supplies. If somebody would like to help me, we can make quicker time."

Menolly and Morio took off with him, as the rest of us retreated to the studio out front. It was no good just standing in the rain. Ivana looked around the shed-cum-apartment with a curious glint in her eye, but she seemed to be comfortable in her silence.

Camille and I retreated to Roz's room, where he found

clean clothing we could both wear. We were cold and dirty, so we headed into the bathroom. There wasn't much time, so we just hopped in the shower together.

Camille turned around so I could scrub her back. She'd put her hair in a ponytail to keep it from getting any wetter than it already was.

"Shade really lost his Stradolan powers?" She glanced over her shoulder.

I nodded, not sure what to say. Everything had happened so quickly . . . it reminded me, to a lesser degree . . . of our night in Elqaneve, caught in the downfall of the city. So much had happened, unexpectedly, in such a short time.

"Do you think that Einar is responsible for the devil-wraith?" I handed her the sponge and turned, offering my back. She scrubbed hard enough to loosen the knots that had formed between my shoulder blades.

"I don't know, but I wouldn't put a link past probability. How? That's another matter. I have no clue how this happened. But I think there has to be some sort of connection. Or maybe . . . maybe it's whoever is trying to control the sword." She traded places with me so I could stand under the streaming water and rinse away the soap. "That's good enough for now, though I hate turning off the hot water. I could stand under the heat forever, it feels like, and still not get warm."

"I know what you mean and I hate baths and showers." I turned off the taps and we stepped out of the tub, drying off with the thick, fluffy towels that Roz had given us.

As we dressed, Camille yawned, and that set me to yawning. "I'm so tired, I could sleep for a hundred years. You know . . . " She paused, staring at the towel. "There's a piece of this puzzle that I feel I have in my hands but . . . I can't for the life of me figure out what it is. Something that happened . . . something somebody said that feels connected to this."

"Can you remember when or where you heard it?"

She squinted, trying to remember. After a moment, she shook her head. "I keep thinking it was at my birthday party, before Daniel got there but then again, I drank a lot so maybe . . . No . . . Everything is such a jumble. But I'll keep trying."

My stomach rumbled. "It feels like dinner was days ago and what we ate at Iris's seems to have vanished into thin air. I guess adrenaline burns through food, doesn't it?"

She gave me a smile, then—the first one I'd seen since bedtime. "Delilah, please trust me . . . Shade will be okay. He loves you and he is bound to the Autumn Lord. Who knows, maybe the Elemental Lord will do something for him to help?"

That was an idea I hadn't thought of. "Thank you for that. I needed some hope to hold on to. At least until we get through this night. I guess we'd better go see if Wilbur's returned."

Camille gave me a sly grin. "What do you think about Wilbur and Ivana pairing up?" By her innuendo, she didn't mean for magic.

I put a stop to that thought right there. "Don't even *go* there!" I shuddered. "I don't want to need a dose of brain bleach."

Laughing, Camille opened the door. "You make a good point. I don't think I could stomach a visual either."

We headed out to the main living room, where—sure enough—Wilbur was back with a large black bag at his feet. Camille stared at it, a curious look on her face. I wasn't the only one to notice her interest.

Wilbur cleared his throat. "I'm going to need some help when we get to Ivana's. This isn't exactly a one-man show I'm pulling here, and while Ivana can free the ghost, I have to do the work from there. Morio, Camille . . . and you, Pussycat. Come with us."

I cleared my throat. "Excuse me, but I don't work magic." I'd give a lot to be excluded from this little party.

"Too bad, but that's not why I want you there. You're a Death Maiden. You cope with the dead in ever so many delightful ways. You're going to be the best help I've got, other than the Prince of Bones, whose ring you're wearing on your finger. And he's out of the game, from what I understand."

That put a stop to my complaining. Shade couldn't go, but if he was able to, he would with no fuss. I wouldn't let him down. "All right."

"Let's be on our way. I haven't all night to waste on gallivanting around." She might be complaining, but Ivana sounded practically giddy. Apparently this was akin to a joyride for her.

She motioned for us to stand back, and then held out her hand. With a swirl of her fingers, she muttered something under her breath and a vortex appeared, a swirl of sparkles filtering out from her hand to form an iris-shaped portal. I blinked. I knew that the Elder Fae could come and go as they liked, but I had no idea how they actually managed it. Apparently, like this.

Ivana motioned to Camille and Morio. "Witch Girl, Fox, you first. And mind your step. There's a bit of a drop on the other side. Pussycat—you after, and then Mad Man. I'll bring up the rear. Never fear, the rest of you. We'll be back with a ghostie in tow who can tame the devil-wraith."

Menolly leaned close to me and whispered, "Her cheerfulness is more frightening than when she's begging for bright meat."

"At least we've never seen her pissed. And I sure don't want to be the one to ever cause her anger." I quieted down as Ivana glanced over at us, and then—as soon as Camille and Morio vanished through the portal, I stepped in behind them.

The swirl of prickling energy sucked me through like a giant vacuum and spit me out the other side. It was totally unlike the portals that transported us to Otherworld. This was more like a giant vacuum cleaner. Hitting the ground with a lurch, I realized that it was about four inches lower than I was expecting and almost twisted my ankle.

"Damn it." I sucked in a deep breath as I moved to the side. Camille was rubbing her left knee, leaning on Morio's shoulder. "You get caught by the drop?"

She nodded. "She wasn't kidding, was she? And that damned portal's like a giant Hoover. I bunged my knee a little, but I'll be all right." As she straightened up, Wilbur came through after me, then Ivana herself.

We were in her garden. Wherever Ivana's home was, it was a replica of a Cape Cod cottage, though larger than they usually were, with a white picket fence surrounding the grounds. On the other side of the fence there was a ravine, and beyond the ravine, a forest. Her garden of ghosts consisted of a colorful barrage of primroses and peonies, marigolds and dahlias. Even in the midst of January they were blooming. Scattered among the flowers were weathered tombstones. Last time we were here, Ivana's garden had been drained of ghosts— Gulakah had sucked them dry. But today, I could feel the buzz and hum of spirit activity.

"My garden, it thrives—can you feel it, girls? I've been busy, busy, busy like the bees, gathering spirits to replace those stolen from me. But idle hands make for idle thoughts, so busy is a good thing. Now then, I'd ask you in for tea, but somehow I don't think you'd fancy my brews." Again, she was positively chipper, the whorls on her face moving as she smiled with a jagged, needle-tooth grin.

Camille quickly declined. "That's quite all right. It's the middle of the night for us. We don't need tea." She edged toward the garden, staring at it warily. "You really have been busy. This place is packed."

"Oh, the ghosts sing to me and I must gather them, you know. That's part of my job, gathering beasties and teaching them manners. And it's also my pleasure. I nurture my garden—my flowers thrive on the pain of the spirits. They grow so big and strong." Ivana leaned down to sniff one of the dahlias—a rust-colored one with a head as big as a dinner plate.

I could smell them from where I stood, but beneath the floral scent, I detected another smell. As a werecat, I could pick up on pheromones, and the flowers—they definitely had grown large on the stench of fear.

Ivana gave me a sly look, tapping the side of her nose with her finger. "I spy, my pretty Pussycat, a look in your eye. You know I speak the truth."

Nodding slowly, I folded my arms across my chest. The more we dealt with Ivana, the more nervous she made me. It occurred to me that perhaps Camille could ask Aeval to fill us in on Ivana's background. We knew a little of it, but it did not pay to meddle with the Elder Fae, and asking too many questions could inadvertently seal you into unexpected bargains with them. And a deal was as good as a blood oath.

Wilbur, however, didn't have the benefit of our experience, and we'd never really thought to discuss the Elder Fae with him. But luckily for us, he wasn't stupid. When he spoke, I could tell he was measuring his words—Wilbur could never be called discreet; he was blunt and direct to the point of being obnoxious. But this time, he surprised me.

"Maiden of Karask, I believe, is the name you prefer?" His voice sounded rough over the words, but for once he wasn't being snide.

"Ivana will do for your use, Mad Man. What do you wish to ask?" She gave him a keen look, like a bird eyeing prey far below.

Wilbur flashed a look over at me, then cleared his throat. "What do we do next, then?"

Ivana began strolling between the rows of headstones in her garden. "Let me find the biggest and best. Oh, it will have to be a strapping spirit! Top of the line and nothing less. You will prepare a spell to control it, but mind you, Mad Man . . . you will not steal any of my other ghosties. I know you are a bone-mage, but lest any spare thoughts linger about wresting my spirits from me, put them to beddy-bye now."

Wilbur shrugged. "I prefer working with zombies and ghouls, to be honest. So don't worry yourself over it. I'll get ready. The ghost can't be under your control when I go after it, so you'll have to free it, and in that moment, before it flees, I have to capture control."

I was beginning to see what they were doing. Ivana could contain them—that was her control—but she couldn't command them once they were trapped. But Wilbur was a necromancer and he could cast a spell on the ghosts in order to control their behavior.

"We understand one another. This is good." Ivana stopped by one tombstone. She lightly ran her fingers over the marble, then turned back to us. "This one. He will do nicely. He is my favorite. Breaking the silence has been difficult with this one. He's strong and willful, though, and wily and I find it hard to force his screams. So prepare yourself, Mad Man, because I predict gaining control over him will not be the slice of teacake you think it will."

Wilbur set out his things in a flat area near the tombstone. Camille and Morio silently helped him arrange the altar. A skull, with the back of the skullcap carved away. In the skull, Wilbur set a red candle.

To the right of it, he set a bottle filled with a purple liquid that looked bubbly and phosphorescent. To the left, he placed a wand. Dark and thin, it was carved from a spindly branch, and blue gems encrusted it, scattered liberally around the surface. A silver wire, thin as dental floss, wound around it diagonally. Wilbur cleared out a place in the dirt and drew a strange symbol on it that reminded me of a Japanese kanji character like I'd seen Morio use.

After he drew the symbol, he sat back, shrugged off his coat, and wrapped a headband around his head. It was woven in blue and yellow, and had what looked like South American indigenous symbols on it. A sapphire the size of a fifty-cent piece sat in the center, right over his third eye.

The headband made me think of the Aztecs, or the Mayans—something along those lines. I knew that Wilbur had been in the Marines down in the jungles of South America, and that was where he'd learned necromancy. Whatever those symbols were, ten to one, they were from whatever shaman had taught him.

Next, Wilbur pulled out a necklace and draped it around his neck. The necklace was made from bone—looking like snake vertebrae interspersed with polished smoky quartz spikes. It began to glow a pale green the moment he put it on. He squatted back on his heels, pressed his hands together, and closed his eyes.

Camille and Morio immediately stiffened and took up

their stances behind him, Camille, her legs spread and her hands raised to the sky, with Morio standing behind her, his hands on her shoulders to brace her up.

Even I could feel the energy wind and coil as it began to grow. I said nothing, but suddenly found myself wearing my Death Maiden robes. Something big was going on here.

You know what you need to do if that thing gets loose. The whisper fluttered through my mind—it was Hi'ran's voice.

I need to perform an oblition if the spirit runs free.

Yes, and you must do so regardless of Ivana's protests.

So the Autumn Lord himself was peeking in on this one. Which meant that, whatever spirit this had been—whoever he had been when he was alive—he'd been a monster. Oblition, or the total destruction of the soul, was saved for the most violent and worst offenders, who had so tainted their soul-stuff that there was no ability to cleanse it. Or they had broken the rules of universal balance beyond easy repair. I wondered who he had been, but then pushed the thought out of my head. I needed to focus.

Ivana looked at us, and her joy turned to silent contemplation. She nodded at Wilbur, who nodded back. Standing back, she raised her silver staff and the sky clouded over, night suddenly rolling in over her house. As the darkening sky raced in, my blood quickened.

And then, Ivana began to grow. She stretched tall—at least ten feet tall rising into the star-studded sky. Brilliant and beautiful, she eclipsed the stars, her hair flowing into the inky depths of the night—silver as the moon with inky streaks racing through it. The wrinkles and warts vanished to reveal angular cheekbones jutting from her face. Gaunt she was, with glowing embers for eyes. She belonged to the night, to earth and fire, to the stars above. Ivana Krask became the Maiden of Karask before our eyes, and her laughter echoed through the dark currents surrounding us.

She raised her silver staff and brought it down, striking the tombstone. A screech of pain ripped out of the marble to ripple through the night, and the agony of that cry knifed through my gut, almost doubling me over. The pain—delicious and dark and terrifying—fed me, even as Ivana let out a whoop of joy and hunger. The flowers rose their heads and a thousand tongues slipped out from their centers to taste the suffering that permeated the garden.

A second time Ivana struck the stone, and a bluish light spiraled up from the marble, snuffling like a crazed animal. The spirit was free.

I stiffened, preparing myself to take it down should need be. But Wilbur thrust his wand into the air as the candle flames lit of their own accord. He no longer looked like the decrepit ZZ Top wannabe, but like the wild-eyed madman Ivana had nicknamed him. He raised both hands as the spirit stopped, turning with a hiss. I had no clue what he was saying, but Wilbur began to chant.

The spirit screeched, resisting, but Camille and Morio took up Wilbur's song, reinforcing his power. They worked in concert, the three of them, while Ivana watched, towering over all of us, a feral laughter ripping out of her throat.

The next moment, Wilbur held up a crystal spike and the spirit—with one final scream—spiraled down into the quartz. The crystal began to glow a pale blue, as Wilbur started to collapse to his knees. Behind him, Moro caught Camille as she stumbled back.

Ivana strode forward, still in her uncloaked visage, and steadied Wilbur. She leaned down, examining his face for a moment like a bird might study its prey, and then without a word, kissed him, her lips plastered firmly against his. He groaned, first starting to push away, then he melted into her embrace with a soft grunt.

I was trying to take in everything that was happening when she let go and stepped back, tapping the ground with her staff again. The night began to fade away, and within seconds, she was back to being Ivana the bag lady. Wilbur, clearly shaken, alternated between staring at the crystal in his hand, and over at Ivana, who seemed to have forgotten all about kissing him.

Unsure what to do next, I waited while Morio and Camille

sorted themselves out. After another moment, Ivana turned back to us.

"I shall miss my favorite beastie. So much fun to play with, and he fed my garden so well. Keep him safe for me, Mad Man. I will give you a vessel in which to trap the devil-wraith. When you have done so, you will call me, and I will come to fetch both my ghostie and the wraith. My garden will be so beautiful this season. You have no idea how much pain I can siphon off a devil-wraith." She laughed, and motioned for us to turn.

Within seconds, the portal had re-formed behind us. "Go now," she said. "The Mad Man knows how to cast his spell, he does. And he knows what will happen should he change his mind about returning my toys."

Wilbur, visibly shaking, turned back to her. "Don't ever worry about me double-crossing you. You'll get your toys back." But he looked a little lost, and he kept wiping his mouth—not as if trying to get any Elder Fae germs off it—but like he was trying to preserve a memory.

Without a word, I motioned for Morio to help Camille back through the portal. Wilbur went next. As I was about to follow, Ivana stopped me.

"I know what you were about, Pussycat. You would have destroyed my toy should the Mad Man have lost control."

I nodded slowly. "Yes, those were my orders."

She gave me a beady-eyed look. "Be cautious and watch the spirit, girl. If something goes awry, destroy him. He was a mass murderer in his life—and I do mean mass murderer. He commanded armies and killed wantonly. He loved the chaos and pain he created, and he craved the bloodshed. Don't you think it a fitting end for him, to find his way to my garden?"

Shuddering, I couldn't do anything but nod. "Yes, actually, I do think it fitting." Before I left, I asked one last question. "Ivana, you can tell me or not, as you like . . . but how long do you keep them for?"

She glanced back at the tombstones. "Oh, girl, a very long, long time. Long enough so that most of them forget who they were. Long enough so that I drain every last ounce of energy and will from them. Long enough so that all that remains when I am done with them is a faint voice haunting the wind with its cries." And then, she motioned for me to leave, and I did.

We found ourselves once again in the backyard behind the house. I was both exhausted yet on an adrenaline high. Wilbur looked like he wanted to skedaddle but all he did was to ask for a chair. Vanzir ran to get one for him.

"So now what?" Camille knelt in the grass beside him. She was shivering. The rain was still pouring down. It was getting so wet there would be flood warnings out before morning. The rivers around Western Washington flooded with alarming frequency, and people knew that if you built on a riverbank, you chanced flooding at some point in your life.

Wilbur gratefully dropped into the chair Vanzir had brought. "Thanks, Vanzir." He regarded us quietly. "I have no idea what the fuck to make of that whole little interlude, but I'll sort it out later. Right now, I have the spirit trapped in this crystal and it has to do what I command it. But I can only give it five commands before the spell wears off. If I were more powerful, I might be able to bind it for life, but after I died, it could really fuck me up good. It's better this way—give him back to Ivana after we're done with him."

I hadn't thought about it before but it made sense. A necromancer who died while still in control of spirits would then be in the spirit world with them, and they could wreak havoc on him because the majority of bindings were broken by the death of the spellcaster.

"How do you need to work this? What do you need us to do?" Camille sounded as weary as I felt.

Wilbur glanced at her, then at me. "I need to go in there, with some backup, please, and release the spirit, then order it to contain the devil-wraith in the vessel she gave me." He held up a miniature headstone. "Seems mighty small for such a massive spirit, but having seen Ivana's garden, I'm going to give that broad a pass on trusting it will work."

"Morio and I will go with you." Camille pushed herself to her feet, wincing.

I followed suit. "I need to go, too. Both Ivana and the Autumn Lord gave me strict orders that, if the spirit somehow manages to get free of Wilbur's control, I'm supposed to blot it out of existence. I know what he did while he was alive. I don't have any more sympathy for him when it comes to Ivana's games."

They both stared at me. Wilbur cocked his head to the right. "Is that so, Pussycat? Then I'll be extremely careful, because if he's that dangerous, I'll be the first target he goes for if he breaks through my control."

"You'd do well to be cautious." I held his gaze for a moment and, for the first time, didn't feel like Wilbur was trying to strip my clothes off in his mind.

Morio motioned for us to follow him. "Let's get this over while we're all still conscious enough to muddle through. It's four thirty and it feels like we've been at this for hours, even though it's only been what . . . ninety minutes?"

We headed toward the house. I really didn't want to go back in there, but then again—I had my doubts whether anybody did. Right now, tentacles and vines appeared to be thrashing out of the windows. We'd have a lot of glass to replace. After the snowstorm in our living room, I had a feeling that any furniture that had survived that deluge would now be ready for the thrift store. Or the dump. Time for a total redecoration.

"So Wilbur, what do you need us to do?" Morio grabbed Camille's hand. I could tell they were starting to build the energy between them even as we were walking.

"Can you create a protective circle around all of us and hold it until I can cast my spell? I don't need to find the central core of the critter. I just have to be in proximity to some part of it. That's one of the better things about the tribe that taught me my necromancy—they work down and dirty. No book learning, no sticking to rules. You do what works and you go in fast and quick." Wilbur narrowed his eyes and I was suddenly glad he was on our side. The man might be crude and lewd, but he was also ruthless and efficient, even if he did like watching *Jeopardy* with his brother Martin. *The ghoul.*

"We can do that. But let us get the circle up before we go in." We were out front now. It was easier to get in the front door than through the back porch.

While they raised the magic for the circle, I lowered myself into as deep a meditative state as I could get. I needed to be ready to shift into Death Maiden mode. Instinct suddenly took hold and I found myself in black panther form, growling low as the lights in the house took on a whole new dimension to me. I could see the aura of the devil-wraith. It raged out from the house, thrashing—hungry and searching for food. I growled again and realized that, while I was on the physical plane, it would be easier to carry out the oblition this way rather than trying to clear my head in my two-legged form.

Wilbur didn't ask any questions. He reached down and lightly patted my head. I didn't want him to touch me, but he wasn't the enemy and I was aware enough to know that, so I gave in, snuffling his hand and giving it one big lick. That would stick with me when I shifted back, but for now it seemed to be the thing to do.

A moment later, Camille spoke. "We're ready. Stay within the circle, both of you. Do you understand me, Delilah?"

I let out a low growl and bobbed my head up and down, moving to place myself firmly within the pentagram that now surrounded us. A mobile star within a circle, it was composed of flaming violet fire—the color of death magic—and as long as we were within the confines of it, we were relatively safe. The moment the pair were attacked or forced to attack, we'd lose the protection, but for now, we were guarded.

"Okay. Step by step, we head up the porch." Morio led the way, hand in hand with Camille. Wilbur and I followed them, pacing ourselves to stay within the flaming magical fire without bumping into my sister and her husband.

We reached the door without incident and I realized that—whatever the devil-wraith was—it couldn't voluntarily leave the house. Somehow, whatever ghost had conjured it had tied it to our place. Otherwise, the damned thing would be out here, attacking us. Enemies didn't generally wait for you to intrude on their domain if they knew where you were and that you were on the warpath.

With her free hand, Camille opened the door. Morio fell back a step, still holding her hand, so they could enter without disrupting the protection. Wilbur and I paid close attention, making certain we didn't lag behind.

We entered the foyer and the noise became deafening. Wails and screeches—screams . . . the devil-wraith was letting loose like there was no tomorrow. As we stepped through the arch leading into the living room, a deep laughter echoed through the walls, and the front door slammed shut and a tangle of vines grew up over the door.

We were locked in.

Chapter 12

"I suggest you get a move on, Wilbur." Morio was shivering. I could tell he wanted to transform into his youkai form—something he didn't have full control over. When anything threatened, it was his nature to change. And if he changed right now, he'd break the spell.

Wilbur fumbled in his pocket, and pulled out the crystal. For an FBH, he was keeping a pretty damned cool head, but then again, he'd been a Marine, and the Marines? They were trained to cope with funky shit in battle. In one hand, he held the crystal with the ghost in it; in the other, he held the miniature tombstone.

As if it knew what he was doing, the devil-wraith roared, thrashing around the boundaries of the pentacle, its vines trying to creep through the circle of protection. A large tentacle came slamming out of the parlor and thudded against the force field that the spell had created.

"I command you, by the Blade of Supay, by the Lord of the Underworld, by the Gates of Death through which you have passed and through which I have reached to control

you, come forth and subdue the devil-wraith, consign it to
this vessel, then return to the crystal and await my orders."
Wilbur's voice echoed through the room, sounding as if it
had been amplified through a loudspeaker. He rose up, his
eyes burning sun-gold, and thrust the crystal into the air.

A blur of fog rushed out of the end of the spike and dove
into the room, heading straight for the tentacle that was
aimed at breaking through our protective circle. Morio and
Camille held tight, and I quivered, ready to pounce if the
spirit broke free.

The devil-wraith roared, and the tentacle vanished, but
with a *dub-dub*, the house began to reverberate as if it had
a heart of its own that was beating. A sloshing sound startled me—it was coming our way from the kitchen.

"Hold fast," Wilbur said to us. "Don't step out of this circle or I can't guarantee you won't be hurt in the crossfire."

Crossfire? But then, I saw what he meant. The spirit had
formed into a vaporous body, and it was holding near the
archway. The sloshing sound grew louder and the reverbera-
tions rocked the walls. Another moment, and some *thing*
dragged its way into the living room behind us. It was huge,
looking like a cross between a tree stump, a blob of goo, and
a giant octopus. It filled the room, squeezing in near the ceiling, and I had the distinct feeling we were seeing only a por-
tion of it. How the hell was this thing going to fit into that
tombstone?

But as I was trying to puzzle out the difficulty of shoving
something so huge into a tiny piece of stone, the spirit Wilbur
had control over aimed himself and went shooting toward the
devil-wraith like an arrow. With a shriek, he pierced the
devil-wraith's skin and drove himself deep, penetrating like a
spear into a whale. The devil-wraith twisted, trying to throw
him off, but the spirit had managed some form of hold and
they were thrashing like wild dogs in a fight.

Wilbur held out the tombstone and closed his eyes. Morio
and Camille were bracing the circle, which felt like it was
beginning to waver. Another few minutes and we'd be in
deep trouble. I looked around for anything I could do in

panther form to help. But I couldn't leave the circle, and if I did and Camille saw, she'd be focused on helping me and that itself would disrupt the magic. I had to sit tight, which was the hardest thing I'd done in a long while.

The violet flame protecting us was beginning to wisp away as the spirit and the devil-wraith clashed. It was thinning, the magic wearing down. Camille and Morio were straining to keep what was left intact. After what we'd all been through tonight, I couldn't imagine how exhausted they were.

Without warning, the floor shifted drastically under our feet, rolling to the left. Camille and Morio went down and the circle vanished. Wilbur managed to prop himself against a chair. I roared—my sensors on overload. That had been an earthquake. I could tell—I knew what earthquakes felt like, and that wasn't magic or anything else but the Earth suddenly deciding to party.

The devil-wraith lurched forward toward us, but the spirit did something—it was hard to tell in the dim glow of the creature—and there was a sudden rush as the devil-wraith was sucked into the tombstone. It vanished within seconds into the marble slab, and the spirit howled in protest as Wilbur held up the crystal, but it returned to the spike and we were plunged into darkness.

As the light vanished, the floor shook again, this time a lot lighter, and then a thin beam flickered as Morio pulled out a flashlight and turned it on. I shifted back to my two-footed form, and we all sat there, silent, in the aftermath of the battle.

The lights worked just fine—they had been shut off by the devil-wraith, but when we flipped the switch, they came on. We were all sitting around the kitchen table. Ivana had come to procure her prizes, and she had taken Wilbur with her to release the spirit in her garden so she could once again capture it. Just what she was going to do with the devil-wraith, I didn't really want to know.

Shade was still asleep down at Iris's. We hadn't wanted

to move him. I didn't even want to think about the ramifications of what he was going to be facing till tomorrow. We were all worn out. The six hours of sleep I'd gotten before the devil-wraith decided to make an appearance had taken the edge off, but we all needed more.

Hanna put on the kettle for some herbal tea, and we plundered the refrigerator for sandwich fixings. The living room looked like it had been pulverized, as had several other areas of the house. The walls were all intact, but the windows were blown out, and we were going to need to repaint after this. Slime had dried on the walls, leaving ugly green trails behind it.

"If something else shows up, can we just tell it to go fuck itself? I'm done for the night." Camille groaned, resting her chin on her elbows on the table.

"I think we're done for a week. Where the hell did that come from? And how did it get through our wards?" Menolly and Nerissa were sitting together, and it looked like whatever fight they'd been having was done for the moment. They were holding hands and snuggling by the window.

"I don't think it actually came onto the land the way most of our enemies usually do." I frowned, pushing a cookie around on a plate in front of me. "I think that whatever ghost brought it summoned it from inside the house."

"But the wards—they would warn . . . wait . . ." Menolly turned to Camille. "Do the wards work against ghosts?"

Camille shook her head. "No, we haven't managed to come up with all-inclusive set of wards yet. And creating too many different kinds of wards in the same area? Not a good idea. It can make all of them go defunct."

"I'm running on what . . . six hours sleep? And I know the rest of you are, too. Why don't we keep watches during the night, just to—"

Camille's phone rang. She answered. "Yes? . . . What happened? . . . Well, where are you? . . . Right, we'll be there, just be careful until we get there." She hung up and I groaned.

"Don't tell me. Somebody needs us. *Right now. Right*

away. Without question." With a sigh, I gulped down the cookie and grabbed a few more.

She nodded. "It was Daniel. There's a ghost in his condo, and he's hiding out in the hallway."

Great. Another ghost. "We might as well all move into the Greenbelt Park District for all the spiritual spooks-capades going on. Okay, let's roll. Who's driving? And who are we leaving here to watch over the place?"

As everybody started to talk at once, I pulled on my shoes and, not for the first time, wished I could just go up, crawl into bed next to Shade, and sleep for a gazillion years.

Daniel had alerted the doorman this time. We were ush-ered right in, albeit with raised eyebrows at the size of our party. We had left Smoky at home, along with Trillian and Vanzir. Trillian was down at Iris's house, along with Shade, Nerissa, Hanna, and Maggie. Vanzir and Smoky were watching over our house. Menolly stayed home, too. With two and a half hours till sunrise—which this time of year was a little before 8:00 A.M.—she didn't want to take the chance of being caught. So that left Morio, Camille, Roz, and me to help out Daniel. Chase decided to come with us. He had wired himself up on coffee and was like a bee hyped up on steroids at this point.

Daniel was standing outside his condo, leaning against the wall. He brightened up when he saw us. "Thank you for coming. I know it's the middle of the night but you would not believe what's been going on."

"Dude, you wouldn't say that if you'd had the night we have had." I gave him a blurry, squint-eyed look and his gaze swept over us.

"Come to think of it, you all do look pretty toasted."

"We were nearly ghost food ourselves. Apparently, there's a special on hauntings tonight—maybe a two-for-one." I pointed to his door. "So fill us in on why you're standing in the middle of your complex hallway at five thirty in the morning?"

Daniel thumbed over his shoulder. "Ghost. In my apartment. One of the Vikings. I got nervous and decided I'd rather wait out here than go back in there." He was in his pajamas and robe, but I knew by the way his hand was in his pocket that he had a gun with him.

"That's not going to work against a ghost, Daniel. You might as well realize that right now." I nodded to his hand.

He slowly withdrew the gun, looked at it, and shrugged, tucking it away again. "I never go anywhere without bringing a friend along, Delilah. I learned that the hard way. So . . . do you . . . we go back in?" A catch in his voice made it clear that was the last thing he wanted to do.

"Yeah, let's get this show on the road. I'll take a Viking ghost over what we fought earlier any day." I motioned for Daniel to step away from the door and, once he was clear, opened it. Even though he'd said it was just the Vikings, we couldn't take any chances.

Inside, the apartment looked unscathed. Part of me grumbled, wishing that sometime we'd get the tidy ghosts. But sure enough, there in the corner of the living room, stood three of the warriors. They were standing at attention, looking as unkempt and grumpy as before. And this time, we didn't have the sword to make them behave.

I gave a nod to the others. "Looks like it's just the boys of summer . . . oh mighty joy."

"Hey guys, Thor called. He wants his posse back," Camille muttered, but she didn't say it quite loud enough for the ghosts to hear.

We edged our way in, but they didn't move. No, they just stood there, staring at us. Daniel hemmed and hawed his way in back of us. He was really out of his element, and it showed.

As we approached the ghosts, Chase suddenly stiffened, then collapsed next to me. I was close enough so that I was able to catch him before he fully keeled over, and I lowered him to the floor, kneeling beside him.

"Camille, call the—" I was about to bark her an order to call the FH-CSI, when Chase sat up again, so fast that I worried he might pull a muscle.

"Return the sword." The words echoed out of his mouth, as if being piped through an intercom filled with static. Only the voice wasn't his, but a low, raspy one.

I glanced up at Camille. "What the hell?"

"He's being used as a conduit. Look." She nodded toward the ghosts.

One of them was standing there, his eyes closed and his hand out, pointing toward Chase. Yep, that would be our Chatty Cathy, I wagered.

Morio looked at the ghost and asked, "Who are you? We don't know what's going on. Help us understand."

"If you do not return the sword, we cannot guard it, and the Blood Reign will begin again. He will rise and scour the land."

It sounded odd to hear words like that coming out of Chase's mouth, but *Odd* was our middle name by now. Then something hit me. I turned to the ghosts. "You guard *against* the Blood Reign beginning again?"

The ghost nodded very slowly. Chase spoke again. "We keep the Blood Reign in check. If Einar the Bloody is loosed now, his powers will be hard to stop. We are the Guardians. The sword must stay in possession of the family. They are the only ones immune to its call."

I turned to the others. "They're not here to guard Einar from *us*. They're here to keep him locked up. They're his *jailors*, not his elite squad."

Camille paled. "They must have thought you intended to free him, Daniel. His family seems to be under protection from the sword's call." She scrambled forward. The ghosts shifted position. "Can you lead us to the sword? It was stolen. Daniel was charmed into taking it by the real thief."

"We cannot find it. Someone hides it from our eyes. Find it, or we will not rest, and neither will any of you." The latter sounded like a warning.

I cleared my throat. "Did you send the devil-wraith to our house? We know a ghost had to summon it."

There was a moment's pause. The ghost channeling through Chase looked at his companions. They all looked rather comically confused, except this wasn't funny and was getting less amusing by the moment.

"We did not. But Einar has the ability. If he has been freed and has found a host, then you have a dangerous and powerful enemy on your hand. He will know you are seeking him—and he will do whatever he can to destroy all of you."

With that, they faded from sight, and Chase dropped back, hitting his head on the floor. He let out a garbled "Ouch" as I helped him sit up again, this time slower. Blinking, he shook his head, then stopped and winced.

"That was . . . what the hell *was* that?" He looked confused and a little bit pissed.

"That was you, learning what it's like to play medium. You were channeling one of the ghosts. Do you remember what went on?" With Morio on one side and me on the other, we carefully helped Chase up and over to the sofa. Daniel headed into the kitchen and returned with a glass of water and some ibuprofen.

Chase nodded. "Yeah, every word that was coming out of my mouth. I couldn't control my jaw muscles." He rubbed his jaw, looking nonplussed. "So . . . that was weird. But damn, it answers some questions, at least."

"Yeah, it does, but it also makes everything more problematic. We have to find that sword. Whoever stole it is out to unleash Einar the Bloody and set him loose. He was bad enough while he was alive; I dread to think what he's going to be like now that he's dead." I frowned, trying to puzzle out the missing pieces, like who had stolen the sword, and why they wanted to free the Viking chieftain.

"You said you'd fill me in on everything. I think right now would be a good idea. Start at the beginning. *Now.*" Chase was starting to look grumpy.

I glanced over at Daniel. We couldn't keep it from Chase—he was as affected as we were because he was living on our land, and had inadvertently been brought into the mess. I'd forgotten we hadn't told him, and on the ride over, he had listened to us in silence. Chase was good at blending into the background. It helped him a lot in terms of being a cop.

"Daniel, we have to tell him." I let out a sigh. "We tried to keep him out of it, but with that thing showing up in our house tonight—Chase lives out there with us. He and his baby girl live on our land. There's no way we can put him in danger by leaving him out of the loop."

"I've spent years covering my tracks." Daniel stared at his glass. "I'm the best at what I do. I can't believe how I fucked up."

"You didn't. You were caught in a trap—someone bewitched you." I thought quickly. Maybe Chase didn't have to know everything. "Okay, Chase . . . you know what an NTK basis means, right?"

He nodded. "All too well."

"Daniel belonged to the ISA. That we can tell you. But now . . . he's a private contractor. It's not safe to give you any info beyond what we're about to tell you. Will you promise not to look into it officially?" I wasn't really lying, but I didn't want to put Chase into a bad situation any more than I wanted to screw over Daniel.

But at the very mention of the ISA, Chase paled. "Got it. I know more than I want to about that agency as it is. Just tell me what you can. I don't want to be on their watch list any more than you do."

Breathing a sigh of relief—the ISA had a pretty rough reputation—I nodded. "Daniel . . . let me handle this?"

Daniel gave me a keen look, then nodded. "Go ahead. I trust you."

"Daniel was charmed and ended up stealing a sword because of the enchantment. The sword belongs to a tech guru in Seattle—it's a family heirloom. As the ghosts said, it needs to be reunited with the owner. That's what we're trying to do. We took it down to the Wayfarer to hide, but you saw what happened there. We had it in the safe room—and now it's gone. Lucias is lucky he wasn't killed. Long story short, we need to find the sword and return it to Leif Engberg, but Daniel's name—and his part in this—cannot leave this room."

I hated having to sidestep legalities, but if Chase knew that he had one of the top-tier art thieves in the world sitting in front of him, he'd be obligated to arrest Daniel. And right now that could lead to a host of bad things happening.

Chase nodded. "So we have a rogue sword—that you were keeping in the safe room at the Wayfarer. Mind telling me more about the sword, if you can?"

"That we can tell you. It belonged to a Viking chieftain during the late eight hundreds or so, in Norway. He was known as Einar den Blodige. Einar the Bloody. Long story short, his own people beheaded him, and he was cursed—he was trapped in the sword."

Camille took over. "Apparently, his family must protect the sword or his spirit runs the chance of escaping. We believe whoever wanted it decided to use Daniel's . . . position . . . to get hold of it. We know they were watching us when we took it—we found evidence of a magical bug. They stole it from the Wayfarer. Given what you found out about Kendell, we believe that the person who is behind this theft is Aslo Veir. I think it's safe to say that Aslo is working for someone who knows magic, given the use of Compelling Powder. And chances are that someone is a necromancer, because of the spell used to summon the devil-wraith. A necromancer must control the ghost who summons the wraith."

Chase glanced over at Daniel, then back to me. "That's a lot to take in but . . . okay, we already have the APB out on Aslo. We know this is a dangerous situation. Aslo is volatile and we know he's not above killing."

I let out a long breath, leaning forward. "We have a lot of questions to answer. First, who is controlling Aslo? Are they partners, or is Aslo just his tool? And why does the unknown necromancer want to free Einar? We can't walk into this situation unarmed."

"So Aslo is Fae, which means . . . silver will affect him? And bullets?"

I knew what Chase was thinking. "Right. He can be hurt by bullets of any kind, and by weapons. He's not a vampire, so we don't need to aim for just the heart. But here's the rub—we don't know what powers Einar has. And the necromancer behind this? We have no clue what his background is."

"Not to interrupt but . . ." Camille cleared her throat. "A thought occurred to me. How do we know they aren't lying? The ghosts, that is. Spirits do lie."

I stopped in mid-sentence. She was right. "Good catch. We don't know if they were lying or telling the truth, do we?"

"Seems to me like this whole mess is fucked up." Morio grumbled. "I have to say, I think you're making one big mistake."

"What do you mean?" Camille turned to him, looking confused.

"I realize why you want to keep Chase out of it as much as possible, but not telling him everything about Daniel? Makes it harder for all of us to watch our tongues. I think he deserves to know."

Daniel glared at Morio, stiffening. "I don't think that's a good idea."

"I just don't want to blurt out something by accident." Morio shook his head. "Too many people in the house know about you. We can't *all* walk on tiptoe. Chase has had to walk plenty of fine lines. This is just one more case. But it puts him on an even footing."

Chase let out a grunt. "What if I don't want to know?" But he was scuffing the floor with his foot, slowly dragging his shoe over the carpet. "I wish there was a way I could work for both sides—the OIA and the Seattle PD. That way I might have some sort of exemption. As it is, I've broken laws to the point of where I don't even know what color hat I wear anymore. I've learned the hard way that sometimes, you do what you have to. I learned that from you girls."

Daniel abruptly stood, pacing the room. "Detective, it's like this. I can tell you what the girls know, and you can try to arrest me. Or I can tell you what they know, and you can conveniently look the other way. They aren't lying with what they said, but there's a lot left unsaid."

Chase shook his head. "Don't tell me now. Later maybe. After we've all had some sleep and a chance to think things over. Meanwhile, what's the next step?"

Camille stood up, stretching and yawning. "We have an

appointment at eleven o'clock today that may shed some more light on the problem. We'll know more after that, one way or another. Until then? Delilah, we should sleep."

Chase groaned, glancing at his watch. "I have to be at work in an hour anyway. I might as well fuel up with coffee and just go in. Can you drop me by the building? I can catch a ride home with Nerissa."

"Sounds good. We'll drop you off. Daniel, do you feel safe staying alone?" I wearily dislodged myself from the sofa. "I have the feeling your ghosts weren't out to get you, not like the creep that showed up at our place."

He warily nodded. "I'm not thrilled about the prospect, to be honest, but I'll be fine. I'll call you later today."

"We'll let you know what we find out after we talk to Leif." And with that, we headed back to the cars.

We dropped Chase off at the FH-CSI headquarters and headed directly home. By 7:00 A.M., we were in bed. Smoky had covered the broken windows with sturdy tarps and had fires going in the fireplaces to warm up the place.

Shade was still down at Iris's, so I left him there. I wasn't up to a heart-to-heart right now and we all needed our sleep. But I lay there, nervous and awake, every noise making me jump. Ten minutes later, Camille peeked in my bedroom.

"Kitten? Come down to my room. The guys will sleep in the study. We can snuggle together." She grabbed my hand and pulled me out of bed. I was about to protest, but she wrapped her arm around my shoulders and propelled me toward the door. "I know you're worried about Shade. And frankly, I don't want to leave you up here alone."

In her room, we crawled under the heavy quilt, and hand in hand, like we had long ago when we were little, we fell asleep as the sun rose behind the thick cloud cover.

Three hours later, we were up again. But thanks to what sleep we'd gotten before the devil-wraith invaded, and the heavy sleep we'd just had, we were reasonably awake. A heavy jolt of caffeine would fix the rest of it.

Camille looked as pulled together as usual, but I just yanked on a tank top, jeans, my heavy denim jacket, and slapped on a little mascara and lip gloss. That was about as much as I cared about. By the time I got downstairs, Shade was sitting at the table, pensively staring into a coffee cup. Hanna waved us over to join him and brought over waffles and bacon.

I sat down, not sure how to start.

"We have to move, Delilah. We've got to be at Leif's by eleven." Camille cleared her throat, and sat down at the opposite end of the table to give us some space. She was gobbling through her waffle like a food shortage was coming, and she picked up a magazine, hiding behind it while we talked.

Shade saved me the trouble of asking. "I know what happened."

I paused, a forkful of food on the way to my mouth. "You do?"

"Yeah, you don't have to tell me." A worried crease appeared across his forehead as he frowned. "I'm going home today. I need to find out just how extensive the damage was. I'll try to be back before tonight. I wish you could come with me, but I really can't take you. Not for what I need to do and where I need to visit. But I'll be back."

"I love you." Suddenly afraid he'd think I would throw him over just because of what had happened, I hurried to reassure him. "No matter what happens, I'm here. I'll go with you if you want me to—you know that, right?" Just as suddenly, I stopped. The idea of me going with him to the Netherworld was ludicrous. His sister barely tolerated me, and I had no clue what kind of an environment he lived in while he was there.

"Delilah, stop." He took my hands and brought them to his lips, kissing them gently. "Everything . . . well, I'm not going to say everything will be all right, but it will be whatever it's meant to be. I know you're here for me, and I know you love me. I love you, too. And this . . . whatever this is, it's not going to change that."

"Thank you . . . thank you for knowing that I have your back." And at that moment, I realized that it was all real. I loved Shade; I knew we were meant to be together and I loved him with a passion that I had secretly been resisting. Whether it was my catlike nature to resist being held too closely, or just fear of what might happen, something had kept a thin layer of reserve there. But it all fell away as I stared into his eyes.

He stood. "I should be going. Thank the gods I can still travel through the Ionyc Seas. I'll be back as soon as I can. I just wanted to stay until you woke up so I could tell you where I was going." Drawing me to my feet, he slipped his arms around my waist and I pressed my lips against his, hungry for him, and hurting for him at the same time. This had to be one of the hardest things he'd ever been through.

Shade let go of me, then walked over to the center of the kitchen. Camille jumped up to give him a hug. "Be careful, dude. My sister needs you. So do all of us. You're *family*, you know."

I could have blessed her for that. Shade brightened just enough to tell me that her words hit home. He knew that I loved him, but right now, it probably helped to know that he was important to the others and not just me.

"Thanks . . . sis." He smiled, grimly, as she planted a kiss on his cheek. "Wish me luck." And with that, he vanished.

Camille and I finished our waffles and grabbed our coats. Smoky and the men were assessing the damage the devil-wraith had caused to the house, so we headed out on our own. Before we left, Camille called Daniel to see if he was okay and put him on speaker.

"Yeah, I'm fine. Nothing else happened out of the ordinary." He also mentioned he'd slept with his favorite gun by his side. "She's a beauty. A Stalley Phoenix. Got her when I was in the ISA, same as my Stalley AR20-14 rifle. They're top of the line, or were when I was in there. For all I know, they may have switched, but to be honest, I don't know why they would." He sounded like he was talking about a couple of girlfriends—there was a life and lift to his voice we didn't normally hear.

"Nice." I tried to force false enthusiasm into my voice. Trouble was, all the bullets in the world wouldn't do any good against a devil-wraith. But Daniel needed his crutch, just like we needed ours. Because sometimes false security was the only roadblock to feeling overwhelmed with fear.

"Ready?" Camille pulled out her keys. "I'll drive."

"Ready as I'll ever be. Let's go see if we can convince Leif to tell us what he knows. And if he doesn't, turn on the glamour. We need as much info as we can gather, and right now, I don't care how the hell we get it."

Chapter 13

Leif lived in an exclusive area, all right. The Vista View Towers were in Kirkland. Waterfront property, the complex was firmly in the *sky-high* price range. Daniel lived in luxury. Leif took it to a new level.

As we gazed up at the twenty-two-story building gleaming chrome and glass, I couldn't help feeling a brief moment of envy. I didn't care about his money—we had plenty thanks to Shade, Smoky, and what our business brought in. But suddenly, the ability to live in a place where ghosts didn't move in, rip up the joint, and camp out seemed delightful. Of course, that was an illusion. Leif had had a ghost living in his place. Whether or not he was aware of that fact, we were about to find out.

"You ready for this?" Camille asked. She was dressed in a chiffon skirt, black leather bustier, and a brilliant purple sash-belt. Her stilettos made me wince—they had five-inch heels and one-inch platforms. If we needed to use glamour on Leif, she definitely would have the edge. I had worn a pair of low-rider black jeans, a gold turtleneck, and

I'd dug out a bronze belt that matched nicely. While there's no way either one of us looked like we belonged here, at least we looked good enough to pass.

"Ready as I'll ever be." We headed toward the front doors.

There, the doorman ushered us through to the lobby with a once-over that made me feel both judged and yet leered at. But he didn't try to stop us. This wasn't quite the same security setup as Daniel's complex, which had seemed aimed at the gated-community crowd.

Vista View Towers resembled a five-star hotel. There was a front desk, a concierge, and the complex included a Starbucks, a deli market, and a bar in the lobby. We stopped by Starbucks and Camille grabbed a venti quad shot caramel latte, while I opted for a chai tea with extra cream. Fortified with caffeine, we headed up the elevator to the top floor.

Two penthouses took up the entire floor. Leif was in Unit 22-A. We paused outside the door. I gave Camille a look and she nodded, so I pushed the buzzer. The faint sound of the bell echoed through the door, and a moment later, it opened. A woman was standing there in a maid's uniform. Thank gods it wasn't the typical French maid's fantasy fodder outfit, or I would have laughed out loud.

"May I help you?"

"Leif is expecting us. Camille and Delilah D'Artigo." Camille smiled graciously at her.

The woman hesitantly smiled back. "Please, come in." She led us into a hallway that opened into a wide living room, but before we reached there, she ushered us into what seemed like a small parlor, off to the right. I had the feeling we were in the waiting room, so to speak.

"I'll notify Mr. Engberg you're here. Please, make yourself comfortable. Coasters are on the coffee table." And then she vanished, shutting the door behind her.

I glanced around. The room was exquisitely furnished— the best leather sofa, perfectly polished end tables, a hand-woven rug that looked like it belonged on the wall instead of the floor. The art on the walls was original, and it looked deceptively simple. Which no doubt meant that it was horribly expensive. But something felt off.

"You know"—I looked around—"there's nothing in here to give the place personality. It feels like a showroom in some upscale furniture store."

Camille gingerly leaned back on the sofa. "Yeah, you're right. I wouldn't know that anybody lived here. The art fits the room, the décor is spot-on . . . but it feels sterile. Even the plants look too cultivated and perfect."

The door opened at that moment. A man, about five-ten, with short curly blond hair and a lean, toned physique stepped into the room. He was wearing jeans that looked so stiff and new, I couldn't help wondering how uncomfortable they were, and a white polo shirt. It had some sort of emblem on the pocket, but I couldn't tell what from where I was sitting, and frankly, I wasn't that interested in finding out. A bandage covered the left side of his forehead, and he had a black eye that looked extraordinarily painful.

"Hello, ladies, I'm Leif Engberg." Leif held out his hand and I shook it, then Camille. He motioned for us to follow him. "Come on in the living room. Would you like something? A drink? Can I get you a glass of wine or anything stronger?"

Blinking, I wondered just how many people drank in the morning. Apparently, our cousin Daniel and Leif were two of them.

Camille shook her head. "Thank you, no."

The living room was three times the size of the parlor, and had a white carpet, black leather furniture, and a wall color that made beige seem interesting. Again, the art all matched the décor, and everything looked perfectly coordinated, but again, seemed sterile. The only thing that seemed out of place were the sterling silver sword hangers on the wall above the gas fireplace. The hangers were empty, and it was my guess that was where Leif's family sword normally rested.

Leif escorted us to the sofa, gesturing for us to sit down, the settled himself in a chair opposite. "What can I do for you, ladies? Have we met somewhere? Did I forget some fundraiser I was supposed to attend?" His gaze was plastered on Camille. Yep, she was our ticket if he didn't want to talk.

I glanced at her, and she gave me a nod. We'd agreed—we'd be straightforward about this, as much as much as we could be.

"Mr. Engberg—" Camille leaned forward, just enough so her breasts swelled over her corset.

"Just Leif, please."

"All right. Leif, we're here to ask you about the theft of your family's heirloom sword. We have some difficult questions, they may seem odd, but it's very important you work with us."

The look on his face was priceless. First, he blinked, unable to tear his gaze away from her boobs, but then a wariness entered his eyes. He knew something was up.

"Family sword? I'm sure—"

I spoke up. "Don't. Just don't. We know your sword was stolen—word gets around through the grapevine. I'm sure you did some checking on us after Camille made the appointment to see you last night. You probably know who we are."

Leif studied my face for a moment and the congenial society smile faded. "Right, so I did. I know you're from Otherworld, I know you're affiliated with the FH-CSI, and that you own businesses in Seattle. I also know there's a lot of talk about the three of you. I gather your sister Menolly couldn't make it because of her . . . nature."

I wondered if he knew about the connection between us and Daniel—that wasn't exactly public knowledge at this point, but if one looked hard enough, they could find out. "You're smart. You catch on fast. Yes, she's in her lair. Vampires can't walk during the daylight hours. Okay, to be blunt here: Leif, your family's sword fell briefly into our hands the other night. We put it in a safe place, but someone stole it from us. We have reason to believe whoever stole the sword *from us* is a dangerous man, with dangerous plans."

Leif paled. "You don't have the sword anymore, then?"

"No. We need to know exactly what you know about your family's sword. We also need to know if you know who took it from you." I wasn't sure how much to ask at first, or how much to throw at him. "Please, Leif, tell us everything you know. We'll tell you why, if you're not already aware of the sword's nature."

He stood, and walked over to the floor-to-ceiling window that overlooked Lake Washington. We were right on the edge of the lake, and I imagined just how beautiful it could be here, especially with the mist rising, or during sunset when the sun vanished slowly below the horizon.

After a moment, Leif turned around. "All my life, my father told me that the sword would one day be mine. He told me, 'Leif, you can sell everything we own, you can sell your soul if you want to. But once you inherit the family legacy, you can *never, ever* sell that sword. It will remain with you till the day you die, and you *will* have a son to pass it down to. I don't care if you have to marry a woman and pay her a fortune in alimony, you *will* have a son. Do you understand?' And I'd nod, and wonder what the hell was so important about the damned thing."

"Did you ever find out?" Camille crossed her legs and leaned back against the leather cushion.

The sofa was smooth and supple, and almost felt indecent when I ran my hand over it.

Leif nodded. "I always knew it was haunted. And then, one morning, about a month before he died, my father came into my room. He told me he'd had a dream—a nightmare about dying. He wanted to make certain I understood that once he was gone, I had control over everything—except the sword. That it was my duty to protect and keep it safe. That I had a responsibility to father a son who would inherit it. I asked him if he believed in the family curse and he said that yes, he had seen the guardians of the sword on occasion, and he knew that if we ever lost it, not only would our family suffer, but a lot of other people, too."

Leif turned back to the window and leaned against it, staring out at the water. "I'm sure you know about its history. You wouldn't be here otherwise. Right?"

"We know about Einar den Blodige. Einar the Bloody.

The sword truly *is* possessed, Leif. Your ancestor is in there, looking for a host body, we think."

He whirled around. "I *always* knew there was something horrible about that sword. I've never been comfortable around it. As a child, I avoided it. When I was a teenager, a friend asked if he could hold it and I wouldn't let him near the damned thing."

"Leif, we're going to ask you a couple of questions that may sound a little nuts, but trust me, they're necessary. Have you ever seen . . . a ghost?"

But he didn't look shocked. In fact, he looked almost relieved. "Yeah. I saw my father once, after he died. But you're talking about the sword, right? Have I ever seen a ghost connected to the sword?"

"Right. Or anything unusual around the sword?" Camille sat up straight. Leif was looking serious now, and the blasé social expression had vanished.

"More than one night I'd wake up and come into the living room—this started when I was young—and I'd see a greenish glow around the sword. I always felt as though it was watching me. Something . . . inside of it. I've hated that sword ever since I was a kid, and I resent having to babysit it now. When I woke up and found it stolen, I was actually relieved, but then my father showed up in a dream, warning me to find the damned thing and get it back."

"So you hired a private detective?"

He let out a long sigh. "Not yet. I have no clue how it was stolen or who hit me—I don't remember anything from that night. I know I had an appointment with someone for . . . something . . . but I can't remember what or who. I looked in my datebook and the evening shows as clear. I guess, there's part of me that just hoped the sword would be gone for good, so I've kept my mouth shut." He dropped back into his chair and leaned forward, elbows on his knees. "I really, really hate dealing with this. Honestly? I'd rather just throw everything over, move to Italy—which I love—and stay there for the rest of my life."

The expression on his face touched me. He looked tired

and harried, like someone who had experienced too much in too little time. There had to be more to his story than this, but I had the feeling it was connected to family drama and responsibility and expectations that he had never been able to meet.

"Has anybody ever tried to take the sword before?" Camille's voice was softer. I thought she could feel his exhaustion, too.

Leif shrugged. "Jay Miles."

Camille stiffened, her eyes widening. "Jay Miles?"

I frowned. "Who?"

"Yes. Why, do you know him?"

She paled. "I know *a* Jay Miles—I'm not sure if it's the same one. Tell us about him."

I wanted to ask her who she was talking about but decided to wait—Leif seemed amenable to talking and so we might as well encourage him while he was up for it.

"Did you read that article that was written about my collection? The article that talked about the sword?" Leif walked over to one of the bookshelves and brought back a print copy of the magazine I'd found online. He flipped through the pages until he found the article and tossed it to me.

"Yeah, I found this online." No use in denying we'd done our homework.

"Yes, well, Davis Jones, the guy who wrote the article? He called me shortly after the magazine hit the stands to tell me that someone named Jay Miles wanted to buy my sword. I met with Miles, just out of curiosity, but of course I refused."

"Someone wanted to buy the sword . . ." I was starting to put two and two together.

"Right. I found that odd, but he said he collected Viking artifacts. When I told him no, he pressed. Hard."

"He was too eager, wasn't he?" Camille was taking notes.

"Right. Something felt off—and of course, I could never sell the sword. I did wonder . . . So yesterday, I put in a call to Jay—I still had his number. He sounded surprised to hear it was stolen and insists he knows nothing about the theft, but I have a feeling he might be lying."

"What does Jay look like?" Camille asked. "Do you think you can describe him?"

"I can do better than that. I have security tapes constantly running and I save the ones that . . . stand out. I decided to file this one away. Something about him made me cautious." Leif stood and motioned for us to follow him. He took us into his office, which was just as perfect as the rest of his house, except here, there were signs of life. Books, half open, a chess set that looked like a game was in progress, half-a-dozen magazines scattered on the sofa that looked like they were well thumbed. There was a TV/DVR combo—a big screen—and it was tuned to a basketball game, but the sound was down.

Leif's desk was casually messy—papers scattered, but nothing piled up to the point of being ready to tip. He had a quad-monitor system set up and his computer was one I'd never seen before. But whatever it was, it looked sleek and sharp and top-notch.

Leif sat down and quickly typed in his password, guarding his keystrokes from our eyes. The next moment, he brought up another screen, which appeared to be a security surveillance system, and then tapped in a date. The next minute, we were watching digital copies of the surveillance cam. And there, on the screen, Leif was talking to someone.

Camille leaned forward. "That's him. That's the man who came in my shop the other day and asked me if I had that grimoire."

"What grimoire?" I frowned.

"Remember I told you something kept bugging me? That I was trying to remember something I said at my birthday party?"

"Right, what was it?" I still couldn't remember much beyond the drinks and the Viking.

"That a necromancer named Jay had been in my shop, asking about a grimoire of Northern European spells that's reminiscent of the Book of the Dead—it can supposedly teach you spells to free the dead and control them. This is the same man. It has to be Jay Miles. He fully intended, even then, to free Einar. Which meant he's the one who put . . . " She stopped abruptly and I realized she didn't want to bring Daniel's name into the picture since Leif apparently couldn't remember him.

"He's the one who stole my sword then?"

"Not from you, Leif, but from us. No, he charmed somebody into doing the dirty work for him—an innocent victim. And then . . . well, never mind the rest. But hey, do you have tapes for the night the sword was stolen?" I wondered why he hadn't just pulled them up and got a view of Daniel himself, but even as he answered, I knew the reason.

"System was disabled remotely. I have no clue how or who did it. I pay for the best and somebody still managed to bypass it." He glanced at us. "Any ideas?"

"Not a clue." I didn't like lying but Daniel was off the hook for now, and I kind of wanted to keep it that way. At least we'd discovered more than I thought we would during this visit. "Is there anything else you can tell us? Do you know anything else about Miles? Maybe where he lives?"

Again, Leif's fingers flew across the board and he brought up another file. "Here we go. Jay Miles. I did some research into him, yes, when Davis said he wanted to buy the sword. One thing my father taught me is to check out references. To the outside world, Jay appears to be on the up-and-up. He leaned back. "What's a necromancer, by the way? Isn't that someone who works with the dead? And the book—can it really free Einar?"

"A necromancer is a sorcerer of sorts . . . someone who works with spirits and death magic." She glanced at me. "Seriously, that grimoire is aimed at raising armies of warriors from the dead, and other such stuff. From what I know of it, it's really a treatise on how to form your own spirit army of ghosts."

I blinked. "And any army needs a king to rally them. An army of ghostly warriors . . ."

"Led by a spirit king gone crazy? That would be bad, really bad."

Leif pieced our conversation together at that point. "You don't mean that Jay Miles tried to buy my sword to release Einar's spirit in order to lead . . ."

"In order to lead an army of ghosts. Yeah. And when you wouldn't sell it to him, he put in motion a plan to steal it, and he succeeded."

"But how did you come by the sword? That's the one part I don't understand yet." Leif pushed his chair back, staring at the images on the screen.

Annnnnd . . . we were back to Daniel again. "A friend. Leif, you're better off not knowing. It's much safer for everybody involved. Can you accept that for an answer?"

He held my gaze for a long while, then looked back at the pictures. "If you can bring me back my sword, I'll be very grateful. And I won't ask questions. But why are you getting involved? What's in it for you?"

Camille looked at me, waiting for me to speak. I ran through a multitude of possible answers, but each one left a lot to be desired. After a moment, I decided to just go with what made the most sense.

"Nothing, except this: Because the sword was in our possession, we're now being targeted by whoever stole it from our keeping. You've seen glowing edges around the sword. We had a full-on invasion last night in our house from the spirit world. We want to prevent your great-great-great-grandpappy, or whatever he is, from getting free from that sword. Because if his spirit escapes, Seattle's going to be his playground and the results aren't going to be pretty."

Leif tapped a pencil on his desk, then tossed it to the side. "What can I do to help?"

"Stay out of it. Let us know if you come across any information on how to find Jay Miles, but for the sake of the gods, don't go hunting him yourself. He's dangerous. Give us the contact information for Davis Jones, and Jay's phone number. We can track him that way." I stood up, not sure what to think. Leif seemed to accept what we were saying. *But,* my mind argued back, *he grew up with tales surrounding the sword, and knowing there was something*

*weird about it. Was it so strange he had come to accept
that there was a problem with it?*

"Tell you what. You head out and do whatever you need
to do. I've got your number, leave me your e-mail, and I'll
see what I can get on Jay Miles. I have access to some of the
best software in the world, and I learned mad computer skills
at my father's knee. I'll shoot you over whatever I find."

"Deal." Camille gave him a broad smile.

"By the way," Leif added as he showed us to the door.
"Just so you know . . . your Fae glamour? For some reason
it doesn't work on me. Didn't on my father either. We've
known about the Supes and Fae for years—long before
they came out of the closet. For some reason, my family's
always had contact with the Earthside Fae. Their glamour?
Never affected us. Neither does OW glamour." He grinned
at Camille. "Not that I wouldn't do you in a minute if you
wanted, but if you were aiming to get answers out of me
that way, your plan wouldn't have worked."

We both blushed. Not too many FBHs were this aware.
Camille stammered out a good-bye while I nodded and we
headed back to the elevator.

"What did you make of that?" Camille waited till we
got in the elevator then turned to me. "And that last statement? My guess is that Leif's aware of a lot more than
we're giving him credit for."

"My guess is that Leif's probably scared shitless of that
sword. I think his encounters with it probably were more than
he was willing to let on. Either that, or he has a highly refined
intuition about what's in that thing." I glanced at the clock on
my phone. "It's noon. You want to drop by Marion's for lunch?"

Camille nodded. The Supe-Urban Café was run by a
friend of ours. She was one of the Koyanni—coyote shifters.
The café had been burned to the ground sometime back, but
she had rebuilt. The arsonist had torched her house, too, and
it brought her and her husband back together again. They'd
been on the brink of separation but tragedy can either push
people farther apart or pull them together, and this had pulled
them back together in a big way.

As we settled in the car, I retrieved my tablet from my backpack. It was a great supplement to my laptop, and I found it much lighter to carry around with me. I began pulling up everything I could on Jay Miles. While I was at it, I put in a call to Chase.

He came on the line after three rings. "Yeah? Johnson here."

"Chase, it's Delilah. Listen, we need you to run records on somebody and see what you can find out about him. It has to do with the sword."

"Not a problem, but then I need you girls to do something, if you're able." I heard him shuffling papers. "Okay, give me the name?"

"Jay Miles. Supposed art collector. May have ties to one Davis Jones, a writer. We think Jay hired Aslo and Kendell to steal the sword from us."

"Do you have a contact number?"

I gave him the phone number Leif had given us for Jay. "We haven't made contact with him yet. We thought we'd wait until you could find out whatever you can on him. If Aslo is working for him, then we don't want to tip him off prematurely. Jay, by the way, is our necromancer we're looking for. He's been in Camille's shop looking for a book on Northern European death magic rites, so be careful if you run into him anywhere."

"Oh, wonderful—yet another big woohoo." Chase let out a sigh, then said, "Okay, I'll run his name. Meanwhile, would you guys drop by Cromby's and pick up a WhosIt-Toggle-Toy for Astrid?"

I blinked. Of all the things Chase had asked us to do, this had to be the oddest. "Stop where for a what?"

"A WhosIt-Toggle-Toy. Iris insists it's a great toy for human babies to encourage their latent psychic powers to grow at a steady pace. Cromby's is a magical toy shop, apparently." He laughed, and I could sense him relaxing a little. Fatherhood agreed with Chase. Even though he missed Sharah desperately, it was easy to see that little Astrid meant the world to him. "Really. Just pick it up for me and I'll reimburse you tonight."

"Will do. Give us a call when you get anything on Miles. We're going to drop by Marion's for lunch." As I hung up, I pulled up the MapsApp and typed in Cromby's. It was on the way to the Supe-Urban Café. "Hey, we need to stop at a toy shop for Chase. He wants a WhosIt-Toggle-Toy for Astrid."

Camille laughed. "Okay then."

She followed the directions I gave her, and we stopped at the toy shop. I ran in to find a woman behind the counter who I could have sworn was part dwarf, but it wasn't good form to ask. Dwarves had mostly migrated to Otherworld, though a few stayed Earthside during the Great Divide. But they were private over here, and tended to do their best to pass even though most of the Supes and Fae were out of the closet.

Rather than poke through the shelves, I approached the counter and asked for her help. She led me to the toy and—as I stared at it—I saw next to it an oddly shaped gadget.

"What's that?" It looked like a box with multicolored light panels on it.

"It's a cerebral stimulator, designed to stimulate learning patterns in Cryptos." She smiled and held it out to me.

I took it, but as I tipped it round and round, and the colors flashed in a seemingly random pattern, I couldn't figure out what the hell to do with it. I handed it back. "Have no clue."

"That's because it's meant for brain chemistry that's different than yours. It's all the rage now in some quarters. Was first developed in Dahnsburg and a version of it migrated here."

A sudden thought hit me. "Would it work for a baby gargoyle?"

The woman laughed. "Oh, yes, in fact, my guess is this would become a favorite among gargoyles. You know they are very stimulated by light patterns."

I hadn't known, but decided to buy it and see how Maggie liked it. As I paid for both toys, wincing over the hundred dollars that vanished out of my checkbook, I suddenly thought about the day when I'd be coming here, buying toys for my own baby. What kind of toys did little Elemental princesses or princes play with? And just how would Shade's dragon DNA play into our child? Or his Stradolan side?

That, of course, sent me back to wondering how he was doing and if he was home yet. But then again, it had only been a couple hours since he'd left. I couldn't expect that he'd found answers in so short a time.

My thoughts whirling, I carried the bags back to the car and slid in next to Camille and belted my seat belt again.

The Supe-Urban Café was always busy, but Marion reserved a table in back for us, in case the rest of the diner was full. And today was one of those days. She saw us as we scooted through the doors. The chill left behind, we were enclosed in a room filled with amazing scents. Hot homemade bread, thick soups full of flavor, sizzling hot fried fish, and—among the rest of the goodies—Marion's famous Big Cinnamon Buns. Her cinnamon rolls had become citywide famous, and stores were starting to stock them.

Marion escorted us back to her private table, and we had menus in our hands and hot tea with lemon on the table before we could say a word.

"It's cold out there," she said. "You need to eat hearty today, girls. Especially with that storm front on the way. You aren't going to want to get caught out in it, so after this, get your butts home and batten the hatches."

Marion was gaunt and tan. She was lean in a spare, hard way. Most Koyanni were like that. She was a fierce friend, though, and would do anything to help that she could for someone on her to-protect list.

"Storm? What kind? Not snow." I was done with snowstorms. I wanted spring and warm weather for a change.

"No, giant windstorm coming in sometime during the night. Dangerous one, the weatherman says. Supposed to be bringing gusts up to seventy miles an hour, and heavy rain." She let out a long sigh and dropped into the chair next to me. "I'm so tired. We've been run ragged since we reopened. We're getting more popular every day and I have to hire more people. Either that or franchise out."

"That's a good thing, though, right?" Camille smiled at her.

"Yes, that's a good thing. Okay, what will you have? I'd better get my ass out of this chair or I'll never want to get up."

Camille ordered chicken noodle soup and a cheese sandwich and one of Marion's cinnamon rolls. I ordered chili and a ham sandwich, and a couple of her chocolate chip cookies. As she took off with our order, I cleared my throat.

"Why haven't you suggested calling Daniel to see if the name Jay Miles rings a bell? Ten to one he's the link between Leif and Daniel."

"Oh, I figured that one out, but if we supply Daniel with Jay's name, our cousin may just decide to head over there and put a bullet through the man. And Daniel going up against a necromancer? Not such a good idea. No, we'll wait for a bit until we can make sure Daniel doesn't do something stupid."

I nodded. That made sense. With a sigh, I turned on my phone, pulled up the WeatherApp, and glanced at it. "Hell, Marion's right. The storm is going to be nasty. Thunder and lightning, the works." I glanced back at the windows. Outside, the rain was pounding down again. "The leading edge has apparently been coming in for a few days and we never really noticed."

"I thought it was typical January weather. Why are you so upset? It sounds bad, yes, but we've been through worse." Camille sipped her tea, cupping her hands around the hot mug with a sigh of satisfaction.

I frowned. Why was I so unsettled? I searched my thoughts, my gut . . . but the answer, whatever it was, lay out of reach. I shook my head. "I don't know. All I can tell you is the storm is going to be worse than they predict."

But the truth was, I had the feeling that somehow the storm was going to help Jay Miles and whatever plans he had for the sword.

Chapter 14

Iris and Hanna had heard about the storm and they were preparing for it by the time we arrived home. We were in an *all hands on deck* situation. Shade still wasn't home, so I went down to Iris's with Camille to help the guys shutter the glass panels of the greenhouse.

Our land was fifteen acres of lovely wooded land, including Birchwater Pond. But the tall timber of the Pacific Northwest had shallow root systems, which made for falling trees during windstorms. The heavy rains would saturate the ground and loosen the roots. There were plenty of trees close enough to both our houses that they could easily smash the greenhouse flat. We couldn't protect against our roofs—that really wasn't an option without clearing out a lot of healthy shade—but we could do our best to protect against ancillary damage.

I still felt uneasy about the storm, though I hadn't mentioned my concerns to anybody else. The rain had let up a little, but it felt like the quiet interlude before something big. As we helped fasten plywood against the walls of the greenhouse, I kept my ear cocked, wondering what I was even trying to hear. By 3:00 P.M., we had weatherized both Iris's house and our home as much as possible.

Camille stood back to look over the front porch. We'd taken down the string of white twinkle lights we always kept around the porch. Smoky and Trillian had unhooked the porch swing from the chains and set it in a sheltered area so it wouldn't smash back against the house.

We'd also remembered to stow the trash bins. We were responsible for dumping our own garbage and recycling, but that didn't mean we wanted it scattered across the lawn if the wind came in and knocked over the bins. Camille had also covered her magical herb garden with another layer of mulch and a plastic tarp with a few holes punched in it for air, weighting it down with bricks along the edges.

"I guess we've done everything we can. Anything else you can see that might become flying debris?" She glanced around the yard. "Make sure all the tools are put away. We should also make certain we have enough water in case the power goes out and the pump stops."

"I'm on it. Vanzir, help me? We need a lot of water for this crew." Morio took off, followed by Vanzir.

"The cars are parked away from the trees, so that's done. Medical supplies are out where we can find them? What about food?" Camille consulted a checklist. I had to hand it to her; she was organized.

"Hanna's taking care of that. Somebody should go check with Iris and Bruce. He stayed home today from the university. He didn't have any classes this afternoon anyway. Make certain they have everything prepped." I glanced over to Trillian. "You want to take care of that?"

"Sure thing." Trillian headed around back.

Smoky cleared his throat. "I'll bring in wood for the fireplaces."

Camille and I glanced at each other. She shrugged. "I guess now we just wait and see if the storm materializes. Let's go make sure enough candles are in place."

As we headed inside, I decided to broach my fears. "Do

you think . . . Ever since Marion told us about this storm, I've had a bad premonition that there will be some sort of really nasty connection to the sword. I don't know how or what, but I'm worried, Camille."

She frowned as we headed for the door. "Do you have any idea of where the connection is?"

Shaking my head, I closed the door behind me. "No, that's the problem. It's so nebulous. I wish I could say, 'I think Jay Miles is going to use it to help Einar escape,' or something like that. But it's just this sense that the storm will be working against us somehow. Not like the sentient storm in Otherworld, but just—it's bad timing, you know?"

As we headed into the kitchen, Hanna looked harried. Her hair was back in a single braid, and she was stirring three different pots of food on the stove. The kitchen was a cacophony of scents, so muddled that I couldn't make out any one thing in particular. The oven was on, too, and three baskets of rolls sat on the sideboard, still warm.

"Need help?" Camille moved in and checked the rolls. "Want me to bag these and put them away?"

Hanna nodded, wiping her forehead. "Please. I watched the weather report after you called about the storm. We're smack in the path, so I've been cooking up anything that might go bad if the power goes out. I've got a pot of chili, a pot of spaghetti sauce, and a pot of stew simmering. If need be, Iris and Smoky can chill down what food is in the refrigerator, but they cannot provide the electricity to cook with and I'd rather limit how much I have to grill. There are lemon bars and chocolate chip bars in the oven. They should be ready to take out in five minutes."

She went back to tending the food while I held the bags and Camille filled them with rolls. Given the rate at which we ate, we bought ingredients in bulk and Hanna and Iris shared the baking duties once a week, making enough bread for everybody.

After we finished up, and went to check on the candle and battery supply, Camille motioned for me to sit down with her in the parlor.

"Let's take a break and I'll go into trance and see what I can find out."

She leaned back, closing her eyes. Her breasts slowly rose and fell with her breath, and the energy around her felt sparkly, like she was vibrating on a different level. I wondered if that's what happened to me when I moved into my Death Maiden aspect.

Five minutes later, she slowly exhaled a long breath and opened her eyes. "The storm isn't sentient, that we know, but it's dark and it's big and it's rolling in. I think, given what I'm sensing, that any necromancer or sorcerer who has access to a supercharged weapon could probably channel the power of the storm. If we were only a few days closer to the new moon, this would be the ideal time to recharge the horn—the extra oomph would probably increase the amount of time I could use it before it drained."

"So you think I might be on to something?"

She thought for a moment. "You know who might be able to help us? He has a great deal of experience with ancient weapons."

I frowned. I had a feeling I knew who she was referring to and I wasn't entirely sure I wanted to go there. "You aren't talking about . . ."

"Yeah, the Merlin. It's a half-hour drive out to Talamh Lonrach Oll. We can get there, talk to him, and get back long before the storm hits. It's not due in until the middle of the night, is it?"

I shook my head. "Are you sure you want to bring him into this? And what about Aeval? You really want to talk to her right now, after what I saw?"

I was scrambling for excuses because I didn't like dealing with the Fae courts. I didn't feel comfortable around them, and I didn't trust them. I knew I had to get over it at some point. Camille was inexorably mixed up with them and that was just the way it was, but right now? Not so thrilled about the idea.

"Until she decides to tell me about her and Vanzir—if she ever does—it's none of my business. I'm not going to bring the fact that I know about them to her attention." She jumped up and took my hand, pulling me to my feet. "The sooner we head out there, the sooner we can get home."

I sighed, letting her push me into the hallway.

"I'll just pop in the kitchen and tell Hanna where we're going and to expect us back for dinner. If we leave now, we should be able to get home by seven at the latest."

As she vanished, I shrugged into my coat, feeling decidedly grumbly. I was worried about Shade, but there wasn't a damned thing I could do right now about it. I grabbed my backpack and made sure I had my phone, and when she returned, I held out her coat.

"All right, but we're taking my Jeep and I'm driving." At least I could focus on the road instead of letting my thoughts wander to places better off left alone. Like what Shade's family might be saying to him, and what the prognosis on his powers would be, and just what this storm might enable Jay Miles to do with the sword.

As we headed out, the rain started in again and the sky was darkening up at an alarming rate. Menolly would be getting up shortly and I was actually glad for that. She was incredibly strong and capable in a crisis, and I always felt safer when she was around.

As we wound through the back roads to avoid rush-hour traffic, Camille's phone rang. She glanced at the caller ID. "It's Chase."

"Maybe he has some info about Miles."

She answered. "Hey, Chase . . . right . . . okay, tell me and then e-mail it to me, please. I'm in the car . . . Talamh Lonrach Oll—we need to ask the Merlin a few questions. He might know a little something about possessed swords."

She laughed. "Really? . . . Okay, what else? . . . Who? You're kidding. Yeah, I remember them, all too well . . . Cozy little club, aren't they?" Suddenly, she didn't sound amused. "All right, thanks, Chase. We'll see you tonight. Have you heard about the incoming storm? . . . Good. Yeah, would be good to have extra men on tonight . . . What? Okay, be sure she lets Menolly know."

As she punched END TALK on her phone, she turned to me.

"Okay, he's e-mailing me all of this in case we space out some of it. First, Jay Miles checks out as human. He's got a shady past, is suspected in several art thefts, etc., and he's suspected of being a fence but nobody has ever proved anything. He also is part of an FBH fraternity—not college, but one of those lodges. He's part of LOT. The Loyal Order of Thunderbirds. They're a magical group, according to rumor, and the membership roster also included—get this—Van and Jaycee."

I blinked and almost skidded across the road. Those were two names I hoped I'd never hear again. Jaycee and Van had been sorcerers who had been running a covert Wolf-briar business until we'd busted their asses and taken them down. Wolf-briar was a drug used on Weres, and it was created by torturing and dismembering alpha werewolves.

"Then whatever organization it is can't be a good one. Not with members like that in their ranks. Especially if it's a magical group. Okay, so he's suspected of being a fence, and he belongs to an underground group that housed known psychopaths. What else did Chase say?"

"He found a couple addresses for Miles. I should have them in the e-mail. Jay Miles has a public persona, though. Delilah, he may belong to LOT, but he also is a board member on the Seattle Race Against Cancer organization. They run a marathon every year to raise funds for cancer research. And Jay Miles is a benefactor of that group. He's friends with a lot of society people, so we have to walk softly on this one." She frowned. "I wonder just how private LOT is. Chase said the only reason he has Miles's membership recorded is due to an informant during the Wolf-briar incident."

Camille pulled her tablet out of her purse. We'd all taken to carrying them, after Roman gifted us with them at Yule. He'd bought the three of us—and Nerissa—iPads, as well as perfume. I wasn't sure what his personal gifts to Menolly were.

She tapped away, frowning. "There isn't a lot on the Net about it. Rumors, looks like . . . hmm . . . searching doesn't

reveal a great deal of info here. Wait . . . ." She paused, click-
ing on a link. "Here's a mention. A woman by the name of
Sandra K.—no last name given—wrote a self-published book
called *Magical Orders of the Fire.* It contains a list of organizations, and LOT is listed in here. I'm buying this book.
Maybe there's more info that can help us."

As she downloaded it, I took the turnoff to Talamh
Lonrach Oll. The rain was growing in intensity, and if it
was this bad now, I dreaded thinking of what it would be
like later when the winds rose. As it was, they were mild
now—about five to ten miles per hour, but I knew what
was coming and my stomach felt unsettled from it.

It took us forty minutes—ten more than usual, because
of traffic—to reach the Sovereign Fae Compound. As we
parked and headed over to the guards, I sincerely hoped
they had a covered buggy ready and able for us. But all of
them were in use.

"I'm sorry, Lady Camille, but with the weather so bad,
all carriages have been in use all day." The guard tipped a
sympathetic smile to us. "We do have one horse left, but he
won't take two riders."

"How far of a walk is it?"

She grimaced. "It will take us a good fifteen minutes at
least. We'd better get a move on. I didn't come all the way
out here just to turn around and go home." With that, she
set off and I hurried to keep up.

We were drenched within the first couple of minutes,
but my sister was resolute. She was wearing heels, but she
didn't complain—the woman could walk in stilettos better
than I could in flats. The pathways were cobblestone, and
slick, but she still managed it without turning a heel,
though I had a feeling she'd be asking for a foot rub later.

It took us twenty minutes rather than fifteen—the rain
worked against us—but we arrived at the great Barrow
Mounds where the Queens held court. The Merlin was stay-
ing in the Court of Dusk and Twilight, where Morgaine ruled.
Except Morgaine was curled in a fetal position in her room.
At least metaphorically.

We approached the gate, and the guards, peering at us closely, recognized Camille. She was well known out here and her reputation seemed to be growing with every month. I had the feeling there were some butt-monkey hurt feelings running under the surface.

Camille was Otherworld Fae, half-human, yet obviously Aeval's pet. She was also destined to become the first Earthside High Priestess for the Moon Mother. A position like that didn't come without breaking a few eggs along the way, even if you didn't realize you were the one breaking them.

"We're here to see the Merlin." Camille shivered, pulling her coat tighter around her, but seeing that our clothes were saturated, it did nothing except squeeze a little water out to run down her arms and legs.

"Come in. Sit by the fire." One of the guards looked furious. "I cannot believe you were allowed to walk all the way in the rain. The gatekeepers are newly trained. I apologize to you, and your sister."

"No, no . . . don't scold them. But if you could find us a carriage back to the parking lot, we'd really appreciate it." Camille brightened as we came to the fire that was burning merrily in the huge fireplace. The guards motioned to a servant, who took our coats.

"Bring towels, blankets, and hot tea immediately." He turned back to us. "I'll tell Lord the Merlin that you're here." Apparently, the Merlin had acquired a new title, too.

"Thank you." I nodded as he turned to go, then pulled Camille over to the bench right in front of the flames. We huddled, warming our hands against the raging heat that filtered out to fill the huge chamber. But no matter how hot the fire, the Barrows always seemed chilly to me during the winter. And they were stuffy during summer. I didn't think I could ever stand living here, and was grateful that Camille's path wasn't my own.

A moment later, a woman brought out towels and a couple blankets for us, and another, a tea tray with tea and cakes. They looked to be woodland Fae, and they smiled

gracefully as they set out the cups and saucers and took the
towels, helping us dry off as best as they could.

The cakes were yellow, with the flavors of apricot,
honey, and vanilla, and they were dusted with what tasted
like powdered sugar.

They melted in my mouth. "Hanna has to learn to make
these."

Camille nodded, licking her fingers. "I'll ask for the
recipe."

At that moment, the Merlin came in. When he went about
the town, he dressed in jeans and a shirt, much to Aeval and
Titania's dismay, but out here, he wore his robes. They were
green, with brown leather trousers. His hair grazed his shoulder blades, a deep burgundy mirrored by his beard. A few
strands of gray mingled in, the only sign that he was as old as
the hills. He had a Romanesque nose, and faint wrinkle lines
creasing his brow.

"Lady Camille, Delilah, what brings your company to
me on such a stormy evening?" He motioned for us to stay
seated, but he remained standing.

Camille swallowed the last of her cake, and gave him a
courteous, but respectful bow of the head. "We need your
advice, if you should have any." As she ran down the events
of the past few nights, including the devil-wraith, the Merlin's expression went from pleasant to nigh-exasperated.

"These meddlesome sorcerers—"

"He's a necromancer, actually." I realized I'd interrupted when he flashed me an irritable look.

"It makes no matter. Necromancer, sorcerer . . . they are
meddling with forces they know nothing about. There's no
respect left in the world for magic. I think something needs
to be done about that. But back to your question . . . So you
have a sword with a spirit trapped in it, and you want to keep
that spirit trapped in it. But the sword disappeared and you
think a *necromancer*"—here he gave me another look with a
gently reprimanding smile—"stole it. And you think he
wants to unleash the dead king to lead an army of the dead
that he might be raising. That about right?"

"That's about right." *And you're a jerk.*

But I kept my mouth shut on the latter thought. No need antagonizing someone on our side, even if he was full of himself. On the other hand, he *was* the Merlin and had a right to his ego. With a sigh, I thought that I was getting far too diplomatic. I didn't want to see the other side of the debate, but it seemed to be coming with experience. I wasn't at "wisdom" level yet, but I was definitely less naïve than I'd been a few years back.

The Merlin—his name was Myrddin, but nobody other than Aeval and Titania called him that—snapped his fingers and one of the servant girls came running. "More tea and cakes for our guests, please."

She curtseyed and ran off, looking a little frightened. I didn't blame her. I wouldn't like having to wait on him either, though I was pretty sure he wasn't a cruel man. He was just abrupt and condescending.

"I have been having a premonition all day that the incoming storm will make things worse." I waited for him to make some snarky comment to me again, but this time, he sat down next to me.

"What do you mean?" He didn't sound snarky.

I told him about the looming sense of doom that had been hanging over me. "I have no idea what it means. All I know is that ever since I heard about the storm coming in, I've been worried about how it will affect the sword and Einar. I can't tell you why . . . it's just a feeling. But I've learned not to ignore my intuition."

"And well you do so." The Merlin looked over at the fire, and the reflection of the flames danced in his eyes. "Storms are like power chargers for necromancers and sorcerers. Even witches, as Camille can tell you. All of us who work with the natural elements gain power from lightning and wind and rain—even snow. It amps us up. If this man has even a rudimentary knowledge of how to free the soul from the sword, the storm may give him an extra boost in being able to do so. You may be sensing that possibility."

"Can you find out where the sword is? Do you have any

way of doing so? Camille tried a spell of Finding on Aslo, but it didn't quite work out."

Myrddin frowned, pursing his lips as the servant girl brought in more tea and cakes. After she left, he continued. "I do have a way of possibly leading you to the sword, but I need to meet the lad. The young man who is linked to it by blood."

"Leif? Why him?" Camille leaned forward, an eager look in her eye.

"Because he bears a link to the soul locked within the sword. There is both a blood tie there and a link via the family curse. That reinforces my chances of finding him. The links are a level deep in the spirit matrix."

Camille looked as puzzled as I felt. "What do you mean, spirit matrix?"

Myrddin closed his eyes and held out his hands. As we watched, a mist rose between them, and then the shape of a honeycomb formed. It wasn't an actual honeycomb, though, no bees or dripping honey, but rather, a diagram. The colors were blue and green, silver and purple, and they sparkled. Then, Myrddin shifted his hands and the diagram became three-dimensional, elongating out. It twisted, a lot like a strand of DNA, and though the image vanished into the mist rolling out from between his palms, I knew it kept going on either side.

"This is the spirit matrix. Each one of those honeycomb sides? Each point where it intersects another line? That's a point where souls intersect. The universe is like a web, yes, in a sense. But soul matrixes bind every being that has come from the same soil, the same source. Animals, people, plants, everything that originated here on this planet—will connect to the planet's soul matrix."

"What about other worlds? Other realms?"

"There will be connections through parallel worlds, yes. The two of you? Are gateways where the soul matrixes from Otherworld and Earthside meet. Leif and his ancestor will be close together on the matrix—they are bound tightly by blood, just as you two would be close together."

With a soft sigh, he clapped his hands and the image vanished, the mist dissipating into the room.

"Everything really is connected, isn't it?" Camille looked around the room. "Even on an infinitesimal level, there will be some connection between some water skipper bug and . . . oh . . . the seers of Aladril back in OW."

"Yes, everything connects. Everything is linked. So bring me Leif, and I can probably trace the sword because the spirit of his ancestor is directly connected to it. But . . ." The Merlin stood. "Not tonight. The storm is rising and you had better go home while it's safe."

"But if we don't find out, the storm may enable Einar to escape." I knew that it was crazy, trying to get Leif and the Merlin together, but the push to take care of this *now* was overwhelming.

Myrddin rested his hand on my shoulder. "Delilah, patience. That may well be the chance we take, but trust me, my instinct tells me that you should go home. The storm is rising, and it will be a wild night. I am needed here. With Morgaine out of action . . ." His words drifted off.

"How is she?" Camille wanted to go see her—I could see that in her face, but the last time she'd asked, Aeval had told her it was better to wait.

"Still silent. I know you blame me for what happened, but destiny will unfold its hand when it is ready. Whether I gave the nudge or someone else, what happened would have eventually played out, regardless of whether I was there." He motioned for the serving girls. "Their coats, please. And make certain a buggy is here to return them to the gate."

"Has she said anything? Even a word?" As much as I had mistrusted Morgaine, her fate seemed horribly cruel, even for her. And with what we'd found out about her, Mordred, and Arthur, I no longer felt so unkindly toward her.

But the Merlin shook his head. "Her maids make sure she's dressed and undressed, bathed and cleaned. They feed her, take her out for walks. But she's retreated deep within her mind. Aeval will not let me see if I can help her."

"Can you? Help her?" Camille slid into her coat. It

looked dry, which seemed impossible for as wet as it had been. But my own coat was also dry.

Myrddin shrugged. "I don't honestly know if I can reach her. I would be willing to try, but I cannot go against Aeval's wishes. The Courts are her domain, not mine. Hers and Titania's. I will be returning to England soon, for a time. I will be flying in an airplane. Your world today? So many marvels. And so many from the past, now dust and lost to memory."

He walked us to the door. "Tomorrow, after the storm passes, contact your friend Leif, and then bring him here tomorrow, if all goes well."

We climbed in the buggy and headed back to the gate. I waited till we were out of earshot, then turned to Camille. "Why won't Aeval let him try to help Morgaine?"

She shook her head. "I have no idea. I didn't even know it was an option. I have a lot of questions for Aeval. I'll be coming out for the New Moon, so I think I have to have a little chat with the Queen of Shadow and Night. If I can keep my head from being chewed off."

By the time we reached home, it was going on eight and the wind was still puttering, but there was an uneasy feel to the air, that pre-storm rustling that sets everybody on edge and raises the hair on your arms. I made sure to park the Jeep by Camille's Lexus, but Menolly's Mustang was nowhere in sight. Other cars were there—Vanzir's beater and Morio's SUV—but Chase's car and Nerissa's were also gone.

"I know that Nerissa is sleeping down at the station in case of any emergencies. As crisis counselor for the FH-CSI, she kind of has to. I guess Chase decided to stay, too." I frowned. "I wish they were both here, though."

"You and me both." Camille glanced around, then shrugged out of her coat. The rain had let up again, and the clouds parted, but they were boiling across the night sky. "It's clammy—if it were summer, it would be muggy. Can you feel the crackle in the air? It's making me want to jump."

"Maybe some playtime with the guys?" Sex relaxed her, and she seemed to be as tense as I felt.

"No, I think . . . I want to be alert tonight. I want to rest, but I don't want my attention caught up in anything. I think I'm feeling what you were. The premonition." She glanced at the house. "Let's get inside and see if Shade is back."

I hung back.

She turned around. "Don't you want to see him?"

"Yes," I whispered. "But what if he's not home yet? What if he's home with worse news than we expected? I don't know how much more I can take today." I leaned against the porch railing. "I'm strong, Camille, but I think I've reached my limit right now. So much has happened, and I just need a break. Some downtime. But we never get any."

"I know, Kitten. I know." She wrapped her arm through mine and we stood there, staring at the sky as the clouds began building again. "I wish we could take a vacation from all of this. The gods know, we need one. But . . . I think right now . . . the best we can manage is a good movie now and then, a bowl of popcorn . . . some cookies . . . a hug from our loved ones. Simple joys. They can make a world of difference."

We watched the sky for another few minutes until first one drop, then another, and the rain came tumbling down again. A flash of blue lightning off to the east lit up the horizon. We counted under our breath but the roll of thunder never came.

"Still a little ways out."

"It won't be for long." Camille shook the rain off her face. "Come on, let's get inside and wait for the storm."

As we headed up the porch steps, the door opened. There stood Shade. He opened his arms and I flew into his embrace. The storm was on the way, but my love was home.

Chapter 15

"Shade!" I buried my face in his neck. He kissed my cheek, then pulled me inside. Camille followed. The house smelled like a food court. Hanna had apparently continued to cook. A fire was crackling in the fireplace and everything seemed incredibly warm and cozy. Smoky was in one of the armchairs, reading. He motioned for Camille to join him. She curled up in his lap.

Roz and Vanzir were playing some video game together. Trillian's voice could be heard from the kitchen—he was helping Hanna out. Morio was nowhere to be seen.

I turned to Shade, not wanting to break the spell that seemed to hover over the family at this moment. It would be so nice to just grab some dinner, curl up, and watch TV. *But . . .*

"What happened? What did they say?" I took his hands, leading him over to the sofa. As I sat down, Shade slid in beside me. I couldn't read his face, couldn't tell whether it was good news or bad.

"Mallen is right." He let out a slow breath. "I've lost all

my Stradolan powers. I'm no longer a shadow walker by
nature. By birth, yes . . . but by nature . . . no. My dragon
side hasn't been affected . . . *much*." The way he stressed
the last word sent a chill through me. That meant there had
been some damage to that side of him, too.

By now, Camille, Smoky, and the others were listening,
too. I steeled myself, not certain just how hard this was
going to be. Shade was strong, but something of this magnitude couldn't just be passed off with an "oh well."

"And . . . ?" I waited.

"My dragon side is still functioning normally, mostly.
But . . . I no longer can travel to the Netherworld in my Stradolan form. I have to take the shape of my shadow dragon
self if I want to visit there without outside help. Once I'm
there, I can shift out of dragon form, but I have to shift back
in order to leave. I found that out the hard way today when I
left here. Ended up bounced abruptly into the Dragon
Reaches when I tried to make it to the Netherworld. I shifted
form there and tried as a shadow dragon, and that time, I
managed it."

I was confused. "But how does that affect your dragon
self?"

"Shadow dragons have a direct connection to the dead.
I no longer have such a strong connection. I'm a shadow
dragon who . . . is mainly just a dragon. My death magic
has been stripped away from both sides. I can still fly, I can
hide in the shadows better than most people, I can breathe
fire. But all the magic that goes with my breed? It's gone.
The devil-wraith sucked it out of me."

Every sound in the room fell away. Camille silently
slipped out of Smoky's lap and moved to a chair next
to him.

Smoky leaned forward, intent on Shade. "You had tests
done in the Netherworld. What about the Dragon Reaches?
Maybe our healers . . ."

"I talked to them, too. The Stradolan sent me back to the
Dragon Reaches after they were done testing me. There's no
cure, no way to rewire me. I'm . . . effectively neutered when

it comes to magic, except for my basic dragon heritage. And I'm only half-dragon, so even that is limited."

The look on his face said what he would not—Shade was devastated. I could see it in his eyes, though his voice was steady. I squeezed his hand, unsure of what to say. Nothing I could do would make anything easier; nothing I could do would make it better.

Vanzir and Roz slowly put down their joysticks and waited for someone to give them a cue. Camille raised her hand to them and shook her head.

Smoky stood. "Shade, come outside with me. We'll have a little chat."

My first instinct was to insist on going with them, but one look at Smoky stopped that. He gently shook his head when I moved to follow them. As they left the room, Camille crossed to my side and put her hand on my arm.

"Leave them. They're both dragon. If anybody can help Shade cope with this, Smoky can. You need to be there with your love and your passion, to prove that he's still the man he was. Let Smoky take care of dealing with the intricacies of dragonhood." She took my hand and led me into the kitchen. Hanna was cleaning the kitchen and laying out paper plates and cups on one of the counters. She'd also made a huge pot of coffee, which was sitting on the stove.

"Dinner is ready. The paper plates are for later, just in case the power goes out and hot water is limited."

Trillian was laying the food out on the table—fried chicken, mashed potatoes and gravy, and coleslaw. "I was about to call you all to dinner," he said, then paused as he looked over our way. "What's wrong? You both look like you've seen another ghost."

"Have you talked to Shade yet?" Camille kissed him, then poured milk in a mug and nuked it till it was warm. She motioned for me to sit down.

Trillian shook his head. "No, he arrived just before you did. Bad news?"

I accepted the milk and slowly began to fill my plate. I still wanted to be out there, talking to Shade, but I knew that at this point, I'd just babble and make things worse. Smoky was right to intervene.

"Yeah." I picked at the breading on the chicken. It was delicious as usual. Vanzir and Roz chose that moment to join us, and Morio clattered down the stairs and into the room.

"Where's Menolly? She didn't go to the bar, did she? Not with the incoming storm?" Camille glanced around.

"Yeah, she did." Roz loaded up his plate. "She said they were going to open for a while and see how things went. She promised to close down early if things get hairy."

"She should have just closed for the night." Camille looked vexed. She glanced around. "Well, while the rest of us are here . . . Shade did get some bad news. Smoky's talking to him now."

I sucked in a deep breath. "I'll tell them. It's my responsibility." I told Trillian, Hanna, and Morio what Shade had said. Better I do it than he have to go through it all again when he and Smoky came in.

"How should we react?" Roz buttered a roll and heaped coleslaw on it. He liked salad sandwiches, which confused the hell out of me, but then I wasn't friends with anything green unless it had an *M* on it or was a gummy-something. "In the living room, I wasn't sure if I should say anything."

"It's not like he's emasculated." Camille passed around the mashed potatoes.

"Maybe not, but he's lost an entire part of his heritage. I still have no idea how his family reacted." I didn't mean to snap at her, but truth was, even I had no clue what to do. I might be growing into my diplomacy but that didn't mean I was good at handling situations like this, and I'd reached the saturation point. I crossed to the window and glanced outside. Smoky and Shade were standing out there, in the middle of the pouring rain, looking like they were having a heart-to-heart. I turned back to the others.

"I don't know what to do. When Menolly was turned, it was such a shock that we were all numb for months on end. Even when she returned home, we all walked on eggshells around her for a couple of years."

Camille leaned back in her chair. "Let's face it, what Dredge did to Menolly? Not a comparison. Dredge raped her; he tortured her for hours. He killed her and turned her. You have to admit, that's far worse than what's happened to Shade. He's still alive, Delilah, and walking, and he still has his dragon heritage. I don't mean to sound harsh, but the truth is: Yes, this is bad, but it could be so much worse."

I wanted to argue, but she was right and I knew it. "Shade's my fiancé, and I love him. I want to be supportive. I don't want to screw up. What do I say? How do I say it? How do I *not* say something stupid that will hurt him?"

"You start by just being you." Shade appeared in the doorway, taking all of us by surprise. He caught my gaze and the stern look slid away. "Okay, let's talk about this—out in the open. I heard what you said, Camille. As much as it stings, you're right. What Menolly went through? *So much worse.* I don't want anybody thinking I'm comparing my fate to hers. Delilah—don't you dare do that either. On the other hand, this isn't going to be easy for me. I've got a lifetime of abilities that vanished in the course of a few minutes. I'm going to probably get frustrated at times. I'll try to work through it, but please, be patient with me while I relearn how to live my life."

He eyed the table. "I'm hungry. Feel free to ask me questions while I eat. With so much at stake, I can't nurse my wounds in private, as much as I'd like to."

Smoky clapped him on the back. "You don't have to. We'll help you."

Shade cast him a grateful smile. "Thank you . . . *Lord Iampaatar.*" The emphasis was deliberate, that much I could tell, but it was also respectful. Whatever Smoky had said, I had the distinct impression that it had helped the issue rather than hurt it.

I handed Shade the chicken. "What about your family, love? Did you talk to them?"

"Yes, I did." Shade filled his plate, as did Smoky. "My mother was understanding and has promised to come visit us because it will make things easier."

Oh joy, that meant that I'd get to meet my future

mother-in-law, probably sooner than I wanted to. After
Lash's reaction to me, I wasn't all that keen on the idea.
"And your father?"

"My father . . ." Shade put down his fork. "My father
has never appreciated my stance on his work. He didn't say
much when I told him what happened. But then, he's never
had much to say to me."

Shade's father was on the Jury of the Damned, which in
the Netherworld was a council deciding the fates of restless
spirits. They were pretty hardcore and ruthless. Shade's sister, Lash, was following in their father's footsteps and the
two had argued over it when she had come to scope me out.

I'd never pried, never pushed, because I figured Shade
would open up when he was ready, but I finally decided
enough was enough. "What are the Stradolan? I've kept
quiet, waiting for you to tell me, but I think . . . if you no longer can be one of them, can't you tell us what you've lost?"

That put a stop to the conversation. For a moment, I
thought I'd just made things so much worse, and I was
ready to creep away from the table, but then Shade pushed
back his chair. His expression was stoic, but his voice was
soft, as if he were feeling out the situation.

"All right. I suppose I should have told you sooner—
but dragons . . . we take our time. The Stradolan are very
private as a race. We mingle . . . *they* mingle . . . mostly
with their own kind and the shadow dragons. How the
ability to interbreed came about is beyond my knowledge,
and only happens if the female of the pair is the dragon.
Hybrids like me? Can never breed with others—"

"You can't breed with others? But the Autumn Lord . . ."
I stared at him. What did this mean for us? Why had Hi'ran
chosen him for me?

"Oh, no worries there. You will bear the Autumn Lord's
child. I'm his proxy, you know that—his energy will . . .
quicken my sperm." He cleared his throat, glancing around.
"This is a weird conversation to be having in public, but I
suppose, given the circumstances, it's not altogether a bad
idea. Delilah, when it's time, the Autumn Lord's energy will

give life to my sperm and change the structure of it. That's the *only way* I can ever get you pregnant. He chose me for several reasons, but that is one of the primary factors. I can never give you a child, so there's never going to be any question of who the father is."

I leaned back, stunned. Hi'ran wanted to make sure I had his child . . . but yet he'd let me sleep with Chase before I met Shade. "I'm confused."

"You'll have to ask him about the rest." Shade gave me a shake of the head. "That's between you and our master. But back to the Stradolan . . . the nature of the race? Very few outsiders even know of us. We are made of shadow stuff. We walk in physical form, but our very nature is composed of the shadows and twilight, of fog and mist and the in-between spaces. The first Stradolan were offshoots of Elemental energy. In fact, they were spawned by the Autumn Lord himself. The Stradolan were originally the children of the Autumn Lord and Grandmother Coyote, in an experiment gone wrong. The only way the Stradolan become mortal is when they are a half-breed . . . and the only time interbreeding happens is with shadow dragons."

The phrase *you could have heard a pin drop* was an understatement. I sat back, not sure what the hell to say. No wonder the Stradolan were so private—they weren't mortal, at least not the full-blooded ones. Whether they were actually Immortals was another question, but they weren't like the Fae or humans or elves.

Finally, Smoky spoke up. "There isn't much to say beyond that. We should eat and let Shade have his rest. As to the permanence of the situation, regardless of what they say, I'm not fully convinced. We will just have to wait and see."

"Thank you. I'm rather tired of talking about it. The tests they put me through were rather invasive, and right now, I just want to relax, eat, and . . . rest." Shade picked up his fork.

I did the same, though my mind was whirling with questions and thoughts. But he needed space now, and even though we had all needed to know what was going down—what affected one of us affected the entire household—it was time to shut up. "Of course, love. Whatever you want."

The rest of dinner went quietly, though Camille and I told Shade what we'd found out from Leif. But halfway through the meal, a loud noise sounded—like someone banging across the roof.

Morio went to go see what it was. When he returned, he was holding part of a tree branch. "The wind's picking up—ahead of schedule. I suggest we turn on the news and see what they're saying about the weather."

There was a small television in the kitchen, precisely for moments like these. Camille flipped it on and tuned to Channel 2—the local news station. The meteorologist was talking.

"Winds that were projected to come in around midnight have made an early arrival. What this foretells for the rest of the storm, we're not certain, but we advise caution on the roads. There have already been reports of two downed trees in North Seattle, and flooding over the road in several parts of Bellevue, Redmond, and even as far south as the city of Olympia. It's a stormy evening out there, folks, so make sure you have your raingear on and don't take chances."

She turned it off. "Well, storm's hitting early. By the looks of that weather map, we're going to be feeling the brunt of it." Just then, the lights flickered and another noise rattled the roof. "We'd better finish dinner and get the dishes washed up."

As we went back to our food, Camille's cell rang. "Hello? . . . Hi, Iris . . . Really? Okay, thanks for letting us know." She jumped up. "Iris and Bruce just lost power. Clear the table while we can see. If anybody's still hungry, you can grab food on a paper plate after we clean the kitchen."

We all pitched in and the dishes were done in no time. I grabbed a handful of cookies and looped my arm through Shade's as we headed into the living room.

"I love you. You know that, right? It's going to take a while to process everything that has happened—and everything you told us—but that doesn't change the fact that I'm nuts over you." I snuggled close to him and he slipped one arm around my waist, pulling me close.

"I love you, too, Pussycat. Thank you for being here. For not trying to pretend this didn't happen, or doesn't matter. And for being honest." He paused. "I'm not ready to talk much about this. But when I am, I'll need you there. I'll need you to remind me of who I am, because Delilah, I just lost a part of my identity. I don't know what to think—this is going to take time to process."

"I'll be here. I'll be ready to listen." I hung my head. "I can't pretend to know what you're going through, but I will do everything I can to make the transition easier. Just don't walk away from me. Don't pull back—I can handle whatever you need me to handle."

He kissed me then, slow and deep, and I could feel the worry and tension in his body as he pressed against me. "I trust you, my love. I trust you with my heart. I know you won't break it."

We settled onto the sofa as Vanzir and Roz readied to fire up their Xbox. Just then, a gust of wind rattled the windows and the lights vanished. The flames in the fireplace offered us enough light for everyone else to finish entering the room and sit down.

"Everybody stay where you are except Trillian—can you go check on Hanna and Maggie and bring them in here? I don't know if Hanna has a candle nearby and she can't carry both that and Maggie." Camille moved to the coffee table, and within minutes, a sparkling array of candles lit up the room.

The effect was magical, and none of us seemed to want to move away from the immediate area. Shade and I curled on one end of the sofa. Camille and Morio curled up on the other end. Smoky took one of the rocking chairs; Vanzir and Roz scooted closer to the fire. When Trillian returned with Hanna and Maggie, he guided her to the overstuffed recliner and gently placed Maggie in her arms, then joined Camille and Morio, sitting on the floor by their feet.

The storm had picked up, and now the sounds of branches skittered across the roof, thumping loudly. Every time some new *thunk* hit, it made me jump. As serene as it felt, all of us huddled around the fireplace, the noises were jarring and I kept thinking about the devil-wraith.

After a moment, Shade must have sensed my tension. "Let's play a game."

I stared at him. "What do you have in mind?"

He grinned. "I shared a lot of secrets with you tonight. I'm willing to share one more, but only if everybody shares something they never told anyone. It doesn't have to be earthshaking . . . just a secret you keep to yourself—about yourself. Not about anybody else. It's a campfire game, I gather, that's making the rounds among the kids today."

"What kids are you talking about?" I shook my head, thinking this could be a dangerous game, but then again . . . we were family. "Okay, I'll go first. My secret is that . . . Camille, do you remember when you made the pumpkin pie last year and everybody thought Maggie accidentally got hold of it and knocked it off the counter?"

She narrowed her eyes. "Yes? Do I detect that this was not the case?"

Grinning, I shrugged. "Cats love pumpkin. What can I say? I was in Tabby form and I leapt up on the counter and started licking it, and accidentally knocked it off. Maggie was in the right place at the wrong time."

It was the right thing to set the mood. After everybody stopped snickering, we went round. When Vanzir's turn came, I waited to see if he'd say anything about Aeval, but of course, that wasn't going to happen. But he did admit to using up Camille's peppermint body wash.

Camille had just finished admitting how she had pushed me into the pond when we were kids because I refused to take a bath—it hadn't been Elan, the bully, but she had done it, and then promptly saved me, but made me go home and take a bath to get the "lake cooties" off—when a loud knock sounded at the door. I started to answer, but Smoky stopped me.

"Not on such a dark night, when a storm is raging. I'll

go." He carried one of the candles with him. We waited and within minutes Smoky returned, Tim Winthrop behind him.

"Tim! What are you doing out tonight?" I jumped up. He was soaked and he looked exhausted. "Is Jason with you?"

He shook his head. "No, he's at home and probably worried sick, but my cell ran out of juice and I couldn't call him. The car broke down about a mile from here. I've been walking in the storm. I figured somebody would be home here. I guess you lost the lights? Is your phone still working?"

I picked up the landline to hear a reassuring dial tone. "Yes. Here, call Jason. Trillian—" I was about to ask him to bring some blankets but he was already on his feet.

"Blankets and food coming up. I'm afraid it won't be hot, but will chicken work for you, Tim?"

Tim nodded. He had gotten a buzz cut, so his curly hair was long gone, and he'd dyed it pale green. Tim had a slender build, but he was fit and lean.

"Chicken is great. Jason does most of the cooking and he's been into paleo lately. I've lost some weight and feel great, but damn, I miss KFC at times." He shook his head at my offer of a chair. "Wait till I dry off a little. I'm soaked."

Trillian reappeared, but stopped before handing him the blanket. "Dude, you're going to be chilled if you stay in those clothes. Come on, you're shorter than I am, but Morio's clothes might fit you. It's either too short or too long—your choice." He led Tim up the stairs. While they were gone, Morio went in the kitchen and fixed Tim a plate, bringing it back and setting it on a TV tray. A few minutes later, Trillian and Tim reappeared. Tim was wearing a pair of Morio's sweats and a sweatshirt. He was using a towel to scrub his scalp dry.

"Thanks, that feels better. You said something about food?"

"Right here. Now call your husband before we do." Morio handed him the phone. "He must be worried sick."

"Maybe. We had an argument. It was stupid, but now I regret it." He put in the call, and a couple minutes later, he and Jason had made up and Tim was ensconced in a chair, eating.

"So why were you out this way?"

"I was trying to reach out to one of the newest Supe Community Action Council members. She's very reclusive, and she's having trouble with her landlords. We could help her with anti-discrimination information, and one of the lawyers in the group has offered to take her case pro bono, but she's nervous about coming into town and I wanted to encourage her to actually take action on this." He bit into the chicken and, within minutes, had devoured everything on his plate.

"Who is she?" I was so out of the loop, I had no clue what was going on right now with the council.

"Feras Dannan. She's an autumn nymph—a wood nymph connected to trees when they begin to go dormant. She hates being in the city and is extremely shy and suspicious of humans." He laughed. "Which begs the question of why she even lets me come talk to her, but somehow we've managed to find our way to a friendship of sorts. Maybe it's because I've always understood what it's like to be an outsider, too."

"Where does she live? I don't think we've ever really met one of the seasonal Fae." They were very much connected with the cycles of the year and tended to fade into the background during the other seasons.

A few had ventured into the open. They were not nearly as quick to out themselves as the more conventional ES Fae, but now—with global warming—they were coming to the forefront and lobbying for immediate action to shift the environmental damage. The government didn't know what to do with them, so they did what they always did—ignored the issue and hoped it would just go away.

"She lives on the other side of Grandmother Coyote's land, actually. They're neighbors, of a sort. Trouble is, Feras has a landlord who wants her off the land. He says she's squatting. She's claiming Fae Sovereign rights. It's a dicey case. Since she's connected with the forest, she has a case, but only if she gets herself a top-notch lawyer and learns to cope with being in constant contact with the FBH world. And that, she's having trouble doing."

Oh gods. Fae Sovereign rights were the big issue affecting the human-Fae communities right now, and the Triple Threat were spearheading it. Some of the Fae who were intimately connected with natural areas, as in they would die if their woodlands or deserts or lakes were destroyed, had begun trying to fight back against the developers.

Years ago, it would have been mysterious things happening to the bulldozers and loggers. Now, fueled by support from Talamh Lonrach Oll, their weapons were court orders and demands for equal rights to a quality lifestyle, which included maintenance of their necessary habitat.

The whole thing was one big ball of wax and would take years to play out. On this issue, the government was walking a tightrope. Paid off by lobbyists who wanted bigger and better shopping malls, but under pressure from Fae Rights groups—along with Supe and Vampire Rights organizations—they hadn't figured out yet what to do about the issue, which was, namely: Humans no longer were top rung of the food chain.

"I take it this is a new cause for the Supe Community Action Council?" Which meant a long, tedious string of speeches and debates about what step to take next.

Tim grinned. "I'm looking forward to it just about as much as you are. Remember, I'm human. But . . . also remember: My *kind* fought for our rights, too. For the right to marry, for the right to not be fired or beat up or discriminated against." He tapped his wedding ring. "I won my battle. I'm sure as hell going to help others win theirs."

And that was all he had to say.

"We're with you, Tim. All the way."

He looked around. "By the way, where is Menolly?"

My phone rang as I was about to answer and I picked up. "Yes?"

"Hey, Delilah." Menolly was on the other end of the line.

"Speak of the devil. Tim's here. We were just talking about you. What's up? We've lost power, by the way."

She sounded irritable as all get-out. "I'm at the Wayfarer. We've *all* lost power—Seattle's black. The storm is taking a nasty turn. Derrick and Digger are outside, in the dark, closing the wooden shutters. But Tolly and Garth haven't shown up yet to guard the portal. So I can't leave here until they get here. I don't dare leave it unguarded."

I didn't like the thought of her staying there alone. "Can't Derrick stay with you?"

"I don't want to ask him to do that. Digger might, though. I'll ask him and call you back." She hung up.

"Seattle's black. Menolly says power is out everywhere." I glanced at my phone. "My bars are low. I'm going to go sit in my Jeep and charge my phone for a little bit. I'll be back after a while, if the wind doesn't blow me away."

I hurried out to my car and slipped into the driver's seat. Turning on the ignition, I cracked the window. Then, I plugged in my phone, sat back, and watched the storm. The clouds were socked in, but churning as the rain lashed the trees. Gusts were growing stronger—smaller branches were starting to rip away from the trunks and sail across the yard. A flash lit up the sky, neon blue and illuminating the night, and immediately, hail stones pelted my windshield, the size of quarters.

"Oh, hell." I was stuck. I could make a run for the house but I'd get bombarded by extremely painful ice bullets. And I'd probably end up falling—slipping on them. As my phone rang, I flipped on the windshield wipers, trying to keep the ice from building up on the windshield.

"It's Menolly. Digger's going to stay here with me for now. But the streets are already flooding and power lines are down everywhere. We may end up camping out on the kitchen level—the city didn't think urban flooding would be such a big deal, but apparently the sewer drains are overloaded already."

"Cripes. Be careful, and if you go out, watch out for the downed lines. Electricity can torch you—and if your clothes caught fire—"

"I know. I'd turn into a torch, and so much dust and ashes. Is this supposed to get much worse?" She sounded exasperated.

"Yeah, a lot. I'm in my Jeep, charging my phone.

Branches are starting to fly off the trees, and hail is going to dent my paint job. If you can't make it home, you'll have to chance the safe room come morning. Shade's back." I told her what had happened and what he'd told us about the Stradolan. "Now we know more about them, at least. But I wish it hadn't happened this way."

"It sucks, but he's alive and he's not . . . well, he was harmed but he's not going to die from this."

"That's essentially what Camille said." I didn't want to tell her that Camille had also used her as a comparison.

"She was right. We'll find a way to help him through this, but I'm just glad there wasn't any worse damage."

A branch went skittering past me, nearly missing my windshield. The hail let up but now a steady hail of twigs and debris were beginning to fly. My phone was charged partway, and I decided that it might be prudent to go back inside.

"Listen, I'm going to head back in the house. Things are starting to get a little wild here. Call in a bit to let us know how you're doing." As I unplugged my phone and went to turn off the ignition, I thought I heard something outside my door, but couldn't see anything out there but blowing branches.

Of course you're hearing things, I thought. *The wind's whipping at thirty-five miles an hour at a bare minimum.*

As I stepped out of the car, a gust of wind blasted me from the side and I leaned against the side of the Jeep. A branch came whirling down from one of the firs to the left of me, and the next thing I knew, it hit me square in the head. I staggered away from the car, but all I could see was a whirl of colors as pain stabbed through my forehead. The next moment, my knees hit the ground, and the world went dark.

Chapter 16

❧ ❧

"Delilah? Delilah . . . can you hear me?" The voice seemed to echo from a long distance and I tried to focus. I couldn't see anything, and there appeared to be some sort of cloth over my eyes. I struggled to sit up, but a wave of pain sent me reeling back and I stopped fighting.

"Delilah? Are you awake?" The voice came more into focus and I recognized it. Camille.

"*Urmf* . . ." It was the best I could muster. I flailed, trying to push the cloth off my face, but a hand grabbed my arm and forced it back down. I ran my fingers over the cloth beneath me. I wasn't sure what I was lying on, but I suspected the sofa.

"We have an ice pack on your forehead. Leave it alone." Shade's voice was low and soothing and I reached out, wanting his hand.

"What . . . How . . ." I tried to find the words to ask how I'd gotten there, and where I was, but my thoughts were too fuzzy. But Shade took my hand then—I knew his fingers by touch—and that calmed me down.

"You got hit by a flying branch. The storm is raging. You've been out for about an hour, but it looks like the bump on your head was the only damage you took. It won't require stitches, but you're going to have one hell of a bruise."

As he spoke, something landed across the roof, very loudly, then skittered along the shingles. The howl of the wind echoed through the window. It moaned like a Bean Sidhe, sending a chill down my back.

Managing to find my voice, I pulled the cloth off my eyes and whispered, "Where am I? Prop me up?"

Someone had stuffed pillows behind my back—in the dim light of the candle's glow, I couldn't tell who it was. But I could see Shade sitting next to me, and Camille's face came into focus. She was leaning on the back of the sofa.

"You're in the living room. We didn't want to chance anybody going upstairs in case a tree decides to topple through the roof. The storm's as bad as they were predicting. Anything outside that isn't nailed down is probably down in Birchwater Pond by now."

Camille was good at sounding normal when things weren't, but even I could tell that something else had happened. The inflection in her voice was a little too happy for the circumstances.

As the room came more into focus, I realized I had one hell of a headache. "I feel like I got run over by a truck."

"The branch that hit you was lying beside you—it was four feet long. You're lucky it didn't split your skull open." Shade motioned to somebody, and as they rested an ice-cold compress over my forehead, a few seconds of intense pain hit, then a wave of relief swept over me as the chilling moisture numbed the pain. "I don't know if you're going to end up with a black eye or not—it's looking like that might be the case—but your temple is nice and purple."

I muttered an "Oh thanks" and closed my eyes.

"Do you feel nauseated?" Morio loomed overhead and I realize he'd pressed the compress to my head.

I frowned. Did I? It was hard to focus on anything except the pain in my head. "No, I don't think so. Woozy, yes, and shaky but . . ." I started to shake my head but that was an extremely bad idea. "No, no nausea. In fact, I could use something to drink."

"I'll get her something." Trillian's voice echoed from my right, near my feet. The flickering shadows from the candle flames weren't strong enough to illuminate much in the room.

As the ice eased the pain, I began to feel a bit more confident, and with Shade's help, I sat fully upright. Camille stuffed more pillows behind me. I reached up to feel the compress. It was already growing warm. Smoky, who was sitting in a chair near my head, took it and—as I watched—breathed a fine layer of mist on it. White dragons and silver dragons could do that—breathe frost and fog and ice. He handed it back to me and it was nice and cold again. I gratefully pressed it back to my forehead.

Trillian returned then with a water bottle. I took a big swig. It was lemon water. "The lemon will be good for you." He also handed me a couple of cookies. "For energy."

I managed a half-grin and nibbled on the chocolate chips, even though I really didn't have any appetite. But the minute I tasted them, I realized that the hunger was there, I just hadn't been feeling it. I wolfed them down.

"So . . . bad storm. Did Menolly call back? Do you have my phone?"

"Your sister is still down at the Wayfarer. She and Digger have been out piling sandbags against the front. She's okay, though. She checked in about twenty minutes ago. Nerissa and Chase are still down at the station—they have generators there. And Trillian went down to check on Iris, Bruce, and the babies. They're fine." Shade looked like he wanted to say more, but then closed his mouth.

"What? What happened? I can see it in both your and Camille's eyes. What went on while I was out cold?" When they didn't answer, I started to push my way off the sofa. "I'll get up if you don't tell me."

Camille let out a sigh. "Daniel called. He thought somebody was outside of his apartment. The alarm system was failing—a massive power surge spiked his condo complex and seems to have shorted the security system. Unfortunately, we got cut off. We haven't heard from him since then, and we don't know if his phone just lost power or what."

"What are we waiting for? We have to go check on him." I struggled to stand, but Shade pushed me back on the sofa.

"You aren't going anywhere."

"I have to—we can't leave Daniel in the lurch. I'm okay."

"You seriously think we should go driving through the storm? Winds are a steady fifty to sixty miles an hour. They've closed the 520 Floating Bridge so they could open the draw spans. Trees are down all over the place, power is out in the entire Seattle area and the Greater Eastside. Lines are down and hot everywhere. It's dangerous out there, Delilah." Morio crossed his arms, shaking his head. "We're risking our lives if we step out that door."

My head was rapidly clearing, even though the pain remained. I cautiously finished the rest of the water, then pushed myself to my feet. Shade knew better than to try to stop me this time—instead he offered me his arm and I balanced on it as I stood. After a few seconds, I knew I wasn't going to topple over, and let go.

"Don't you think we owe it to him to try? He's our cousin." I turned to Camille. "What if Aslo is after him? What if Jay Miles sent Aslo back to Daniel's for some reason?"

She looked half convinced. "You might be right."

"Why would he go back to Daniel's, though? Daniel stole the sword in the first place. Why give him another crack at it? If they have it, that is?"

But my instincts were urging me to go help him. I tried to puzzle through the headache. Why would Aslo and Jay return for Daniel? The ghosts wanted to keep Einar from emerging. So that meant going back to Leif, not Daniel. They hadn't urged Daniel to get it back. They'd urged *us* to find it. They just picked Daniel's house as the venue for their appearance.

"Wait! I think I'm on to something." The pieces were beginning to fall into place. "Daniel . . . he was affected by the sword—remember, he said he thought it was making him want to rampage through town with it? That it sparked off a flashback from when he was in the ISA?"

Camille nodded. "Yeah . . . so how does that play into events?"

"Einar needs a host—a host he can control, if he's to exit the sword and return to life. He has to have a living body to possess. But Jay wouldn't be a good host—he wants to *control* the king who controls the army. He wouldn't want Einar to control him. And Aslo . . . he works for Jay, but would a necromancer want a toadie of his having that much power? However, Daniel . . . The sword—Einar—liked Daniel and was able to influence him. Ten to one, Jay knows this. What if they're—"

"Looking to force Daniel into being an unwilling host for Einar! You have to be right on this. Jay figured out that Einar wants Daniel." Camille whirled to face Smoky. "Delilah's right, we have to go over there now. We can't let that happen."

The others now looked alarmed, which is precisely what I'd hoped for. "We go, then?"

Nodding slowly, Camille stood. "We get dressed and head out. And hope to hell we can navigate this storm. Delilah, are you sure you're up to coming with us?"

"You can't make me stay home so don't even try." I frowned. "Shade, can you bring me some clean, warm clothes?"

He nodded, heading for the stairs.

Camille followed him. She was wearing a bathrobe and nightgown. "I'll change, too."

Twenty minutes later, we were dressed and out the door. We left Shade and Roz home to watch over Hanna, Maggie, and the house. Meanwhile, Smoky, Trillian, Morio, Vanzir, Camille, and I all piled into Morio's SUV. It was safer to take just one car. If the word *safe* could even be implied.

As we stepped onto the porch, a blast of wind busted past and I grimaced as the cold sting of rain hit against the bump on my head. The storm was raging, and it sounded like it was getting worse. Seattle wasn't a target for hurricanes, but occasionally we hit the lower levels of gale-force winds, and this was setting up to vie for the record.

Without the lights in our house, or the lights along the drive, it was so dark we could barely see the house. We carried flashlights—and our weapons—but even the beam of a flashlight wasn't strong enough to thoroughly pierce the darkness. Camille and I inched down the stairs, holding on to the rails. The constant howling from the wind was loud enough to disorient me, and it took me a moment to figure out when I was on the actual ground.

Morio held out his keychain and the SUV's lights blinked as he unlocked the doors. We cautiously made our way over to the vehicle, and—once there—slid into the car. Morio and Camille sat in front. Smoky and I sat in the middle seat. And Vanzir and Trillian took the rear.

"Hold on and keep your eyes open. There aren't going to be any streetlights on, due to the power outages, so I'm taking this slow and easy." Morio wasn't always so cautious on the road, but tonight, he inched down the driveway, and every time anybody started to say something, he hushed them.

"I need to focus, people. We don't want to get caught in a bunch of downed power lines. That's just asking for trouble."

We quieted down. As we reached the main street, Victoria Road, Morio turned left. "We have to go around Lake Washington to I-405, then south to Bellevue. With the 520 Floating Bridge closed, there's really no other option. I don't want to try to drive all the way through a blacked-out Seattle to the I-90 bridge. That would be a recipe for disaster."

He managed to navigate out of Belles-Faire, to 205th Street, which would run a long stretch before we had to turn. It was a heavily wooded road, which meant we had a good chance of running across a downed tree, but for now it was our best bet.

The wind was blasting against the sides of the car, a streaming whistle as we cautiously ate through the miles. Morio turned on his high beams so we would have the best chance of seeing danger before we got to it. All the while, we kept our mouths shut, giving him the space in which to focus on driving. The streets were a hazard of littered branches and tree limbs, and Morio swerved time and again to miss them.

Eventually, we came to a T-junction. To our left was Cedar Way. To the right, the street ran as 37th Avenue NE. Morio turned right.

"We follow this to 40th Place NE, then shortly after shift on to 197th." Morio had the ability to look at a map and remember the directions almost by rote.

The road remained a two-lane street, curving through the heavily forested suburb. Here and there, we would see one house with lights—which told us just who owned generators out here. A short while later, we came to a fork in the road, where we turned to the left onto 197th.

Our luck continued to hold as we sped along, and 197th turned into 201st Place. Around the Puget Sound area, it seemed that city planners had no problem with naming the same street two different names, depending on whatever whims befell them. So streets turned into avenues turned into places.

At yet another junction, we bent to the south on 55th Avenue NE, then onto a street that made me giggle. We were on Cat's Whiskers Road, which would finally take us to Highway 522 and eventually lead us to I-405. As we approached Highway 522, however, a noise thundered in back of us and the road shook. Morio pulled over to the shoulder of the street.

"What's going on?"

Trillian ducked out of the car, then right back in. "We just missed being creamed by a huge freaking fir tree. It's covering the road. We're not going home the same way, I tell you that much. A minute later, and we would be under that trunk."

I sobered, suddenly realizing just how dangerous this storm really was. "Get a move on. If any other trees around here have unstable roots, we don't want to hang around to find out."

He nodded and eased back onto the road. Five minutes later, he suddenly swerved hard to the right, and the wheels screeched as he struggled to bring the car out of a skid over the watery pavement.

I glanced out of my window as we passed to see another tree lying halfway across the road. Morio had managed to miss it, but we hadn't had much room to spare. I caught my breath and whispered a prayer to Bast that she get us there safely.

Another two near misses and we reached the interchange, where Morio took the exit south, and we were on the freeway. It was nearly empty, which was good, and it was also relatively safe, given the circumstances. The lights were out there, too, but at least we were on a wide swath of asphalt and there weren't many other cars around to worry about.

We managed to find our turnoff and eased into Bellevue, where the streets looked like a war zone. They were covered with branches, and the wind was even worse over here on the East Side. Morio had to bypass the route we would have normally taken to Daniel's—we got halfway down the street and a huge old cedar lay stretched out across it, sparking power lines everywhere. Camille leaned forward.

"Smoke. I think one of the power lines is starting a fire on the tree." She called 911 and reported it. "We should get out of here before the fire engines block off the street."

Morio cautiously backed into one of the driveways, turning around, and we headed back the way we came. We managed to swing out just before the fire trucks came roaring down, hanging a right onto the street we'd just vacated. We watched them speed into the dark night.

After two more blocked streets we finally found a way through to the Lakefront Village Condo Community. The security guard was keeping watch as best as he could, given the security systems were off-line. He checked our names on the printed-out list of acceptable visitors and waved us in, then locked the door behind us. He handed us a flashlight and pointed to the stairs. The elevators were out of commission, of course.

We hiked it up to the fifth floor, passing one person who was on the way down from the third floor. He seemed groggy, though, and was carrying a beer, and as we passed, he let out a low "Shit, man," and continued on his way.

Fifth floor. Camille, who was first, eased open the door to glance down the hallway. She glanced back. "I don't see anybody in the hallway. Come on. Daniel's apartment is at the other end, near the elevators."

We headed down the hall, but as we drew near, we slowed. Morio, next to Camille, reached out to stop her. He glanced back and mouthed, "Door open," then crept forward. Another moment, and he motioned us forward.

In the beam of our flashlights, we could see that Daniel's apartment was a mishmash of clutter. A fight had taken place, that much was obvious, and I thought I saw a couple bullet holes in the wall. Considering Daniel used a silencer, it wasn't surprising the neighbors hadn't reported gunshots—if they had, the police would have been here. But why hadn't they reported a scuffle? The chrome and glass tables were a mess of shattered glass now, their frames bent. I mentioned my concern.

Camille shook her head. "Listen."

The wind rattled the windows, howling outside. Even from here, the steady thunk of branches hitting the street could be heard. The sounds of a fight would barely register over the noise of the windstorm. We checked through the entire apartment, though, and finally verified there was no sign of Daniel or his assailant.

Morio righted a pedestal that had held a very pricey vase. The vase was no longer in any condition to be placed back atop it. "We have to find Jay Miles and Aslo."

I picked up a broken figurine of a water nymph. "The Merlin said he can trace the sword through Leif. We're going to just have to go get Leif, beg him to go with us, and take him out to Talamh Lonrach Oll."

"The Merlin also explicitly refused to do so before the storm is over. You know how he is—there's not a chance in hell he'll help us tonight." Camille looked around, her shoulders sagging. "We can't do anything until morning. Or whenever this fucking storm decides to buy it."

A crash shattered our conversation as well as the balcony window, and a huge branch came whirling through. Daniel had double pane windows, so the gust that sent the limb into the air must have been hellacious.

"Crap. He's going to just love that." I headed into the kitchen, looking for a broom. At least he had hardwood floors and not carpet. Finding a whisk broom and dustpan, I headed over to clean up the mess.

"What are you doing?" Vanzir joined me. "Housecleaning?"

"I have to do something. If we can't make it out to Talamh Lonrach Oll now, then I need to keep myself busy."

"I think you need to sleep. Tomorrow we'll track down your cousin. Fretting all night isn't going to do anybody any good." He quietly took the broom and pan from me and set them aside. "Only one of the sliders was busted. Smoky and I can move an armoire in front of the broken panel, and we'll lock the door on the way out. That way, it won't be easy for any thieves to make it inside."

I relented. Vanzir was right. My head hurt like hell, we were all tired, and the storm was showing no signs of slowing down. I glanced at my phone. It was nearing midnight.

"Fine, let's go home. We'll get some sleep, and when we wake up, the storm will have moved through and we can focus on finding Daniel." With a grunt, I moved past Camille, who hugged me as I did. She waited till everyone was out, then locked the door behind us. We headed back to the stairs, and out past the doorman. We couldn't tell him Daniel was missing—he'd want to call the cops and there wasn't a damned thing they could do about it. So we just said good night, and returned to the SUV.

By now, the wind felt like it had been howling forever. I was tired of the sound, and when we got in the car, I leaned my head back against the seat and closed my eyes. I must have drifted off, because the next thing I knew, we were home again and Smoky was gently shaking me awake. He helped me out of the car and we all trooped inside to find Menolly waiting there. She jumped up.

"You're safe. I was going to call you but decided to save my bars. The street is flooding in front of the Wayfarer, but it's only edging over the sidewalk and I'm hoping the sand-bags will hold most of it at bay. Where were you?"

We told her everything, including our theory for why they wanted Daniel. Menolly groaned, dropping back into her chair.

"That sounds so horrible you have to be right. With our luck, he's being invested with Einar's soul right now and we're going to be walking through a remake of *The Exorcist*."

"Except Daniel isn't as cute as Linda Blair was." I rubbed my head and she noticed the marks.

"What the fuck happened to your head, Kitten?"

"Got attacked by a rogue branch. I wonder if we've lost any trees on the property yet." Suddenly infected by worry, I turned to Shade, who was just entering the room. "Have you checked on Iris and Bruce? Are they okay? And has Chase or Nerissa pinged us lately?"

"Iris and Bruce are snuggled up tight. I went down there about half an hour ago and they're fine. They're up, with the babies—they don't want to stay on their second floor right now, but the kids are sleeping and they had every-thing in hand when I dropped by. As far as Chase is con-cerned, I haven't heard a word from him or Nerissa for a while." Shade stoked the fire, adding another log. The flames flickered up, licking the edge of the new wood and crackling hold of it.

But Menolly set me at ease on that score. "Nerissa called me about twenty minutes ago. They're okay, but it's a good thing she stayed. They've had several fires to deal with—Supes who are now homeless. She has been having to track down shelter for them, and arrange for transportation."

"Then, I guess we just try to get some rest. Where do we want to sleep?"

Camille offered up her study to Shade and me. "If a tree

does come through the roof, it will be through the roof to your rooms. So stay on the second floor and you should be fine. Menolly, can you keep watch through the night? Call us if anything happens."

Menolly nodded. "Not a problem. Hanna isn't sleeping well—storms make her nervous, so I'll keep her and Maggie company. Maggie's up in arms because of the noise."

As we trailed up the stairs, the pain returned full force, and before I went to bed, Camille ran back downstairs and found the pain salve that Iris made. She rubbed some into the knot that had formed, then handed us blankets and pillows. The sofa in her study pulled out into a bed, and before long, Shade and I were in our PJs and snuggled beneath the covers.

"How are you doing, love?" I turned to him, slipping into his arms. We curled together, snuggling beneath the blanket. A battery-operated candle sat on the table next to us, providing a safe light source.

He sighed. "With so much going on, I think it's going to take me a long time to process all of this. But whatever happens, as long as we're together, I'll be all right."

I wanted to take away the worry in his voice, but love— as strong as it was—couldn't cure all ills. So I just kissed him silently and moved back over on my side of the bed. I liked my space when I slept, and thankfully, Shade was not a clingy person.

Taking one last glance at my phone, I saw that it was 1:00 A.M. I flicked the switch on the candle, and even though I didn't think I'd manage to fall asleep amid the constant roaring of wind and branches whipping against the house, within minutes I managed to drift off.

Camille woke us up by tapping on the door. She peeked around the edge. "It's eight o'clock. The storm's over and we should get a move on finding Daniel."

I yawned. My head throbbed but not as badly as the night before. As I slipped out from beneath the covers, I realized it was cold. "Jeez, turn up the heat, maybe?"

"Right. And I'll bring you Shadow Wing's head on a stick while I'm at it." Camille laughed as she entered the room. She was dressed in her spidersilk skirt and tunic from back in Otherworld, and wearing a leather corset over the top. She was also wearing knee-high soft leather boots with flat heels, which told me something was up.

"Heat? What heat? The power's out everywhere. We're going to have to light up the fireplaces for real. Smoky's outside, firing up the grill so we can heat water for coffee. The power company predicts it will be days before we're up and running in the outlying areas. They haven't even begun to assess the damage."

"Can't we just get some coffee when we head out?" I shivered. My flannel alley-cat kitty PJs weren't warm enough to stave off the chill. As I glanced at the window, I noticed it was still raining. "I thought you said the storm was over."

"The windstorm is. It's still raining. Morio got up early this morning and took our cell phones out to charge them in the car. He said the WeatherApp calls for drenching rain through the rest of the week. Going to be more trees falling from oversaturated root systems and wind damage."

"Any chance for a hot shower? Maybe?" I was hopeful, but Camille shook her head again.

"The well's out. Electric pump. Roz will look into buying a generator for it today but we kind of suspect they'll be sold out. So use wet wipes for your face and your hoo-haw, and come down to the kitchen. Hanna's also using the grill to heat up breakfast for us." She turned to go, but then glanced back. "Oh, minor damage to the roof but we lucked out. Vanzir scouted around the land—a number of downed trees but nothing that hit either our home or Iris's. The studio got clipped but it won't be a huge fix. The men will cut up the trees for firewood. We'll be set for a couple of years."

Shade watched her go, then slid out from beneath the covers. He was fully at attention and looked at me hungrily. "Do we have time before breakfast?"

I glanced at the clock. "Not much, but if you don't mind down and dirty and quick . . ." Then, I stopped. Truth was, my head still hurt. And I was cold. And hungry. "On second thought, do you mind if we just wait? I'm not in the best of shape and my head is throbbing."

He laughed, free and easy and with an understanding smile. "Not now, honey, you have a headache?" But he was teasing.

I grinned. "Yeah, I do. One hell of a headache."

"Let me see that bump of yours." He took a long look at it. "That tree really did a number on you. Okay, let's get dressed and get you downstairs for breakfast."

We headed up to our room, where we changed quickly because, even though heat rises, when there's no heat to begin with, there's nothing to rise to the top levels of the house. When we were sufficiently clothed, we clattered down the stairs. A rush of white darted by and I laughed—Camille's spirit kitty, Misty, was extremely playful. I usually wasn't very good at actually spotting more of her than a vaporous blur, but she stood out clear as crystal this morning.

"She has to go somewhere fast."

"Ghostly activity rises during power outages. Didn't you know that?" Shade cocked his head expectantly, but I just gave him a blank stare. "It's true. When the power is out, there's less electromagnetic interference and the spirits can run free easier."

As I thought over what he said, it suddenly occurred to me why I'd been so worried about the storm's effects on Einar. "That means, if the power outage is widespread and takes several days to repair, that Jay and Aslo will have a better chance of freeing Einar from the sword. The ghosts will be more active and easier to summon!"

A dark look washed over Shade's face. "Crap. You're right. Let's get down there now. We have to move on this."

As we were entering the kitchen, there was a knock on the door and I turned back to answer it. I opened the door to find myself staring at the Merlin.

"Um . . . come in?" I stepped back. "What . . . why . . . well . . . what can we do for you?" What did you say to the High Priest of the Hunter God when he arrived on your doorstep in full regalia, carrying a staff with antlers attached to it?

As he entered the foyer, he ignored my question. "I need to talk to Camille. We have a serious situation out at Talamh Lonrach Oll . . . and we need her out there immediately."

Chapter 17

Oh crap. Just what we needed. I led the Merlin into the kitchen. Camille was setting out paper plates and—on the back porch—Trillian had the grill fired up, and a tea-kettle was over the flames. He had a huge pan heating and a big bowl of eggs ready to scramble. Smoky had kept the contents of the refrigerator cold with his ice magic, and so we hadn't lost any food so far.

The house felt eerily quiet with the lack of electricity, almost like an underlying irritation had been eliminated. However, it made it chilly and I was annoyed that I couldn't use my laptop. The battery hadn't fully recharged on it and I didn't want to waste what was there.

Camille stopped short when she saw the Merlin. "Well, that solves our problem in coming out to you. We need to find Leif and have you help us—"

Myrddin held up his hand. "Yes, definitely bring him to me. But I need you out at Talamh Lonrach Oll. There has been . . . an incident. Aeval has summoned you and she asked me to make certain you understand—this takes priority over everything else."

Camille slowly set down the plates, a look of trepidation washing over her face. "Yes, of course. What about Leif?"

"Have one of the others bring him out. You are to come with me now." He paused, then glanced over at me. "You might as well come with her; this involves all three of you girls to an extent. Menolly cannot, of course, given the daylight hours." He crossed his arms, waiting.

Nodding, Camille glanced around the kitchen. "Hanna, be a dear. Can you fix a bag of rolls and cheese for us to take? We need food, and I need coffee, so fill a thermos. I'm going to grab my purse."

"I'm on it." Hanna bustled over to the counter and began quickly preparing a to-go breakfast for us.

"Should we take my car?" Camille asked Myrddin.

He grunted. "That works. But make haste."

She passed by me, tapping me on the arm. "Let's get our coats and purses." As we left the kitchen, she added to Morio, "Please go find Leif, tell him who you are, why we need him, and then drive him out to Talamh Lonrach Oll. Get him out there if you have to kidnap him. In fact, leave someone here to watch the house, but the rest of you come out."

Morio gave her a quick nod. "Of course."

I followed her into the living room, where we gathered our purses. "What do you think this is about?"

"I haven't the faintest idea, but Aeval wouldn't make me come out there with the roads like this unless it was important." She paused, closing her eyes. "Something huge is about to shift, Delilah. I can feel it. I don't know what it is, but it's going to be . . ." Another stop, then she shook her head, looking frustrated. "I can't quite pick it up, but something happened during the storm last night."

Slowly, I nodded. I was feeling the same thing—my body felt like it was vibrating from the energy, and I never felt this way except when I was in my Death Maiden aspect. "That storm brought in more than wind and rain. I'm afraid it's going to increase Einar's ability to jump from the sword to

Daniel, and every minute that goes by without us finding him is another step closer to losing him and gaining a blood-thirsty spirit for a cousin." I told her what Shade had told me.

It sounded funny, but truth was, I had started to grow fond of Daniel and I didn't want to see him hurt. He'd been through so many harrowing situations and I had no doubt that he'd faced down a barrage of weaponry, but then enter one rusty old iron sword possessed by a decrepit Viking chieftain and he was down for the count.

Camille didn't laugh, though. She took my hand and squeezed it, kissing it gently. "I know, I'm worried about him, too. Okay, let's get this show on the road. The sooner we find out what Aeval wants with me—with us—the sooner we can go hunting for Daniel."

We called for Myrddin and headed into the yard. The lawns and gardens were covered with debris—branches, branches everywhere. I saw at least one tree down near the driveway but it wasn't fully blocking it and we were able to ease out past it.

Camille drove cautiously. The roads were covered. The area looked like a hurricane had come through, and here and there, we saw downed lines but they ran along the edge rather than over it. But as we drove past the side roads, I noticed wires and trees everywhere blocking the narrow lanes. As we passed the nearest strip mall, I realized that nobody had power—not even the stores. There were no lights inside, but several stores had handwritten signs sitting outside their doors, indicating they were open for business.

An ambulance came roaring by, sirens blaring, followed by an equally loud fire engine. Camille pulled to the edge of the road until they had passed, and I wondered where they were going and who was hurt. Given the number of broken power lines, and given the number of candles and fireplaces going full force out there today, common sense predicted some nasty fires.

"So what do you think of the world today?" I decided to break the silence, which was becoming deafening.

But apparently, the Merlin wasn't in a chatty mood.

"As barbaric as ever," was his abrupt answer. I glanced back, but he was staring out the window. Every time we met, I liked him less, though he had promised his help against Shadow Wing. I had the feeling, though, he was used to being treated like the center of attention and now, in the modern world, he wasn't. But then, when I really thought about it, given the representations of him—from the comedic wizard in Disney's *Sword in the Stone*, to the power-hungry machinations of Merlin the Conqueror, he had been given a pretty rough reputation.

Camille pointed to a roadside fruit stand that we normally passed on our way out to the Fae Sovereign Nation. "Look—Sandro's . . . The stand is a mess. That sucks." She frowned. "They barely get by as it is."

The fruit stand was trashed. It was a freestanding structure, much like a newsstand, with a place for the cashier in back of the counter. Wide tables held the fruit or vegetables or whatever else they might be selling. A large fir had crashed down on top of it and split the stand in two, destroying the tables with the branches. Rhonda Lopez—Sandro's wife—was standing there, staring at it. Her kids were milling around, looking confused. Sandro was nowhere in sight.

"I wonder if they have insurance." But even as I said it, I knew how ludicrous that sounded. The family was poor, but they worked their asses off to build their business. "I wonder if we can help."

"Why don't you start up a phone tree with the Supe Community Crisis Center—tell them that one of our own needs help. Sandro and his family are Weres. I forget what they shift into, but I remember they were at a meeting last year. Maybe we can organize a community drive to help them out." She changed lanes. We were near the exit to Talamh Lonrach Oll.

"You know, I'd totally forgotten they were Were. I'll do that." I made a note on my list. I'd found it best to write things down when they occurred to me or they'd vanish under the ever-growing to-do list.

Another ten minutes and we managed to make it to the

gates of Talamh Lonrach Oll. A carriage was waiting for us, and Myrddin silently motioned for us to get in. He remained silent as we approached the Barrow palaces.

Camille gasped as we rounded the bend, and my own jaw dropped. There was a heavily armed contingent of guards standing in front of Morgaine's barrow. The carriage slowed and Myrddin hopped out. The guards escorted us down the steps, as the Merlin, still silent, waited for us. He turned then, and—with us in tow—headed into the barrow.

As we passed through the halls, the Fae had gathered in small groups, and they were all whispering. The moment we came into view, however, the / fell silent until we'd passed. Myrddin looked neither to the right nor to the left, just led us on through the maze until we came to the outside of a large chamber that was heavily guarded. One of the guards stood back, allowing us access to the door.

Myrddin opened the door and motioned to Camille. "Go in. Aeval is waiting for you." He shook his head when I started to follow. "Lady Camille first. You will be called in after Aeval has her say."

One of the guards brought me a chair and I settled in to wait. I tried to gauge the mood of what was going on, but it was almost impossible. The guards here were stoic, and they gave nothing away in their expressions. The Merlin was even worse.

Fifteen minutes later, the door inched open and there was a whispered exchange. One of the guards motioned for me to go in. Both curious, and a little wary, I entered the room to find myself in Morgaine's bedchamber. To the right of the bed, Aeval was sitting on a bench. Titania was standing near her, and Camille was sitting between them on a chair. She looked stunned.

It was then that I noticed Morgaine. She was in the bed, lying back against the pillows with her eyes closed and her hair streaming down over her breasts. She was wearing a gown of purple and blue . . . delicate and shimmering with beads. She didn't open her eyes when I came in. Something struck me as odd, and I looked at her again. It was then that I noticed that Morgaine wasn't breathing. She was still as a sculpture . . . still as ice . . . still as the grave.

I walked over to her and leaned down. There was no breath. And her face was paler than usual, the alabaster of her skin shimmering with a faint bluish cast.

I didn't need to ask. I had seen enough corpses in my life to recognize death. Uncertain how I felt—I'd never really liked her, but I sure hadn't wished her any harm—I sought for something to say. "How did she die?"

"Her own hand." Titania sounded incredibly distant. Her voice was like the tinkling of summer flutes on the wind. I turned around and found her staring at me, with a soft, sad smile. "Morgaine poisoned herself. She managed to get hold of some Bellavonna."

Bellavonna, a drink made from belladonna, hemlock, wolfsbane, and honey, was a deadly mixture with a sweet taste, and was the drug of choice for Supes who had lived so long they were tired of the world.

"Did she *really* kill herself?" Morgaine had been a fire-cracker, a take-no-prisoners, no-holds-barred type of woman. It was a hard image to reconcile with the idea that she'd killed herself. "The Morgaine we knew wouldn't let anything beat her down."

Aeval let out a soft sigh. "She was not the Morgaine you knew. Not since Arthur and Mordred died. She's been sinking deeper and deeper into her fugue. The only times she seemed to surface was when she would find something of theirs—a shirt or a belt or a photo. Then, she would sit and cry for hours. Morgaine could handle anything except the loss of the two people who kept her going all these years. She lived to take care of them. Once they were gone, so was her reason for living. When we found Mordred's body, it was the final straw."

Her words hit me, then. I slowly sat down on the edge of the bed beside our long-distant cousin, feeling unaccountably sad. Camille rose and joined me, on the other side of the bed. She took one of Morgaine's hands, and I held the other as we whispered our prayer for the dead.

"What was life has crumbled. What was form, now falls away. Mortal chains unbind and the soul is lifted free. May you find your way to the ancestors. May you find your path to the gods. May your bravery and courage be remembered in song and story. May your parents be proud, and may your children carry your birthright. Sleep, and wander no more."

Camille silently replaced Morgaine's hand, folding her arm so it rested on her chest. I did the same.

"Camille, you should tell your sister your news." Aeval sounded both relieved and yet pensive. "Delilah, the only ones who are to know this are you, Menolly, and Camille's husbands. None of the others—not yet. We cannot risk this news getting out yet, and the implementation of it will take a long while yet."

I frowned. What the hell was going on now? I turned to Camille.

Camille glanced over at the two Fae Queens, then, with a look that read both petrified and awestruck, she came around the bed and sat down next to me, taking my hands. "Aeval and Titania . . . they've decided that eventually I'm to take Morgaine's place. I'm not only going to be the first Earthside High Priestess for the Moon Mother, I'm going to be the Queen of Dusk and Twilight."

Of course, that shifted my entire focus. While I was worried about Daniel, he fell to the background as I tried to take in what she'd just said. I looked at Aeval, then Titania, and they both nodded.

"When . . . How did you . . ." I didn't know what to say. The idea was so huge, so life-shifting, that it felt like there was suddenly an elephant in the room and I had no clue how it got here.

Aeval stood, and by the look on her face, I realized this wasn't up for discussion. "The Hags of Fate have decreed it so. And Titania and I concur. Camille's destiny has led her here, and it is here that she will make her home when the time comes."

"It will take quite some time, of course. She must be properly trained, and you must get through this war first. But Aeval is correct. Camille is ours. She belongs to Aeval's court until then, but she will have her own as time passes." Titania beamed me a smile so warm that I almost forgot my hesitation.

Camille hadn't said a word, and I wanted to ask her how she felt, but I was smart enough to realize this was neither the time nor the place. She had to walk a tightrope here, and if she had any hesitations or fears, it was better she express them in private.

She caught my gaze, and I could tell she was pleading with me to just let it be for now. Given that they weren't talking immediate coronation, I decided to bite my tongue and keep my misgivings to myself for the moment.

"I really have no clue of what to say. That's . . ." I let my words drift, hoping it would sound like something other than what I was thinking.

"As I said, you, your sister Menolly, and Camille's husbands are the only ones who may know." Aeval gave me a long look and I suddenly felt like she was probing into my energy, searching for something.

A thought occurred to me. I could be playing a dangerous game here, but if we knew, then the whole household would find out. There was no way to exclude the others.

"Lady Aeval . . . surely the rest of our family needs to know. Rozurial and my fiancé, Shade, Nerissa and . . . *Vanzir.* You understand how hard it can be to keep *secrets* from getting out." I met her gaze and her eyes burned like glowing coal as she stared me down.

In that moment, I noticed someone standing behind Aeval. I started to say something but then I realized I was staring at Morgaine, who was glaring down at the Fae Queen. She looked up, blinked as she saw me looking at her, and let out a crafty smile as she headed my way.

Aeval let out a huff. "Very well. But make sure it goes no further for now. Raven Mother must not know." Disconcerted, because Morgaine's translucent form was now standing beside me, and she was giving me a snarky look, I stammered out, "Thank you. And we'll make sure she doesn't find out." I glanced at Camille, who was giving me a cautionary shake of the head. She didn't seem to see Morgaine. I decided the best thing to do would be to beat a hasty retreat so I could figure out what the hell was going on. "We have to go find our cousin Daniel. He's in danger."

Aeval gave me an odd look, as though she sensed something was up, but then she shrugged nad nodded. "Go, if you need to. We will notify you when we arrange the service for Morgaine. I'm sorry she wasn't strong enough to manage the shock. Morgaine had her faults, but she was growing on me."

At that point, Morgaine gave Aeval the finger and stuck her tongue out. I burst out with a snicker and Aeval blinked, staring at me for a moment before saying, "I understand you have asked the Merlin for his aid."

I forced myself to regain some semblance of control and nodded. "He has the power to trace something we're looking for."

"Then go, and be off to your duties." The Queen of Shadow and Night was still watching me closely as we crossed to the door. "Delilah?"

I turned, to find her right behind me. The Fae Queens moved as silently as the creeping dusk.

"Yes?" I might be taller than she, but she scared the hell out of me when she got this close. The Elder Fae might be loco bananas, but the Fae Queens knew exactly what they were doing and that seemed almost more frightening.

"Be cautious. Curious kittens often find themselves caught up in a tangled skein of trouble. Watch your step, that you don't make a wrong turn. Is my meaning clear?" Her voice was low, but the threat echoed clearly in my ears.

"Yeah . . . I hear you." I tried to break off eye contact, but she held me fast. I inhaled a slow, deep breath. "Loud and clear."

"Good. We understand one another, then." She motioned to Titania. "Come. We have a funeral to plan, sister."

At that, both Camille and I whirled around. Camille,

who had been silent during the whole exchange, asked, "*Sister?* Are you sisters, then?"

Aeval laughed. "In the long distant past, yes. We were born to parents who stood outside of the Summer and Winter courts and we were parted when we were young. I can barely remember those days, they were so long ago."

Titania looped her arm through Aeval's. "Too true. But the world changes, the Wheel turns, and we adapt. So now, we are three queens instead of two, and we find that a much healthier balance. Camille . . . you will join us and the Barrows will thrive as Talamh Lonrach Oll takes its rightful place in the coming world." With that, the pair followed us out of the room. I glanced around, but Morgaine had vanished, too, and I wondered if I'd really been seeing her ghost, or if the bump on my head had been more serious than we thought. On the way to the outer chamber, I wanted to tell Camille what I'd seen, but the chances of being overheard were far too great.

Camille and I found the Merlin standing in the corner, watching us closely as we crossed the hall to him. Impatient, I wanted to get all of this over with so Camille and I could talk. But Daniel's life was in danger and so I focused on the immediate business at hand.

He waited till we were near to speak. "So you know."

I nodded, glancing at Camille. Speaking out in front of Myrddin was problematic, too, because we were in no way clear as to where we stood with him.

"Cat got your tongue?" He smiled at me.

"I think we should focus on Daniel for now," was all I said.

Camille backed me up. "Kitten's right. We have a lot to think about, and a lot to process, but first we have to take care of Daniel and the sword."

Myrddin scanned our faces, and once again I felt like we were being probed for our reactions. I remained as stoic as I could, trying to give away none of my thoughts. I didn't feel safe here. The politics ran thick and deep, and even though we were half-Fae, our Earthside counterparts were used to hiding their agendas and keeping under the radar. That made them stealthier than we were and, therefore, more dangerous.

After another moment, Myrddin let out a disgruntled sigh and motioned for us to follow him. "Morio is here, with the man. And the others. They are waiting for us."

We wound through the barrow. It was obvious the news was out—everywhere the Fae looked stricken. We might not have taken to Morgaine much, but it looked like her people had appreciated her. As we walked, a low drumming began to filter through the halls.

"The drummers will continue until her burial rites." Myrddin escorted us into his chambers, but stopped before we were fully into the living space. "Something you need to know about your cousin: Her destiny was originally slated to be glorious and magical. What happened to her was not approved by the Hags of Fate. It set up an imbalance in the web and changed the history of the Fae here, Earthside. The Hags cannot repair it to what it should have been, but Camille—you are their answer to bringing it back into stability. Do you understand what this means?"

She caught her breath, and again, I saw the wash of fear race through her eyes. But she inclined her head. "Yes, Lord Myrddin. I do."

"Then let us take care of your current problem. There is all the time in the world to discuss your future." And with that, he led us into the living room, where Morio, Smoky, and Vanzir were sitting there. Leif was waiting with them.

"Trillian and Roz?" I looked around.

"Home with Hanna and Maggie. Nerissa called. She's going to be practically living at the station the next few days, given the damage that's been done. A lot of houses are sporting holes thanks to all the trees that fell." Vanzir stretched, but he kept a careful eye on Camille. "You okay? You look a little pale."

Smoky noticed the interaction, but instead of grumbling at Vanzir, he scoped out Camille, too, and apparently noticed the shift in her mood. "Are you all right?"

"We'll talk later. Right now, we need to deal with the sword."

I walked over to Leif, who had a glazed expression on his face like he'd just climbed through the looking glass. He was sitting very straight and very still. "You doing okay?"

"I feel like I just wandered into an alternate universe. I knew about this place—everybody does—but nobody I know has ever been out here." He lowered his voice. "I'm afraid of offending somebody and getting my head chopped off or something."

I snorted. "We're half-Fae; do we really seem like monsters?" But I was grateful we weren't dealing with the Elder Fae right now. No use giving the poor guy a heart attack. "Leif, we think we can track the sword but we need you here, because you are connected by blood to Einar."

"What do I need to do?" He still sounded nervous, but seemed eager to help. As one of the serving girls wandered by, his gaze flickered to her ass, but he immediately reined himself in, as though he sensed I was watching.

"Come here and sit in front of me, put out your hands, and *do not move*." It was obvious that Myrddin was done with small talk.

"He's not familiar with magic, Lord the Merlin. You might want to explain what you're doing. Especially if you have anything wiggy going on there." I had a horrible vision of Myrddin drawing a dagger out for part of the spell and Leif shrieking his head off, thinking he was going to be sacrificed.

That actually elicited a faint smile from the druid. His gaze flickered to Leif, then back to me. "You might be on to a good idea there."

While he began to explain to Leif what he was going to do, I wandered over to Camille. She still looked a little shell-shocked. I still wasn't sure whether to tell her about seeing Morgaine's spirit, but first I wanted to find out how she was. "You okay?"

"I guess. I have no fucking clue what this is going to

mean for my life. And . . ." She glanced around, then lowered her voice. "What will Smoky, Morio, and Trillian say
when I tell them that, *'Guys, one day in the future you have
to move out to the Fae nation with me because I get to play
Fae Queen?'* I mean, I know it's quite a ways off. There's so
much I have to learn first, and my first duty is to the Moon
Mother as a priestess. But . . . this changes the game on
everything."

A sadness crept into her voice and I suddenly realized
that both destinies—ES High Priestess, and ES Fae
Queen—came down to one inexorable conclusion: Camille
would never be returning to Otherworld to live.

"You're here for good." The words slipped out before I
could stop them.

She gave me a melancholy smile. "Yeah, I knew that
already, when I was told I'd become the first Earthside
High Priestess, but it never really sank in. Not till now. Not
till Aeval brought it glaringly home today."

"We're ready." Myrddin called us over. "Just stand back
far enough so you don't interfere with the weaving of the
spell." He shooed everybody else out of the way, and then,
with Leif sitting in a chair in the center of the room, the
Merlin began to cast his magic.

Using an antler-handled dagger, he drew a triangle
around Leif, weaving a trail of green light that sparkled
out from the tip of the blade. As he closed the triangle, he
began to draw other sigils in the air, swirls and what looked
like staves from the Celtic Ogham, but I had a feeling they
predated the runic alphabet by a long, long time. After he
finished, he began to sing, and it was then that I understood why Áine—the Merlin's girlfriend who was forever
locked within dragon form—had fallen in love with him.
His voice lilted over the words, the melody trilling and
hypnotic as it wove a spiral that turned into a labyrinth,
that invited us to follow it into the core of the song.

My panther self responded, not in defense, but I wanted
to transform and follow this man into the woods, deep into
the forest wild. There was something primal about his

nature. The magic that rolled off the Merlin was feral and wild and rose up like the Antlered God. Camille was drawing closer, too, her eyes rapt as she watched him, and Morio had inched forward, a look of wonder on his face.

Myrddin rose up, the mask of humanity falling away, and he stood there, against the shadow of the Antlered God. He was the chosen of Herne, of the Horned One who danced through the forests and called all witches and wild creatures to follow in his wake. Passion rolled off him, and strength, and the musky scent that drove forth the desire to rut, to mate, to burn.

Leif was staring at him with a radiant look on his face, like someone who has just found his reason for living. Tears ran down his face as the Merlin circled him, whispering in a language I did not understand. It was old and guttural and yet . . . beautiful.

The guards who were watching had set down their weapons, equally enthralled. As I watched Myrddin, I realized that the arrogance and the singular focus—it all went with his position. He was the High Priest of the Hunter; he had to stand outside the rules. His focus was on the bigger picture.

Suddenly wishing Shade were here, I slowly dropped to one knee. Camille was already down on her knees, entranced by the spell and magic. I closed my eyes, still listening, and that was when I made the connection.

You understand now?

Hi'ran was there, sweeping around me, his words a whisper on the wind. I realized then: His energy stemmed from the same core as the magic surrounding the Merlin, except for being from a different season. The Autumn Lord's fires were the same as the bonfires around which the witches and celebrants danced. Everything was entwined. The Hunter, he was the heart of the forest, whether it was summer or autumn or winter or spring. Hi'ran ruled over the autumn winds of that forest. Though not the same entity, they were connected by the underlying energy of the forest and the turning of the Wheel.

I think so . . . I think I'm on the edge of it.

You are beginning to perceive the threads of the web that interconnect everything in this universe. You and your sister Camille are not so different. She follows the wild goddess and the wild god . . . you are pledged to the Autumn spirits. But they are of the same essence. The Wheel may turn with the seasons, but the world is still the same world. Remember this . . . it will play into your own transformation.

I thought about Shade. *Can you help him? What will happen to us?*

Shade will rise triumphant out of this. Remember: All transformations happen for a reason. The Hags of Fate weave the web, and even seemingly disparate shifts fit into the tapestry. Now be at peace. The cycles move, the Wheel turns, and each step builds on the last.

And then, with a feather's touch, he was gone. I opened my eyes. The Merlin was doing something with his hands—playing with a ball of energy or something. As I looked closer, he stretched the thin mist into a wide ellipse and the fog began to shimmer. As we watched, the image of the sword appeared in the center of it.

"Mark and set." The Merlin clapped his hands and the image shimmered once, flared, and then vanished. The triangle of energy around Leif disappeared and the room returned to normal.

Feeling like I'd just tumbled down from a drugged high, I blinked and stood. Morio helped Camille to her feet. We walked over to Myrddin and Leif, who had a radiant look on his face.

"What happened?" I glanced from one man to the other.

Leif started to speak, then burst into tears and shook his head.

But the Merlin smiled. "You'll find the sword—and Daniel—at 37501 Sythica Street."

"That sounds familiar . . ." Camille frowned. "I can't remember why, but I know that address."

"I know, same here. But I can't find out why until we go outside." We couldn't use our cell phones in the Barrows—

the energies disrupted them, but she was right. I knew that address, too, but couldn't quite place it.

Morio stepped forward. "I know exactly what that address is. It's smack in the heart of the Greenbelt Park District. That's the address of the Greenbelt Asylum. Or rather, the ruins of the mental institution. The one that burned down during an inmate riot. They're keeping Daniel there. It would make sense—with so much ghostly activity there. And with the power out all over town . . ."

"It's going to be jumping with spirits. All the better to feed Jay's army of the dead he's trying to raise." My stomach lurched. The most haunted district in the city was a dangerous and frightening place. And while we had never had the misfortune to enter the ruins of the asylum before, it looked like now we were going to have to. And that was going to be one *hell* of a trip.

Chapter 18

❧❦❧

"We'll need to take Leif with us, in order for him to claim possession of the sword once we put a stop to whatever's going on. But I don't like putting him in danger." Camille frowned. "We'll have to make certain to watch him." She looked at me. "Shade . . . he has no powers over the dead anymore, right?"

I knew what she was asking. We'd come to count on his ability to—if not outright control, at least understand—what kind of dead we were up against. "No powers over them. But let me call and find out if he can still get a good read on them. That would be a huge help, considering where we're going."

Camille gave me a solemn look and then glanced at Morio. We'd almost lost him to angry ghosts sometime back, a grim reminder that we were all vulnerable, for all of our powers and abilities.

I headed out of the barrow and, in the pounding rain, put in a call to Shade. I'd have to charge my phone in the car again—the bars were getting low. He answered after a couple rings.

"My phone's getting low, love. I was about to go out to your Jeep to charge it. What do you need?"

"Everything at home okay?" We always checked. It was our first priority when any of us called home anymore.

"Everything's fine. Cold, but fine. I've been putting piles of rocks around the different rooms in heatproof bowls and firing them up so they at least emanate some heat. Iris and Bruce are okay. What did you find out? What's going on?"

"So much . . . I can't even begin to tell you, but what I need now is to ask you something and it might sting a little, but we need to know." I rushed on, telling him what we were facing and asking if he could still sense ghosts, even if he couldn't control them.

Shade hesitated, then said, "Yes, I can. I can sense them but I can't do anything against them. I may be able to still talk to them, but I don't know yet."

"Love, I talked to Hi'ran. I'll tell you what he said later, but this is all in the scheme of things. We need you now. Meet us at the ruins of the Greenbelt Asylum. We'll be there as soon as we can. We're bringing Leif—he has to be there."

At that moment Camille and the others emerged from the barrow. The carriage was waiting—two, in fact—and we climbed in and rode back to the parking lot. Neither Myrddin nor the Fae Queens joined us.

Camille and I rode in one of the carriages, Smoky, Morio, Vanzir, and Leif in the other. Camille started to say something, then closed her mouth, pointing to the roof, where the driver sat. The chances of being overheard were still too great. So we rode in silence till we reached the parking lot.

"The guys are going in Morio's SUV. I don't want to tell them about . . . you know. Not yet. Not till I've had time to process the news."

"What about Morgaine?"

"Oh, we have to tell them about her. But about me . . . hold off. We'll talk to Menolly tonight, though." She started the ignition and we pulled out of the parking lot, followed by the men.

After a couple minutes, I told Camille about what the Autumn Lord had said to me. "Things are changing for all of us. I wonder where we'll all end up." And then, hesitating, I told her about Morgaine's spirit. "I have no clue what it means."

"You're a Death Maiden—maybe it's something to do with her death. I'm glad she seems back to her old self, though. Anything's better than the fog she was lost in." She glanced at me, then back at the road. "Do you think you'll end up raising the Autumn Lord's child Earthside or in Otherworld? If it was over here . . ." The hopeful note in her voice told me she was thinking just what I was: If I raised his daughter here, we wouldn't be separated. She didn't want to be split off from me and Menolly any more than we wanted to be broken apart from her. Our destinies were vastly different, and we had our loves, but we were sisters—and we'd been tightly bonded since childhood.

"I hope so." I smiled at her. "But that's a while off, I think. So let's focus on taking care of this problem before we dive into solving another."

"Can you call Carter while we're on the road and ask him for anything else he might have on the Greenbelt Asylum? Ask him if he has any floor plans for it. Granted things shift over the years, especially when you're a pile of rubble . . . but it would be nice to know what we're headed into."

I plugged my phone into Camille's charger and then punched up Carter's contact number. He was a demigod of sorts. He was half-demon, half-Titan. His father was the Titan Hyperion, the father of the sun and the moon. And he had devoted his life to the Demonica Vacana Society.

I put him on hold and—in a flash of inspiration—called Smoky. "I'm going to bring you into the call with Carter, but don't put it on speaker phone—you have Leif in the car. We don't want any potential secrets spilled in front of him. But you can tell the others what they need to know after we're done."

"Can do," Smoky said, and I tapped Carter back in so we were on a three-way conference call.

Carter swore when I told him what we were facing. "Wonderful. Just what we need to stir up things again. But I can't get on the computer. Power is out here, too. I'm going into withdrawal. I have to figure out a solution for outages—there's no place for a generator in a basement apartment without suffocating oneself. But I can check that scrapbook I showed you sometime back to see what I have on the asylum."

For someone who lived in a rather antiquated apartment—he was retro beyond the point of retro—Carter was extraordinarily tech savvy.

"Before I go prowl through the filing cabinet, I have some news for you. Unwelcome news on the Shadow Wing front."

I let out a long sigh. Shadow Wing had focused his efforts over in Otherworld for a while now, and we'd had a chance to breathe here—well, breathe as far as he was concerned. But now . . .

Camille darted a quick look my way.

"Let me put you on speaker so Camille can hear what you have to say."

"Can you all hear me?" His voice sounded tinny through the speaker, but he was clear.

"I can hear you," Smoky's voice crackled through.

I nodded, then realized neither of them could see me. "Go ahead. And can you e-mail all of this to us when you get power back? Whenever that happens." I was already getting tired of the storm damage. As it was, we still didn't know just how widespread the storm had been, or how bad.

"Sure. Okay, here's the thing. There's a new demon general on the rise. Shadow Wing is being very closemouthed about him, but I'm looking into matters. I'll let you know as soon as I find out what you're facing. All I know is this is worse than any you've faced before. This may be the vanguard before Shadow Wing himself manages to break through." Carter sounded worried, and when Carter was worried—it meant there was reason for it.

Camille swerved to avoid a large branch in the road. She had the windshield wipers going full steam and the rain was still pounding down. "Worse than Gulakah? And do you know if he—she—is in the area yet?"

"Yes, and I have no idea. Whoever it is, they might already be here. I don't even know if Shadow Wing has located another of the spirit seals and that's why he's sending out someone new. I'm not sure. I wish I had more to give you on this, but with everything down, there's not much I can do. Okay, now I'll go find that scrapbook. I think I know where it is. I'll be right back."

We continued along. The roads weren't that cluttered with traffic—people were still feeling the aftermath of the storm. And the rains were continuing to cause havoc. As we passed one side road that sloped down, I saw that—at the bottom—it was covered with water and a tree was sprawled across it.

"Being on the roads today? Dangerous."

"Back." Carter came back on the line and we could hear him flipping through pages. "As we discussed before, the Greenbelt Asylum was in operation for fifty years before an inmate burned it to the ground. The owners were abusive. They also owned five hundred acres buttressing the grounds of the asylum, the majority of which has been sold off over the years."

"Do you have floor plans?"

"Not at hand, just on the computer. But I do know that the basement contained the boiler room, and that's where the explosion happened. There were over three hundred and fifty deaths, and even more patients, so the asylum covered a large area. The building was—in its heyday—five stories high, not counting the basement. You'll find some of the old ruins still there. A good share of it was lost to the fire, but parts of it still exist, including one of the west wing towers. I think."

"You said that atrocities happened there?"

"Right. Electroshock therapy, starvation therapy, and there's a lot of reports that the owners raped, abused, and outright murdered the patients. There were rumors that some medical experimentation was practiced and covered up. The hauntings in the area are thick—even with you having defeated Gulakah, it's going to take decades for it to settle down, and with the energy hangover from something like the asylum, I don't know how much it ever will."

"Anything else you can tell us about the actual asylum's layout? Where was the entrance?" We needed every scrap of information we could cull on the area. Going blind into a burnt-out shell of a building wasn't easy under the best of circumstances. And with the power outage giving the ghosts a one-up, I had my doubts we'd have luck on our side.

"From what I can tell, the entrance was on the Sythica Street side. Do you need the address?"

I double-checked my notes. "No, we have it—37501 Sythica, right?"

"Yes. The main entrance was on that side. From what I remember, the dining hall was on the main floor, and the medical facilities were supposed to have been on the fourth floor. I guess they didn't want to risk any of the inmates' relatives figuring out what was going on. I think one corner tower still stands that might have had some of those rooms."

Carter let out a deep breath. "To be honest, I think the entire thing should be razed and then bring in a group of various exorcists from different religions to sweep through and clear the area. But the city considers the Greenbelt Asylum an historical landmark. As hideous as it was and as broken down, they aren't going to tear it down anytime soon. Plus, I still think it's owned by family."

I glanced at Camille. "I guess . . . that's it then. Thanks, Carter. If you think of anything else that might be helpful, let us know."

"Be safe, girls. I can only warn you that the asylum holds more dangers now than it did when it was fully functional. Because the ghosts cannot be so easily stopped, whereas humans can be, once you know what they're up to." He signed off.

"We're walking into a powder keg." I glanced at the clock. It was going on eleven. "At least it's not the middle of the night, but that doesn't guarantee us anything in terms of the ghosts."

Camille slowed down. We were coming off the freeway, back into Seattle, and none of the streetlights were working. People were out and about by now, looking for coffee and hot food, but there were no coffee shops open. Nothing was open. Well, almost nothing. One supermarket appeared to be running on generators and its doors were open. Would be cold as hell in there, but they were getting food to their customers.

"Want to make a bet they're sold out of candles and flashlights?" I pointed at the store as we passed.

"Want to make a bet they'll be sold out of canned goods and batteries, as well? I hope Roz can find a generator, but given the circumstances, I wouldn't bet on it." She cautiously proceeded through an intersection.

Most of the drivers seemed to be taking extra care, but I wasn't sure how long it would last. People could be gracious until they were tired of being put out, and then they turned nasty. With luck, we wouldn't reach that point before the electric company managed to get things up and running again.

While I was thinking about it, I flipped on the radio and tuned into a local station. The news was not good.

"Over two million households along the Western Washington coastline are without power at this point. There are no estimates on when power will be restored, but fifty crews from neighboring states have been dispatched to help with the recovery. Be careful—there are downed power lines everywhere, and hundreds of trees fell during the windstorm. The rain has saturated the ground so much that meteorologists expect more falling trees throughout the day, as root systems weakened by the windstorm give way. Seattle should expect heavy rains today through Wednesday. Rains will taper off on Thursday, and the weekend may bring some dry weather."

I glanced over at Camille. "Not too promising, is it?"

She shook her head. "We need to rethink how we heat the house."

"Yeah, you're right." I quieted down as the announcer continued.

"There have been at least three deaths from the storm so

far—a car was hit by a falling tree over on the Maple Valley Highway, killing the driver and injuring the passenger. A brother and sister were killed when their house caught fire. The parents managed to make it out with minor injuries but the house was engulfed by flames before anyone could rescue the children. The cause of the fire is suspected to be stray sparks from the fireplace. Police are issuing a warning: Do not use lighter fluid on the logs in your fireplace. On to other news, we are working on getting a list of stores, restaurants, and hotels that still have power for our next update. Meanwhile, if you spot downed power lines, please call Puget Sound Power at the following number . . ."

I flipped the radio off. "Yeah, this is going to be a big old bundle of fun." The thought of a hot meal sounded really good right about now. At least we could grill on the back porch, and we had dragons to warm up next to. It occurred to me that now would be a good time for a vacation, but I decided not to even trot that idea out until we were done for the day.

We entered the Greenbelt Park District and immediately the energy shifted around me. I noticed an upswing in foot traffic along the sidewalk, and at first, I wondered why so many people were out wandering around through the storm damage, but then it hit me. I stiffened as I realized they were shadow shapes. I was actually *seeing* spirits walk along the sidewalk.

"Camille . . ."

"Yeah?" She swerved to avoid another large limb lying in the street.

"Do you see anything . . . out of the ordinary?" I knew it wasn't my imagination, but—even with seeing Misty and Morgaine so clearly—I still wasn't sure of myself. I had seen some pretty wacky things, but seeing ghosts casually walking by? Not really my forte.

"Not in particular, not counting the debris all over the road." As if she heard the underlying hesitation in my voice, she pulled over to the curb. "What's wrong, Kitten?"

I watched a woman walk by a chain-link fence enclosing a dirt lot. She was wearing a dress from what looked like the 1930s and she seemed oblivious to everything. She was also translucent and vaporous. I pointed in her direction.

"What do you see?"

Camille followed my finger. "A dirt lot. Fence. Litter on the sidewalk. Why? What do you see?"

"I see a woman . . ." I described the spirit to her. "And she's not the only one. I'm seeing people everywhere on the sidewalk. I don't know what's going on, and to be honest, it's making me a little nervous."

Her hands clutching the wheel, she squinted, still staring straight ahead. "I don't see anything. Maybe if Morio and I were together, I would but . . . Kitten, when did this start?"

"This morning, with Misty. Then with Morgaine and now, as we entered the district." I thought back to what I'd been talking about with Arial. And how Hi'ran had mentioned several times that I was growing and evolving in his service. "I think . . . it has something to do with my being a Death Maiden. This is connected to the Autumn Lord."

Camille's next question startled me. "Can you speak to them?"

I hadn't even considered that. I didn't really want to find out either. Most of our interactions with spirits were hostile, to say the least. "I don't know. Want me to try?"

She glanced in the rearview mirror. "Morio has pulled over in back of us. Why don't you get out and give it a go. If you need help, we'll be here. I'll come with you."

We slowly got out of the car. At first, the shadow shapes on the sidewalk didn't seem to notice, but then one of them—a man in a business suit—glanced over. I caught the man's gaze and he stopped in his tracks, tilting his head to the right. I slowly moved forward, my hands up to show that I wasn't armed. Although what the hell I could do to a ghost with my dagger, I wasn't sure. The spirit stood there as I advanced, looking more and more confused.

"Hello, can you hear me?" I had no clue what to say but that seemed as good a choice as any.

All hell broke loose. Half the shadow shapes I saw on the sidewalk suddenly stopped and whirled, staring at me. Then, before I could even blink, about fifteen of them began rushing toward me, and a cacophony of voices filled my head. The thundering of shouts sent me reeling and I staggered, hands over my ears, as they surrounded me. The clamor was so loud that I couldn't think, could barely breathe.

"Help! Stop, please stop . . . please be quiet!" I struggled to speak through the cacophony that filled my head. Their voices were like angry bees, out of phase and too quick for me to understand.

"Kitten . . . Kitten! Are you—" Camille was waving her arms through the spirits, but they didn't pay any attention to her. I did the only thing I could think of and sent out a mental cry for help to Greta, my trainer. The next moment, she was standing there, and blessed silence filled my ears. The ghosts were on the outside, pounding against the invisible barrier she had created around us. She leaned down and helped me to stand.

"Where are we?" We appeared to be on the sidewalk, but now it was Camille who looked out of phase, rather than the spirits.

"We're between the world of the living and the dead. Don't worry about your sister—this is taking place outside of time. She won't think you've disappeared." Greta smiled then, and let out a long sigh. "So this has come already. I didn't expect it for a while yet, but then again, you are still alive so your evolution can't be measured against the rest of the Maidens."

"What has come? What's happening to me?" Whatever it was, I wasn't so hot on it. "I can do without a migraine brought on by spirit chipmunk chatter."

Greta snorted. "Leave it to you, Delilah, to turn a major milestone in your path into a cartoon reference, and yes— before you ask—I know what you're talking about. They only sound like that because you haven't learned how to listen to them yet."

"Yet?" I had a feeling I knew what was coming. "You mean I'm joining the *I-can-see-dead-people* ranks?"

Greta nodded. "All Death Maidens reach a point in their training where they gain the power to see the dead. As I said, it usually comes later, but then we've never had a living member of the group. That said, it's going to make things problematic for you until you learn to turn it on and off."

"You mean I don't have to see them every which way I look? Because this is getting creepy." I stopped. Foot-in-mouth struck again. Greta was a spirit, and so were the rest of my Death Maiden sisters.

But she just grinned. "Creepy, perhaps, but you'll learn to control it. We'll have to start training you as soon as you've finished what you need to be doing here. Pretty soon, it will be like turning a light switch off and on."

"Is it just ghosts . . . or other astral hauntings? I'm not so familiar on the world of the spirits." And then it hit me . . . Shade would know a lot about this. "Shade can help, too . . . except . . ."

"I know what happened. We'll talk later. But for now, I can mask your hearing for a short time. And I can give you a sort of invisibility to them—they will not know you can see them, unless you want them to. I cannot mask your vision, but I think that may come to your aid more than your detriment. But this is not permanent—it won't last long. Within a few days, you must travel to Haseofon for the next step in your training."

She gently stroked her fingers across the tattoo on my temple, then over my eyes and ears. As she did so, it was as if a heavy pressure lifted and I was able to breathe again.

Greta smiled. "There. You will be fine for a day or so, though you'll have to get used to seeing them around. But come to me as soon as you can. The training will be intense and will take you several weeks. I hope you don't have plans for the next month."

"Not any of my own making. But I can't vouch for what happens to us on the demonic front with Shadow Wing." I

closed my eyes, relishing the silence that had descended.
"I feel so much better."

"You'll learn how to control both vision and sound, and
how to use the power when it's appropriate. You cannot
walk around the world of the living constantly open to the
spirits. Without warding, without boundaries, you'd go
crazy. Come to me when you can—but don't wait long. No
more than a couple of days." She stroked my cheek. "You'll
do fine." And then, she vanished.

The next moment, I opened my eyes, and I was standing
there, next to Camille, feeling dazed. Behind us, Morio was
getting out of the car. I realized that fractions of a second
had passed between me calling for Greta's help and now.
The spirits still wandered the sidewalk around me, but now,
they didn't seem to notice me and I couldn't hear them.

"Kitten, are you okay? Answer me!" Camille sounded
frantic.

"Yes . . . yes . . ." I shook my head, trying to clear the
cobwebs. "I'm all right, it's okay now."

Morio jogged over to us. "Everything all right?"

"Yeah." I rubbed my temples, the remnants of the headache starting to dissipate. "I'll be okay. You know what?
It's nothing—I'll explain later. I know what happened and
why, but we have a job to do. It won't interfere. I talked to
Greta. Let's just go, all right?"

The thought of Daniel, caught with Einar's ghost bear-
ing down on him, hit me like a sledgehammer. Whether it
was premonition, or empathy derived from what I'd just
been through, I wasn't sure, but I only knew that I wanted
to get in there and stop whatever was going down, because
my instincts were screaming bloody murder.

Camille nodded. "Let's go." She motioned for Morio to
return to his car. "We're only a block or so away."

We jumped back in the car and cautiously edged back
out into the street. I cringed as we drove through a couple
of the ghosts, but they didn't seem to notice. Yeah, Greta
was right—I'd have to get my ass in for training or I'd
never be able to drive again.

Camille maneuvered down the wind-blasted road, skirting broken limbs that had blanketed the asphalt in a splintered trail of green and brown.

"Care to tell me what went on?" she asked as we neared the crossroad right before where the Greenbelt Asylum had once stood.

I sighed, then explained what had happened. "So apparently, I'm starring in my own version of *The Sixth Sense. I see dead people.* But Greta helped me shut down the voices for a little while, and they don't know I can see them. She will train me how to turn it on and off, and how to cope. I gather Death Maidens see and talk to ghosts as a matter of course." Even as I laughed, I realized that I was trying to comfort myself. The prospect scared me stiff. I didn't like ghosts. I didn't like fighting them. The thought of being on a permanent chat line with them gave me the willies.

Camille grunted. "Seems like we've both got some changes in the works, huh?" She flashed me a sympathetic look. "I don't know who I feel worse for—you, or me."

And then, she crossed the street and we eased up in front of a building that, to make an understatement, had seen better days. Huge, the building took up an entire block.

The original asylum had sat on the family estate, which had been five hundred acres. The land left still ate up two full city blocks, but was a fraction of the original estate. Maybe nobody wanted to buy the remaining land because the thought of building a home over an old mental institution was just asking for trouble. Whatever the case, the city hadn't stepped in to do anything about it.

The tangle of vegetation had crept in around the gated hospital, and now was cascading over the walls and into the ruins. The fence was ten feet tall, solid iron bars, which meant going over it was out of the question. But it wouldn't be a problem, because from where we sat in the car, we could see that one of the gates was off the hinges and lying on the ground. We'd just have to watch our step.

The neighboring areas—originally part of the massive estate—had been built up into solid little houses, sturdy in the 1950s suburban fashion, but they were weathered now, and I wasn't sure how many were still inhabited. Cars were sporadically parked up and down the opposite curb, but they, too, were weathered. Every time we came to the Greenbelt Park District, I felt like we'd stepped into an archaeological dig from sixty years back. I wondered if our mother had ever walked down this street, and if so, what had it been like back then?

As Camille parked, Morio swung in behind us. Shutting the door behind me, I stared up at the gray remains of the building. Thank gods Greta had muted the ghosts' ability to know that I realized they were there, because a whirl of spirits surrounded the place and I really really didn't want to be at their mercy. But I couldn't help wondering, as I gazed at the misty figures wandering through the crumbling tower and broken brick, how many ghosts were running around here? How many of them were still fighting against cruel overseers who had kept them in check with electricity and starvation, brutalizing them at the drop of a hat?

As if sensing my thoughts, Camille sidled closer to me and reached out to take my hand. "I can smell death here."

I knew she wasn't talking about blood or bodies . . . but the actual presence of death. A sense of loss and decay and violence had imprinted itself on the very walls and in the air of the asylum. Atrocities had happened here, to people who could not defend themselves, who could not speak out. The criminally insane had been locked up alongside those who were in need of help but had never turned their illness on others. The caregivers had been harsh wardens, and the entire building had been a pressure cooker, until that storm-ridden night when the inmates took over and Silas Johnson blew the place sky-high.

As we slowly approached the gate, a figure stepped out of the shadows, so quickly that neither one of us had time to react. At first I thought it was another ghost, but then I was relieved to see that—not only was it *not* a ghost, it was Shade.

"I made it before you, but didn't feel like heading in there on my own, though I doubt much of anything in there could hurt me if I turned into my dragon shape." Shade held out his arm, smiling, and I slipped into his embrace gratefully. He kissed me, but then looked over his shoulder at the building. "There are horrific things in there, and I can feel the sword. I know Einar's energy from holding it. It's there, all right, and I'm betting up in that tower."

Just then, Morio and the others joined us. Leif stared up at the ruins, a terrified expression on his face. "*Of course* Jay would come here. Why didn't I think of it before?"

"What do you mean?" My gaze was riveted to the asylum. Pins and needles raced through my arms and the back of my neck as I watched the spirits move around us, whispering and talking, going about their shadowed existence. They knew we were here—some of them—and they watched us warily.

Leif let out a long sigh. "Jay Miles is the great-great-nephew of the man who owned and ran this hospital. He's the one who owns the land here now."

And there was the last piece in the puzzle. He must have grown up playing here, feeling the spirits, being drawn to necromancy. And perhaps . . . being twisted by the memories that haunted this place.

My stomach lurched. "There's an army of ghosts right here. Ten to one, Jay plans to harness the spirits of the patients. Einar will be their king—as cruel as the owners and staff were. And Jay will control Einar. Not only were the inmates shackled in life, but they'll be controlled during their death. What kind of freak is Miles? And what does he hope to gain?"

The wind gusted up and caught my words, spinning them into the air. It was time to go stop a madman who came from a long line of cruel nutcases. That is, if we weren't already too late.

Chapter 19

"What's the plan?" Morio asked me.

I gazed up at the tower. "Shade, you said you can feel the sword. Can you guide us to it through its energy signature?"

He nodded. "I think so. I have no idea if Einar is free yet, but I think we'd better be prepared for an ugly question. If he *has* already possessed Daniel, and if he *can* control the ghosts in this place, then how do we get rid of him? I can't exorcise him . . . not anymore. Morio and Camille, do you have anything to send him packing?"

Leif shot us a strange look. "Daniel . . . Daniel *who*?"

I cleared my throat. "Jay Miles has kidnapped our cousin. His name is Daniel. He's trying to free Einar to possess Daniel's body so Einar can lead the asylum ghosts on a war through the city." I turned back to Shade. I knew what his actual question was. He was asking if we had to, would we be willing to kill our cousin to prevent further bloodshed. And I wasn't prepared to answer that. We'd been forced to do a lot of things we didn't want to, that we still hated to think about, but we'd still done them.

Camille glanced at Morio, who shrugged. "I don't know. It's hard to tell what we can do without knowing just how powerful Einar is. The only thing we can do is go in swinging and play it by ear. There's no way to find out anything else at this point, and we don't have time to waste."

I glanced at our group. "Someone has to keep an eye on Leif. Okay, here's the battle order. Shade, you're up front with me. Morio and Camille—back of us. Vanzir, you keep an eye on Leif after them. Smoky, will you bring up the rear?"

Leif cleared his throat. "What should I *do*? I'm out of my element here and I'm not even sure what the hell we're walking into, other than ghosts are involved, and this building scares the shit out of me."

I turned to him, catching his gaze. "Listen and listen good. Yes, we are heading into a dangerous situation, but we have to take you with us because of the sword."

Leif nodded. "Because Jay's in there, with my sword and your cousin. And he's working on freeing Einar from the sword to lead an army of the dead. Right?" Leif had a good memory; that I'd give him.

"Right. To be able to do that, Einar must take possession of a living body. Apparently he finds Daniel to his liking." I glanced up at the ruins. "Trouble is, we don't know if Jay's already managed to free Einar. If he has, we could be facing a nasty-assed bunch of not-right-in-the-head ghosts."

Leif barely blinked. "Got it. So tell me what I should do."

"You do whatever we tell you to. You jump when we say jump, duck if we say duck, get out of the way if we say get out of the way. And if you recognize Daniel . . . Leif—do nothing except what we tell you. Don't even ask why I'm saying that right now. I hope we all come out of this in one piece, but you stand a better chance if you just react without questioning. Whatever you do, don't try to play the hero. That's usually a recipe for disaster. Got it?" I felt sorry for Leif. He hadn't asked for any of this, but because of Einar, he was saddled with it.

If he was having second thoughts, he didn't let on.

Instead, he straightened his shoulders. "All right. You can count on me. But when this is over, promise me one thing?"

"What's that?"

"That you'll help me destroy that goddamn sword for good. Father always pushed me to have a son. *You have to have a son to inherit the sword.* But I'm not about to drape that albatross around another person. If I have to die childless, that's fine. I'm not giving another generation the headache of always knowing that thing is there, waiting, on the wall."

Morio clapped him on the shoulder. "We'll help you. Now, get in line, and let's take this inside."

We stepped around the fallen gate, Camille and I cautiously avoiding the iron bars. The grounds of the asylum were overrun by a thick blanket of fern and huckleberry. Scavenger trees had seeded through where the original forest had been logged. Cottonwood and alder—pulp mill trees—grew in dense stands. The tangle of vegetation was interrupted only by a thin path that looked recently cut back. Which meant somebody had come through here and not long ago.

I jumped as the spirit of a young woman raced by, a terrified expression on her face. She glanced over her shoulder, as if to see how close whatever pursued her was, but I could see nothing behind her. And then she vanished into the forest. This was going to take some getting used to, all right.

"Are you all right?" Shade leaned close. "Did you just see . . ."

"What you saw? Yes. I'll tell you about it later." I kept my voice low. "Right now, we need to focus on Einar and Daniel."

He gave me a searching look, then nodded and turned back to the ruins, scanning along the edge of the giant complex. The hospital had been huge—five hundred people can fit in a small enough space, but the structure had been dizzyingly big, taking up over half a city block. I wondered, how much money had the original owner made from taking in the patients?

"This is a grim place," Morio said from behind me. "The despair's imprinted onto the very grounds. It's everywhere."

The walkway to the building was relatively short, but every step felt like it took us deeper and deeper into a mire. Camille made a sound behind me, and when I turned, she just shook her head. I knew what she was feeling because it was starting to hit me, too—as if we were walking farther and farther away from safety. We were outside, but we might as well have been in an enclosed box, for all the feelings of claustrophobia. The closer we came to the ruins of the asylum, the less I wanted to go in there. It felt like a dank cave, like an open mouth waiting to slurp us up and chew us into bloody pieces.

I skirted a large chunk of charred brick. "Whatever went down here, this is bad. No wonder this place never attracted any buyers."

Doing my best to ignore the ghosts moving every which way, I slowly led the way with Shade toward the burnt-out shell. A man in a straitjacket wandered by, whispering aimlessly to himself, and then, to my right, a woman, naked except for a sheet draped around her shoulders, stumbled past, a vacant look on her face like nobody was home. Were they really ghosts? Or were they just flickering images from the past, impressed on the very currents of the air? I couldn't tell—maybe Greta would be able to teach me how to know the difference, but right now, I had no clue exactly what I was seeing.

We managed to make it to what had been the large double doors leading into the building. I glanced at my notes that I'd taken from Carter. This would be the main floor, the entrance into the building where the public had come through. If what Carter said was correct, then when we entered, to our left would be the wing leading to administrative rooms, residents' rooms for the sanest and most pliable inmates, a smaller dining hall, and a recreation room.

To the right, we should find the remains of a medical room where the families of the inmates were allowed to observe psychological exams. But that's not where the real medical procedures had taken place.

Most of the residents' quarters had been on the second and third floors, along with another dining hall and recreation room. And the fourth floor—that was where the owner and his son allowed doctors to experiment on the patients. It was also where electroshock therapy had been performed, along with other treatments now considered barbaric. The boiler and maintenance rooms had been in the basement. Staircases were on either end of the building, as well as the central area, and elevators—of course no longer in use—had been strategically placed throughout the building.

The entrance loomed ahead. The doors were still there, but the glass was long gone, and the brick surrounding the area was heat-blasted. Parts of the building were entirely leveled, but here, and to the right—where the medical facilities were—the walls and roof had remained intact, if somewhat precariously so.

"Somebody should have just leveled this thing long ago." I gazed to the right. With the way the building had been shattered, it was now a tower.

Shade stared up at the sooty brick. "The sword's up there."

"Well, at least it's not a basement this time." The last thing I wanted to do was head down into the basement where the explosion had taken place. Silas had been incarcerated here for killing his mother, father, wife, and three kids. Yet he had complained to the doctors that "voices" told him to harm the other patients. I didn't want to run into his ghost, because I had a feeling he wouldn't be one of the passive ones.

We pushed through the entrance, and into the inky darkness.

The daylight vanished as we entered the silent tomb. I could feel spirits passing by now, brushing past me with no sense that I was there. Behind me, Camille and Morio began to chant in a low voice. I wasn't sure what they were doing, but whatever it was, I welcomed anything to take the looming sense of weight off our shoulders. The building felt like it welcomed us, and that alone was unsettling. I didn't want to feel welcome here. Welcome here could easily mean, *Come in and die.* I wanted to get the hell out of here as soon as possible.

A pale violet light flared and a pentacle surrounded our group. Immediately, a wash of protective energy flowed over me, and grateful, I glanced back and smiled.

"We need light to see by," Vanzir said. The next moment, he had turned on a heavy-duty flashlight and handed it to me, producing another for himself. Between the two of us, we managed to shed enough light for all of us.

There wasn't much to see, though. A lot of charred timbers, and ashes that had been hardened into chunks by rain. I briefly wondered if the police had recovered all the bodies, but then decided I didn't want to go there.

"Over there." Shade pointed to the right. I flashed the light in that direction to reveal a staircase going up. The heavy metal door lay on the ground nearby, ripped off its hinges by something big and nasty. Lovely, whatever had done that had plenty of force behind it—and hopefully was long gone.

"We go up, then." I led the way over to the stairwell. The stairs were concrete, against the brick of the wall, and it looked like the fire had channeled at least partway through the passage because when I put my hand on the railing, it felt dusty. I pulled it away to see that my hand was covered with dirt and soot and whatever else might be living on the rail.

"Do you think Jay knows we're here?" Vanzir's question drifted forward and I glanced over my shoulder. He had moved Leif in back of him, between him and Smoky. We were single file at this point, still protected by Camille and Morio's protection spell. I was familiar enough with it now to know that it would hold as long as they maintained their focus and kept holding hands.

"I think there's a pretty good bet he does. He's a

necromancer, which means he can probably communicate with the dead, and trust me, there are so many spirits here that he has to have eyes and ears among them." I tried not to flinch as a man came racing down the stairs at me—or rather, a ghost—and then dashed right through us. A shiver raced down my spine as a blast of cold air lingered in his wake.

We turned the bend and passed the exit to the second floor. I paused, looking at Shade. "Are we there?"

He closed his eyes, then shook his head. "Higher."

"Then up we go." We climbed past the third story, then at the entrance to the fourth—which still had its door intact—Shade nodded. "Here. He's here. Einar . . . the sword . . ."

Camille and Morio broke hands and drew their weapons. Camille had brought her dagger, Morio had brought what looked like a wand, but I didn't recognize it.

At my look, he grinned and held it up. The wand was thin, slender, and straight, wrapped with silver wire and inlaid with numerous gems—what looked like smoky quartz and sapphire in the glow of the flashlight. A pale crystal spike was affixed to the end, and it had some sort of fur wrapped around the hilt.

"I made this," he said. "It's focused on disrupting magical energy. It seemed like it might have a place in tonight's fight, though frankly, I'll probably resort to my youkai form when push comes to shove."

"Don't underestimate your intuition." Camille gave him a quick smile. "You know what you need."

I stared at the door. Beyond here, I had no clue of how the layout went. Carter hadn't been able to send us any schematics. I placed my hand on the door handle and cautiously turned it, easing the door open, but I could have just as easily slammed it wide for all the good my attempts at silence did. The door let out a long squeak as I opened it. If they didn't know we were on the way before this, they did now.

"That takes care of that. Let's go." I pushed through, followed by Shade and the others, to find myself in a hallway. The hall was dimly lit by the light filtering through some of the windows that hadn't been boarded over, but my focus hit the end of the hallway, where an archway led into what appeared to be a large room. There must have been doors at one time but they were long gone.

Shade took off running. "It's there!"

I caught up to him, and the others were close on our heels. But as we pushed through the entryway, I realized that we were too late. The room was a swirl of ghosts, but they looked determined, no longer lost. They were surrounding Daniel, who stood there, shirt off, chest bloody but from no wound that I could see, with the sword in hand. Behind him stood another man—it had to be Jay. To his left stood Aslo.

Leif let out a gasp. "Daniel—I remember." But he kept his word and did nothing.

Skidding to a halt, I realized they had been waiting for us. The host of ghosts filling the room looked different than the others I'd seen—not only did they look like they had purpose, but they had shifted. Their auras flared with a pale green light, and their eyes gleamed with a dangerous glow.

"Daniel!" Camille's voice echoed from behind me.

Daniel raised his sword, and as one, the ghosts fell to their knees. He slowly pointed it toward us, and they rose, turning in unison, and began to move forward. I suddenly realized that the others might not see what I was seeing.

"Ghosts, incoming! I can see them—more than I can count and they look dangerous." I kept my eyes ahead on the advancing army of spirits, but motioned for the others to move back and spread out.

Camille and Morio stepped to the left and joined hands and they began a chant. I watched in fascination as whatever they were doing emanated out like a mist to roll over the ghosts, whose auras flared brightly.

"We can see their outlines now," Camille said. "Delilah can see the ghosts full on, guys—trust what she says."

"Right. Vanzir, protect Leif." Smoky moved up to my right, between me and Shade, and we all formed a semicircle in front of Vanzir and Leif.

The ghosts advanced with Daniel following behind, a

cruel smile across his face. I didn't even bother speaking to him—it was obvious Einar was in possession of his body.

"How do we fight them?" Hell, we didn't even know what they could do.

"I wish Ivana was here to gather them up." Camille took Morio's hand and they began a low chant, building the energy between them.

Smoky let out a long breath, and an icy wind swept through, followed by a hail of sleet. The weather didn't faze the ghosts, but managed to engulf Jay, Aslo, and Daniel. The former two stumbled, but Daniel kept his footing, and raised the sword again. As the ghosts reached striking distance, a noise echoed from behind me and Vanzir let out a shout.

I turned to see the Viking warriors—the guardians of the sword—appear. They silently moved forward to meet the oncoming spirits. There was a pause, a moment where everything felt poised on a fulcrum, and then Daniel brought his sword sweeping down, and with a cry, the ghosts were on us.

The spirit of a young man was facing me. I wasn't sure what to do to him, but when he raised his hands and grabbed me around the neck, I started to choke. Fuck! I'd better do *something* and I'd better do it fast. I brought Lysanthra up and stabbed him in the head. The ghost groaned as the magical silver hit his aura, and he stumbled back, but did not dissipate. I jumped back a step. At least I could affect him.

He glared at me and then did a double take as I flipped him off. At this point, I didn't care if they realized I could see them. Maybe it would give them a little scare, though as to what a ghost might be frightened of . . .

"That's it! What can scare a ghost?" I held Lysanthra out, aimed at the ghost who was giving me a dirty look now.

"Well, they aren't afraid of dying, I can tell you that!" Vanzir, his usual smart-assed self, answered from behind me.

"Oblivion. Delilah, can you use your powers of *oblition* on these spirits?" Camille stumbled back, no longer holding hands with Morio.

"No, I can't—it's not allowed—" I stopped as Camille let out a shout and then went flying back against the wall as a burly ghost hit her head on in the stomach. Arms out, he was headed toward her throat.

"He's going to try to choke you! Move!" I wanted to help her, but the ghost on me took another lunge and I darted to the right, unable to get past him. I couldn't see what happened to Camille but I heard her scream and then caught a glimpse of her once again flying through the air. She looked alive, though.

As I tried to duck out of reach, the guardians of the sword moved in to begin fighting the biggest ghosts in the group. They tangled in what looked like an eerie WWE match.

Meanwhile, Shade pushed his way over to an open area in the large operating room and rapidly shifted form. It never failed to amaze me when I saw him in his dragon shape—a skeletal dragon, bones an earthy brown, with glowing topaz eyes. Every step he took, his bones clattered and moaned, and he was as terrifying a visage as anything we'd ever come across, except he was my lover and there was no way I could fear him. I was simply in awe of his natural form.

He let out a loud roar, and this time, not only did Jay and Aslo fall back, looking petrified, but Daniel along with them.

"*Drage! Drage!*" Daniel stumbled back, his eyes wide.

So Einar could be frightened of something—good to know. Shade bore down on him and I had the sudden fear that he'd eat my cousin whole. Because, Einar's soul or not, the body belonged to Daniel.

But I had turned my back too long, and the next moment, my ghost attacked me again, his hands burning with an icy fire as he once more grabbed me by the throat. I stabbed wildly with Lysanthra, but this time he evaded my attack, his grip tightening. I struggled to breathe and dropped my dagger, instinctively reaching to loosen his grip but I couldn't latch hold of him.

Then he was gone—vaporized, as one of the ghostly warriors broke through and stabbed him with a flaming axe. He looked down at me, then smiled softly and moved on. I grabbed my dagger and staggered to my feet, trying to figure out what was going on.

The ghosts were thick and fighting with the warriors. Their single-minded focus told me that Einar was fully in charge of them—they might as well be zombies on a spiritual level.

Morio held out his wand—I wasn't sure what he was doing but I could see tendrils of energy flowing from the crystal on the end. Camille looked ragged, but she had charged over to his side, and clapped her hand over his. Together they began to chant something that made my stomach shift.

Vanzir was protecting Leif from a ghost that was trying to get at him. Shade was plowing through the spirits—he seemed to be able to disperse them with a touch in his dragon form. Smoky had managed to work his way over to Jay and Aslo, and the two were running like hell from him as he gave chase.

Daniel, on the other hand, was in the middle of his ghostly brigade, and his focus was on Leif. I knew then, Einar's goal was to destroy Leif. Because if he did, there would be no one to watch over the sword should we be able to re-imprison the chieftain.

My throat burning, I jumped between Daniel and Vanzir. He stared at me, a twisted grin on his face.

"Daniel? Daniel! Snap out of it." I had to try—I couldn't just mow him down without trying to dislodge Einar from him.

He muttered something, but I didn't understand what he was saying, then he raised the sword, and I realized that Daniel couldn't hear me—wherever he was, it wasn't behind those calculating eyes.

I dove to the left as he brought the sword whistling down, and then stretched out my leg to hook my foot around his ankle. As I fell, I gave a yank and Daniel fell with me, the sword tumbling out of his hands. The flat of the blade bounced against my cheek, the iron burning with a sharp, fierce pain. I let out a scream, even as I scrambled to subdue my cousin. I straddled him, pinning him down between my legs, and forced his arms over his head.

He struggled, trying to flip me off. Leaning back, I brought my head down against his, headbutting him so hard I saw stars and the bruise on my forehead sent a shockwave of pain through me.

Even though Daniel was possessed by a ghost, the fact remained that I was stronger and bigger than he was, and I was half-Fae. His eyes closed as I knocked him unconscious. I looked up and noticed that, in all the mayhem, Aslo was trying to sneak out of the room.

"Oh hell no, you don't!" I shifted fast, so rapidly that it hurt, but seconds later, I bounded across the room in panther form. Aslo turned on me, a very big knife out, but he was no match for me. I leapt, knocking him to his back, and as he struggled, I caught his throat in my jaws and bit deep. The blood spurted into my mouth, warm and fresh, and the thrill of the chase set me off. Aslo gurgled out some last words, but I didn't care, and was off again, piling into the fray.

The ghosts were still moving forward, which told me that Einar still retained control, unconscious though he might be. As I considered what to do next, Camille and Morio raised the wand overhead, both of their hands linked around it, and they let out a loud shout. A swirl of energy rose out of the tip, from the crystal, to spiral down and through the mayhem. It headed toward Daniel, and I realized what they were doing. I shifted as quickly as I could, groaning as the pain hit full force when I landed back in my two-legged form.

"Leif, grab the sword—take the sword!" I screamed as loud as I could so he could hear me over the mayhem.

Vanzir heard me, though, and he shoved Leif forward, toward the sword. Leif snatched it up and teetered back as Daniel's eyes shot open and he abruptly sat up. His focus was solely on Leif now, and he was on his feet before I could reach them. Leif looked terrified and he turned to run, but Daniel was on him, struggling with him for possession of the sword.

At that moment, the energy from Morio's wand hit the pair, swirling around them like a tentacle, catching them both. They rose into the air, held aloft by the energy, and the sword was in both of their hands.

Suddenly realizing what was going to happen, I lunged forward, trying to intervene. But I was too late. There was a horrible flash, and the smell of sulfur and burning embers, and Leif collapsed as Daniel let go of the sword, dropping to the ground. The sword landed near him, but he sat there, looking confused, not attempting to reach for it.

I landed by his side. "Daniel? Is that you?"

He blinked, squinting at me. "Where the hell am I?"

Morio and Camille knelt near the sword. Smoky strode over, motioning Camille away from it. I looked around for Jay, then saw his body, limp on the floor, neatly eviscerated. I didn't say a word—Smoky made his own rules.

Smoky picked up the sword and stared at it. "I think . . . they are both in here."

Camille winced. "We didn't mean for that to happen. Is there any way we can free Leif?"

I looked around. The ghosts had gone back to being their normal selves, and the warriors moved forward, eyeing us cautiously. "Is his body alive?"

Vanzir leaned down to check for a pulse. "Yeah, he's alive. Let me try to wake him up." But try as hard as he might, he couldn't shake Leif awake. "I think . . . he's in a coma."

Feeling dazed, my throat still raw, I tried to close my vision to the milling ghosts that thronged around us, once again back to their lost lives. But they wouldn't go away. "I don't know what to do. We promised Leif we'd destroy the sword, but if we do, then we destroy him in the process."

"Maybe Wilbur can help? He's a necromancer. Maybe he can figure out how to separate Leif and Einar?" Camille limped over. She was covered in bruises. Being tossed through the air a couple times certainly hadn't helped.

"That's the only thing I can think of." I shrugged. "Why do I feel like we won the battle but lost the war?"

"Because . . . we did. Okay, then. We're done here. Let's go see Wilbur. And maybe . . . just maybe, we can salvage something out of this mess." I motioned to Leif. "Somebody bring his body. Somebody not Camille or me carry the sword, and for the gods' sake, keep it away from Daniel."

Camille and I helped Daniel to his feet, and we all staggered toward the stairwell. I watched the misty figures pass around as we went, and felt a wave of incredible sadness sweep over me. Most of these people had died here. And now they were just as trapped as they had been in life.

"When we get the chance, we're coming back here and clearing out this horror show. And we're not handing these spirits over to Ivana. We're freeing them to go on, to leave, to finally have some peace."

Camille nodded as we helped Daniel down the stairs. It felt like a million years since we'd first entered the asylum. And it felt like I was leaving a little part of myself behind. Now that I knew there were so many spirits everywhere, my world would never be the same. I'd never again look around, and think I was alone. And that . . . that was a scary thought in itself.

Chapter 20

❦

The drive to Wilbur's took a good twenty minutes, dodging power lines and trees and emergency vehicles. But we made it. Camille groaned as she climbed out of the driver's seat.

"I'm going to hurt like hell for days. I need an Epsom salts bath, that's for sure." She winced as we headed up the steps to Wilbur's house. I knocked, and was surprised when Martin opened the door. I don't know why it startled me—Martin often acted as the butler for his brother. The fact that he was a ghoul shouldn't matter, I guess, but it still gave me the creeps.

Morio and the others were right behind us. We made sure Daniel was far away from the sword, but I could tell that it was still working on him. He was watching every movement Shade made with it.

We explained to Wilbur what had happened, and he let out a "Hrmph" and leaned down to look at the weapon, running his hands over the blade but not touching it. That was one thing I would say about Wilbur. He might be crass and rude and lewd, but he was far from stupid.

"So you want the boy's soul returned to his body. What

about the other one?" He finally sat back, contemplating the sword.

"What about it? Can you do anything about it? Ultimately, we'd like to destroy it—and the sword with it." I leaned forward. If Wilbur could help us, then I'd gladly be in his debt. I was so tired of collateral damage that I'd even give the old coot a kiss if he could fix this mess.

He gave me a long look, almost as if he could read my thoughts, and I blushed. With a guffaw, he slapped his knee. "Yeah, I can take care of this. Morio and Pussycat, I'll need your help—the rest of you will just get in my way. You say you want the other soul destroyed?"

"And the sword, if possible." Camille frowned. "It's dangerous to leave around. It can entrap spirits and we can't handle it since it's iron."

Wilbur arched his eyebrows. "I know men would pay a pretty penny for this thing." He whistled as he picked it up. "Oh yes, I can feel them wriggling around in here, like snakes in a tube. Or my snake when I see you chicks in a pair of tight pants."

Camille groaned, shaking her head. "You had to destroy the moment, didn't you?"

"I do my best, honeypot. I do my best." He motioned for Morio to follow him, the sword casually in hand. "Bring Leif's body with you, Fox."

Morio carried Leif and I followed. When Wilbur had rebuilt after the fire, he'd built his laboratory on the main floor to avoid having to use the basement. Now, we entered and he motioned for Morio to place Leif on a flat metal slab. I didn't want to think about what other bodies Wilbur had put there.

"I have some powder . . . it should free your buddy out of there. Then . . . I can use an alchemical spell to transmute the sword. It should destroy the Viking's soul in the process. But Pussycat, I need you here because if he gets loose, you have to disintegrate him or whatever it is you do as a Death Maiden. That's the only option if he manages to survive the spell."

I didn't like using my powers without permission, but we had no choice at this point. If we didn't get Leif out of there now, Einar might be able to destroy his soul. "All right." I stood back, changing into my panther form. It would be the quickest way for me to react if I needed to.

Wilbur and Morio worked in silence. I had no clue what they were doing, but that wasn't my department. I just had to be prepared. They set up several beakers and poured powder and some sort of liquid into two of them, then Wilbur motioned for Morio to go stand by Leif's body. The necromancer lifted the sword, holding it up to the heavens, then he laid it back down and poured the liquid that was bubbling into the powder. A puff of smoke hissed up as the liquid frothed and foamed, and Wilbur silently began to pour it over the sword, while whispering in that same language he'd spoken before. By now I had the feeling it belonged to the South American shamans he'd learned his craft from.

Morio shouted and I looked over to see Leif convulsing. Just then, I saw two forms emerge from the sword—Leif was racing away from Einar, who looked as mad and blood-thirsty as we thought he was. They were both translucent, and I realized that they'd been freed by whatever the liquid was—it hadn't destroyed Einar. Leif passed by me, heading toward his body, with Einar on the run.

I jumped in between them, looming up, growing wild and feral and snarling at Einar, who stopped in his tracks. *"Nei nei,"* he whispered. *"Nei, nei. Bli borte, Valkyrie."* His eyes were wide and he looked absolutely terrified.

I transformed back into my two-footed shape, but cloaked in the dress of the Death Maidens, and I reached out to touch his spirit. Without knowing what I was going to say, I opened my mouth to speak. "You must rest, Einar. You must travel through the veil for good. You have lived long past your time and you must go meet your fate. Go to your gods and answer for your actions."

The moment my hand met his spirit, he screamed, and then a rift opened—I could feel the autumn winds blow through it—and Einar was sucked through. It slammed shut, closing with a final sucking sound, and Einar the Bloody was gone from our realm forever.

I let out a long breath and turned to see Leif opening his eyes. Wilbur let out a crowing sound and held up a metal cube.

"Here's what's left of your sword and sheath. Neither will ever be able to entrap anyone again."

Feeling both relieved and exhausted, I turned and walked out of the room without saying a word.

Camille and the others were waiting as I emerged from the back. They sat up, looking expectantly at me. "It worked. Leif is safe. Einar is gone. The sword . . . it's toast."

Smoky and Shade suggested we go home but I shook my head. "I want to wait until we find out how Leif is doing.

Daniel had fallen asleep, and Camille looked close to it. Vanzir was resting his eyes, too. Martin shuffled over and repeatedly tried to turn on the television. At least he wasn't getting miffed about the darkened screen, but it was almost mesmerizing to watch the single-minded focus. After another ten minutes, Camille grumbled and marched over, leading Martin back to a chair, where she pushed him in it.

"Stay, boy."

Martin started to stand and she pushed him back to the seat.

"I said *stay*!" She leaned over him, hands on her hips, sounding for all the world like Iris.

Shade glanced over at Smoky and laughed. Smoky just shrugged and shook his head. "Don't even ask."

Another five minutes and Morio and Wilbur brought Leif back into the room. Leif was on his feet, looking no worse for the wear.

"It's okay," Morio said before we could ask. He held out a huge slag of iron. "This is all that's left of the sword. I'm going to go chuck it in the Sound where nobody can find it."

"I removed the magic from the blade first. You girls owe me one. I'll happily take it in trade." Wilbur looked at Martin, frowning. "I'm surprised he's not trying to turn on the television."

Relief sweeping over me, I walked over to Wilbur, grabbed him in a big hug, and planted a big ol' kiss on his forehead.

"You grumpy old lecher. Thank you. And we owe you one, yes . . . we'll take you out to dinner when the town gets its power back."

As I stood back, I suddenly noticed a misty apparition standing next to the burly biker. Startled, I glanced over at Martin, who was staring straight ahead, then back at the ghost. It was Martin's spirit, and he was smiling at his brother with the kind of love reserved for someone who always pulls you through the hard times. He glanced at me, and I realized he could tell that I saw him. He raised one finger to his lips and shook his head, then turned and walked through the wall.

I glanced at Martin again . . . maybe the dead really *didn't* care what happened to their bodies. And even if Wilbur didn't know it, his brother was with him in spirit, as well as body.

Turning to the door, I motioned to the others. "Come on, guys. Let's go home. I'm worn out." As we trooped out of the house, the rain soaked in again, and I shivered, wondering how long it would be till we got our power back.

Thanks to Shade and Smoky, we were all able to take reasonably good sponge baths with piping hot water. It wasn't the same thing as a long shower, but at least we were clean. Camille was bruised up, but she would heal. Leif was asleep in the parlor, and we planned on keeping him around until we made sure he didn't have any aftereffects from being in the sword. Daniel was sleeping on the sofa. He, too, was exhausted.

Camille and Menolly and I gathered on Camille's bed, Maggie playing quietly between us. The fire in the fireplace was blazing, and Smoky had heated up some stones and wrapped the blankets in them till they were toasty. They'd chill down soon enough, but it was enough to take the edge off being so damp and wet. Battery-operated candles lined the shelves—for safety given the number we needed—and the room was beautiful and glowing in the dim light. Outside, the wind had picked up, but at least it wasn't storming again like it had.

Camille and I held cups of hot chocolate, and a plate of cookies sat on the nightstand, out of Maggie's reach. Hanna had managed to fix tomato soup on the grill, as well as grilling French bread and sprinkling it with a heavy coating of parmesan, so we'd eaten a hot meal earlier. The power was still out, and would be for days, the news said.

"How's Shade doing?" Menolly didn't need the blanket, but she huddled under it, too, because it made everything seem cozier.

"It's going to be an interesting road. We still don't know whether or not he can regain what he lost, but we'll figure that out as we go along. With my new abilities, he's going to have his hands full, so we'll have to help each other adjust. Tomorrow I'll head out to Haseofon, after a good night's sleep, and begin training on how to handle all of this. It's disconcerting, to say the least." I turned to Camille. "How do you feel? You got tossed around like a rag doll."

"It hurts but it's not like I'm permanently bruised." She paused. "Menolly, I need to tell you what happened out at Talamh Lonrach Oll."

"You told us at dinner that Morgaine died . . . did something else go down?" Menolly frowned. She had been bummed at being left out of the action, but the vampire thing was just a reality of her life. Daylight and vamps didn't mix, and unfortunately, it left her out of the loop at times.

"Yeah . . ." Camille took a deep breath. "I haven't told anybody else this yet—Delilah knows but that's all. I'm slated to take Morgaine's place."

Menolly stared at her. "What?"

"I'm destined to become the Queen of Dusk and Twilight."

After a pause, Menolly sputtered. I half listened to her diatribe—apparently she had some strong thoughts on the subject. I zoned out of the conversation. I was tired and just wanted to curl up in Tabby form.

As my attention wandered, I glanced over to the edge of the bed, where Maggie was giggling. There, in the dim light, I saw the faint shadow shape of a very large woodland gargoyle. Maggie's mother. We'd seen her before once or twice, when she'd come to check on her baby. Now she glanced up and saw me watching her. She raised one of her hands and I gave her a broad smile and nodded. With a soft *mooph*—whether it was Maggie or her mother, I couldn't tell, Mama 'Goyle leaned down and nuzzled her baby. Then she stood, and as Maggie paused, watching, she silently vanished.

I came back to the conversation as Menolly was practically scolding Camille for not saying no.

"Stop."

"What?" Menolly looked at me, and so did Camille.

"Enough bickering. Enough mulling. It's a cold, blustery evening, and we're lucky enough to have some downtime to spend with each other. Can we just stop and enjoy it? I want to sit here with the two of you and just let everything be." I reached out and took Camille's hand in my left, and Menolly's in my right.

Menolly laughed. "All right, Kitten. I'm sorry—I get fired up and forget to stop, don't I?"

Camille squeezed my hand. "I'm up for just relaxing."

So we sat, hand in hand, as the wind whistled at the windows. The candles flickered softly and the fire danced in the hearth. We had a new demon general to find and destroy. Both Camille and I were facing major changes in our lives. And Menolly? I had the feeling she'd have to face her own inner demons soon enough, with what Nerissa had told me.

But for now, we could push the world out. Lovers were wonderful, but sometimes we needed sister-time. To have a moment when it was just the three of us, each with our own lives, but still united.

I looked over at the fire. The ghosts were walking tonight. They filled the world, hidden and unseen by most. But in my world they were now very real and very visible. Every day, it seemed, I slid more into the realm of the Autumn Lord.

But *right now, at this moment*, I was just Delilah. Just Kitten, and Menolly and Camille and I were safe and together. We generated as much light as we could to face the growing darkness, and what kept us going was the love that united us in blood and in spirit. And so we sat in silence, with only the crackling fire singing its song to us as evening turned into night.

CAST OF MAJOR CHARACTERS

The D'Artigo Family

Arial Lianan te Maria: Delilah's twin, who died at birth. Half-Fae, half-human.

Camille Sepharial te Maria, aka Camille D'Artigo: The oldest sister; a Moon Witch and Priestess. Half-Fae, half-human.

Daniel George Fredericks: The D'Artigo sisters' half cousin; FBH.

Delilah Maria te Maria, aka Delilah D'Artigo: The middle sister; a werecat.

Hester Lou Fredericks: The D'Artigo sisters' half cousin; FBH.

Maria D'Artigo: The D'Artigo sisters' mother. Human. Deceased.

Menolly Rosabelle te Maria, aka Menolly D'Artigo: The youngest sister; a vampire and jian-tu: extraordinary acrobat. Half-Fae, half-human.

Sephreh ob Tanu: The D'Artigo sisters' father. Full Fae. Deceased.

Shamas ob Olanda: The D'Artigo sisters' cousin. Full Fae. Deceased.

The D'Artigo Sisters' Lovers and Close Friends

Astrid (Johnson): Chase and Sharah's baby daughter.

Bruce O'Shea: Iris's husband. Leprechaun.

Carter: Leader of the Demonica Vacana Society, a group that watches and records the interactions of Demonkin and human through the ages. Carter is half-demon and half-Titan—his father was Hyperion, one of the Greek Titans.

Chase Garden Johnson: Detective, director of the Faerie-Human Crime Scene Investigation (FH-CSI) team. Human who has taken the Nectar of Life, which extends his life span beyond that of any ordinary mortal, and has opened up his psychic abilities.

Chrysandra: Waitress at the Wayfarer Bar & Grill. Human. Deceased.

Derrick Means: Bartender at the Wayfarer Bar & Grill. Werebadger.

Erin Mathews: Former president of the Faerie Watchers Club and former owner of the Scarlet Harlot Boutique. Turned into a vampire by Menolly, her sire, moments before her death. Human.

Greta: Leader of the Death Maidens; Delilah's tutor.

Iris (Kuusi) O'Shea: Friend and companion of the girls. Priestess of Undutar. Talon-haltija (Finnish house sprite).

Lindsey Katharine Cartridge: Director of the Green Goddess Women's Shelter. Pagan and witch. Human.

Maria O'Shea: Iris and Bruce's baby daughter.

Marion Vespa: Coyote shifter; owner of the Supe-Urban Café.

Morio Kuroyama: One of Camille's lovers and husbands. Essentially the grandson of Grandmother Coyote. Youkai-kitsune (roughly translated: Japanese fox demon).

Nerissa Shale: Menolly's wife. Worked for Department of Social and Health Services. Now working for Chase Johnson as a victims-rights counselor for the FH-CSI. Werepuma and member of the Rainier Puma Pride.

Roman: Ancient vampire; son of Blood Wyne, Queen of the Crimson Veil. Menolly's official consort in the Vampire Nation and her new sire.

Queen Asteria: The former Elfin Queen. Deceased.

Queen Sharah: Was an elfin medic, now the new Elfin Queen; Chase's girlfriend.

Rozurial, aka Roz: Mercenary. Menolly's secondary lover. Incubus who used to be Fae before Zeus and Hera destroyed his marriage.

Shade: Delilah's fiancé. Part Stradolan, part black (shadow) dragon.

Siobhan Morgan: One of the sisters' friends. Selkie (were-seal); member of the Puget Sound Harbor Seal Pod.

Smoky: One of Camille's lovers and husbands. Half-white, half-silver dragon.

Tanne Baum: One of the Black Forest Woodland Fae. A member of the Hunter's Glen Clan.

Tavah: Guardian of the portal at the Wayfarer Bar & Grill. Vampire (full Fae).

Tim Winthrop, aka Cleo Blanco: Computer student/genius, female impersonator. FBH. Now owns the Scarlet Harlot.

Trillian: Mercenary. Camille's alpha lover and one of her three husbands. Svartan (one of the Charming Fae).

Ukkonen O'Shea: Iris and Bruce's baby son.

Vanzir: Was an indentured slave to the sisters, by his own choice. Dream-chaser demon who lost his powers and now is regaining new ones.

Venus the Moon Child: Former shaman of the Rainier Puma Pride. Werepuma. One of the Keraastar Knights.

Wade Stevens: President of Vampires Anonymous. Vampire (human).

Zachary Lyonnesse: Former member of the Rainier Puma Pride Council of Elders. Werepuma living in Otherworld.

GLOSSARY

Black Unicorn/Black Beast: Father of the Dahns Unicorns, a magical unicorn that is reborn like the phoenix and lives in Darkynwyrd and Thistlewyd Deep. Raven Mother is his consort, and he is more a force of nature than a unicorn.

Calouk: The rough, common dialect used by a number of Otherworld inhabitants.

Court and Crown: "Crown" refers to the Queen of Y'Elestrial. "Court" refers to the nobility and military personnel that surround the queen. "Court and Crown" together refer to the entire government of Y'Elestrial.

Court of the Three Queens: The newly risen Court of the three Earthside Fae Queens: Titania, the Fae Queen of Light and Morning; Morgaine, the half-Fae Queen of Dusk and Twilight; and Aeval, the Fae Queen of Shadow and Night.

Crypto: One of the Cryptozoid races. Cryptos include creatures out of legend that are not technically of the Fae races: gargoyles, unicorns, gryphons, chimeras, and so on. Most primarily inhabit Otherworld, but some have Earthside cousins.

Demon Gate: A gate through which demons may be summoned by a powerful sorcerer or necromancer.

Demonica Vacana Society: A society run by a number of ancient entities, including Carter, who study and record the history of demonic activity over Earthside. The archives of the society are found in the Demonica Catacombs, deep within an uninhabited island of the Cyclades, a group of Grecian islands in the Aegean Sea.

Dreyerie: A dragon lair.

Earthside: Everything that exists on the Earth side of the portals.

Elemental Lords: The elemental beings—both male and female—who, along with the Hags of Fate and the Harvestmen, are the only true Immortals. They are avatars of various elements and energies, and they inhabit all realms. They do as they will and seldom concern themselves with humankind or Fae unless summoned. If asked for help, they often exact steep prices in return. The Elemental Lords are not concerned with balance like the Hags of Fate.

Elqaneve: The capital Elfin city in Otherworld, located in Kelvashan—the Elfin lands.

FBH: Full-Blooded Human (usually refers to Earthside humans).

FH-CSI: The Faerie-Human Crime Scene Investigation team. The brainchild of Detective Chase Johnson, it was first formed as a collaboration between the OIA and the Seattle police department. Other FH-CSI units have been created around the country, based on the Seattle prototype. The FH-CSI takes care of both medical and criminal emergencies involving visitors from Otherworld.

Great Divide: A time of immense turmoil when the Elemental Lords and some of the High Court of Fae decided to rip apart the worlds. Until then, the Fae existed primarily on Earth, their lives and worlds mingling with those of humans. The Great Divide tore everything asunder, splitting off another dimension, which became Otherworld. At that time, the Twin Courts of Fae were disbanded and their queens and the Merlin were stripped of power. This was the time during which the Spirit Seal was formed and broken in order to seal off the realms from each other. Some Fae chose to stay Earthside, others moved to the realm of Otherworld, and the demons were—for the most part—sealed in the Subterranean Realms.

Guard Des'Estar: The military of Y'Elestrial.

Hags of Fates: The women of destiny who keep the balance righted. Neither good nor evil, they observe the flow of destiny. When events get too far out of balance, they step in and take action, usually using humans, Fae, Supes, and other creatures as pawns to bring the path of destiny back into line.

Harvestmen: The lords of death—a few cross over and are also Elemental Lords. The Harvestmen, along with their followers (the Valkyries and the Death Maidens, for example), reap the souls of the dead.

Haseofon: The abode of the Death Maidens—where they stay and where they train.

Ionyc Lands: The astral, etheric, and spirit realms, along with several other lesser-known noncorporeal dimensions, form the Ionyc Lands. These realms are separated by the Ionyc Seas, a current of energy that prevents the Ionyc Lands from colliding, thereby sparking off an explosion of universal proportions.

Ionyc Seas: The currents of energy that separate the Ionyc Lands. Certain creatures, especially those connected with the elemental energies of ice, snow, and wind, can travel through the Ionyc Seas without protection.

Kelvashan: The lands of the elves.

Koyanni: The coyote shifters who took an evil path away from the Great Coyote; followers of Nukpana.

Melosealfôr: A rare Crypto dialect learned by powerful Cryptos and all Moon Witches.

The Nectar of Life: An elixir that can extend the life span of humans to nearly the length of a Fae's years. Highly prized and cautiously used. Can drive someone insane if he or she doesn't have the emotional capacity to handle the changes incurred.

Oblition: The act of a Death Maiden sucking the soul out of one of her targets.

OIA: The Otherworld Intelligence Agency; the "brains" behind the Guard Des'Estar. Earthside Division now run by Camille, Menolly, and Delilah.

Otherworld/OW: The human term for the "United Nations" of Faerie Land. A dimension apart from ours that contains creatures from legend and lore, pathways to the gods, and various other places, such as Olympus. Otherworld's actual name varies among the differing dialects of the many races of Cryptos and Fae.

Portal/Portals: The interdimensional gates that connect the different realms. Some were created during the Great Divide; others open up randomly.

Seelie Court: The Earthside Fae Court of Light and Summer, disbanded during the Great Divide. Titania was the Seelie Queen.

Spirit Seals: A magical crystal artifact, the Spirit Seal was created during the Great Divide. When the portals were sealed, the Spirit Seal was broken into nine gems and each piece was given to an Elemental Lord or Lady. These gems each have varying powers. Even possessing one of the spirit seals can allow the wielder to weaken the portals that divide Otherworld, Earthside, and the Subterranean Realms. If all of the seals are joined together again, then all of the portals will open.

Stradolan: A being who can walk between worlds, who can walk through the shadows, using them as a method of transportation.

Supe/Supes: Short for Supernaturals. Refers to Earthside supernatural beings who are not of Fae nature. Refers to Weres, especially.

Talamh Lonrach Oll: The name for the Earthside Sovereign Fae Nation.

Triple Threat: Camille's nickname for the newly risen three Earthside Queens of Fae.

Unseelie Court: The Earthside Fae Court of Shadow and Winter, disbanded during the Great Divide. Aeval was the Unseelie Queen.

VA/Vampires Anonymous: The Earthside group started by Wade Stevens, a vampire who was a psychiatrist during life. The group is focused on helping newly born vampires adjust to their new state of existence, and to encourage vampires to avoid harming the innocent as much as possible. The VA is vying for control. Their goal is to rule the vampires of the United States and to set up an internal policing agency.

Whispering Mirror: A magical communications device that links Otherworld and Earthside. Think magical video phone.

Y'Eírialiastar: The Sidhe/Fae name for Otherworld.

Y'Elestrial: The city-state in Otherworld where the D'Artigo sisters were born and raised. A Fae city, recently embroiled in a civil war between the drug-crazed tyrannical Queen Lethesanar and her more level-headed sister Tanaquar, who managed to claim the throne for herself. The civil war has ended and Tanaquar is restoring order to the land.

Youkai: Loosely (very loosely) translated as Japanese demon/nature spirit. For the purposes of this series, the youkai have three shapes: the animal form, the human form, and the true demon form. Unlike the demons of the Subterranean Realms, youkai are not necessarily evil by nature.

PLAYLIST FOR *PANTHER PROWLING*

I write to music a good share of the time, and so I always put my playlists in the back of each book so you can see which artists/songs I listened to during the writing. Here's the playlist for *Panther Prowling*:

AJ Roach: "Devil May Dance"

Android Lust: "Saint Over," "Here and Now," "God in the Hole"

Awolnation: "Sail"

The Black Angels: "The Return," "You on the Run," "Evil Things," "Black Isn't Black," "Young Men Dead," "Manipulation," "Phosphene Dream"

Black Rebel Motorcycle Club: "Feel It Now"

The Bravery: "Believe"

Broken Bells: "The Ghost Inside," "The High Road"

Crazy Town: "Butterfly"

The Cure: "From the Edge of the Deep Green Sea," "The Hanging Garden"

Death Cab for Cutie: "I Will Possess Your Heart"

Eastern Sun: "Beautiful Being"

Eels: "Souljacker Part 1"

Faun: "Iduna," "Hymn to Pan," "Arcadia," "Sieben," "Rad"

The Feeling: "Sewn"

Foster the People: "Pumped Up Kicks"

Garbage: "Queer," "#1 Crush," "I Think I'm Paranoid"

Gary Numan: "I Am Dust," "Here in the Black," "Everything Comes Down to This," "A Shadow Falls on Me," "Splinter," "Haunted," "Melt," "Cars (re-mix)," "Petals"

Godsmack: "Voodoo"

In Strict Confidence: "Silver Bullets," "Snow White," "Tiefer," "Silver Tongues"

Kyuss: "Space Cadet"

Lady Gaga: "Teeth," "I Like It Rough," "Paparazzi"

Ladytron: "Destroy Everything You Touch," "I'm Not Scared," "Ghosts," "Black Cat"

Mark Lanegan: "Methamphetamine Blues," "Phantasmagoria Blues," "Gravedigger's Song," "Riot in My House," "Black Pudding," "Pentacostal"

Morcheeba: "Even Though"

Nick Cave and the Bad Seeds: "Red Right Hand," "Ain't Gonna Rain Anymore"

REM: "Drive"

Screaming Trees: "Where the Twain Shall Meet," "Dime Western," "Gospel Plow"

Stone Temple Pilots: "Sour Girl," "Atlanta"

Tamaryn: "While You're Sleeping, I'm Dreaming," "Violet's in a Pool," "The Waves," "Afterlight," "Transcendent Blue"

Tom Petty: "Mary Jane's Last Dance"

The Verve: "Bittersweet Symphony"

Voxhaul Broadcast: "You Are the Wilderness"

Warchild: "Ash"

Zero 7: "In the Waiting Line"

Dear Reader:

I hope you enjoyed Panther Prowling. *I love writing this world—seeing it develop and grow with each book. As I finish another volume in the series, I grow a bit closer to my envisioned end. For a long time, I didn't have an end point in mind, but now I do, though it won't take place in the next book. The characters are developing and changing along with their world in ways that make me both smile and a little teary. Please note: there will only be one Otherworld book this year and next—so look for* Darkness Raging *next year, around this time.*

However, I'm thrilled to announce the beginning of the Otherworld spinoff series—the Fly by Night Series. Follow the exploits of Alex Radcliffe, the gorgeous expat Aussie vampire who owns the Fly by Night Magical Investigations Agency, and Shimmer, a blue dragon shifter who was exiled from the Dragon Reaches and must go to work for Alex. They take on all manner of beasties while trying to keep their escalating love-hate relationship under control. The first book in this series will be Flight from Death, *coming this year, in July 2015. I'm enclosing the first chapter here as a teaser, to give you a taste of what's coming up for Alex and Shimmer.*

And then, this autumn, you'll get to read Autumn Thorns, *the first book in yet another new series I'm writing. The Whisper Hollow Series follows the story of Kerris Fellwater, a shrine keeper who attempts to put the dead to rest. Kerris returns to her hometown of Whisper Hollow, Washington, after her grandparents die and leave her their home. Located near Lake Crescent on the Olympic Peninsula, Whisper*

Hollow is a town where ghosts walk among the living and Bigfoot makes house calls. In Whisper Hollow, not only do monsters hide in the shadows, but so do secrets of the heart, and love can be as dangerous as anything else that lurks in the dark.

For those of you new to my books, I hope you've enjoyed your first foray into my worlds. For those of you who have followed me for a while, I want to thank you for once again revisiting the world of Camille, Menolly, and Delilah, and invite you all into my two new worlds later this year. Check my website, galenorn.com, for information on my short stories, for release info, and to find the links to where you can find me on the web.

> Bright Blessings,
> The Painted Panther
> Yasmine Galenorn

"Hurry up, damn it! Get a move on, woman!" Alex shoved me toward the stairwell and jammed the door by shoving a wooden wedge beneath it, but that would only buy us a little time.

"I'm trying but the camera's stuck!" I yanked on the strap, which had got caught in the door as we'd beat a hasty retreat from the apartment where we had been spying. We couldn't afford to lose the camera—we needed the pictures on it. Not to mention, if we lost it, the cost for it would come out of my salary. I wasn't about to leave it behind.

"Oh, for cripes' sake, Shimmer. Just cut the bloody straps! For the love of . . ." Alex grabbed the straps out of my hand and yanked out Juanita, his trusty big-assed bowie knife. The blade glittered dangerously in the dim light. Alex sliced through the leather straps like they were butter and, bingo, the camera came free in my hands. I managed not to play fumble-fingers and drop it as we returned to beating a hasty depar-ture. Someone was pounding on the door behind us but we knew who was on the other side, and we weren't about to let him in because he wanted to do really bad things to us at the moment.

"Get your ass down to the parking garage." Alex bared his fangs, looking pissed out of his mind as he shoved me toward the stairs. I didn't protest, just raced down the steps with the vampire following.

We made it to the third level of the garage and piled into Alex's sedan that he used for stakeout work. As he revved the engine and we swung out of the parking spot, the door to the garage slammed opened and Jackaboy Jones came barreling out, his eyes glowing—and he wasn't alone. His pack of good ol' boys followed. They were shifting into wolf form even as we managed to swerve toward the exit. With the wolves racing behind us, we hit the streets of Seattle.

Lucky for us, it was 2:00 A.M. and there was no traffic to speak of. Alex made a sharp right turn at the intersection and we left Jackaboy in the dust, his cronies now gathered behind him.

I let out a long sigh and leaned my head against the seat. "That was close."

Alex grinned at me. "Not really, love." He still had a slight Australian accent, even though he'd been over in the U.S. for almost one hundred years. It was charming, in a boyish sort of way. "I've been in far tighter straits. We have the pictures and that's what counts. His wife will be able to press ahead in her case, we'll get paid, and we have one more divorce notched on our belts."

With a twinkle in his eye, he began to whistle. "But next time you get the urge to wear a pair of stilettos on a case, maybe rethink the idea? I'm not advocating Birkenstocks but . . ." He laughed and held up the broken heel from my sandals. It had come off on the stairs and I'd left it, but apparently Alex had noticed.

Blushing, I tried to hide my embarrassment. "You're a dick, you know that?" I had picked up Earthside vernacular pretty damned quickly.

"Oh, sweet pea, I've known that for years. I'll grow on you. See if I don't." He switched on the MP3 player and

AC/DC's *Highway to Hell* came blaring out. As we headed back to the office, I couldn't help but think that he was all too right. Alex Radcliffe *was* growing on me, and I couldn't afford to let that happen.

"Holy fuck, what the hell are they doing in there?" I grimaced as another crash interrupted my conversation with Bette. We were eating lunch—well, what passed for lunch. It was midnight, but since our office hours were 8:30 to 5:30 A.M., this counted as our noon meal.

Bette sat behind the receptionist's counter of the Fly By Night Magical Investigations Agency. A fine gray marble veined with rich gunmetal, the counter stood between the back office and the waiting room. Bette was our official meet-and-greeter, and as unconventional as she was, people liked her. She netted us a number of new clients just by the way she welcomed them when they came through the door. Something to do with pheromones, she said.

I was sitting beside her, counting the crashes. "That's how many? Four?" The sound of breaking glass would have alarmed me and sent me running into Alex's office if I hadn't known who was in there with him.

Bette cackled. "Three. Something's got her knickers twisted, that's for sure." The older woman—well, she *looked* like an older woman, even though she didn't act it—grinned and winked at me. "Glenda can be a real bitch when she gets worked up. And she gets worked up a lot."

She leaned over her plate and enthusiastically bit into the hamburger. Dripping with bacon grease and secret sauce, the sandwich smelled wonderful, and the look on the Melusine's face told me just how much she enjoyed it. We had that in common, at least. Snake shifters and dragons both were major carnivores. There, though, any resemblance ended.

Bette was a sight, with her long gray hair curled into a bouffant and eyes the color of a green leaves with sunshine sparkling on them. She routinely dressed like a biker mama. Today she had on skintight jeans, a glittering gold belt, a V-neck

T-shirt stretched so tightly over her ample boobs that the material looked ready to tear, and a pair of Doc Martens. All that was missing was a leather jacket, and *that* was hanging on the back of her chair. At least she didn't smoke while she was eating—that would have killed my appetite.

We made quite the pair. When I'm in my human form I'm six feet tall, with long black hair streaked with blue. The streaks are natural, not dye. My eyes are the same royal blue, leading to a lot of people asking: "Do you wear colored contacts?" It's just easier to say yes. Add to that I'm strong and muscled, and—like Bette—I have big boobs, and I get a lot of interesting looks and a few too many hands I have to slap.

As I finished my fish and chips, another crash split the air. This time it was followed by Alex shouting, and Glenda shouting right back at him. The argument was escalating, all right. Apparently it had reached match point because the door to his office slammed open and the succubus came storming out as fast as her formfitting pleather skirt would allow her to walk. She glanced over at us, glowering.

"Don't even ask. Just mind your own business, bitches." And then, without another word, she vanished.

Alex peered around the corner of the heavy steel door. "She gone?" He looked properly cowed, but the twinkle was still hiding there in his eyes. It wasn't like this was the first time the pair had fought up a storm.

Bette nodded, licking her fingers. "Sure is, *precious.* I'll get a broom and dustpan after I finish my lunch." She paused, then before he could disappear back behind the door, she added, "There was a call that came in while you and Miss Prissypants were occupied. Patrick Strand needs to talk to you."

Alex slowly emerged from his office. He was about my height—six feet, and had wheat colored hair that was always lightly tousled. It reached his shoulders, and a stubble of beard covered his chin. His eyes were frosty gray, and he was fit, with a fine spread of pecs and abs. I knew that from seeing him without his shirt a couple times.

He could also be the most annoying man I'd ever met,

except that he wasn't exactly a man. He was a vampire. And he happened to be my boss so I had no choice but to put up with him. He owned and ran the agency, and I had been assigned to him for a five-year stint, so I did my best to get along with him, even when he drove me up the wall. I didn't have a choice.

"Patrick Strand? You're sure it was him?" He looked puzzled. "I haven't heard that name in a long time." He leaned against the wall, gazing at Bette, his expression thoughtful.

"Twenty some years, if I'm on my game." Bette polished off the last of her meal and wiped her hands on a paper napkin, then tossed the bag and container in the garbage. "The last time you two talked, it ended up with a major argument, if I recall correctly."

I perked up. I hadn't heard this story. I'd only been around a few months. And so far, with what I *had* heard of Alex's exploits, I had come to realize that I was dealing with someone as volatile and chaotic as myself, which was in itself a scary proposition.

"What happened?" I had no shame when it came to butting in.

Alex glanced at me, a smirk on his face. "Patrick conned me out of a thousand dollars that I happened to need very badly—"

"You lost it in a poker game, sugar. He won fair and square. But you know that's not the real reason." Bette snorted and tapped out a cigarette, shoving it in one side of her mouth. She smoked like a chimney stack and smelled like one, too.

"That was reason enough. Patrick cheated—"

"You choked!" Her laugh was raspy as she lit up. The NO SMOKING sign above her desk never deterred her. She ignored it, just like she ignored just about everything Alex told her. But she ran the company with an iron fist. There was no doubt who held everything together for us.

"You old bitch . . . I never choke." Alex snorted.

"Sure you don't, sugar. Sure you don't." She laughed. They teased each other constantly. It was their pattern. "Why don't you run along and call him. Patrick needs your help, and you two need to settle the past and put it behind you. It's not like it was with Julian. Trust me on this one. Let the past go."

She held his gaze and I had the feeling there was something being said under the surface. Instead of arguing, he let out a grunt, turned, and went back into his office. And just like that, we were back to work.

So . . . I'm Shimmer, if you're wondering who I am. And I happen to be a dragon. A blue dragon, specifically. If you don't know what that means, here it is in a nutshell: I'm a water dragon. I'm connected to the element of water in more ways than you'd think, and I'm most at home when I'm in a lake, ocean, swimming pool. Hell, even a bath makes me feel more secure. Trouble is, I got myself in a really bad jam and—long story short—was exiled from the Dragon Reaches for five years and stripped of some of my powers.

The Wing Liege—one of our main council members and the advisor to the Emperor—commuted what could have been a death sentence and sent me Earthside. He assigned me to work for his friend Alex Radcliffe. That the Wing Liege even admits to *knowing* a vampire still boggles my mind. And he didn't give me a choice—it was accept the punishment or face assassination. This was by far the better option.

So I've been here about five Earthside months, and I'm slowly acclimating myself to human culture, but it's not easy. I don't understand a lot of the mores and customs, and I'm still not sure how I'm supposed to fit in. I don't even understand the other Supes very well. I miss the Dragon Reaches, but since I was never accepted there in the first place—long story, best saved for another time—I guess . . . maybe this might be for the best. It's a new chance for me, and one I'd never get at home.

So, I'm giving this stint my best because, really, there isn't much else I can do. I'm on probation. I screw this up, and I get sent packing to a fate that might well include my execution. Working for Alex can be a little scary, but it's not as scary as having an assassin on my tail.

Oh . . . last thing. As to what I did? Well, let me give you one piece of advice: never, ever steal from a white dragon. Even if you think he might have clues as to who your parents were. Being an orphan is rough, especially in the Dragon Reaches. Being dead? Even harder.

I was just finishing up entering some info on a case we'd recently solved when Alex called me into his office. I made sure I had my iPad and headed in to see what he wanted.

Alex's office always gave me the creeps. The ceilings were high—which I *did* like. At about twelve feet, they gave the room an open, airy feel. But against one wall, a line of trophies faced the door. A rhino, a hippo, a giraffe, and a crocodile all jutted out in 3D living color from their mounting plaques. Over his desk was a giant swordfish. Occasionally I'd hunted them when I was in dragon form underwater, but I never thought to stuff one and stick it on the wall.

At one point in his two-hundred-some-odd years, Alex had taken up big game hunting, and this was the result. He had told me when I'd questioned him on it that while he'd never do it again, he wasn't going to disrespect the animals he'd killed by dumping the trophies in a thrift shop or just tossing them away.

The rest of the office was a mixture of brilliant wall colors, old wood, and chrome and glass. Glass-covered cases displayed the numerous blades Alex had collected. He even had a bow and arrow slung over a coat rack. I wasn't sure if he could use it, but chances were, he could. Alex was rough-and-tumble. He'd never pass for a cowboy, but he sure could pass for Mad Max.

I slid into a chair opposite his desk, looking around. Two of the vases that I had liked were gone, and one of the panes of glass on the display cases was also missing. No doubt the victim of Glenda's temper tantrum. But I wisely avoided that subject and leaned forward, readying my tablet.

"Ready. What you got for me, boss?"

He laughed, folding his hands against his stomach. He had

a flat stomach. Nicely flat. Way too nice. As he stared at me, that damned grin of his showed the very tips of his fangs.

"What are you laughing at?" I squirmed a little. His gaze was cool, and yet there was always an underlying heat between us that made me uncomfortable. Half the time, I wanted to smack the guy. I conveniently ignored what I wanted to do to him the other half of the time.

"You. You're always so to the point when you come in here, love." He leaned forward. "You need to learn how to loosen up."

"I just . . . You're my boss," I muttered. Truth was, I'd almost staked him a couple months back. Granted, I'd been under a charm at the time, but the end result? I'd just about dusted my boss and any chance I had at making a go of things. I still was amazed that he wasn't holding a grudge.

"I'm also your friend. Okay, here's the deal. Patrick Strand? He's an old friend of mine. We go way back."

"He a vampire?" Usually vamps associated with their own kind.

"Actually, he is, yes. At least now. He wasn't when I knew him. He runs a B-and-B joint up in Port Townsend geared toward Supes—especially vampires. He bought it a couple years ago, but just recently got around to converting it over. That's when the problems started." Alex winked at me. "Patrick always did know how to pick 'em, whether it was women or houses or jobs."

Considering Alex had once been involved with Bette, and now he had a succubus girlfriend with anger management problems, I wanted to point out the obvious hypocrisy in that statement, but decided to save it for later.

"What kind of problems? And what's the name of the place?"

"The High Tide Bed-and-Breakfast. It was supposed to open last month but a series of accidents forestalled that. There's more, though." Alex frowned, staring at his notes. "Patrick thinks . . . he thinks he's being haunted."

Ghosts. Wonderful. I had very little experience with spirits and wasn't eager to add to my repertoire.

"And what makes him think that?" I tapped in a few notes on my iPad.

"Strange noises, poltergeist activity . . . cold spots. Typical stuff. I told him we'd come up and investigate."

Annnnd . . . there we had it. A real case landing at my feet at last. Over the past few months, we'd taken on some low-key items, but nothing out of the ordinary or that proved to be much in the way of dangerous. Mostly taking pictures for divorces or court cases. Supes were really good about knowing when they were being followed. It took another Supe with a camera to manage the necessary proof. But until now, Alex hadn't thrown me into anything major. He had told me that business was in a lull, but I suspected he'd been turning away clients until I got my wings about me. Now, it appeared, he thought I was ready.

"Sure thing. Anything I need to bone up on?" I still wasn't used to the concept of being a professional spy, but then again, I'd spent my life breaking into people's—well, dragons'—houses and rifling through their stuff. I had a decent amount of experience at getting myself into tight places.

"Not really. We'll head up tomorrow night. Find the ferry schedules, would you? We need to go from Coupeville to Port Townsend. We'll leave first thing after sunset, so pack a bag for a few days. You might want to do a little reading up on the town. It's an odd place. Supposed to be spook-central, from what I gather. I'm telling Ralph to pull all the stops and bring all the ghost-hunting equipment."

"Equipment? But . . . you're a vampire. Ralph is a werewolf. I'm a dragon. What do we need equipment for?" I knew that the agency had a store of EMF meters and EVP recorders and whatever else that humans had managed to create in their quest to prove that ghosts were real, but *really*?

"Listen to me. Always go in prepared. We probably won't need it, but better to have it with us than not. I may be a vampire, but that doesn't mean I know when there are ghosts around. Same with Ralph and you. Not all Supes are created equally psychic."

"True. You have a point."

"Patrick said the house belonged to a friend of his in his pre-vampire days. Guy by the name of Nathan Striker. We're going to need to look into that but I figure it might be easier up there, where people knew both of them. Meanwhile, I'm going to do some online shopping and buy Glenda something to appease her. I have no idea what to get." He rolled his eyes. "We had a bit of a tiff today."

"Well, that's the understatement of the year." The words spilled out before I could stop them. I clamped my mouth shut and stood up.

Alex gave me an odd look. "You know what they say— no relationship's perfect."

I nodded and headed for the door, but inside, I wanted to shake him by the shoulders and say, *Wake up! This is about as far from perfect as you can get.* I glanced back. "Alex . . ."

"Yes?" He looked up, already engrossed in his Werewyx Search—the newest Supe search engine.

I paused, my hand on the doorknob, but then decided against saying anything more. Shaking my head, I gave him a gentle smile. "Nothing. Never mind." As I closed the door behind me, I realized that I was beginning to care about Alex. Maybe a little too much.

New York Times bestselling author **Yasmine Galenorn** writes urban fantasy, mystery, and metaphysical non-fiction. A graduate of Evergreen State College, she majored in theater and creative writing. Yasmine has been in the Craft for more than thirty-four years and is a shamanic witch. She describes her life as a blend of teacups and tattoos, and lives in the Seattle area with her husband, Samwise, and their cats. Yasmine can be reached at her website at galenorn.com, via Twitter at twitter.com/yasminegalenorn, and via her publisher. If you send her snail mail, please enclose a self-addressed stamped envelope if you want a reply.

Don't miss a word from the "erotic and darkly
bewitching"* series featuring the D'Artigo sisters:
half-human, half-fae supernatural agents.

From *New York Times* bestselling author
Yasmine Galenorn

WITCHLING
CHANGELING
DARKLING
DRAGON WYTCH
NIGHT HUNTRESS
DEMON MISTRESS
BONE MAGIC
HARVEST HUNTING
BLOOD WYNE
COURTING DARKNESS
SHADED VISION
SHADOW RISING
HAUNTED MOON
AUTUMN WHISPERS
CRIMSON VEIL
PRIESTESS DREAMING

Praise for the Otherworld series:

"Galenorn creates a world I never want to leave."
—#1 *New York Times* bestselling author Sherrilyn Kenyon

"Thrilling, chilling, and deliciously dark."
—*New York Times* bestselling author Alyssa Day

facebook.com/AuthorYasmineGalenorn
facebook.com/ProjectParanormalBooks
penguin.com

*New York Times bestselling author Jeaniene Frost

M192AS0414

FROM *NEW YORK TIMES* BESTSELLING AUTHOR

YASMINE GALENORN

◁**THE INDIGO COURT SERIES**▷

NIGHT MYST
NIGHT VEIL
NIGHT SEEKER
NIGHT VISION
NIGHT'S END

PRAISE FOR THE INDIGO COURT NOVELS:

"Excitement at every turn…a great read."

—*Night Owl Reviews*

"Lyrical, luscious, and irresistible."

—Stella Cameron, *New York Times* bestselling author

galenorn.com
facebook.com/AuthorYasmineGalenorn
facebook.com/ProjectParanormalBooks
penguin.com